S

Go

Down

Suns Go Down

by Shirley Sikes

Sunflower University Press®

1531 Yuma • P. O. Box 1009 • Manhattan, Kansas 66505-1009 USA

Cover art, Mike Boss, Hill City, Kansas.

Layout by Lori L. Daniel

ISBN 0-89745-240-2

Sunflower University Press is a wholly-owned subsidiary
of the non-profit 501(c)3 Journal of the West, Inc.

Presentiment is that long shadow on the lawn,

Indicative that suns go down,

The notice to the startled grass

That darkness is about to pass.

Emily Dickinson

*For Bill
and
Stephanie*

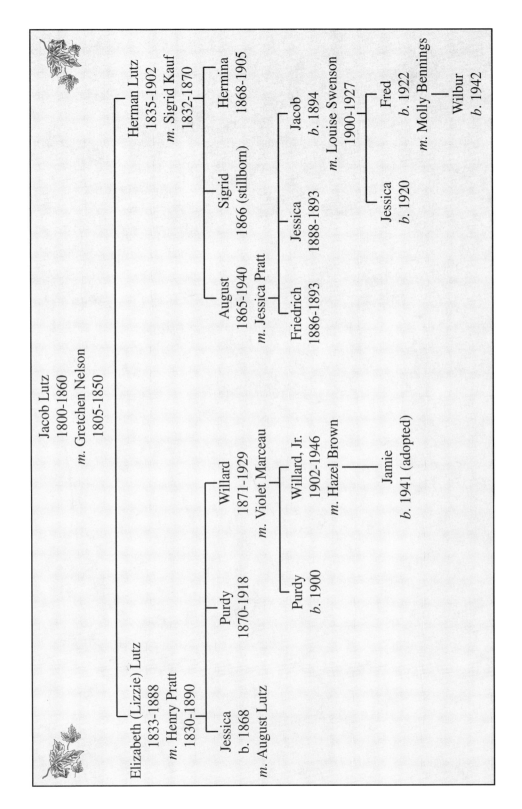

Jacob Lutz
1800-1860
m. Gretchen Nelson
1805-1850

Herman Lutz
1835-1902
m. Sigrid Kauf
1832-1870

Hermina
1868-1905

Sigrid
1866 (stillborn)

August
1865-1940
m. Jessica Pratt

Jacob
b. 1894

Jessica
1888-1893

Friedrich
1886-1893

m. Louise Swenson
1900-1927

Fred
b. 1922
m. Molly Bennings

Jessica
b. 1920

Wilbur
b. 1942

Elizabeth (Lizzie) Lutz
1833-1888
m. Henry Pratt
1830-1890

Jessica
b. 1868
m. August Lutz

Purdy
1870-1918

Willard
1871-1929
m. Violet Marceau

Purdy
b. 1900

Willard, Jr.
1902-1946
m. Hazel Brown

Jamie
b. 1941 (adopted)

Jake

1958

Chapter
One

*H*E WAS GOING TO DIE. His best friend had just told him so.

Will, "Doc" Harvey, the country doctor who had been friend and companion of Jacob Lutz for more than sixty years, had stabbed a finger at Jake's chest and said: "It's here, Jake, damn it to hell. Right here."

They were sitting in Harvey's tiny office in an old building on the main street of Atlas City; the biopsy report had come back from the specialist Harvey had sent Jake to see, and now they both stared at Harvey's identifying finger as if expecting the cancer, confronted, to flee.

Jake ran his fingers over his gray hair, felt down the Western shirt tentatively, gently removing his old friend's hand, afraid suddenly that pressure might dislodge more of the malignant cells into his body. He studied his hands as he placed them, one on each knee, against the cotton twill of his pants. He moved one booted foot over the other.

"You're sure?"

"I'm sure."

"Operation?"

His voice, he noted, was high and unsteady, as if it possessed a will of its own, like the thing Doc had told him was eating away at his flesh. For a moment Jake felt a pang of regret: he had ignored the terrible cough, the occasional sputum mixed with blood. If he had come in earlier, would Will now be telling him something else?

Moving his hands together slowly, Jake clasped them in his lap. Harvey was speaking.

"Operation?" Doc repeated. "Well —" he paused, "we could. Won't change things — maybe delay. It's —" now his voice trembled, sounded alien too, "it's already spread, Jake."

"I see."

The two men turned their glances from the dark interior of Will's office to the brightness of the summer day outside. It was almost noon — an oven already — the heat rising in long curls from the asphalt.

"Distorts things."

"Uh-huh."

The dusty pavement of the street in front of them intersected the highway just a few buildings down, but there was seldom much activity along either thoroughfare. Now only a few people braved the Kansas heat, strolled along the sidewalks or crossed the street to the post office beside Harvey's office.

"Your town has changed," Will remarked.

Doc used the possessive from habit; because of the Lutz family enterprises, the townspeople had sometimes called Atlas City "Lutzville."

Jake drew himself more erect in the chair. "Remember how it was when we were growing up, Will? The town, I mean?"

Will nodded.

"We thought it was the best place on earth."

"I remember," Will said, smiling briefly.

"You could go down to the blacksmith shop and watch ol' Louie welding or making horseshoes, or you could go down to the newspaper office and bum candies from Madge Kaufmann. . . . You could wander all over the place."

"Yes."

"And now . . . " Jake's voice trailed off.

"Gone," Harvey finished. "All gone." Harvey looked away from Jake for a moment, then turned back to face his friend. "I wish I could tell you different," he said.

"Uh-huh."

Jake suddenly thought of Jessie, his daughter, and Fred, his son — his and Louise's children — Louise had died thirty-one years ago. How would he tell Jessie?

And there was Jamie Pratt — adopted into the Lutz family, but like a grandson to Jake.

There was someone else as well, Jake abruptly remembered, someone whose memory the years had obscured, but whom he could never have rooted out of his consciousness, even if he'd wanted to: Ilse. They'd been lovers, but nothing, finally, had come of it.

Recalling, Jake started in his chair so that Will reached out a hand to touch his arm. But Jake removed his friend's hand and put his own fingers on the brim of the Stetson resting on Harvey's desk and spun it around. "Jessie doesn't know?" he asked at last. There was a plaintive quality to his voice he realized.

Will shook his head.

"Good."

"You'll tell her?" Harvey asked.

Jake got up, unwinding his tall body from the position in which he had slunk. "Uh-huh." He reached out a hand to take the Stetson from the desk. "In a little while. Gotta think it over — get used to it myself."

"Sure."

Will placed both of his hands on Jake's shoulders and pressed firmly. Then he let his hands fall to his side and coughed.

"I wish —" Jake began, then stopped. He felt awkward suddenly, as if they had become strangers. He opened the door, blinked against the stringent light.

"Yeah," Harvey said.

Jacob Lutz had lived in Atlas City for all of his sixty-four years. He knew every square inch of it, from the little red brick railroad station, which sat in spurious authority at one end of Main Avenue, to its other end, where the water tower — bean can on stilts as they called it in the town — jutted up against the sky.

Along the railroad tracks, twice a day, in opposite directions, a train rocketed. In the mornings, it was the Comet, splitting the mists which had descended on the little town in the darkness; at night, the Golden Express came rushing out of the setting sun to glide with haughty splendor into a panting, impatient stop at Atlas City. The train always gave the impression of tremendous haste, its gleaming sides seeming to expand with annoyance at the dingy reality of the town. Watches were studied, passengers stared with dismay out the window, the steps were barely extended for people to get off when, as if sensing a mistake, the conductor would consult his timepiece again and fold the steps back in with a bang.

The train station had a brick platform on its south side, where the tracks were, a small baggage room, and a smaller waiting room, where the odor of wood polish and dust competed. Oscar Smith, the agent, had been in the job for years, it having been passed down to him from his father and *his* father before that. Oscar had a deep awareness of the importance of his work: he always wore a green-visored cap, his sleeves held up with rubber bands, his chest blooming in a floral-printed vest. He had a habit of making pronouncements about the trains: lifting his eyes heavenward as though he had received his information directly from God, his voice high and slightly pinched. "Train late out of Kansas City." Or, "You'll have to have a *rese*vation" — he never sounded the "*r*" — "for Kansas City."

The whistle of the trains and the wail of the city siren, at noon and six o'clock, on the hour, were the only sounds to disturb the otherwise pristine stillness of the town. A tractor-trailer might occasionally roar by, sucking up dust and spewing it out behind, as it followed the concrete highway that ran at right angles to the main street. But most times, you could walk along the tree-lined city streets and fail to see another soul stirring. In summer, the houses were shut up against the sun; in winter, against the cold, the same drapes pulled at the windows, showing their fading backsides.

The town was spread out for a population of five hundred. As though the city fathers had expected a great ingress — the "Pride of the Plains," someone termed it — the streets were wide and pleasant, carefully planted with trees, the lawns generous, bespeaking benevolence and hope. Even the cemeteries seemed to have invited settlement, for they too were wide and spacious: choice lots for departed beloved.

Atlas City was inbred. The settling Swedes and Germans had married and intermarried and a newcomer was well advised to keep his counsel, to withhold his opinions on the city and the people because a person never knew when he was speaking to the aunt or first cousin or even brother of the one he discussed. And though the families themselves might feud, they rallied around each other with a particularly defensive fury when an outsider offered comment.

The streets were not named, they were identified by the people who lived on them. "Gracie Grauss? You know where Aunty Espy lives? Hard by her house, just over the hedge." One street was still known as Grady Manning Street, though Grady had shot his head off with a twelve-gauge years before. And there was Lindstrom Street — where that *Lindstrom* girl lived, whose morals furnished adventure for every red-blooded farm boy for miles around, and who finally ran off to the "city," wherever that was, with a soldier.

Johnson's Hardware was on the east side of Main Avenue, then an empty building, then Parson's Cafe, which, in the forties, had moved down the street from its original spot opposite the Lutz General Store. Parson's was the one place where there was almost always activity — in the mornings, men wandered in for coffee or perhaps an occasional beer — lulled by the dark interior with its wooden booths and floor, lit up only by the glittering beer signs: Hamm's cool waters glistening above the counter.

Beyond Parson's, across the street, was the post office, where tiny knots of people would gather in the morning for the early mail and the latest gossip. Beside this was the Manor, the town's one hotel, the only rather elegant structure it could boast — white-frame, two-story, with endless leggy geraniums and ancient men in rockers languishing on its wide front veranda. The last paint job having been several years before, the Manor was now "looking its age." But it furnished a home for those not able to take care of themselves — though not so far gone as to need the *Jesus Saves Boardinghouse* of Purdy Pratt.

August Lutz had built the general merchandise store for the town, making it a trade center, and Jake had donated land for the city park and built a swimming pool.

Now, 1958, Atlas City seemed on the brink of something: there were strangers in town, soldiers' families from the military fort nearby, and corporation executives who came in and out of the village, having bought up some foreclosed farms in the months before. Some of the farms had oil. The town seemed stunned.

"Somethin's gotta give," Oscar Smith prophesied, regarding the newcomers who sometimes boarded his train now. "Things be changin'."

Chapter
Two

*J*AKE WENT STRAIGHT to his pickup as Will told him goodbye, yanked open the door and slid into the seat, turned the key he'd left in the ignition. The door slammed as the motor ground into action, then Jake jerked the pickup around, made a U-turn in the street, tires screeching like a teenager's, and headed out the highway toward the lane that led to the ranch.

As if it were a horse, the pickup nosed its way home.

He could see the ranch now: the two double-story houses, one frame, one stone, with porches on three sides, nestled against the backdrop of the low hills. Beyond and in back of the houses, a mile away, on top of the hills, the big bluestem pastures ran, on and on it seemed, into infinity. Balls of trees rose around the houses, a steel windmill behind them groaning against the sky, its blades turning mightily in the sudden breeze, the words "The Aermotor, Chicago" emblazoned on the tail. Jake could see the shaft of the pump going up and down, water being poured into the metal tank below. The tail was pointing, quivering in the wind like a finger, turning away from the wind then, as if undecided, switching direction only to swing once more to its old position.

As Jake approached, he could see the brick silo gleaming in the sun, its huge maw empty now and ready for the fall feed corn. Still closer, the outbuildings sprang into view. His quarter horse was out in the big barnyard, nosing the dirt as if expecting to find something, then retreating out of the hot sun to his stall inside, flushing some barn swallows from the rafters of the building as he made his way in.

In front of the house stood a wrought iron fence with elaborately carved spikes. Tendrils of grass which the lawn mower had missed clung to the wrought iron at its base, a rabbit springing from one clump as Jake pulled the pickup into the drive and shut off the motor.

He sat for a moment, soaking in the shade of the cedars that lined the path on the north, the coolness a respite, the stinging odor soothing.

He put his head and his hands far up on the steering wheel and sighed. Then, reluctantly, he leaned over to open the door, ease out. He found himself thinking — foolishly — that he should move slowly and carefully . . . *What the hell difference did it make?*

Feeling like someone had hauled off and socked him in the gut, Jake stood looking at the house, as if he expected it to have changed, reflecting his own devastating news. But the structure looked noncommittal, almost abandoned in its imposing presence. Lucky for it, he thought, maybe lucky for him, that something in the world had permanence.

Straightening, Jake moved further up the walk, up the steps and across the wooden floorboards of the porch, which lay almost completely exposed now to the morning sun and bore the scent of warming wood. As he walked, the boards creaked and moaned, puncturing the air along with the screech of the windmill, the sound alerting the old Collie who was snoozing in the fast-disappearing shade of the overhang. At the noise, Prince lifted his gray-tinged muzzle and thumped his tail in greeting; he probably hadn't smelled him, Jake thought, he was just trusting all was well.

"Hello, ol' boy," Jake said.

Again the thump.

Jake paused at the door, drawing in his breath, anticipating the questions that would await him. Fred and Molly would be there; they would have decided which one of them would tackle him.

Delaying, Jake reached out, touched the antique brass handle set in the middle of one wooden panel of the door. His mother had had it fashioned for the house; it was Swedish, perhaps cast by the same ironworker who made the fence — turn the handle and it rang a bell.

Now, perversely, Jake took off his hat and turned the knob, letting the resultant sound shatter the stillness of the house. It was as if he were simply selling something, had no function here.

It was Jessie whom Jake had hoped to see as the door swung open. Instead, Fred stuck his head out. When he saw his father he couldn't seem to refrain from blurting, his voice betraying his uncertainty, "How was your visit with the doc?"

He hadn't even waited for him to enter the hallway, Jake thought . . . he was that anxious.

If it had been genuine concern, Jake would have been touched. But with Fred it was more likely to be the thought of an inheritance than love of his father.

Behind Fred, her round face a white moon in the darkness of the vestibule, hung Molly.

"How was it, Dad Lutz?" she repeated, her voice high, insisting once again on using the phrase "Dad Lutz" that Jake hated. "What did you find?"

Apparently, Jake thought as he swung in the screen door, the frame banging behind him, she expected — perhaps even hoped for — the news of illness.

"I'm great," he said, watching Molly's face as she cast a hurried, disbelieving glance at Fred, who now walked beside him.

Fred coughed, then laughed nervously. "Really, Dad?" He cleared his throat. "You see, I've been thinking . . . things here sorta depend on your good health. We oughta make plans . . ."

Plans, Jake thought, and flushed.

"I'm an Olympic specimen," he asserted. Then, "Where's Jess?"

Molly raised her brows and said, as if it were a joke, "See? He only cares about Jessie. If we were lying here dead . . ."

But Jake brushed past her into the living room, looking around as if he expected Jessie would be there, somewhere among the early American and flowery chintz furniture Molly had insisted would look "ideal."

"She's not here, Dad. She's checking fence," Fred said.

Behind him, Molly was trailing complaints. "I've been working all morning on lunch," she said, "and it's so hot and I'm so tired. My back hurts today. Think I'll go see the doc . . ."

"If you would open the windows," Jake said. "It's stifling in here."

"Open windows let in dust," Molly pronounced.

"Hmmph," Jake said, and fled into the kitchen.

But Molly tracked him, stood looking at him now as if she were a setter, sniffing out a wounded bird.

Something was steaming on the stove.

"What the *hell's* that smell?" Jake growled, able, momentarily, to fend off the despair that had seized him.

He pointed to the casserole dish sitting on the counter by the stove; tiny pieces of fish lay exposed in a bed of rice like shriveled flesh.

"I've fixed a shrimp casserole," Molly said. "*Gourmet* magazine recommended it and it's divine."

"Hmmph," Jake repeated.

Molly was always trying to be something other than what she was, Jake thought. Though attractive in an overblown, nineteenth-century barroom manner, with a rather uncontrolled sensuality, she seemed bent on being someone else. She liked to subscribe to fashion and cooking magazines, and she tried to emulate the ideas, but somehow the latest outfits, designed for skinny women, always looked out-of-place on big-bosomed Molly, and her gourmet foods seldom worked out. She had come from a farm family that had never made good; she seemed determined to erase that.

Molly tried to please Jake, however, and he took a delight in refusing to be pleased.

"Why don't you just stay in your own house and leave me alone?" Jake often told her when confronted with another of her "creations."

"You know I abominate that place," Molly said.

"Oh, yes."

"Abominate" was one of her favorite words. She "abominated" the Kansas weather, the "bumpkins" in Atlas City and, most of all, the house she and Fred lived in — the frame one, not stone like the original farmhouse Jake and Jessie had. But it was larger than Jake's house, and it had the distinction of being one of the first semi-prefab houses he knew of, built in 1905, all the ready-cut siding coming from Chicago. Jake had pointed that out to Molly — the homeplace having been quarried from nearby hills — thinking she would like that because she certainly didn't like anything native to Atlas City. But of course she didn't; it seemed to be a principle with her that she never be content.

For a moment, Jake considered speaking to Fred alone. But would Fred listen to him?

As if Fred had read his mind, he said, "We'll make plans later, Dad," and Jake turned away.

He brushed past Molly and Fred to go back into the hallway, starting up the stairway to his own room, on the southwest of the house. "Did Jessie say when she might be back?" he asked.

"After lunch I think," Molly said and, apparently, moved the casserole dish closer to the kitchen door so that more of the odor rose on the air, pursuing him.

He hurried up the staircase, his heart pounding as he reached the top. Putting a hand to his chest, he thought as he opened the door to his room that he would have a heart attack. Then he remembered.

Carefully closing the door behind him, he went over to sit in the rocker by the window. He had to absorb what Will had told him; he had to handle it somehow, as he always tried to handle problems.

Easing into the rocker, he began to sway, back and forth, keeping a rhythm. He looked at his room, hardly changed since his mother's day, when Old Jessica and August slept here — the pottery pitcher and washstand, the crocheted bedspread, the high walnut headboard, the bare wood floors polished and gleaming. They came closer, retreated, as he rocked.

The motion calmed him as it always had. The rocker had been handmade by his grandfather. It had been in his grandfather's room when Jake was growing up. He and Jake had shared the room for a time, beginning when Jake was six and ending only on the day his grandfather died.

Now, once again, Jake felt like that little boy.

When Jake first went to see Will Harvey, he'd supposed Will would tell him to stop smoking so many cigarettes and stop drinking so many beers.

Well, Jake thought.

He looked out the window to see if maybe Jessie was coming. He knew she'd probably taken Coalie, the black Morgan mare, to ride fence. Fred didn't ride. That was one of the reasons Fred ran the general store and Jake and Jessie the farm.

"He didn't have to be so sassy," Jake heard Molly say now, her strident voice winding up the stairs. "He's always so sassy!"

"Maybe he doesn't feel well," Fred said.

Why was Fred being understanding, Jake wondered. What in God's name did Fred really feel about things?

What did *he* really feel about things?

Jake blinked his eyes open suddenly, found he was clasping the arms of the rocker as if in a vise. He wanted very badly for Jessie to come. But how would he tell her?

He sat for a moment, his hands on the rocker arms. Then he pushed himself up and out of the rocker, over to the window. It was probably a good thing he hadn't remarried, he thought. He'd had chances . . . even Molly seemed at times to regard him as a possible substitute for Fred, those times when Fred was perhaps not sexually up to her. *Oh, God!* Surely he was wrong about that.

Yet he supposed it would have been flattering to some men to have a younger woman interested in them . . . and there were plenty of women closer to Jake's age who'd wanted to tie him down. One almost succeeded. But he didn't want to abandon Jessie, and he felt he would be. She'd had enough sadness in her life . . . first her mother dying . . .

Fred and Molly grew terror-stricken when Jake became interested in another woman, and so did his mother, Old Jessica. They certainly didn't want to see the family holdings passed on to other hands. Old Jess had never liked the idea of Jake's marrying — not when he married Louise, not when he got involved with Ilse, never.

Jake sighed. *Ilse.* Oh, God, he couldn't think of that now.

It was because of Ilse that his mother had stalked out of Jake's house twenty years before, removing herself to Atlas City and Purdy Pratt's boardinghouse. She issued orders from there.

Well, Jake thought, the Lutz family had never been easy to be a part of; if there was any kind of family cohesiveness, it had to be in their very divisiveness.

Jake looked out the window again, but there was no Jessie. He put a hand to his chest, pressing in gently now as if he were afraid that it would collapse, like cardboard. It was easier to think of what was going to happen when he was here in his room; there was a continuity in the stillness.

But was he accepting this verdict too readily? Could Will be wrong? He had heard of that — mixed-up tests — could it be?

But Will would examine that too, wouldn't he? Doc Harvey would have been no more willing to accept the biopsy report than he was.

Suddenly Jake turned, and, leaving his Stetson on the dresser, strode out of the room and down the stairs. He passed Molly and Fred, huddled together in a corner, whispering.

"Where? . . ." Fred asked, startled.

Jake didn't answer, banged the screen door behind him.

He could sense their eyes on him as he made his way through the heat into the barn. Dust circled in the air inside, motes catching the light and whirling to the ground, his big sorrel regarding him curiously as he approached.

Jake put a hand on Duke's neck, reached out the other to grasp the bridle hanging on a peg beside the feedstall, gently pushed the bit into Duke's mouth. Duke turned his head to look at him again as the saddle blanket went on, then Jake sighed and heaved the heavy Western saddle up on Duke's back. For a moment the effort exhausted him. He leaned against Duke while Duke's head affectionately brushed against his back and rested. He felt a cough coming on and turned his face into the heavy woolen blanket, lungs in spasm. He hadn't had such pain since the First World War, when he had been wounded in France.

When the paroxysm finished, Jake leaned under Duke, seized the girth, fingers trembling, and cinched it. He put a knee against Duke's belly, pulled the girth tight — again, the cough.

Leading Duke from the barn, Jake touched the pommel, swung up into the saddle, leather groaning and, slapping Duke fiercely with the end of the reins, wheeled him into the direction of the upper pasture. It was the first time ever that Jake had left the corral gate open.

Duke plunged past emerging milo, almost-yellow wheat, flecks of sweat appearing on his withers; he began to slow, but Jake whipped him again and the horse, surprised, leaped from his gallop into a still faster gait. Jake sensed the power between his knees and he bent over the pounding shoulders until his own face was wet from Duke's exertion. On and on they went, Duke tearing over the shallow creek now, under a low tree, beginning the ascent up the rocky hillside to the top of the pasture.

Suddenly Jake reined him in, letting the horse pick his own way up, turning in the saddle and putting a hand on the strong, rounded haunches that struggled to push them forward, the flesh hot and sticky.

When Duke reached the top, as if he sensed Jake's urgency, he spread his thundering legs into the breakneck gallop of the moments before. They flashed through the tall bluestem, Duke beginning to breath heavily but refusing to stop until, as abruptly as he'd begun the mad dash, Jake pulled the horse to a stop. Duke stood trembling, sides exploding. On a walk, Jake turned him toward the pond blinking in the distance.

The scene was empty. No Jessie. No cattle in view. It was as if he and his horse were alone in the world. Jake felt the wind in his face, the breeze brushing off his own perspiration and the flecks of white foam on Duke's neck, chest, and legs, the froth thick on the tender skin that linked the legs to his belly.

Here there was flint six inches below the grass, the land still much as it had been one-hundred years ago, in his grandfather's day. Grazing did not destroy it; plowing would, for the topsoil would all blow away in the stiff Kansas winds.

The ground was like a plateau, dipping here and there into a ravine where one or two stunted trees stood beside man-made ponds. The edges of these ponds were pocked by the hooves of the Herefords that came here to water themselves. Sometimes the ponds closer to the woods, which crawled up the sides of the rocky cliff, would have the mud indented with raccoon claw prints, or deer hooves, or coyote tracks.

Off in the distance — still on his land, which stretched for three-thousand acres — he could see the oil pumps, dipping like gooney birds into the earth. "Well, you've finally done something sensible," Old Jessica said, amazed, when Jake allowed the oil wells to go in. "I assumed you wouldn't want to complicate the landscape."

He didn't tell Old Jessica the reason he'd relented was that it allowed him to buy more land, to help prevent what was happening to some poor farmers in the vicinity. Beyond the pumps was Peterson land, which had recently been bought by a corporation. The first thing the corporation did was plow it up and try to sow wheat.

Jake wanted this land in private hands, with people who would live on it themselves.

Jake dismounted, led Duke to the pond, let him drink. At first Duke merely brushed his lips over the water, stirring it with his nose, then reached in and sucked deeply and noisily, sides groaning.

"I almost winded you, boy," Jake said then, patting him. "I'm sorry."

Jake stood there a moment watching the horse. He lifted his eyes to see a hawk dip on the horizon, rise a few seconds later with something in its talons. A field mouse no doubt, Jake thought, or a baby rabbit. With a shriek of victory, the hawk wheeled in the sky and headed for its nest.

He could smell Duke, the leather, the grass, the air. Breathing as deeply as he could without coughing, Jake soaked it in, put his foot in the left stirrup, and once more settled in the saddle.

Jake released Duke in the corral, watching the horse roll in the dirt, erasing the glistening saddle marks. He turned, walked into the house.

Fred and Molly were still in the kitchen, sitting at the table, looking as ever like conspirators. Though Molly didn't speak as Jake moved word-lessly past them, Fred took a deep breath — almost a sigh — and got up to follow his father as Jake made his way back to his room. When Jake reached the top stair, Fred said, "Wilbur's coming home," as if that were great good news.

At sixteen, Wilbur was staying with a relative of Molly's in Denver, working and attending high school. "So much more civilized," Molly was fond of saying. "Denver will cure his high spirits."

Wilbur's "high spirits" were a little more than that. Wilbur had been kicked out of the local high school for being a disruptive influence. In point of fact, he had vandalized the band room, destroying several expen-sive bass horns, and Fred had had to pay the damages.

Jake was silent.

"He's coming to see you," Fred added.

Now Jake was suspicious. "Why?" he managed to ask. "Why now?"

Fred was noncommittal. "He just wants to see you . . . that's all."

But when Fred had closed the door and left him alone, Jake thought: *I am going to die after all.*

Even his family could smell it on him.

Chapter Three

"HELLO, DEARIE," Purdy had called out just moments earlier. "Your breakfast will be ready in a minute."

Then she had barged into Old Jessica's room, hurled at her, "I have news about Jake. Something's up!"

But, like the idiot she was, Old Jessica thought, Purdy had announced this and, inexplicably, had turned and backed out of the room, leaving Old Jessica furiously pondering the interruption.

Now Old Jessica stood looking out the window of Purdy Pratt's boardinghouse. The house was flaking paint, like so many in Atlas City, semi-white, a frame house with a sagging front porch and tilting cement walk. There was a fence, broken down, and a gateway, but no gate. Over the arch of the gate was a sign with home-made letters on it, the letters out of proportion to one another, like a first grader's, one "e" sliding upwards as if some tenant of crazy Purdy's had pushed her hand as she printed. *"Jesus Saves,"* the sign read.

Jesus saves, indeed, Jessica thought bitterly. Jesus was apparently busy saving everyone but herself. Why else would He allow her to be doomed to the insufferable house of Purdy Pratt?

Jessica yanked closed the torn lace curtains and went back to the walnut chair by the dresser and sat down. She cocked her head, waiting for Purdy's call. But there was nothing. Just like her, Jessica thought sourly. Purdy had all the organizational abilities of a two-year-old.

Outfitted for breakfast, Old Jessica wore a black gabardine suit with a shiny "seat-sprung" back, black shoes, black hose. She had years ago vowed she would honor her dead husband by wearing black for the rest of her life, and though Purdy often told her that she looked ready for burial herself, she was determined to fulfill her promise.

Jessica was familiar with the house in which Purdy rented rooms. *"Rooms for rent,"* a sign outside said, below the *"Jesus Saves,"* in the same untutored lettering; the house had belonged to Purdy's namesake and aunt — to Jessica's sister.

Jessica had never liked the house. She had never really liked her sister Purdy either. And the dislike only deepened when their brother Willard named his first born after Purdy and not herself. Such a disagreeable name!

Now Old Jessica got up and moved about the room. Though she had never liked the house, she *did* like her room. Her own personality had managed to overwhelm Purdy's here: tall, lead crystal bottles with spectacular stoppers, full of the Paris perfume she sent away for regularly, lined the left back of Purdy's old walnut dresser. Powder, in a Chinese enameled box, sat beside the Shalimar, Chanel No. 5 beside this, a Chinese fan beside that. A silver-framed portrait of herself and August, taken immediately after their marriage in the German church, decorated the right side of the dresser. Lipsticks, all a dark, winey red, were neatly arranged in one of the small wooden drawers on the right side of the chest. Below the cosmetic drawer was her lingerie, folded precisely, her hose and slips and gowns in the bottom drawer.

Moving to the closet, Old Jessica opened the door and regarded her clothing: hung up in military order, seasonal clothes separated by a small space, suits and coats in one area, dresses in another,

But though she wore only a few of her clothes now, she never threw anything out. Her son once told her she was like a princess entombed in a castle.

"Why don't you just grow long hair, hang it out the window, and I'll climb up?" Jake had asked.

Going back to the chair, Old Jessica took a long, deep breath of frustration. No telling when Purdy would be ready. She had probably burned the bacon and made rocks of the eggs.

Jessica pulled her arms tightly about her, though it was hot in the room and the suit was long-sleeved. It was one of Jessica's dictums that old women, with "skin like elephants," should not wear short sleeves. However warm she became, Jessica seldom perspired; she willed herself not to.

Purdy, on the other hand, paid no attention to any ideas of dress, decorum, or interior decoration. Her home was like herself, constantly askew, with a kitchen made up of antiquated appliances. No electric stove for Purdy. . . . Her aunts's wood stove still stood against the middle of one wall, as it always had. Neither was Purdy about to trade in her "trusty" old foot-driven sewing machine for one of those things "that are always about to fly off into the room in pieces." She would not have an electric refrigerator, nor water other than what came from her "little white pump." She still had the white enamel table and chairs that Jessica's sister Purdy had plucked from some junkyard in 1900.

She could open a museum in the house, Jessica thought, as she waited for Purdy's raucous voice to tell her breakfast was finally ready.

And Purdy herself could be part of that museum. A dumpy woman with a lurching gait, Purdy dyed her hair black every Saturday night in the little pantry behind the kitchen and then had the gall to declare it was natural. *Natural!* Wood-shaving curls, flying off in every direction — a kind of ancient Shirley Temple! Jessica wouldn't have been surprised if someday Purdy would get some baby-doll shoes, do a two-step, and render "The Good Ship Lollipop."

She was ridiculous.

And her clothes. Purdy made her own, of course, used selvages as hems, plaids going off in all directions, zippers aslant, buttons off. And then she would slap a black straw sailor on her head to take off for town as if she were the Queen of the World.

She was so coarse. Like everyone else in her stupid boardinghouse, Jessica thought.

There was the adopted Jamie. Taken in by her nephew, Willard, Jr., Purdy's brother, Jamie had been shifted to Purdy's when Willard and his wife were killed in a car accident. Jamie was five then, which was perhaps all right; but now he was seventeen, with all the drawbacks of adolescence. Jamie had shot up in height the past year as though he meant to puncture the sky, his blonde hair darkening to brown, his body slowly thickening, his features clean-cut and distinctive enough, even with the huge glasses he wore, to attract some of the female trash in the town. Brazen girls kept calling Jamie and he would flush, go to the telephone, toe the floor, turn red, go up to his room and no doubt do all sorts of things to himself. Adolescent boys did, she knew.

And there was Ned, the idiot circus aerialist, who was always going off and climbing up into the trees and swinging like an ape from the branches. Ned and Jamie had been like Siamese twins ever since Jamie first came to Purdy's, clinging together as though they were somehow attached by the flesh. They had a train set in Ned's room, and twice a day they went to the railroad station to greet the real train. Ned was convinced Rita Hayworth was coming on the train and he didn't want to miss her!

And the way Ned dressed! Overalls without a shirt, one strap down so that the brown nipple was exposed to all, shoes without socks, the shoes being worn husks which did not bend to accommodate the huge feet thrust within them. The whites of his eyes were too large, Jessica thought; one look at them and anyone could tell he was a madman.

When Jamie and Ned weren't going to see the train or Ned wasn't having a fit, they played like children in that room, Jessica having to listen to the constant "Toot, toot!" that old Ned sang out as a whistle for the train, while the cars themselves went around and around the dimestore metal track.

She was encased in a hotbed of lunatics, Jessica thought. Rooms for rent, indeed. It was an asylum.

Jessica sighed.

And added to the gaggle of Purdy's undesirables were Nellie Nameless and Lars Larson. Nellie, who had a penchant for going nude, would simply take off her clothes and saunter down the stairs, surprising whomever might be visiting Purdy. Nellie had come from the Manor Hotel and no one could remember her name or her age, and Nellie wouldn't tell, so Purdy, with typical creativity, called her Nellie Nameless.

Old Lars was a relic Swede left by somebody or other to rot at Purdy's. He was always going off too, but unlike Nellie, he didn't take off his clothes and unlike Ned, he didn't fly off into the trees — Lars would leave the house and run out into the fields, imagining he was chasing his cattle. Purdy and Jamie would go out to find him, if no one had called Purdy already, and then Purdy would bring him back, hands on hips and say, "Now Lars Larson, what you be doing?"

"Chasing cattle," he'd mumble.

Purdy: "Now you know you ain't got any cattle."

Lars: "Hmm."

"Where be you? Name of city?"

At this point, usually old Lars' memory would come sailing back and he would say, proudly, "Atlas City."

"Right! Name of place?"

"The 'Jesus Saves'."

"Right. Now you go, do right. Sit in that rocker and rock a bit."

Once Old Lars tried to commit suicide by jumping out of his window. "Goodbye, world," he had yelled before he leaped. Unfortunately for Lars, Purdy had so much junk in the yard — old dollbuggies, rusting bathtubs, wheels, hand lawnmowers, all overlaid by lumpy old mattresses — upon which he landed that he didn't even break an arm.

"As any sensible old man would do," Purdy later told him.

Oh dear, Jessica thought as her mind switched back to the present; what had she done when she allowed herself to be forced out of Jake's house? And he — the renegade — would not even condescend to ask her back. He was waiting, he said, for her to make up her mind. As if she could just retract, like that!

. . . Jake would no doubt be coming on his weekly "duty" visit, Jessica mused, leaning forward in the chair and quickly looking at herself in the dresser mirror. And what would he tell her? . . . What did Purdy have to reveal?

Nothing, probably, she thought. Purdy was always wanting to turn up rocks, see what wriggled out.

Jessica's gaze narrowed on her reflection; hastily she looked away. "I'm old," she once told Jake. "I keep forgetting that."

And, of course, just to defy her, Jake would go see Jamie if he came to Purdy's, for he had taken to that boy from the moment Jamie appeared at the Jesus Saves, treating him almost like kin.

It infuriated Jessica; here he paid no attention to Wilbur, who was a dear boy, if a little wild. Wilbur wrote lovely letters to his great-grandmother and he sent flowers on her birthday. But Jake gave all his affection to a waif like Jamie! It was part of his very stubbornness — just like his father, August. Like father, like son. Oh gracious, would it never end? . . . Because she really would like to leave Purdy Pratt's, Jessica thought now, other than in a pine box. But she certainly couldn't simply appear on

Jake's doorstep, belongings in hand, like an orphan in one of those melo-dramatic novels.

If Fred could only help. . . . But he was such an incompetent in emo-tional matters, and Molly was even worse. Jessica just never had been able to count on anyone, she acknowledged to herself, indulging in a rather pleasant sense of doom.

"'Jesus Saves'," Jessica muttered as she cocked her head to listen once again for Purdy. "Like *hell* He does."

Still Purdy didn't call.

Jessica was impatient, wanting to eat and then come back to her room for her morning nap. She was accustomed to taking several naps a day, after breakfast, and again after lunch — never mind Purdy called it "dinner," showing her country ways. Old Jessica had an oscillating fan and she liked to powder herself, turn the fan full on her, and lie on top of the bed with the breeze caressing her. It was probably her only concession to pampering herself, she thought, with the exception of the long, hot baths she took in Purdy's ancient tub. Purdy always complained about this: "Runs my water bill up like mad, you bathing in there like you was in the county reservoir." Naturally Jessica went ahead anyway.

With perfumed salts to cut Atlas City's hard water, the baths were relaxing to Jessica and very possibly one of the few things that kept her from swallowing a handful of the tranquilizers Doc Harvey had given her long ago. Was it after August's death? She wasn't certain. She would never actually have taken enough pills to kill herself of course. Just enough to frighten people.

But the baths and the naps and the letters she wrote from time to time to her old college roommate were the things she clung to, to keep her sane. She liked rituals, and at least Purdy's house afforded her that; she could make up her own routines and — everyone else either throwing them-selves out windows or hanging in trees or taking clothes off or chasing ghostly cattle — there was no one to disturb her or pay her any atten-tion.

Elsie McDonald and she had taken to each other from the moment they had entered the state land-grant college. Elsie came from Kansas City and she was "cultured" and "far-seeing." She had become an artist, in New

York City, where she actually sold some of her work. To Jessica, that was immensely intriguing.

Jessica put a hand over her eyes momentarily; this was always the painful part of thinking about Elsie. Elsie had died some forty years ago. But Jessica couldn't bear to think of her as dead — or grown old — so she wrote her letters, and reread those that Elsie had sent so many years ago. They were all in a shoebox marked, not "Elsie," which might have encouraged the snoop Purdy to peek at them, but rather "History of Chinese Agriculture." Jessica thought — rightfully — that would be enough to ward off Purdy forever.

It was very warm in the room; Jessica stirred on the bed, letting the fan touch parts of her body that had been heated by the bed covers. The fan felt like a hand, brushing over her body, cooling it. Jessica shivered.

Suddenly she became aware someone was knocking at the door. Before she could speak, Purdy burst in.

"Hello, Dearie," Purdy greeted her.

Purdy seemed distressed, Jessica thought, more haphazard than ever, as if thought and feeling were jumbled and colliding within her.

Purdy spit out: "Jake's ill, I think. I just told Jamie. Rosa Mae Harvey saw him go into the Doc's this morning, early, like he was aimin' to go in before Doc Harvey opened, before anyone else was there."

Old Jessica stood up, shaking, leaning on her lion-headed walnut cane and pricking her way toward Purdy. She didn't care right now to challenge Purdy's telling the orphan Jamie before she told her.

"*What?*" Jessica demanded.

"Yes'mm," Purdy said, shaking her head up and down. "Now what be going on?"

Old Jessica tried to recover her equilibrium. She felt as if someone had assaulted her. "Well," she stated finally, "what's wrong with Jake's going to Will Harvey?"

But her son *did*n't go to doctors, she knew, not even to his friend, Will.

"Nothing's wrong with Jake's going. But Jake never did doctor much, did he?" Purdy inclined her cracked-nut face toward Jessica. "Just thought he might have something really wrong, thought he might have told you."

Instantly, Jessica was irate. "You would like for him to! You mean little gossips could then just relish every detail!"

"Now, Dearie."

"Don't you 'Dearie' me!" Jessica commanded. "Give your gums a rest!"

"As you wish it, Dearie," Purdy needled, backing out from the room. "But do come down to breakfast and maybe we can chat."

"*Hmmph!*"

Jessica waited for Purdy to start down the stairs, then she took her cane and slowly began to follow her. What could possibly be wrong with Jake? And why hadn't he told her? And if something were really wrong, how in God's name would she ever escape from the clutches of Purdy Pratt?

Chapter Four

HEN JAKE LEFT, Will Harvey returned to his desk and put his head in his hands. He had read the biopsy report before Jake had come in, had felt his stomach and throat tighten as he read it, as though he were being informed about himself. He knew from his preliminary examination of Jake and Jake's delayed reporting of his symptoms, that the prognosis was not good. Nevertheless, Will had hoped he would be wrong.

He and Jake were such good friends. Will's father had been the Lutz family physician before him and a friend of Jake's father; Will could not remember when he and Jake first met, but supposed it may have been while they were in baby carriages.

Will got up and strolled to the window, put his finger between the dusty slats of the blinds, and looked out. Jake had gone. The street was empty.

After they grew up, Will and Jake both felt a special obligation to the citizens of Atlas City, Will as its doctor, Jake as its entrepreneur and leader.

Only last year Jake had gone at his own expense to Washington, to see the Kansas Senators. He wasn't directly involved, but he wanted to lobby against the proposed extension of the nearby military reservation into grasslands belonging to Atlas City farmers. He was eloquent, insistent; nevertheless, this time Jake's mission had not been accomplished. The lands were taken and the farmers disenfranchised, just as they had been five years earlier when the Army Corps of Engineers had taken land for a dam purporting to be for flood control.

"They want the blasted thing for amusement," Jake had said then, referring to the citizens of Harper, the county seat. "The businessmen there know a big dam means recreation, which means money."

Jake, Will, Jake's daughter Jessie, and a few others were for smaller dams on the farmers' property, less damaging to the environment, equally effective.

But for the first time, it was the urban areas, not the farmers, who determined the outcome.

Will remembered that Old Jessica and her grandson Fred had been on the other side of the dam issue, even the military reservation proposal. But this familial disagreement wasn't unusual; in August Lutz's day it was Old Jessica and August who differed in what they thought was good for Atlas City.

The thing was, Fred and Old Jessica seemed to be in tune with whatever the present times were; he and Jessie and Jake apparently were not.

And now Jake was dying.

Will let the blinds go. Dust rose in the air and he sneezed.

He and Jake had been through so much together. They had fought beside each other in World War I, Will even being wounded and Jake attending to him. They had returned to Atlas City as "war heroes" and they had together tried to adjust to civilian life.

He and Jake were in each other's company when Jake met Louise, and Will had stood up with Jake when Jake married her. It was Will who had to tell Jake they'd found Louise's body when she drowned in the summer of 1927.

"I want to see her," Jake had said.

"No," Will said. "You don't."

Jake had sat on the shore of the lake, silently watching motorboats throb over the water, the dredging boats now gone. He had stared out over the lake, his gaze fixed on the far shore.

Will had put a hand on Jake's shoulder. "Come on, Jake. I know how you feel."

Jake had turned on him, his face contorted with anger. "Goddammit!" he shouted. "No one knows how I feel!"

Now Will went back to his desk and sat down.

He had even been a part of another phase of Jake's life: the involvement with Ilse after Louise had died and Ilse came to take care of the home and the children.

"Tell me how Ilse is," Jake had written from London.

He had been in England — with Army Intelligence — for almost a year before he came home in 1940. His father had died. And then, Jake said, he had "reached out for someone." That someone was Ilse.

"Do you love her?" Will'd asked Jake.

"I love Louise," Jake answered, and flushed.

"Louise is dead."

Jake was silent.

"Ilse's a fine, strong woman, Jake."

"I still love Louise. It wouldn't be fair."

"Ilse is like Louise, Jake. Quiet, but assertive."

"I know."

"You were never interested in anyone else."

"I know." Jake had looked straight at Will then. "I'm going to offer her my name. I owe her that."

"She won't accept that, Jake."

"I know."

As Will predicted, Ilse did not accept Jake's offer of marriage. Then Will lost touch and he didn't know what had become of her.

Will remembered when Jake met Louise, right after they returned to Atlas City, in 1918. He and Jake were still "battle-weary," and sometimes a loud noise would cause them both to duck and hit the floor, as if they were being shelled. But the hardest thing to adjust to was the fact that they had come back and others didn't. Oscar Smith's second son, Ronald, was one of those — killed in one of the last attacks of the war. The sad, aching looks that Oscar gave them when they saw him on the streets of Atlas City only made them feel more guilty. Why had they survived and Ronald hadn't?

Strangely enough, it was Old Jessica who finally got them both on track: "Why don't you go to the dance at the American Legion Hall in Harper?"

It was an unusual suggestion for Jessica because she seemed to want Jake under her thumb all the time, even while she ignored him.

"I don't want to," Jake said.

But they went.

Will still remembered that he had said, "We oughta wear our uniforms," as they went in to the Legion Hall door, hearing the orchestra inside fill the night with strains of "Pack Up Your Troubles." "That would really impress them. Girls are crazy about uniforms."

"You know we can't," Jake said.

But he laughed, the sound heartening to Will because it was always Jake who was serious about things, and it would be Jake who would be last to forget his war experiences.

He and Jake were dressed in dark suits, white shirts, and black ties. Some of the women there were in formal gowns, others in long skirts and shirtwaists. They had headed for the punch bowl.

"Do you suppose they put anything in this?" Will asked.

"Are you kidding?" Jake replied. "They know we're veterans and we aren't going to take to lemonade."

A swan cut from ice floated in the crystal bowl, the bowl surrounded by matching cups. On the handmade crocheted cloth covering the table where the punch bowl rested were tiny sandwiches and cakes.

"Is this a ladies' tea?" Will asked then, chagrined.

But Jake had come prepared. He slipped a flacon from underneath his suitcoat and poured. "Take a taste, Will."

"Bootleg," Will said, and whistled. "That's better."

Both men stood at the table a moment, orienting themselves. Someone had decorated the hall with red, white, and blue streamers and the band was playing, "Over There." The audience cheered.

Will was still surveying the women lined up near chairs in the corner. One brunette — Will had always been partial to dark-haired women — lounged in a large, white wicker chair, almost hidden behind two other women as if she were seeking cover from the crowd. She was idly swinging one long leg, crossed on the other. Her hair shone in the light from the revolving chandelier in the ceiling; even from a distance Will could see her face was lovely, lavish makeup accentuating the eyes. Will liked women to be bold as well as beautiful.

"Excuse me," Will said.

Will had seen Jake grin as Will strode purposefully toward the girl only to have some other man cross his path just as he reached her. Will stopped short, shook his head a moment, then stood with arms folded as he watched the two begin to dance. He gave the man only a second with his chosen partner however, before he cut in. Will remembered saying something stupid to the girl, the girl dipping her head coyly, then swinging it back to gaze up into Will's eyes. He had been smitten immediately, Will recalled.

The band finished its number and Will and his partner applauded; from the corner of his eyes Will saw that Jake was ducking out the back door, apparently having found no one who interested him.

Jake returned moments later though, a stunning blonde in tow. Even Will had been impressed with her looks.

"Well," Will said as Jake came over to them. And, lower, to Jake, "I see you did all right."

Louise Swenson extended a hand first to the brunette, then to Will. She smiled, a broad, friendly smile. "I'm pleased to have met you." And she moved away.

Jake, caught unawares it seemed, could only glance at Will and trail after her.

She had firmness, Will thought. He was glad. Any girl interested in Jacob Lutz would have to have because there was Old Jessica to face, and she was unlikely to admire anyone Jake did.

Will had been right about that; Old Jessica reacted to the news that Jake had a girl as though she'd been stabbed. But he'd also been right about Louise. As Jake related to Will, Old Jessica had looked the girl over upon hearing Jake wanted to marry her; her look was positively "venomous" Jake had said when his mother met Louise. She followed the look with a dry, "So soon?" — the intimation plain that they were rushing things. "Why not, if we love each other?" Louise had asked.

And Louise had challenged Old Jessica when little Jessie was born.

"I want to have the baby in the Harper hospital," Louise told Old Jessica when her time was near.

"I can handle babies," Old Jessica insisted. "And hospitals are for sick people. You could pick up something terrible there, to say nothing of the poor baby!"

"If it's a girl, I'll name her for you," Louise said, and went right ahead and had the baby in the hospital.

Now Will laughed, remembering.

"Well, I guess Louise is right for you," Old Jessica told Jake after the baby was born. "She'll provide you with heirs, anyway."

For Old Jessica, that was a compliment.

"Louise is a perfect mother," Jake told Harvey one day. "She loves to bathe and feed the babies."

"Like your mother?" Will had joked.

Instantly, he was sorry he'd said that, for Jake's face fell. "Hardly," Jake said. "Mother is world-oriented. She's always too busy fighting the City Council and the ignorance of the natives to take care of her family. Henrietta Olson did all the hugging and kissing and taking care of me when I was little."

And it was Henrietta Olson's daughter, Ilse, who came to help the family when Louise died.

"I can see Ilse as a friend for Jessie," Will had told Jake then. "But she's barely older than Jessie. Isn't she too young to take over a mother's duties?"

"Ilse has worked since she was eight years old," Jake replied. "You know Henrietta's arthritic. Ilse has been running the household for years."

It was true; Ilse knew how to do everything connected with a home — cook, sew, clean, do laundry — and she seemed possessed of an irrepressible energy. She could do everything but replace Louise.

Damn, Will thought now. Jake was not only dying, he would die in pain.

For the first time, he felt his being a physician was going to cost him dearly.

Chapter
Five

"*I*LSE OLSON?" the minister had said, running his finger down the baptism book. "Yes, of course she was a member here, but we don't have a current address. Perhaps someone else in the parish could help you?"

Fat chance of that, Jake thought, for the populace had rightly blamed him for the involvement with Ilse. She was so young, after all.

And yet — Ilse's mother still lived on her little farm in the valley and perhaps, just perhaps — she would tell him where Ilse was. He had to find her. He wasn't certain if it were to ask for Ilse's forgiveness, to make amends, or whether he wanted to see himself again in the eyes of one who had loved him . . . as Louise had loved him.

The black Cadillac he drove was Fred's idea. "An image, Dad, it helps to have an image." Jake had to admit it rode and handled well, and it provided him with room for his long legs. But he was far more fond of the pickup. The only reason he took the Cad was that it would upset Molly and Fred to think he might not return it. He might sell, trade, drive it into the north fork of the river — anything.

Sand and rock hurtled out from the back wheels as Jake rounded a corner, the road descending slowly into the river valley where Ilse had lived. As he drove, angling the car around the curve, he nearly struck a startled chicken who had strayed onto the path. Clucking, feathers flying, the chicken thrashed its way back to the safety of the weeds along the side.

Jake remembered coming to the Olson place years ago to try to hire Ilse. And long before that, as a child, he had sometimes come there to stay with Henrietta, while his mother worked at the Lutz Store. Henrietta had been as young as Ilse when she first started working for Old Jessica.

"Hello, Mr. Lutz," Ilse had said that day. She looked up at him with startlingly blue eyes, her long, very blonde hair like a cloud hugging her face. Though only sixteen, her body was full and round, her legs long and slim. She seemed much older than his daughter Jessie.

"Hello, Ilse. Your mother has told you I need help?"

"Yes."

Ilse had a way of bending her head when she spoke — a mannerism that reminded him of Louise. Even then Jake had felt a stab of something — pain, pleasure — he wasn't sure.

"She's a hard worker," Mrs. Olson had said.

Jake had taken Ilse back to his home for her to appraise the situation, decide if she could handle it. When he opened the car door for Ilse to get out, Jake remembered that his mother's face hung in the upstairs window, as if disembodied. She wore a malevolent look, evidence of a hostility that remained carved on her face as long as Ilse was in the home.

Jessie, too, seemed oddly out-of-sorts.

"This is Ilse, Jessie," Jake said as he ushered Ilse into the front hall.

But Jessie had only nodded bluntly and brushed past them, calling to Jake as the screen door banged behind her. "Going riding," she stated.

"Be back for dinner, Jessie," her father ordered. "At five-thirty sharp."

Jessie grunted and stalked off.

Jake turned back to Ilse. "She'll get used to you," he said, and flushed.

"I hope so," Ilse said.

Later Ilse offered to help Jessie with her homework. It was a course Ilse had already taken, but Jessie shook her head. "I don't need help," she said.

"You can help *me*," Fred piped up.

"Ah," Ilse said. She turned to him and smiled, her mouth wide. "All right," she said softly. "What are you studying?"

"Arithmetic," Fred said.

"You don't need help with that," Jake laughed. "That's one thing you do without any trouble at all."

Fred's face grew dark. "I can't ride horses," he told Ilse soberly. "But I like these kinds of problems."

And he thrust his arithmetic book at Ilse.

"All right," Ilse said. She bent her head into the book with Fred. "If I buy ten dozen eggs . . . "

Jake had stolen out of the room and gone upstairs to read, feeling secure about leaving for the first time since Louise had died.

"She may be pretty," his mother said the next morning at breakfast, "but she won't last. They never do."

They sat alone in the kitchen, the children having gone to school. Ilse had not stayed the night; she was to let Jake know this day if she would be coming, living in during the week, returning home on weekends.

"Why not?" Jake asked.

He smiled over at his mother, who still insisted on buttering all the toast for everyone, never mind Jake wanted to do his own. The kitchen was warm with the heat from the oven — Old Jessica insisted that toast done in the oven was better than that in a toaster. The air was sharp with the odor of the fresh oranges Old Jessica sliced for them every day.

"She's bound to get married," his mother said now.

She leaned across the table toward Jake, trying to press her words into him. "She's too pretty, you know."

She made it sound sinful.

Jake almost laughed. "You need to occupy yourself with other things," he said then and got up from the table and poured himself another cup of the strong coffee he'd made — Old Jessica preferred tea. "Ilse can run this house for me now."

Old Jessica frowned across the table at him. "You mark my words, that girl is trouble."

Jake, unperturbed, smiled.

Now, as Jake drove toward Ilse's home, he felt the same kind of serenity he had felt when Ilse had told him she would take the job. Jake had been relieved. If only Ilse would still be there, he thought now, waiting for him; if somehow she had never left. She would smooth things over once more as she had always tried to do.

The valley Jake was threading into was like a flat tongue pressing through the rolling hills around it. Apple, peach, pear, cherry trees thrived on the river bottom land — even corn grew here. The hills themselves were thatched by bluestem pastures like his — tall grasses that raced on indefinitely, pastures that had grazed cattle from Texas long years ago.

The Smoky River coiled through the bottom of the valley, brown and shallow. It writhed around and through the land, doubling back upon itself, twisting in the mists which rose from it in the morning like smoke. These same vapors settled back onto it in the evening, like spirits returning to their favorite haunt. Cottonwoods lined the Smoky's banks, the bed of the river clearly visible from a distance when, in late summer, the heat had dried up most of the surrounding vegetation. The line of trees crowding the water then was like a green necklace on the throat of the land. These cottonwoods were the first to flash pale lime in spring, and in fall brilliant ochre, the color so bright it hurt your eyes to look at them.

It was a day like this, Jake remembered, when Ilse and Jessie had their first real argument — or Jessie had gotten angry anyway, since Ilse had such a placid disposition she never seemed to argue.

Jessie had had a date and had come in late. She apparently had been startled — and irritated — to find Ilse waiting for her.

"What are you doing up?" she'd demanded of Ilse furiously.

Jake had heard her come in, was standing on the stair, but Jessie hadn't seen him and had gone into the living room to confront Ilse.

"I'm waiting for you," Ilse said. "Why are you so late, Jessie? It's after midnight."

"You're not my mother!" Jessie shouted. "You think you are and you may try to be, but you're not! You'll never be!"

And then Jessie had streaked out of the living room, raced past Jake and up the stairs and, without speaking, slammed her bedroom door so hard that the hallboards rattled.

Ilse was in tears. She apologized to Jake as he walked into the living room. She pulled her bathrobe firmly about her and reached for a balled-up Kleenex stuffed in the pocket. She wiped at her eyes.

"I know she'll be going to college soon, but I just don't think she should. . . ." Ilse had abruptly stopped, apparently aware she was speaking to Jake in a manner that suggested they shared an equal task in taking care of Jessie and Fred. ". . . I'm sorry," she finished.

Jake had sat down. "I don't know what gets into Jessie," he said, shaking his head. "Too much like her grandmother I guess. They fly off and you never know what it is that sets them going."

"Oh, I know what it is," Ilse said.

Across the room, the Kleenex arrested in mid-air, Jake thought how beautiful she looked, how much at home she appeared to be, how right it was that she was here.

"Well, what is it then?" Jake asked.

Ilse stared at him, a flush beginning. She seemed about to cross the room to him, thought better of it, sank back into the easy chair she'd been sitting in when Jessie had attacked.

"It's not just that I'm almost her age," Ilse began.

She seemed to be appealing to Jake to help her, but he was honestly puzzled.

"It's that . . . well . . . you know, she's been close to you." Ilse's voice grew faint, pulsed back stronger. "Since her mother died, she's tried to be . . . almost everything to you."

Her voice dropped at the last and she looked over expectantly at Jake. Jake felt his face turn hot. He hadn't thought of Ilse as anything other than a helper and companion for the children, but he found himself reacting to her now not as though she were a child, but as an immensely attractive woman. His impulse was to stride over to Ilse and take her in his arms. *Impossible*!

He got up and turned his back to her. "Ilse . . . let Jessie go. As you say, she'll be off to college soon, she's growing up, she must learn to manage her own affairs."

"But . . . "

"No," Jake said softly, almost a whisper. "Jessie has to work some things out herself. Let her go."

Abruptly Jake realized he was going to say what would be the hardest thing of all. But he couldn't stop himself: "I don't ever want anything to come between my family and me."

He felt somehow damned when Ilse at last said, "I understand."

Now, thinking of that comment, Jake felt a pang. Why, he thought, did he always say the wrong thing? Would he get a chance to correct that?

Henrietta's home was modest. Jake remembered how well she had taken care of him as a child; his mother had never thought Henrietta very capable, but she had given Jake much needed affection and attention at an early stage of his life. When she took him home for the night, she let him stay up late, a treat that Jake looked forward to, something his mother would never let him do.

Henrietta's house was a tiny, stone farmplace, built in the 1880s. Little had changed on the farm itself, except the road had been paved and, later, the main road moved farther away. The horses once used to cultivate the land had been replaced by tractors and mechanized farm implements. Now Henrietta rented the land to others and lived alone in the small house nestled between orchards of apple and cherry trees.

It had been a long time — occasionally, those years ago — since he had driven Ilse home. He'd always felt a sense of peace coming here. The valley had been a cool place to drive to in the summertime, before he put air conditioners in his and Fred's homes, the colder air hitting his cheeks as soon as the car nosed downward into the river basin. The rejuvenating air was mixed with a pungent stench of weeds and dust. A fine white powder sifted over the bushes and trees along the gravel road every time a car passed by.

As Jake approached the house, he felt a tremor of fear. He didn't know what the reception would be, but he didn't expect it to be friendly. Henrietta had never come into the store since Ilse left; indeed, she had seldom set foot in Atlas City, and that only to visit some old friends who had left their farms and moved to town. Jake felt a strong cord to his childhood had been cut; it had been years, but the years may only have added to Henrietta's bitterness. And then there was Ilse's father . . .

The car purred to a stop and Jake shut off the motor, shifted in the seat, another sharp pain stabbing him as he did so. Putting his hand to his chest, he sat for a moment, massaging the flesh.

It really was there, wasn't it, waiting for him?

Jake looked down at his chest. It seemed impossible, really impossible, that something so deadly could be operating within him — without his permission. Why him? Other people smoked and didn't get cancer.

A wave of anger passed over him and he sank into the seat, pounding on the steering wheel suddenly until it hurt his hands. Goddammit! *Goddammit!*

Jake gripped the wheel for a moment, as if ready to drive off. He wondered if he were wrong to come here, to stir up old memories, if he should forget the whole thing. Perhaps he should take a cruise around the world

— something he'd put off all his life until "retirement" — or fly to some foreign, exotic place so that he could say he had seen something different from Atlas City in his sixty-four years.

As he sat there, pondering, he heard footsteps. Looking up, he saw a worn, bent-over woman approaching him. She had on a sunbonnet, just as they wore years ago, and a rather long print dress. She was smiling, frowning into the sun; she seemed pleased she had a visitor. Who could Henrietta have living with her?

"Hello . . ." the woman called.

Jake knew that voice; he realized this spectre was Henrietta, that she could barely see — no wonder she hadn't recognized him, though he'd changed too he was certain. Great cataracts now clouded her once fine, blue eyes, the eyes the image of Ilse's. Her face was seamed with wrinkles.

Jake felt suddenly that he should flee, that he should not disturb this now-ancient, kindly woman with his probings. He should let well enough alone.

But she clutched his sleeve as he turned to move back in the car, to start the engine. She pulled on his arm urgently. Jake slid out of the car and towered beside her.

"Are you lost?" the woman inquired.

Jake got a whiff of uncared for teeth, saw caverns between the pointed stalactites of those that remained. There was a faint odor of urine.

"I'm Jake Lutz," he said limply.

"Jake Lutz?"

Henrietta frowned, as if trying to recall what the name meant to her, a twinge from the past. But her memory came up empty: she could not recollect.

"Henrietta," he said then. "I'm looking for Ilse."

"Oh, she's a good girl," Henrietta said. "Yes, she is. Come in."

Momentarily, looking at Henrietta's smile, Jake saw her as she was when she was younger, when she cared for him. He felt familiarity and affection wash over him suddenly. Perhaps all would be well, after all.

And then he wondered if Ilse were here. Could she have come back? Jake's heart pounded as he quickened his pace, for Henrietta was urging him through the dry dust of the yard to the house. He discovered Ilse's mother still had the springy strength she'd always had, in spite of her mental — and visual — failings.

"We'll have coffee and ost-kaka."

Jake found his head whirling — it had been eighteen years after all — Ilse would be forty. Would he recognize her? Would she recognize him? It was all happening too fast.

But of course there was no ost-kaka; there was no Ilse either, Jake finally realized. All that had existed in Henrietta's mind. Henrietta began talking rapidly, not sorting images out, offering them to Jake in the chaos with which they materialized: aunts, cousins, her father, and then, finally, Ilse.

"She writes," Henrietta said.

Jake wanted to escape, afraid to hope once again, but Henrietta began a search of the kitchen into which he'd been ushered and was unturning this, upturning that, ransacking the worn Bible which lay open on the white enameled kitchen table where they sat.

"A letter here," she said, as if to herself.

As she spoke, a bony, liver and white pointer picked himself up from a rug in front of the stove and moved beside her as she tracked about the room, reaching out for the hand she swung beside her, licking it. He trailed her briefly, timing her trudging steps with his tail, then turned, duty done, and flopped back on his bed. His eyes were clouded too, Jake saw, and he stared momentarily at Jake as if deciding whether to bark or not, gave up, eyes folding shut, lips puffing out as he exhaled and sank into slumber. A long snore issued. In moments, his paws twitched as he raced after rabbits, raccoons, whatever, in the rich pastures of his dream.

Henrietta was approaching Jake, hands trembling, holding a letter at her fingertips and pushing it toward him.

"Ilse," she said.

Jake hardly dared look. What if she lived thousands of miles away? But a glance at the return address calmed him briefly: Granada, Kansas. She had not gone far then — a mere one-hundred miles west of Atlas City.

Pulling out a check blank, he wrote down the street address. He noted that Ilse either had not married, or had been divorced and reassumed her maiden name, for the envelope said, "Ilse Olson."

"Did you like the coffee and ost-kaka?" Ilse's mother asked then.

He realized she lived so much in her mind that she probably could invent whole scenes, whole dinners. Glancing quickly around the room, he looked to see if there were food in sight. She really shouldn't be living alone in this condition — didn't Ilse have any idea?

And then Jake noticed that the stamp was old, that the paper the letter was written on was yellowed. Looking at the postmark, he saw it had been mailed in 1953.

Oh God.

Chapter Six

*I*N HIS ROOM, Jamie lay on the bed, looking up at the brown water spot on the ceiling. Soon he would go into Ned's room and they would play with Ned's trains, as always, before they went to see the real train. For a moment, however, he wanted to think about something: what Purdy had told him about Jake's being ill.

He couldn't remember the beginnings of his going over to Jake's and Jessie's, but it was as if it had been destined since his coming to Atlas City and so was lost in familiarity. He often went to Jake's for Sunday dinners — Fred and Molly like outcasts in their own family, for they always sulked on the periphery of his and Jake's and Jessie's conversations.

Jake had taken to Jamie and had let him go in the cutter when there was snow; he had even let Jamie ride Cannibal, the meanest, fastest, wickedest stallion he had on the ranch. Jake had promised Jamie a colt by Cannibal, but Purdy's face had screwed up in horror and she'd declared she wouldn't have a stupid horse dropping manure all over *her* yard. Jake had laughed and told Jamie he'd will him one when he himself was beyond Purdy's clutches.

Jake had promised, but Cannibal was dead.

Jake had taken Jamie for long walks on the pastures of the ranch, cutting across the tall bluestem with his bluejeaned legs striding like a pioneer. He'd shown Jamie the fresh springs that spurted up everywhere in the flinted hills — he'd fished in the river with him, and he'd swam, and they'd talked until night had swung over the sky and drowned the earth in darkness.

He'd read the books Jamie had — *Walden Pond*, *War and Peace* — the ones Jamie brought with him from his parents' library and loved to leaf through. They were stuffed up in Purdy's dusty attic now, where, in Purdy's mind, "they couldn't do no harm." Jake listened to Jamie tell how he was going to go back to the city someday and be like his real father, the one he imagined — who also lived in Kansas City.

"The city!" Jake snorted — the only time Jamie had heard that kind of roughness in his voice. But then he'd laughed and said, "I guess a fella can't try to make everyone same's him."

Jake hunted rabbits and squirrels with Jamie, waded in duck blinds. There was just about nothing he and Jake hadn't done — he thought he just couldn't stand it if Jake were sick.

And yet — now Jamie got up from the bed, went to the west window, pulled the finespun lace curtains aside and looked out in the direction of Jake's house — what could he do about it? If Purdy was right — if for once she'd got her damnable gossip straight. . . . But it couldn't be, Jamie told himself. It just couldn't be.

Jamie went from his room to Ned's.

"Toot, toot!" Ned sang in his high-pitched, sing-song. "Toot, toot!"

The train set had been given to Ned the last Christmas by Jamie and Purdy. Ned had made some primitive wooden elevators and silos and houses to put beside the tracks to make it look as though the train was spinning around the countryside, just like the real one that pulled into Atlas City twice a day. And everyday he and Jamie would watch it go.

Ned, big beside Jamie, had a shock of thick, white hair which sprang upwards from his face like a patch of weeds. His eyes were deep blue and thickly lashed, giving a deceptively feminine look to a face that was tanned and furrowed and heavily boned. His hands, hairy and big, rested on his thighs, and as he watched the train, a smile widened his face and he jumped up. "Toot, toot, Jamie! Hear the train?"

"I hear."

Jamie crouched beside Ned, eyes gleaming behind the large glasses, took one red-painted railroad car from a stack on the floor, and set it on the tracks. Then Ned, his face glowing with pleasure, poised one huge finger over the electric switch and turned to Jamie, eyebrows raised. "Now, Jamie?"

"Now."

Ned squealed with pleasure.

In those early days, when Jamie was afraid at night — and there were many nights at first when the room seemed to be housing bears, snakes, dragons, when the awful dreams came back in which he saw his parents lying beside the car, bleeding, Purdy only telling him to "get some starch in that backbone, boy, nothing to be feared of" — Jamie would go across the hall and creep into bed beside Ned. There, arcing up against the huge warmth of Ned's broad back and buttocks, he would feel safe and would at last drop off to sleep. In those moments, it seemed to Jamie that surely everyone was wrong about Ned, that he really *was* all right in the head, that he was not different. Ned would reach back and pat him, pulling him even closer against his own body, and Jamie would swear, "I will always be true, Ned. I will always be true."

And then Jacob Lutz started asking him to Sunday dinners. . . .

"Time to go see train?" Ned asked.

"Time."

Ned carefully picked the engine and the cars off the track and set them down beside the depot. They had not yet built a roundhouse, but that, Ned promised, was coming.

They went down the stairs, Purdy glancing up at them momentarily, then going back to the steady pushing of the pedal on her sewing machine.

Outside it was hot, the dry oppressive heat they had learned to expect in the summer. The trees seemed to bend over, backs to the sun, birds swirling in the sky, looking for the reflection that would catch their eyes and tell them there was water. But there was none, the puddles that came with the rains of spring long since gone. There was only the river.

Overlaying the heat was the constant rumble of the grain elevator — sucking up the ripened wheat like a giant vacuum cleaner, drying through the night. The sound was continuous in late June and July — pickups swollen with wheat lining up to be weighed, the wheat tested for moisture. If dry enough, the wheat would be scooped up into the maw of the elevator. Too much moisture and there would be a penalty for storage.

In October, the scene was repeated, but this time it was milo being taken up, not wheat.

"I get tired of hearing that elevator," Jamie said to Ned then, but Ned didn't answer, apparently too intent on thinking about the train they would soon see.

Twin lines of perspiration started down the sides of Jamie's neck. He wiped at them, then he and Ned turned onto the main street. It was deserted in the heat, only one hound lay in the shade of the cottonwoods, a horde of flies circling above it. No one was on the porch of the Manor Hotel. Usually some old men sat there, looking as wizened and dry as the geraniums languishing in wooden planters at either end of the flooring. At intervals, one of the men might disappear, only to be replaced by another frail figure.

"Train on time, Jamie?" Ned asked him.

"I don't know. I suppose so."

It was a ritual question. Just then they both heard the whistle, vibrating on the thick hot air, coming from Darby's Crossing. Ned sped up, the limp arm of his overall strap flapping around as he walked.

Jamie always told Ned, "Someday you and I are goin' to take that train!"

"Train, train," Ned sang.

"We're gonna get on that, just like those other people, and we're gonna ride down those rails as far as that train will go."

Ned would only cock his head, listening to the hoot of the engine.

That was a wonderful dream to Jamie. He had hardly been thirty miles away from home, and that in a decrepit old car that belonged to Old Lars. The car was now resting in Purdy's backyard, as though lying in state, on four bricks set at opposite ends of the two axles. The trip had been to Harper to get some medicine for Lars, and Jamie had sat in the front seat in order to read the signs for Purdy and tell her where to turn because she couldn't see well enough! They had inched along, people passing them and glaring at them, on a wickedly hot day with the wind streaming in the windows and under the front windshield of the ancient car. It had taken them nearly an hour to get to Harper, the car coughing and hacking all the way, as though it were an extension of Lars, who sat coughing in the back seat.

"No, sir," Jamie said. "We're going to get on that train just like anybody and go!"

"Train's coming!" Ned sang.

"Hey," Jamie said. He lifted his face up to Ned so that one bright lens of his glasses reflected the sun, his brows knitting together against the probing rays. "Did you know you can tell a train is coming by listening to the rail?"

Ned's head swung slowly around. "Rail?" he asked.

"Yeah. You don't have to hear the whistle. Or even before you do, you can put your head down and hear it — like this."

They were at the station now; Oscar Smith, busy, was folding the inevitable note he always had for the engineer onto the triangular apparatus fashioned for the purpose. Jamie crossed the brick platform, ran onto the track, bent over, and put his head on the rail. "See? Like this."

Ned watched a minute, then ran with a laugh beside Jamie and thrust his large head down too. He waited, a big grin spreading over his face and he sat up, said, "It talked to me, Jamie. Different!"

"Sure — didn't I tell you?"

Ned was about to put his head down again, but Oscar, who had finally noticed them, put his hands on his hips and yelled: "Hey you two, train's coming. Get the hell out of there."

Ned looked at Oscar and then down the track. Coming through the gathering light was the big engine, a diesel, the whistle sounding again. Ned pulled away from the rail and stood beside Jamie, his face glowing and his hands trembling.

"It talked to me, Jamie," he said. "Different."

Though Ned was always happy when the train came, running beside it until it stopped, even going up to the engine and trying to pat it though it was hot, to Jamie there was something sad about it, when it was finally there. Perhaps it was because it always had to pull out of the station and leave him; perhaps because hardly ever did anyone get off. Once in awhile, someone in town would board that train, but they never seemed to return. There were several passenger coaches and a Pullman, but most of the people didn't even get off to stretch their legs and, when the train pulled out, only turned their heads a bit, as though they'd rehearsed it for days, looking out the windows at the station. The white faces peering into the dusk from behind the windows looked to Jamie like the ducks in a shooting gallery. Someone, he thought, was pulling them along on an invisible string, and they were not real faces at all, but cardboard.

In the winter, lights would be on inside the train. That picture had hit Jamie with a special pang: it was another world in there. People were eating in the dining car, they were reading, they were self-contained in the coaches the train pulled. The only person who emerged from the train was the conductor, who looked up and down the track to see if anyone would get on — the only thing moving, the mailbag, tossed out of the baggage car with such force that it often hurtled against the wall of the station, to collapse downward like a wounded bird. The people in the train appeared so well dressed; one woman even had furs wrapped around her, and Jamie could almost smell the subtle perfume she would wear, so unlike the dimestore pungency of Purdy's "Atom Secret."

As the train moved out, its metal sides gleaming in the station lights, the people would stare, almost in disbelief, at Jamie, Ned, and Oscar, as though they were wax figures in a museum, some ancient setting with which the passengers had nothing to do. Jamie would say to himself: there is where I will sit. Right there. By the window. And the next time it would be a different place, and then another, until he had sat everywhere in the coach and been all the places they were going.

Ned would run after the train until he got to the end of the railyard, then he would come back, his face unhappy because it would be another twelve hours before he would get to see a train again.

Jamie walked off the brick platform, dragging his feet in the dust. Oscar called, "You guys wanta chat awhile?"

Jamie didn't even turn around and Ned only giggled and said, "Train talks to me."

Jamie looked up Main Avenue where the sun was blazing, drying to an even harder crust the clods of dirt.

Was Jake really ill? He and Jessie were the only good things, besides Ned, in Atlas City!

"This is a stinko town," Jamie said.

Chapter Seven

"STAY OUT OF THE WATER, Louise," her grandmother had said to Jessie's mother that day they left for the Ozarks. "You don't swim well."

When her mother died, Jessie felt a great gaping hole within her, and nothing to fill it. She had watched with her fists balled up to her mouth as her father dived again and again. . . . But she didn't cry.

Now Jessie bent her head over her coffee cup, blowing on the tendrils of steam that issued from it, looking out the kitchen window toward the spine of the hills where she'd been riding. She'd just missed her father apparently. The Cadillac was gone.

"Where's Poppa?" she'd asked Molly when she first came into the kitchen.

"How would *I* know?" Molly answered testily. "He didn't spend five minutes talking to us." She shrugged, rolled her large, round eyes to the ceiling. "He saw the doc this morning, and I don't know what Harvey found . . ."

Her tone was ominous.

Jessie had felt a tremor, put her hand over her stomach. It was not like her father to go off without telling her — he knew she'd been riding fence — and, as usual, anything that threatened the stability of their life together — hers and her father's — was frightening. But Jessie was not about to confess her fears to Molly; instead, she took the offensive.

"You'd better put that casserole in the refrigerator, Molly. It's not safe to eat if it's been sitting out."

Useless advice, Jessie knew. Because Molly could seemingly eat anything without ill effect. Her sister-in-law, who complained so mightily about her health, had the armored body of a tank. Jessie thought Molly could probably eat live salmonella and rout the bacteria with ease.

"Don't you worry about it, Jessie," Molly had said stiffly. Then: "Your father's ill . . . oh, yes. His color isn't good."

Jessie ignored her, picked up the cup with both hands, took a tentative sip. "So you don't know where he went?"

But Molly was off on a tangent of her own. "My back's been hurting today," she said. "All this kitchen work."

"Hmmph!" Jessie offered no sympathy.

"You'd think he would appreciate all we've done for him — cooking and all — and he treats us like strangers. Not a word to Fred and me. And us just as anxious as can be. You would think he might say, 'Molly, Fred, let me tell you what I've been through.' But, oh no." Molly folded her arms across her chest and jerked her lips into a tight line. "He wants us to read his mind."

Now she rolled her eyes to the ceiling as though this were the final blow.

Jessie walked over to the kitchen stove, looked at Molly's noontime shrimp congealing in the casserole, the little pink pieces somehow reminding her of human flesh. Her stomach wrenched. Shuddering, she reached for the casserole top, put it on. "Take it home," she ordered Molly.

"Happy to," Molly said. She flounced over to the stove, picked up the casserole, went to the door. "I know when I'm not appreciated. When your high and mighty father comes in, he can damn well fix his own food."

"I'm sure he will," Jessie said. "You don't *have* to cook for us, you know. We didn't ask you."

Now it was Molly's turn. "Hmmph," she threw back, as she swung out the door.

Jessie turned to the coffee, looked in the cup as if some answer would appear there. Jessie remembered when her father first confessed to her that he was going to see Doc Harvey. As a patient.

"I've had a little trouble," he'd finally told her a few days ago. "Just a little cough and cold. I'll get some syrup."

They had been in her father's room — he sitting in the rocker and pushing it back and forth at a rather wild gait, as if trying to indent the rungs in the floor, she standing beside him.

"Oh," Jessie'd said. She'd glanced at him, but his face was unreadable. "Are you feeling any better today?" she'd asked at last.

"I'm great . . ." Jake said. "It's just —" and then he returned her look with such a penetrating glance of his own that Jessie felt cold gather inside her. "It's just that I realize I'm not immortal. I always thought I was, didn't you? I mean — death is for other people, isn't it?"

Jessie hadn't known what to say. "But Poppa," she started.

He held up a hand. "I'm just a little tired, that's all," he said.

Now Jessie looked out the window. She could see that a breeze had started up, that clouds were pulling themselves together in the sky; it was going to rain — hard. The cattle she could see on the high pastures were gathering into bunches, backs to the wind. Even old Prince had sensed the storm; he wanted into the kitchen.

"Come on, fella," Jessie said, letting him in.

Prince gave her a grateful lick on the hand, flopped onto the floor beside her. "That will please Molly," she said to Prince. "She loves to have you inside."

Prince wagged his tail, thumping the floor.

Large drops of rain began to streak the windows and the trees in the backyard tossed. "I hope Poppa's watching the weather," she said to Prince.

He started snoring.

As she sipped the coffee, she thought about Molly and Fred: two peas in a pod, they were that much alike. Fred was the ambitious young businessman who had a deft way with profits and Molly was as shrewd about money as he was. There was some justice on Fred's side for his uncertainties with his father she knew; their father had always dominated him — her too probably — except that when he went too far with Jessie, she fought back. Fred didn't seem to be able to. He fought in another way; he couldn't face Jake directly, so he tried to erode his power gradually, in innuendos to townspeople about his father's "foolishness" and lack of attention to business, or remarks about his aging. Well, Jessie thought, maybe Fred would finally have it all his way.

But perhaps she was being unfair again, she thought as she took another sip of the coffee. Fred and Jake were so different, each foreign to every notion and idea of the other's. Even Molly had her good points: she'd been a good wife to Fred, solicitous of him, and she was generous to those less fortunate than herself. It was Molly's idea to give the clerks in the store Christmas bonuses and huge turkeys at both Thanksgiving and Christmas. And it was Molly's idea to organize an Easter Egg hunt for the workers' children.

More, Jessie had to admit that once Fred had left the family partnership — the farming end — to try enterprising on his own, being solely responsible for the Lutz Store, he had done well. Their father truly didn't manage money as well as Fred; Fred had restored the profits to the Lutz Store all by himself.

Suddenly Jessie heard the back door open, the wind rushing through as Fred and Molly swept into the kitchen.

"That dog!" Molly said, pointing to Prince.

"Let him be," Jessie said, her voice steely. This was not Molly's house and she was not going to decide things for Jessie!

"Jess," Fred said, the voice conjoling so that Jessie knew he'd thought of something, "we need to talk to you."

Oh God, Jessie thought. Fred has thought of something and she felt vastly unprepared to weigh it in her mind now. Wisdom, she knew she'd read somewhere, comes at the wrong end of the line.

Jessie sucked on her lower lip. She pushed the coffee cup away from her, took a deep breath, held it for a moment, then pushed back her chair to face Molly and Fred. For some reason, whenever they were together they had the look of accomplices.

"Jess, we've been thinking," Fred began.

He held out a chair for Molly. Just allowing Molly to be seated made Jessie feel she'd somehow compromised herself.

"Yes," Molly affirmed. "We've been thinking."

"About what?" Jessie countered.

"About Poppa," Fred inserted, confiscating Jessie's word for Jake. "If he's ill."

"He just needs to give up smoking and rest," Jessie said. "That's all."

Fred and Molly looked at one another.

"That's all, dammit," Jessie said then, angry. She glared at Fred. "Did you come in just to get a bulletin on his health? Am I to issue them every fifteen minutes or something? What the hell's wrong with you two?"

She sounded exactly like Jake in his worst moments, she knew, but god*damm*it, what was wrong with them?

"Look, Jessie," Fred said then. "We're a little concerned about . . . well. . . ." But he stopped, folded his hands in front of him, suddenly propelled himself out of the chair again and asked, "Do you want more coffee?"

"Dammit, *no!*"

Fred sank again into the chair, cleared his throat. His glance swung to her. "We were thinking about the will," he said finally.

Jessie laughed scornfully, "That figures," she said.

They had thought about August's will before he died, wanting him to leave it all to their grandmother, who could be counted on to favor Fred. But August, perverse, had given most of it to Jake.

"Now, Jess — not in an acquisitive way."

"Taxes?" Jessie offered, unable to purge her voice of sarcasm.

Fred didn't answer right away. Then: "We've been thinking," he went on at last. "It's time we considered the possibility of Dad's no longer being with us."

Jessie gazed at him. "Poppa agrees," she said.

"Oh?" Molly's interest was piqued. "What did he say?"

"Just that he realizes he's not immortal, must make plans."

"That's it!" Fred snapped, a little too readily. "That's the very thing!"

"*What* is?" Jessie turned to him, bewildered. "I don't get it."

"We're afraid that he might not . . ." Fred's voice dropped; inaudibly, he muttered something as he studied his hands.

Molly picked up the refrain, leaning back in the chair rather belligerently. "We're afraid he'll give you . . . more than us. And we need it . . . Wilbur and all."

She was nodding in time to her words, stapling them on the air.

"I see." Now Jessie sprang up, happy to be released. "If that's all you're worried about, you can rest assured that I will not take more than my fair share."

"But . . ." Molly began.

Fred put up a hand to silence her. "What do you consider your fair share?"

"I don't want the store, if that's what you mean."

Fred's face relaxed abruptly. He must have thought, Jessie decided, that she would get a portion of it and he couldn't bear that — the only thing with which he felt some affinity, some measure of control.

"You see," Molly asserted, "Wilbur might want to help out. He's coming home, you know."

No wonder her father took off, Jessie thought. If there were anyone he got along with less than Molly and Fred, it was Wilbur.

"Why is Wilbur coming home? Why now?" Jessie asked.

Molly's eyes searched the corner, the side of the refrigerator, the ceiling. Her voice was wispy. "Oh — just to check in, sort of. In case things happen." The eyes whipped back to Jessie, challenging. "Things *do* happen, you know. Even with people like Dad Lutz."

Jessie ignored the "Dad Lutz."

"One thing," Jessie said then, "I want to make clear. I want the ranch if Poppa gives it to me — and I don't mean soon — I think he's all right — or I want to run it alone if he gives it to both of us. I'll buy you out in that case, Fred."

"Okay. But . . ."

"And I'll make a cash settlement for the difference of what your share would have been if Dad doesn't do it — assuming of course," there was no point in being *too* altruistic, "I get some compensation for no shares in the store."

"Well, of course," Fred said, beaming.

Molly seemed less certain. "We would have to do some figuring," she began.

But Jessie interrupted her. "I think we're being quite premature," Jessie went on, getting up. "Poppa is very much alive and I don't think we need to worry. Not just yet."

"Well . . ." Molly said.

Jessie was saved from further inquiries by the ringing of the phone. Fred went over to answer, his voice suddenly becoming very pliant, almost little-boy like. From the other end emerged the most strident, self-assured voice Jessie could remember and she knew, without asking, that it was Old Jessica and that she was issuing instructions.

"Tell her hello," Jessie said, "and then come with me and finish fixing some fence. I need some help and Poppa's gone."

But Fred wasn't even listening to her. He was grinning foolishly, as though their grandmother could see him, nodding his head vigorously while Molly inclined her head as though to intuit whatever it was Old Jessica was saying.

Jessie sighed. She didn't bother to tell Fred and Molly that she too had been doing some thinking: she'd gotten a letter that day, a letter which stirred up memories of long ago. It recalled a terrible incident in which Fred had been involved — indeed, in which he was the perpetrator. She had never forgotten the event, nor forgiven Fred for it. If she answered the letter, her whole life might be changed.

Jessie leaned over the table, saw the image of her father diving and diving . . .

"It's never too soon to plan," Molly mused behind her.

Chapter Eight

*O*LD JESSICA went down the stairs of Purdy Pratt's boardinghouse, her wooden cane preceding her, beating an impatient tattoo on the ancient floorboards. Fred had called back just now — said he couldn't talk when she'd called because Jessie was there . . . Jake could not be found. He had packed and left. Jessica was furious: partly with Molly, who seemed unable ever to help Fred form a plan of action, partly with Jake. What right did he have to just go off and leave chaos in his wake?

Purdy Pratt — the imbecile — was busy sewing in the downstairs room.

"You going *out*?" Purdy called to Jessica as she heard her tap across the kitchen. "Mercy sakes!"

"And what business of yours is it, pray?" Jessica returned waspishly. "Can't I go out for a walk if I want?"

Purdy, her face drawn up like one of her seams, came out of the sewing room and accosted Old Jessica. She looked her up and down.

She probably thinks I look funereal, Old Jessica thought, for she was swathed in her customary black and, to add to the gloom, had chosen a black parasol. But she had also snapped on a huge pearl brooch, fastened to the right lapel of her dress. She thought it broke the pall.

"Well of course you can go wherever you want," Purdy said. "Only it beats me why anyone of *your* tender years would want to be out walking on a day so hot chicken fat would melt in the sun."

Hmmph!

Jessica not only disdained Purdy for her boardinghouse — never mind she was in it — her lifestyle, her very self, she could not abide the homely "wisdom." "Smile and the World Smiles with You," was embroidered in red thread on one wall of the dingy living room, and "If at First You Don't Succeed . . ." faced them on the dining room wall. Unfortunately for the pithy thought, Purdy had framed it without ever finishing the embroidery.

Jessica stomped her cane down on Purdy's floor. "Get out of my way."

"Well, I never!" Purdy exclaimed.

But Old Jessica ignored her.

Once outside, Jessica almost reeled from the heat and the brightness of the sun. Nevertheless she forged her way down the narrow wooden steps of Purdy's back porch, turning toward the street. The idea! Having to tromp all the way across town just because that idiot son of hers couldn't figure out what to do . . . had just taken off and let no one know *what* he was thinking. It wasn't like Jake to do anything without talking first to Jessie, and Fred maintained that Jessie didn't know either where Jake had gone. What was going on?

Putting the parasol firmly over her head, pointedly not glancing at the sewing room window to meet Purdy's inquisitive eyes — which she just *knew* were there — Jessica made her way down the cinder drive, noting how the heat radiated up at her as if she were lurching down the blacktop highway. Perhaps it would be cooler when she got to the sidewalk, she thought; at least the trees would have shaded the cement. It didn't occur to her to turn back.

It *was* cooler under the trees, but her passage along the uneven slabs of sidewalk was no easier. Old Jessica found herself having to get off the cement and into the dust of the curbing. She would write the city officials, Jessica told herself as she worked her way along. She would write them and complain, even though she knew nothing would come of it — they were accustomed to her diatribes.

Jessica walked past the Johnson house, did not look in, kept her eyes firmly fixed on the ground. If she were to stumble, fall, break a leg or hip, she would be at Purdy's mercy, a fate she certainly didn't desire! Wouldn't Purdy just love to have her incapacitated — she would fawn and fuss over her from dawn to dusk until at last, defeated, she would go insane and die.

The idea!

Jessica worked her way along, her black shoes now coated with dust, until she came at last to the main section of the town. It was bleak — she'd always thought so — the frame stores with the paint peeling off like powder on ancient faces.

For a moment, her simile displeased her, and she put a defensive hand to her own face. She was accustomed to still think of herself as a beauty; she could only resent the ravages of age.

Now Jessica shielded her eyes and studied the stores that lined Main Avenue: their fronts looked blanched, like bones abandoned in the sun, their windows dirty and fly-specked. Of course the merchants claimed it was impossible to clean in the heat, but Old Jessica remembered *she* had washed windows in one-hundred-degree weather when she worked at the Lutz General Store. It wasn't impossible.

Atlas City looked like a forsaken movie set, as she made her way along the sidewalk; someone could shoot a Western here and not have to change a thing.

For shame.

She knew the ignorant storeowners of Atlas City could do better. They could upend themselves from their backsides and at least apply a coat of paint, at least rinse the windows. Atlas City would never be a beauty spot, but it needn't be an eyesore.

She had waged such battles with the all-male City Council before, and she had never won. They considered her a meddler, someone sent to disturb their ease, and it all came to nothing. No one, except the Lutz family and maybe Doc Harvey, seemed to care. Even Jake had been ignored when he tried to get the townspeople to take more pride in their buildings.

Old Jessica stabbed the pavement with her cane, looking around — she was in enemy territory — noting, with satisfaction, that no one was afoot. She had already decided that if, heaven forbid, she met anyone on the street, she would only nod. Years ago she had made attempts to "fit in"; she had tried to start a literary club for one thing, was flabbergasted when no one would read the books but wanted to discuss them! Later she suggested the townspeople get together for a work day and clean up the town. Three people showed up. Finally Old Jessica had had enough. She knew she was never going to get along with most of the citizens of Atlas City and there was no point in trying.

"They don't want to help themselves at all," she complained to Elsie in one of her letters. "They want God — or the Lutzes — to do it all."

And then the townspeople tried to shut her out — laughing at her behind her back when Jake and Ilse carried on, to say nothing of the relish with which they spread rumors about Jessie and Pete Johnson — who turned out to be a distant relative of the Johnsons here in Atlas City. They said nothing to Old Jessica of course; they never did anything openly. It was the way they turned their heads when she walked by or broke off their conversations that demonstrated their contempt.

Well, she'd shown them she didn't care. She didn't need anyone calling on her — which they seldom did anyway, apparently feeling she needed no friends. She'd survived alone. And she would continue to survive — with her family, or without them.

Eventually she detested the local inhabitants as much as Molly did. Almost as much as she detested Molly herself, Jessica thought. Why oh why did Fred have to be so careless and get involved with the likes of her?

"Marry in haste, repent at leisure," Old Jessica thought. And then she flushed, again caught off-guard by her thoughts: the adage was true of her as well, was it not?

Not wishing to pursue the direction her musings were taking her, she returned to the more comfortable feelings of martyrdom.

She'd apparently been selected by God — or Satan — to direct the Lutz family lives, and the role was certainly taxing. Right now she had her hands full trying to figure out what Jake was up to. Obviously he wasn't well — Fred and Molly were certain he was extremely ill — could it be he decided he would have a last fling before he got so decrepit he couldn't? Or, heaven forbid, had his male hormones got him all out of whack again so that he had to go running off to the city to be satisfied?

Unlike some people, Old Jessica thought, the physical nature of man was something she hardly tolerated — except for, well, she would think of that later. August had always been pawing at her, it seemed, and she submitted to what she called his "carnal caresses" with all the grace of a martyr being burned at the stake. When he was through with his love-making, she mentally circled the date on the calendar so that if, prompted by God knows what lust, he too often sought another encounter, she could inform him that his "quota" was actually up.

But there was a wild streak in her family, Jessica thought, aiming her cane at an insect crossing her path, disemboweling it with one blow, if it wasn't Jake hopping like a satyr into the hay with someone, it was Jessie. Why couldn't they just have restrained themselves? It was much less messy.

There was the trouble with Ilse, and there was the trouble with Jessie.

Not content with one slaughter, Old Jessica now went out of her way to impale a caterpillar on the metal point of her cane. Walking over to the high curbing which went along the business district, she rubbed the still wriggling body off on the cement. For a moment, she felt ashamed of herself.

At least Fred had mostly tended to business, and though she supposed the hussy Molly tried — and did, heaven forbid! — seduce him from time to time, Old Jessica knew Fred would not be tempted to stray. Why would he want to put himself in the arms of another woman when living with Molly had probably soured him for life?

Damn her . . . damn Jake, Jessica thought.

She saw a figure approaching her from across the street; someone had sneaked up on her while she was dispensing with the bugs. Well, she had no intention of being engaged in "pleasantries."

Pulling her parasol firmly down, holding it against the person who by now had drawn alongside her, she shielded herself.

"Afternoon, Jessica," she heard someone say.

It was a male voice, sounded very much like Will Harvey, but Jessica wasn't going to be tricked into looking. He was an enemy too, a cohort of Jake's.

"Hmmph!" was all she would say.

She passed the Lutz store, holding the parasol this time against the window pane so that no one inside could see her — the store her "loving" husband had passed on to Jake instead of to her. It had made her a beggar, except for the money set aside in the past, what she termed a shabby sum — $25,000 — from August. No doubt the family liked it that way.

They'd changed the store all around since she left, moving the yard goods and ready-to-wear into the back room, and putting furniture in the front. Fred had decided to have a drawing every Saturday night and give away some inane prize, trying to erase whatever she might have done, she thought; but it would never be as well-organized as when she was there.

In moments, Jessica had safely traversed the mined no-man's zone of the business district and was back into the shade of the residential section. She put her hand to her chest momentarily; she was getting very tired. Stopping a second, she rubbed the hand across her forehead: it was wet with perspiration. Damn Molly and Fred, she thought. Molly had probably urged Fred to call her — Molly would kill his grandmother if she could!

Her anger revived her, as it always had, Jessica moving through life by the adrenalin of ill-humor, her catalyst since childhood. She had all the equanimity of a rattler, she supposed, drawing the analogy with pleasure: she was ready to strike and not too careful to issue a warning beforehand.

Well, she thought, now she was rattling on down to extricate little Freddy again, or to try to. But Jake and that damn Jessie often outwitted her! Even charged up with wrath she could not count on defeating them.

Well, she would try. She would do what she could and she would coil up — ready to inject her venom into the nearest object.

It happened to be Fred: "So what do you intend to do about it?" she accosted him when she found him in the kitchen. Then, softer: "Can't you do anything? Track Jake down somehow?"

She'd been disappointed that Molly wasn't there because she really had wanted to vent her anger on her. As if sensing a fight, Molly appeared from the dining room; she seated herself at the kitchen table with Fred and Old Jessica, barging in as usual, Old Jessica thought.

"Oh, Gran Lutz," Molly began. "Maybe it's like the elephants."

Old Jessica was so astounded at what seemed to be a complete non sequitur that she forgot to tell her — for the millionth time — not to call her Gran Lutz.

"Whatever do you mean?" she asked.

Fred, too, seemed puzzled, staring with raised brows across the table at Molly as though the heat must have gotten to her and she had gone mad. "Yes, Molly, what?"

"Elephants. You know. How they all go away into the forest and die."

"You booby!" Jessica said, lips tight, banging her cane on the floor. Glancing down, she saw a piece of the dead caterpillar still clung to the tip of the cane. Jessica felt like picking up the cadaver and flinging it at Molly. "What in God's name do you think Jake is? If he *were* an elephant, he would have run you through!"

Molly's face sank, but she shot out, "He may have cancer you know. Just like August."

In spite of herself, Jessica felt wounded. The old adversary's aim was just a little too good; she would have to watch herself.

"What do you mean?"

Fred interposed, "Molly, let me handle this. Let me talk to Grandmother."

"Of course!" Molly said, lunging back from the table, though she did not usually let Old Jessica know she'd reached a sensitive area. "If you insist on keeping death in the family."

"But we don't know that," Fred went on quietly. "We haven't heard anything for sure."

"He went to see the doctor though," Molly insisted, putting off her exit apparently, but edging toward the door of the dining room as if she thought Old Jessica just might fling the cane at her. She had undoubtedly noted how impatiently Jessica was stabbing the floor with her offensive instrument.

"That doesn't mean he's in his final agony!" Jessica shouted. "I simply want to know why he's taken off like this — what's behind it?"

"So do we all," Molly said.

Fred, impatient for once, signaled her to leave. Reluctantly, turning back to look like a chastised but curious schoolgirl, Molly left the room.

"Honestly, Fred," Old Jessica said.

Fred didn't know whether Jessica meant Molly by her remark, or the entire situation. He guessed.

"Don't always be after her, Grandmother," he said.

"*Hmmph.*"

Old Jessica pulled her arms together, still holding the cane in readiness. She hadn't quite realized what a weapon she had; she could beat off most anything, she thought, anything in the family anyway. There wasn't a one — excepting maybe Jake and Jessie combined — who was formidable, who was her equal.

"We just don't know where he's gone or why," Fred said then.

He was half-heartedly drinking from a glass of iced tea — Jessica still insisted on hot tea no matter how warm it was outside. "It's uncivilized to drink iced tea," she'd once stated, and she followed her dictum to the letter.

For a moment, Jessica was silent, the heat suddenly seeming to reach out and smother her. If the air conditioning was on, it wasn't reaching her; her forehead, again, was damp. Even her armpits were wet. There was also a faint pain in her chest — a persistent pressure — like a fist gripping her. It was the only thing she had any respect for, she thought, and it was a recent development. The fist held her when she had heard Jake left, and now her fury with Molly had brought it about again. She would wait for it to loosen.

"Are you all right, Grandmother?" Fred inquired then. "You look pale."

For once, she didn't want Fred's sympathy. "I'm fine, thank you."

They sat there a moment, then Old Jessica said, "You may have to drive me home. But I just want to rest now. I haven't been in this house — " she realized her voice was lapsing into nostalgic tones, "for ages. Just let me be a minute. Please."

The "please" apparently frightened Fred, for it was not like her to utter it, Old Jessica knew. She'd always tried to keep up a pretense of self-sufficiency, of strength, but she felt drained. Fred sipped pensively at his tea, nervously glancing over at her as she let her eyes sweep around the room. She could feel a bit of the angry glitter going out of them as she looked; images of past years were whirling before her, and she abruptly recalled that she had had some happy memories here. There had been arguments — there were always arguments in her life, she thought, most probably her own fault — she and August constantly immersed in opposite opinions. She used to pick at August for his smoking or his eating or something, and August always obliged her with a verbal assault of his own. But there was life then; she was really alive. And what was she now? . . . An old woman practicing to be a ghost!

"What is he up to?" Old Jessica murmured as if to herself. She did not seem to be aware of Fred's sitting opposite her, and her grandson evidently understood that she did not want to be answered.

For something had abruptly occurred to Old Jessica, something which she could not discuss with anyone, least of all Fred. He would only get upset about it, and he was incompetent enough in emotional matters when he was clear-headed.

"Take me home," Jessica said then. She lurched up, almost collapsed, Fred reaching across the table to support her, then she brought the cane down on the floor and began a rambling walk to the door.

Fred looked bewildered, she thought.

"I've never seen you look so wilted, Grandmother," he confessed.

Old Jessica stabbed a finger at him. "You make me sound like a fern," she snapped.

Fred, surprised at Old Jessica's unusual attack on him, was speechless.

Chapter
Nine

*F*ROM THE LETTER Henrietta had given him, Jake had learned that Ilse had stayed at a Frau Grummacher's in Granada. But before he set out for the return address listed on the envelope, he had stopped to check with Henrietta's neighbors to see if they were aware of her plight.

He learned that they took care of her, bought food for her and the dog, looked in on them every day. But when he asked, offhandedly, about Ilse, they looked blank.

Frau Grummacher also gave him no information when he stopped at her large, rambling frame home in Granada; in fact, she seemed to resent his presence. He had driven away from there somewhat puzzled by her hostility.

Jake drove to the highway, looking for a motel to stay in while he searched further in Granada. There was one — the U'll Rest Well, which looked as if it had probably been built in the thirties as a "cabin camp" and then converted, poorly, into a motel. A few sparse, dried-up elms offered splotchy shade in a central court, a slump-block pool, complete with plastic liner and filled with water almost as dirty as that of the Smoky River, and two broken-down, wooden deck chairs with faded denim slings. Jake had gotten back in the car and driven to the courthouse square again. There, opposite the courthouse, was a brick hotel called the Palmer House, whether in ignorance of the renowned Chicago hotel or in spite of it, he didn't know.

But it was clean, the lobby filled with huge, overstuffed couches, relics of earlier days, the carpet a somewhat worn Oriental. The desk clerk looked as if he had come with the hotel: a tiny, scrofulous man with a quick look but a seemingly slow mind. He reminded Jake of Wilbur.

The clerk showed Jake, rather ostentatiously, to his room, giving him the key with a grand flourish, as if the Presidential suite surely awaited him.

Jake had spent two nights in the room since he engaged it; yesterday he left it early to go to the newspaper office. He had searched — fearfully — in the newspaper morgue for the obituaries; he had not found Ilse's. Next, he went to the courthouse, looked through the voter register and the tax rolls, found nothing. It was as if, except for Frau Grummacher, Ilse Olson had never set foot in Granada.

It was boring in his room, only the radio for company and the Granada paper which he had bought but which contained almost entirely unre-markable local news. And the room was hot. Jake had flung the windows open to suck in what breeze he could, but as he was on the first floor, there wasn't much. It was noisy. He could hear cars screeching around the square during the night, restless teenagers no doubt, who, as in Atlas City, drove their cars for sole relief to the tedium. He almost felt like joining them.

Thinking of the teenagers made him remember Jamie. It was Sunday tomorrow and Jamie would be coming to the house, as usual, to eat. Then he would discover that Jake was not there, had left no explanation, and would probably be as upset and puzzled as the rest of the family. And no doubt Old Jessica was having a fit. To think that he had sneaked out from under her without a word as to his destination and intentions! It would infuriate her. But then, he thought, amused for a moment, everything did — himself . . . and his father.

August's "inventions" particularly irritated her: a collapsible cardboard carton that had been patented years before, a gravestone "monument" made by writing in wet cement — none of them ever worked out.

But it didn't discourage August.

"I'm going to set this world on fire," he would tell Jake while Jake sat, wide-eyed. "No matter how much cold water your mother pours on me, I will."

And Jake was certain he would.

He and August had been "accomplices" — Jessica's word — since Jake had been a toddler.

"Keep that child away from your infernal contraptions," his mother would explode at August. "You'll maim or kill him!"

Kill him!

Well, Jake thought now, lying back on his bed, hands behind his head, the morning sun glaring in the window so that the room was already heating up, his mother couldn't have foreseen the end that awaited him and neither could he.

Jake put one hand over his eyes, shutting out the light. He couldn't keep his mind from going back over the family's past.

Jake had long suspected, as a child, that a great battle — one of many between his mother and father — was being waged over his own consciousness, how it would be shaped.

"You should encourage your son to take part in civic life," Old Jessica would assert. "Instead, you keep him tagging along with you on your stupid 'inventions!'"

"I'll strike it rich someday, woman," August would retort. "You wait and see."

When he was very young, Jake had covered his ears to shut out the fighting; the quarrels had been frightening to him, and he had somehow felt responsible for them. It was only later, as a young adult, that Jake realized contention was a way of life for his mother and father; it seemed necessary to them both.

"I love your mother, damn it," his father once said to Jake. "And that's a curse! Marry someone easy to get along with!"

But August's "visions" were right in one way: he had bought land for the partnership, diversifying assets, and now the land was returning far more as an investment than the store. Neighbors had told August that raising cattle was an investment in the future, and August had loved walking over the bluestem pastures looking at his herds. He really hadn't liked being tied down to the store business; that was for people like Fred, who hated the outdoors life.

Fred. He managed the store well now, but it had not earned the partnership as much as it had in the early years. It was the times, Jake was certain.

Perhaps that was why Fred had wanted to talk to him, to "make plans?"

August had had cancer too.

Jake coughed, turned on his side. He had spent two bad nights here, coughing, trying to smoke, trying not to smoke, finally flushing all his cigarettes down the toilet. The morning sun was now glaring in the room, and the air was heating up. Jake became aware of the pain in his chest; it seemed daily to be growing stronger, grinding away without his bidding.

Suddenly Jake felt such a hopelessness descend on him that he wished he had brought his .22 pistol with him. Maybe it would be better to finish it off that way; it would be neater — Jessie and Jamie and Will Harvey wouldn't have to stand around and watch him succumb by degrees.

He had never felt more isolated.

He remembered how Doc Harvey had taught him to give pain shots to his father. August never complained about his getting the disease, but sometimes he raged about the terrible pain that wouldn't release him. Jake remembered sterilizing the puncture spot — as though it mattered — inserting the needle, watching his father's agonized face slowly relax as the morphine took hold. He remembered Doc Harvey saying, "Some fools worry about drug addiction at a time like this — as if it made any difference! Who the hell wants to keep a patient in pain just to prevent something that isn't going to matter a damn anyway?"

Would it have been different if he had sought help earlier?

That must have occurred to his father because August had said, "You make your bed and you lie in it. The only thing a man has going for him is to accept that without complaint."

Jake was considering packing up and going back home, when there was a knock at the door. He opened it to face the desk clerk.

"What?" Jake said, surprised.

"You have a visitor," the desk clerk said.

"A visitor? I don't know anyone here."

The clerk smiled broadly, as though he had a scenario in mind.

"This lady must know you. You Jacob Lutz?"

For a wild moment, Jake thought it might be Ilse. He had mentioned her name in the newspaper office. But no one had seemed to know her.

"Yeah. I'm Jake Lutz."

"Well. . . "

And the clerk turned around to indicate Jake was to follow him.

She was seated in one of the lobby's large sofas, almost lost in it. His visitor was in her late thirties he judged, small and dark, very beautiful. She had an elaborate upswept hairdo which looked out-of-place with her white uniform. She was clutching a large purse.

"Mr. Lutz?" she inquired, getting up.

She barely came to his chest.

While the desk clerk pretended to busy himself with the ledger, actually spying on them with quick, surreptitious glances, Jake said, "Would you care to go into the dining room and have some coffee?"

"Well — yes — all right," she said.

He helped her sit down at a corner table, watched her pull something from the purse, put it in her lap. Then she set her purse down on the floor beside her.

He waited until they both had been served coffee and some very dry rolls, before he asked, "You wanted to see me?"

"I knew Ilse Olson," the woman blurted out.

It was so sudden that Jake almost felt he'd been stabbed. So she existed somewhere, she wasn't lost in the past! He could barely keep the excitement out of his voice as he asked, "When? Where?"

"Here," she said, taking a sip of her coffee, "in Granada. I am a hairdresser, Mr. Lutz." As if to verify her statement, she put a hand up to her glistening black hair.

"I see," Jake said.

He felt hope for the first time. But he didn't want to rush her.

"Ilse was too."

"I beg your pardon?"

"A hairdresser. We roomed together at Frau Grummacher's" — few people who knew Frau Grummacher well would address her in any other way.

The "Frau" had convinced him of her absolute sincerity.

"My name is Maria Sanchez," the woman went on. "Frau Grummacher was disturbed after you left and she called me up. She didn't want me to give you any information, but as a friend of Ilse's — and knowing how she felt about you — " now she gave Jake a penetrating glance, seeming to sum him up, "I thought it only fair I help you."

"I appreciate that," he said, aware his voice was flat. Then: "You were friends?"

"Yes. Good friends. It was all too bad."

She shook her head, apparently remembering something.

Suddenly Jake felt pain lance through him and he thrust his napkin up to his face, coughing unmercifully until Maria leapt up from her chair and began pounding him on the back. The waitress came over to assist, but Jake waved them back, his face anguished and red.

"I'm — I'm okay," he managed to say, downing a glass of water which seemed — thank God — to end the spell.

"Look," he began. He hadn't brought his Stetson with him, as he had left so abruptly; now he missed tossing it around as he spoke. It had become a habit with him, as reliable and steadying as the rocker or . . . the cigarettes.

But Maria held up a hand to stop whatever he was going to say. Blowing on the coffee to cool it, she said, "Ilse loved you very much, Mr. Lutz. She admired you, and I think that this was a good deal of what she called love, but there was overwhelming affection too."

Momentarily, Jake couldn't speak.

"She saved your letters. I have brought them to you."

And Maria extended a packet she extracted from her lap. "These were letters you wrote to the children when you were first called up in the service. There is one from the time you were out of town buying cattle, in the earlier years. Everything you wrote."

Jake was astounded. He didn't remember he had even written the letters, but he took them from Maria's hand, looked at them. There were only three or four, but they were tied up with a rubber band and there was a slip identifying them, the writing Ilse's: neat, rounded.

"Thank you," he said. "I offered to marry her," he said, almost defensively.

"When a woman is deeply in love with a man," Maria said, almost as if to the air, "she wants that love returned. When she sees it cannot be, she will not accept less."

Jake couldn't think of anything to say.

"But I can see why she would be attracted to you," Maria said now.

Jake flushed. He felt pleased — and foolish.

Then Maria straightened in the chair, as though she had made up her mind about something.

"Ilse is dead, Mr. Lutz. She died five years ago."

Her voice was cold, uninflected.

"Oh, no!" it was almost a cry.

If he had thought of that, he hadn't really prepared for it.

"I have something else," Maria went on, as Jake sat there, stunned.

She leaned over to her side, reached for the large purse on the floor, pulled something from it. Then she pushed it across the table to him. Her eyes filled with tears.

"I was with her with she died," Maria said. "It was polio — bulbar polio. A very rare case. She became ill while we were driving back from a picnic out in the country. I was driving — we had a flat tire. Ilse was already struggling for breath and I — I tried to help but I couldn't. She couldn't breathe. I got back in the car and drove on the rim of the flat tire as fast as I could to get her to a doctor. I wasn't in time."

"I'm so sorry," Jake said. "So sorry."

"I watched her die, Mr. Lutz! I couldn't save her. To go through all she had gone through and then — so suddenly — so terribly — I just —"

"It's all right," Jake said then. He got up, went over to Maria's chair as he spoke, put a hand on her shoulder, pressing down. "I understand. I had to watch someone die once, and I was powerless to help her."

If Maria understood, she gave no indication. The revelation of Ilse's death seemed to have calmed her. Now she said, "Take the book and keep it. I think Ilse would have liked for you to have this."

She caressed the top of the book with her fingers, pushing it further toward Jake.

"I'm glad you were such a fine friend to Ilse," Jake said then, standing up as Maria pushed back her chair and prepared to leave.

"Are you okay now, Mr. Lutz?" Maria asked.

"Fine, fine," he replied.

Maria shook her head, as if ridding all the confusion and uncertainty of years of Ilse's secrets, and of the agony of revealing them.

"The baby was a little boy," Maria said.

"Baby?" Jake said, astounded.

But Maria was already threading her way out of the dining room and did not turn back.

Back in his room, as Jake read the diary, a suspicion began to grow in him. There were not many entries, some were even in Swedish, which he could not read, but the last, in a rather shaky hand, read: "He was born today. I have gotten money to give my baby away. I can't bear it — but I must. My baby needs a home."

The date was March 22, 1941. *Oh God*, Jake thought.

Jamie's birthday.

Old
Jessica
1885...1926

Chapter
Ten

*I*N LATER YEARS the Lutz family would peruse the wedding picture: Jessica staring sourly out at the camera, looking as if someone had just told her that her entire family had perished, August looking bemused. They would study the wedding party — seated, the best man holding a hat in his hand and wearing large tassels on his shoes, August — black, handlebar mustache, thin, wiry body — dressed in a black suit with a bow tie at the collar and a sprig of flowers springing inexplicably from the first suit button. In the photo, August's elbow is cocked on the back of Jessica's chair, the right hand resting insouciantly on his right knee. Jake once decided that his father's pose was saying, "What's all the fuss? I'm just getting married, that's all." Yet August looked like a young man in love. He was.

Jessica, however . . . in spite of the lovely white lace dress, the cumbersome tiara-like spray of pale roses pinning the veil to her thick, vibrantly red hair — which looked almost black in the picture — Jessica seemed to have suddenly been assailed by a disturbing thought: *What in the world had she done?*

In the beginning, Jessica did not feel doubtful. No, when she and August exchanged their vows in the German Evangelical Church that hot summer day in 1885, their pupils dilating to take in light because the outside brightness had almost blinded them, Jessica only seventeen and her mother weeping bitterly in the family pew, Jessica had had a feeling of triumph. She had left many broken hearts, not just her parents', but the fact that thrilled her most of all was that she had shocked the populace for yet another time. August Lutz, first cousin, "mad inventor," was the most unlikely man the people of Atlas City could ever have imagined for Jessica, and therefore she had to have him.

In 1886, young Friedrich was born, the testament to the wedding night. In 1888, the "wifely duty," as Jessica now termed it produced a daughter.

Both children were unhealthy, subject to colds, fevers; they were frail. In 1893 the frailty became serious and the children — two days apart — contracted diphtheria and died.

Jessica was never to forget the sight of the tiny coffins mounted on the burial wagon that cold, gray day in 1893 as she and August followed behind in their buggy.

That day Jessica told herself she would never have another child; it was better not to care about anything.

But she *did* have another child. The funerals of her children had caused a sudden change in Jessica: for once in her life she wanted August — really physically wanted him, masking the pain of her — their — loss in desire. She had been so fierce in her lovemaking that August was amazed. He felt he had at last ignited a passion in her to match his own, but it was not well-founded and it died out, of course, just when Jake was born, in April 1894.

August considered himself an inventor. And his latest disaster — as Jessica would term it — was born of his trip to the Chicago Exposition in 1893. There he had seen the Sullivan exhibits and a recent book on modern architecture, with pictures of the Paris Exhibition of 1889. The pictures of the Eiffel Tower actually set him off: he conceived the idea of erecting the same structure in Atlas City.

One morning, his body trembling with enthusiasm, moustache

twitching, he announced his intention to Jessica at breakfast. "I'll make it out of windmills."

Jessica, aghast, had known he would come up with *some*thing after his recent trip — he always did — but she hadn't expected this.

"You'll make it out of damned contrariness!" Jessica snapped. "You'll make your baby and myself the laughingstock of the whole town!"

"Hmmph!" August said. "You have no vision! If you could just see the things that I see!"

And August began waving his coffee cup around as if visions lurked everywhere in the room.

"If I could see the things you see," Jessica hurled at him, "they'd have me in the steam baths in a nuthouse!"

Jake, hearing voices raised, began to cry. Jessica swooped over to him and picked him up. "Now see what you've done, August Lutz! You've frightened your son with your talk."

"If he understands me at *his* age," August countered, "he's a genius and should be working with me!"

"Get out, get out!" Jessica shouted.

And August turned and stomped out of the room, to the barn, where he housed his "inventions." Jessica heard him slam the door.

"The darn fool," Jessica said, holding Jake to her for a moment. "I hope he blows himself up."

Then, worried he might be working with chemicals, she thought, "God forbid. He'll kill us all."

Jake, though he had stopped crying, held a fist to his mouth. His little body was taut.

"Now," Jessica said, putting Jake down so that he began to cry again. "Be a little man. We've got a lot to endure here."

She firmly detached Jake's arms from around her legs. She wished — really wished — she could hug him, but she just couldn't.

Jessica and August seemed always to be arguing, many of the arguments over Jake.

"I don't want him out there in that stupid barn watching you do terrible things," Jessica said. "You'll kill him."

"Thanks for the vote of confidence, Jessie," August said. "If I ever fail to invent something, I'll be sure to thank you!"

Jessica didn't answer.

But Jake, as he grew older, wanted more and more to be with his father as he worked on his "inventions."

"Go barn," he would say.

"No," Jessica would order.

But when Jessica wasn't looking, Jake was likely to struggle with the back door, succeed in opening it, and race out to where his father was working.

"Daddy do," he would say as he ran. "Daddy fix things."

August *was* fixing things — he was continuing to work on his Eiffel Tower. He had been delayed somewhat by Jessica's initial opposition, but he had not been dissuaded, she knew.

Jessica had gone out to the barn one night after August had retired and, lamp held high, looked for the marvelous "invention." What she saw made her gasp: there, laid out on the floor of the barn, were several windmills, in various stages of being torn apart, some pieces now rewelded and riveted on top of each other to make the replica of the Eiffel Tower.

It was on a modest scale — it had to be, Jessica reasoned, for him to be able to get it out the barn door — but it *did* resemble the structure in Paris. Jessica didn't know whether to be relieved or irritated.

When August started bragging about the idea, however, Jessica pretended disdain.

"Listen to this," August said, quoting from a recent book on architecture and its quotes from the Paris papers: "Before the accomplished fact — and what a fact — one cannot but bow down. I too, like many others, said and believed that the Eiffel Tower was an act of absurdity. Certainly this immense mass crushed the rest of the Exhibition. . . ."

"I'll bet it'll crush more than that sometime," Jessica scoffed.

She snatched the book from August and, triumphant, read him a contrary view. "*Seigneur et cher compatriote*," she began.

"You needn't try to impress me with your French," August said sarcastically, interrupting her. "I know you have a college degree."

Jessica had been able to complete her schooling while August had been forced to quit and return to Atlas City to rescue the family business.

"Oh, shut up," she sniffed, and resumed reading. "We writers, painters, sculptors and architects, fervent lovers of the beauties of Paris, hitherto unblemished, protest with all our might in the name of slighted French taste against the erection, in the heart of our capital, of the useless and *mons*trous" — while Jessica's voice underlined "monstrous," August stared sullenly at the ceiling "— Eiffel Tower, which public ill-feeling, often inspired by good sense and the spirit of justice . . ." — Jessica fell heavily on "good sense" and "the spirit of justice" — "has already christened the Tower of Babel."

Hmmph.

"And just who," Jessica now asked August, trying to pin him down with a look, as he steadfastly refused her gaze, "who is going to help you finish this insane enterprise?"

If she'd made a mistake in using the word, "finish," August failed to note it. "Cousin Willard, " August stated petulantly.

"That figures!"

August and Jessica shared Willard as a relative because of their first-cousin relationship: brother to Jessica, he was cousin to her husband. This unusual circumstance had caused few family objections; only Jessica's parents had voiced any misgivings about cousin marrying cousin, possibly because all parties thought they deserved each other. August's mother had died in 1870 and his father, Herman, shared August's impractical vision. He wouldn't have objected to *any*thing.

"The apple doesn't fall far from the tree," Jessica's mother had warned her. "August will be just like his father."

But Jessica had ignored her.

"Cousin Willard has some vision," August said, stubbornly. "Unlike some others I know."

"Oh, yes, vision. That's why my brother can't even farm his half of our place. That's why he forgets how many cattle he has and where they are . . ."

"He doesn't forget them," August countered. "He just doesn't always count right."

"And if he'd buy some equipment instead of trying to harvest in such old fashioned ways!" Jessica went on. "He could save paying those harvesting crews. Better yet, he ought to give up farming his own land and join them! He'd make more money."

August didn't answer, pulled on his moustache.

"Oh, don't tell *me* about the Pratt side of this family. They are my cross in life!"

"You blame the Pratts for everything!" August roared.

Jessica suspected he was defending them for two reasons: one, he was not related to them, and two, he liked to argue.

But the outburst was useless: Jessica stomped out of the room.

She stood trembling outside the door for a few moments, trying to calm herself. Though August liked to argue with her, he also seemed to revere her: he didn't smoke in the home — she objected to the odor — and he always removed his work clothes in the "mud area" off the kitchen pantry before venturing into Jessica's immaculate house.

"You'll burn yourself to death out there in that barn," Jessica recalled telling August one day, hoping it would deter him. "Your clothes reek of smoke. And," she went on bitterly, "you'll probably take Jake with you!"

"Nonsense," August shot back. "One of these days I'll make you rich."

". . . A rich widow," Jessica had said.

"If you used some of your verbal abilities to create ideas like mine, you and I could go far. You could do the selling."

"God forbid!" Jessica had said.

Now, standing in the hallway, Jessica only hoped the whole venture would soon be over.

It was. At least the secrecy of his invention was. The idea had become public knowledge.

August was interviewed by the local editor days after he confessed his plans to Jessica; in the next edition of the paper was a sarcastic editorial — much like the one about the original Eiffel Tower. The Atlas City *Gazette* declared: "A nameless local citizen, of some repute in our fair city, has elected to construct a monument to brighten the skies of Kansas. We assume it will be visible for miles, attracting tourists and the curious and dignitaries to visit our environs. We look forward to being known as the prairie town with the Tower, though we trust viewers will not confuse our Tower with that of Biblical times. We have enough trouble here under-standing each other without adding the confusion of many tongues."

Jessica cut out the editorial remarks and showed the clipping to August.

August was silent, reading.

"I suppose you'll say he has no vision," she mocked.

"Damn right! He's a pinhead!"

And August went right on building.

The collapse of the tower, with August spread-eagled upon it, occurred at the point where the third windmill was to be taken up piece by piece and riveted onto the other two. While Jessica held Jake's hand, so that he could not approach his father and endanger himself even more, August climbed up the side and rigged up a kind of pulley system to carry up the steel. Willard was loading the pieces on the rope and August was hoisting them up.

As the third piece of steel was jerked aloft, the structure began to tremble; first it shook — rather like a dog getting rid of water — then a strange crackling noise criss-crossed the frame, then the sides crumbled together and fell inward like a house of cards. August went flying down with it; fortunately, he was not pinned in the wreckage. He clung to the skeleton of the tower like a surprised spider as it went down, then was pitched aside as it struck the ground.

"Daddy, Daddy!" Jake screamed.

He wrenched himself free from Jessica and raced over to his father.

August sat up, scratched his head, and tried to hug little Jake. He groaned with pain.

"You didn't even break your back," Jessica told him later as he lay in the county hospital in Harper, trussed up and suffering with a concussion, a broken nose, two broken legs, a broken arm. "You must have a charmed life. Or there's a protector of fools in Heaven! Now I hope you'll give up climbing all over like a demented monkey!"

August didn't answer.

But Jessica saw to it that he gave up climbing. He did not, however, relinquish his role as architect, not just yet. His next project, he told Jessica, mistaking her concern for collusion, would be a dome. He would again employ Willard, who was willing, if untutored, and certainly not wise.

"He seems determined," Jessica wrote Elsie when August confided her latest idea to her, "to inflict some monstrosity on Atlas City."

August was enthusiastic, as usual. He held Jake in his lap at the breakfast table, feeding him pieces of toast, and then showing Jake the egg that Jessica had placed in a cup on his plate. "It will take this shape, Jake," he explained, as he pointed to the hard-boiled egg. "Nature's perfect shape," he went on in his fast intense speech while Jake ran his fingers over the warm, uncracked egg. "It will sit on the earth as the head of man — our greatest asset — sits on his neck."

"I don't think that applies to everyone," Jessica said with irritation.

"And now quit playing with that egg, Jake, and sit down in your place and eat your breakfast!"

Smiling — for Jake seemed to let his mother's disapproval pour off his back — Jake did as she ordered, cracking the egg smartly so that it nearly broke in two.

"Careful!" Jessica said.

As the weeks wore on, the dome plans proceeded.

The dome was to be constructed of extremely thin strips of wood, the ribs placed closely together, then mortared. "It'll look like a roundhouse," one of the local wits scoffed. "We can't corner anyone there."

The strips of wood were to be twenty feet long, soaked in the creek back of the farmhouse until pliable, then bent around a huge wheel and let dry.

The first bit of lumber that August tried to apply his method to bent well, Willard holding one end and August the other. Suddenly Willard went springing into the air like a projectile from a slingshot; the board had curved, then straightened out. They tried again. This time August was propelled through the air. While Jessica stared out the kitchen window, hanging on to Jake's overall straps so he couldn't run outside and get close to it all, the two men picked up their lumber, stacked it beside the barn, and went back to consult August's drawing, in his "study" in the barn.

"Daddy fix," Jake said.

"Daddy fix, my eye!" Jessica scoffed.

"I hope you ask the horses what they think of it," Jessica told August through the kitchen window. "They may know about circuses."

August gave her a thin-lipped smile.

But the revised drawings never came to any conclusion; August couldn't think of a new way to build his dome, and grew tired of the people who flocked by to see his "cracked egg" — or was it, they inquired, guffawing, something else that was cracked?

When her family was criticized, Jessica rallied behind the victim. Jessica knew August was not discouraged. "They may laugh at him," she told her sister Purdy one day while August was working on the Lutz Store books, "but our profits show him not to be a fool! They may simply be jealous of all he's earned!"

"And *I* helped you earn that," Jessica went on. "You have to have a good saleswoman and manager, you know."

August agreed, but he was already off on another tangent. "I'm just taking a rest from inventing," he mused, more to himself than to Jessica. "I'll get back to it someday."

"Oh . . . *dear*," Jessica murmured.

The family partnership, which she, willy-nilly, had become a part of, was another source of irritation to Jessica, as it would later be for her grandson's wife, Molly. Her brother, Willard, and his wife, Violet — French and Catholic, two strikes against her, Jessica avowed — shared in it, as did the original homesteader of the farm, Herman. But Herman Lutz was no longer an active partner by 1897: his eyesight, hearing, mind, all were failing, and he spent most of his time up in the northeast corner of the family home, muttering to himself about days long past. He had divested himself of his shares in the family partnership: he had given two-thirds of his shares in the ranch and store to August, one-third to Willard. The action had made both Jessica and Violet furious, Jessica because she thought the only son should have had it all, Willard just to be a working member, and Violet because it wasn't equal. One or other of the female sides of the partnership was constantly unhappy.

"He's careless and lazy," Jessica told August about Willard, no matter he was her brother. "And so is Violet."

"Oh, well."

August didn't seem to care — as long as he could count on Willard helping him with his schemes.

"And he's ignorant. He didn't go to college."

Jessica always pulled this card out last — the "final proof of his unsuitability." She herself made sure to wear her college pin when visiting the cousins' reunion they held every August.

At least, Jessica thought, the store was run by her and August alone. Willard would have ruined it; in fact, Jessica often thought, if her brother Willard had been an alchemist, everything gold would have turned to lead in his hands. And if August were not cautious about selecting hired hands on the farm and clerks in the store, and if they had not been hard workers themselves, both enterprises would have gone under. Willard, like August, was a dreamer, the difference being that Willard didn't want to put out any effort to attain his dreams.

Willard did try a few ventures, however. "He *says* he's going to write a family history," Jessica told August one day, having nailed him in the barn where he was scratching his head, working on yet another idea. "Anyone who begins such a project with the words, 'Our forefathers were Germans from Germany,' is doomed to mediocrity."

"I suppose so," August answered, but he wasn't really listening. He had come up with another inspiration.

"This one," he confided to Jessica, "will make us rich and famous. I'm going to put a sleigh on wheels."

If he had expected her to faint with enthusiasm, Jessica thought, he was disappointed.

August's reasoning, apparently, was that sometimes, when driving in the late spring on a snowy road, the sleigh would run into patches of bare dirt, which is hard both on the sleigh rails and on the horse pulling it. If the driver had a mechanical gadget to lower a set of wheels . . .

"You're *not* going to try to sell that," Jessica said when August confided his newest project.

"Indeed I am!" he snorted.

Willard Pratt was employed again and once more they bent their heads over drawings, assembled nuts and bolts, screws, old bicycle wheels, and wagon axles. They even put it together.

"Daddy fix, Daddy fix!" Jake shouted with glee, as though the words were an incantation.

On a cold Sunday morning in the winter of 1897, Willard and August tried out the invention with Coalie, looking rather startled, in the shafts of the sleigh. The two men and the horse went down the lane to the gate and onto the main road, Jessica shaking her head all the while. Jake, standing beside her on a chair in the living room, pointed and clasped his hands. "Daddy go," he said.

"Daddy's gone all right," Jessica said.

When they hit the sand road leading into Atlas City's downtown, August gave Coalie a smart crack with the whip. "It was to show off, of course," Jessica wrote Elsie McDonald, later, "and damned if the wheels didn't come down with a bang and frighten Coalie so much she bolted. They went lurching through town, first the sleigh rails down, then the bicycle wheels, and didn't stop until Coalie came shuddering into her stall in the barn!"

August and Willard, unfortunately, did not follow Coalie into the barn: the sleigh hit the too-narrow barn door, wedged there, while the shafts broke off, trailing the stampeding horse.

After this disaster, August could never get Coalie hitched to anything.

But August didn't entirely abandon the sleigh: he removed the bicycle wheels and hung a picture of William Jennings Bryan on the back of it. Why he did this, as well as a good many other things in his lifetime, Jessica was never to know.

"I'm married to a madman," she announced to no one in particular.

Chapter
Eleven

*I*F SHE TRULY was married to a madman, Jessica began to feel, she'd better see that she was financially secure. So, in the spring of 1900, just before Jake's sixth birthday, "To stave off starvation," as she put it, Jessica rented Jake's room out to a Swede visiting from the "Old Country." Olie Olson moved his steamer trunk, his Swedish New Testament, and himself into Jake's old room on the northwest corner of the house while Jake, protesting, was transferred onto a cot in his grandfather Herman's room.

Herman's room was oppressive, Jessica had always felt: towering high-back walnut bed, glazed china washbasin and matching pitcher on a dark walnut washstand, almost black, varnished wood sills, and a tall walnut wardrobe with carved doors and drawers. The room didn't get the favorable southwest breezes in the hot summer, but managed to collect the full blasts of the cold plains winters. Jessica supposed that Jake must have felt abandoned, but she could see no other way to assure herself that there would always be money for necessities.

By the time Olie Olson arrived, Herman had become a bit of a problem. Sometimes, mind wandering, he would go down the stairs and out the front door and roam around the town looking for his "dog" or "cattle." Usually he was found before he got too far, but many times Jessica had to send Jake out to look for Gramp.

"Is Gramp looking for Whitey?" Jake would ask.

Whitey had been Gramp's favorite dog, a liver-spotted pointer who had never been a very good hunter but who Gramp adored.

"That dog knew when hunting season was coming," Herman used to tell Jake while Jessica made up his bed. "He would begin to quiver when October nights got cool."

"Oh, *Herman*," Jessica would protest.

Jessica had long grown tired of Herman's stories, and thought she probably knew everyone of them by heart. She wished that the burden of his care could have been shared by August's sister, Hermina, but Hermina was far out on the West Coast and declared *"She could not do it."*

Nevertheless, Herman was not demanding. It was just that sometimes now he was incontinent, and Jessica would have to clean the bed soon after she'd made it. Then she would have to take a washrag and the little washstand, fill it with warm water, and clean Herman too.

"Gramp has a present," Jake would sometimes tell Jessica when she was downstairs preparing supper.

"Oh, God."

Jessica knew that Herman's presents were not to be desired; Jake had begun to call the stools Herman inadvertently passed the same thing that stupid Violet called her baby Purdy's: presents.

Jessica said, "If there's anything this dirtiness is *not*, it's a present."

But she always cleaned up the mess.

Jessica was a worker. She rose early every morning, at five, to begin the day's cooking, starting with the breakfast — eggs, bacon, *pie!*, toast, and coffee — for Herman and Jake and herself, carrying Herman's breakfast up to him on a tray. At dinnertime, the noon meal in Atlas City, the Lutz and Pratt families ate together and Violet was supposed to help Jessica, but she was always "under the weather." She begged off most days. Violet seemed to find some excuse so that she would not have to prepare the grand repasts, even though she shared a housekeeper with Jessica — Henrietta, who was almost abysmally stupid but who could at least serve what was prepared, and, if instructed carefully by Jessica, could follow directions and cook. Henrietta's duties at Violet's were simple: wash and iron, one day a week.

After breakfast, Jessica would wash the dishes with Henrietta's help and prepare to go to the store to work. Jessica was a good manager and full of energy; she could prepare endless meals with seeming ease and then put in a full day at the Lutz Store.

Now, seated at another noon meal, August was, as usual, taking charge. The new renter was shy and, sensing this, August seemed determined to tease him.

"Olie's got a girl friend," he said this day.

It wasn't true, of course, but August got the desired reaction from his reticent boarder: Olie's face flushed red from the tip of his chin to the top of his forehead, where his blonde hair curled over his eyes. Olie was very good-looking, tall, muscular, blue-eyed, and he had caused quite a stir among the eligible young women in the community.

"Oh, shut up, August," Jessica said as she served him his fried chicken. She tried to give Olie an encouraging smile.

"I've heard how all the young girls are going to church, now that they know Olie will be there."

"August!" Jessica said, and stamped her foot. "If you don't stop right now, I won't give you any more food!"

"Oh, bother," August said.

Jessica knew he would cease because if there was one thing August liked, it was eating. He could stuff himself until he could hardly ease back from the table. And there was plenty for him to eat, no thanks to Violet: three fried chickens, mounds of mashed potatoes, a huge boat of gravy, sliced pickles and tomatoes and cucumbers, steaming green beans, slabs of fresh bread stacked so high the top leaned over in imminent fall.

Yet no matter how high the bread was piled, hands reached out so quickly when the warm slices were set upon the table that the plate was empty immediately and passed to Henrietta or Jessica to refill. Jessica would frown, sigh, get up and slice more bread.

August dominated the conversation. Olie would mostly say, "Ya, ya," from time to time, encouraging others to talk but offering little input of his own.

"Let someone else talk for a while," Jessica would tell August.

"Anyone wants to say anything, let 'em interrupt!"

And August would roar — a more robust version of the cackle Grandfather Lutz emitted from time to time, always at the beginning of some tall tale, which, Jessica supposed, he thought was entertaining.

"Did I ever tell you about the Mexican green bananas?"

August was stabbing a leg of chicken into the air, using the piece of meat to emphasize his words. He took a bite, chewed thoughtfully a moment, organizing his story.

"Of course you've told us," Jessica said, "we've heard it a hundred times."

August ignored her. Like Grandfather Lutz, when he wanted to talk, he did.

"Well, I ordered half a carload — think of it — half a carload from Mexico."

"August, please," Jessica said, putting yet another bowl of potatoes on the table near him, thinking that might end the recital.

She was wrong. Flushing, her face perspiring, pushing her hair out of her eyes, she realized August would continue. She looked over at Olie briefly, wanting to give him a look of sympathy, was startled to see that he had been watching her all along.

"So they came in. . . . Green? Why I shout to heaven, they were green! They looked like they'd never been on a tree, like them damn Mexicans just shaped them out of clay or somethin'. *Well . . .*"

Again like Grandfather Lutz, Jessica thought. Dramatic pauses — or boring, depending on how you looked at it — were their stock in trade.

Jessica sat down at the table, aware that Olie was following her every movement. Jake began tracing his fork on the tablecloth, indenting it. Jessica reached out and pressed his hand down so he could not move it. He looked up at her and she shook her head. Olie: watching.

"So I decided as how I would ripen those stiff little things. So I take 'em down to the basement, build me a tent over the coal furnace we got going there. . . . Know what happened?"

No one asked.

"The damn things blew up on me! Damn furnace and all was belching out black smoke like we was in the bowels of Hell!"

"*August!*"

Like his father, Jessica thought, August repeated the story the same way every time. And also like Herman Lutz, Jessica played her customary part in the story.

"August! Clean up your language!"

Briefly, August would look down and pause. Jessica noticed that Olie looked over at August for a moment, then back to her, as if he wanted to say, "I understand. I understand you."

"I ripened them up all right — they looked like pieces of coal by the time I got through with 'em . . . and so did I!"

"It's not funny," Jessica said, her voice level but furious. "*I* had to do all the cleaning up and we lost a lot of money on that deal of yours. I don't know what *you're* crowing about, nor why you have to tell that story over and over!"

"Because I like it!" August shouted.

"Now eat your food and be quiet," Jessica would order, and, surprisingly, August did as she instructed.

After the meal, Olie always stayed to help; Violet sometimes stayed, but never for long, and Henrietta and Jessica would clear off the dishes. Olie seemed to linger around her indecisively, Jessica thought, then August would say, "Time to get back to the store."

One day August told the assemblage: "I've taken in a new partner!"

August had the controlling interest in the family partnership — the farm, the store, and all assets of these enterprises. But he seemed to forget, at times, that there were others. His announcement surprised Jessica.

She looked at him and waited for clarification.

"Guess who?" he prompted.

At the table, Olie bent his head.

Recognition was coming, Jessica saw, and it must have been Olie since he was flushing. She noted too that apparently Olie didn't know how to avoid the attention. She felt anger rising in her.

August now pointed to Olie. "Him," he said. "My new partner, Olie Olson!"

Jessica bit her lip. "You could have asked *me*. I'm a partner too."

Then, because she didn't want to hurt Olie's feelings, she briefly put her hand over his, causing even more redness to creep over Olie's face so that he looked as if he might blow up.

"It's just — it's not that I don't want you," Jessica said, her voice strangely soft. "It's just that I don't know how we're going to split the profits more ways."

"Amen to that," Violet said.

Willard seemed expansive — as usual. "Oh, we'll manage," he said. "Don't we always?"

"I — I do not want interfere," Olie said, the words emerging sing-song from him, and with effort. "It — it August's idea."

"And a good one," Willard said, while Jessica stared at her brother. "That's great news."

"Well, we'll see," Jessica said, her voice tight.

Yet Jessica seemed to enjoy Olie: he was a respite from the commonness of the townspeople and he was a hard worker. He wasn't really a partner — August, as usual, had overstated the facts — but he shared some of the profits. And all of the work. He not only helped at the Lutz Store, he helped with the wheat harvest in July.

And it was hot — a dry, relentless, pressing heat which reminded Jessica of a song Herman Lutz used to sing, to a tune of "Tannenbaum":

> *I've reached the land of corn and beans*
> *At first the crop looked fine and green*
> *But the grasshoppers and the drouth*
> *We'd better pull up and go south*
> *Oh Kansas sun, hot Kansas sun*
> *As to the highest knoll I run*
> *I look away across the plains*
> *And wonder why it never rains*
> *And as I look upon my corn*
> *I think but little of my farm.*

Well, Jessica thought, it wasn't corn harvest — August was generally smart enough not to plant corn on upland — and though the weather was good for a wheat harvest, it was difficult to endure.

"I hate it," Jessica told Henrietta, who was helping her prepare the huge dinner for the harvest crew. "It's so hot. There's so much work. And we never have a day off, not even when the crew brings along a few cooks to help us. After they go, it's still the same old grind!"

Henrietta nodded. She and Jessica had to get up even earlier — at 4:00 a.m. — to prepare for the larger harvest meal.

And though the crew's hired cook helped in Jessica's kitchen now, she could barely tolerate him. It seemed he was continually in the way whenever she went over to see if the fried chickens were ready, if the potatoes were mashed — she didn't care if he was only thirteen — he was supposed to know what he was doing.

"Where did you come from?" Jessica asked the boy now, pushing back her hair so she could see into the oven where the bread was browning. "Have you been with the crew long?"

"Came from Oklahoma, ma'm," the boy said in what Jessica later termed a "hillbilly" accent — halfway between a drawl and a twang. "Been on the crew most of the summer. We done Oklahoma."

"*Did* Oklahoma," Jessica corrected as she carefully shut the oven, wiped her hands on her apron, stared at the shy young man. "You *did* Oklahoma. If you ever want to improve yourself, you'll have to learn proper English."

"Yes, ma'm."

"And don't just 'Yes, ma'm,' me. Get that fork there and mash those potatoes."

"Yes, ma'm."

Henrietta looked at Jessica with her dull gray eyes; she had a half smirk on her face, which Jessica would have liked to wipe off with the back of her spoon. Instead, she inserted it in some of her homemade cherry jelly, emptying the jar in a dish. "It won't last two seconds," she predicted. "I know harvesting crews."

The men worked with the binder, Olie helping Jake — bless his heart, Jake *tried* — and August, who attempted to keep up with the wide swaths the binder cut in the ripe wheat. The field wasn't large, but it took time. The threshing machine was placed in the center of the field and the shocks of wheat were fed into it. The Atlas City postmaster once complained that the whistle the threshing machine used sounded just like the train whistle. "Damn farmers who aren't harvesting," he told Jessica, "damn farmers come in wanting their letters!"

Jessica just laughed.

No one helped the women, however, she told herself, as she surveyed the table to see that all was in readiness — there were few hands offered in the kitchen. Each farm wife had to resort to her own initiatives, and whatever household help she had, to feed the hungry men who, like locusts, settled first on one farm, then another, cleaning it out. The smallest child had to help: Jake, at six, was big enough to do quite a few things for her when he wasn't out in the field — peeling potatoes, slicing tomatoes. Of course Jessica worried that he would cut himself, so she hovered over him most of the time, making him feel awkward no doubt, and taking her time away from other chores.

"Here they comes," Henrietta said this day.

"Here they *come*," Jessica corrected, throwing her hands up in despair. "Lord Almighty, doesn't anyone in this God-forsaken town speak English properly?"

Henrietta blanched at the words "Lord Almighty" and "God-forsaken." "The Lord's name shouldn't be taken in vain," she said primly.

"I'm not taking it in vain," Jessica said. "The Lord ought to try to fix this kind of a meal!"

Henrietta cast a downward glance as she went to the door to let in the hot, dirty, tired men.

"Wash up in there," Jessica ordered before they could set their filthy feet in her kitchen. "And get the chaff out of your shoes! I don't want to have to sweep up after you!"

The men, bold and aggressive with each other, immediately obeyed Jessica. August laughed. "See what a tyrant I live with?" he said. "A regular she-cat!"

"Fudge!" Jessica said.

Olie came in last, gave Jessica a tentative smile, went in to carefully wash himself. Jessica felt sorry for him in his overalls: the itchy wheat chaff got in every possible opening and the clothes were not washed until the harvest was over. All the men could do was rinse off in the horse tank each night — although August said that felt wonderful, the cool water sloshing all over and helping to soothe the irritated flesh — and at the end of the ordeal, dunk the overalls and prepare them for the next harvest.

The men settled down to eating as quickly as they were in the chairs, knowing August did not offer prayers. "All I pray for is a good harvest," August said. "And I don't always get that, so I'm not asking for more."

The men ate like animals, Jessica thought. She always went into the parlor, as far away from them as she could get, letting Henrietta serve them for a few moments, then coming back to see that the fool hadn't let something awful happen. Henrietta was so careless she was likely to spill hot coffee on someone, or drop the jelly in someone's lap. Jessica wished she could have someone elegant to wait on her, as Elsie McDonald had told her *she* had in New York.

Elsie would be coming soon; her parents still lived in Kansas City, and when Elsie visited them, she always made a pilgrimage to Atlas City to see Jessica. Elsie's coming was a pleasant thought.

"*Tak*, Jessica, thank you," Olie always told her, before he returned to the field.

"You're welcome, Olie," Jessica answered.

Later in the day, Jessica and Henrietta would take a "lunch" out into the fields, around four o'clock, along with cold water or lemonade, so that the men could rest a bit before going back to work until the sun set.

Jessica was always glad when the harvest season was over. It made the Fourth of July — if harvest had come before it — all the more enjoyable.

But what was she doing *on a farm* in Kansas, Jessica often asked herself as she crawled, tired and hot, into the bed beside August. It was hardly what she had thought of that day so long ago when she married him in the dankness of the old German Evangelical Church. Perhaps her mother knew this when she had opposed her marrying August.

Lucky Elsie. She had never had to live in a place like Atlas City.

Chapter
Twelve

MMEDIATELY AFTER graduation from college Jessica began writing Elsie McDonald. Elsie had moved to New York because she was an artist; she felt a need to be in a place where art was not only "understood, but appreciated."

Writing Elsie transported Jessica out of Atlas City; sometimes she even wrote her in French, her college major. Usually she wrote her letters to Elsie on Sundays — ensconced in her upstairs bedroom, secure in her rather set-apart environs — even August entered with a knock when Jessica was there — but for some reason, every once in awhile she didn't want to stay home and compose her epistle. She chose the bookkeeper's office, at the Lutz Store, where she had taken over the chore for August. He detested working with figures.

From Monday through Saturday everyone worked long days at the store: Lon Nelson, grocery manager, opened the doors by seven o'clock every morning. Even then, customers complained they'd been waiting "for hours." And they worked until seven at night Monday through Friday and until twelve on Saturday night!

Sunday was a day of rest for everyone but Jessica, because she prepared the family meal. Occasionally Violet kept her family in her own home, but more often they simply showed up, ravenous, precisely at the moment Jessica was ready to serve her own family.

It was a schedule that would have killed a Hercules; yet it was only in the past year that Jessica had noted she wanted to slow down, was tiring of her work. She had wanted more from life. Sometimes when she felt overcome by boredom or had had a particularly irritating customer (like Mrs. Kunzler, who was always ill and wanted Jessica to "Feel here — see that lump?" or "Look into my eyes — see the sickness?") she would come up to the small room where her desk and August's were and lie on a cot that August had brought up from the basement for some project or other and which he mercifully had never carried out.

Sometimes, lying there, Jessica would indulge in self-pity. "The family uses me," she was fond of saying. "I have to do everything."

Yet she was violently unhappy if she wasn't involved in everything. Certainly no one else ever did anything well enough or quickly enough to suit her.

This was not the first time Jessica had come down to the store when everyone was gone; sometimes on a Sunday afternoon when the family dinner was over, or on a week night when August was occupied with Cousin Willard and some damn foolishness, Jessica would sneak into Lutz's. She would stand near the hat counter and, one by one, try them on — the most outrageous ones, with ostrich plumes or swollen roses, plunk them down on her glowing red hair, and admire herself in the hand mirror left on the counter for customers. And she would stare into the three-cornered mirror near the yard goods counter, with some satin fabric, perhaps, held up before her so that it looked like an elegant dress, a great hat swaying on her head. She was in New York, she told herself; she and Elsie were striding down the street and everyone was admiring them. They were still beautiful young girls.

Jessica decked herself with the counter's jewelry; she tried on new boots and coats; she invented a whole life apart for herself.

But this night she was preoccupied with writing to Elsie. The correspondence, though wavering somewhat, was still important to her as Elsie was, after all, the only one to whom she could confide. She told Elsie McDonald things she would never have confessed to anyone else. Even so, Jessica kept the letters three days before mailing so she could be certain she had not revealed anything that might later prove embarrassing.

"My dear Elsie," she began that evening. *"I've had to take over Baby Purdy's care. August thinks she isn't walking as well as she should by now — she's about 18 months — so he has come up with some of the most wretched schemes for helping her walk. She's never been exactly quick, if you know what I mean, and she seems to be taking her time developing as well. One of the horrible ideas August has come up with involves those damn bicycle wheels he used on the sleigh, the same ones that ruined Coalie for hitching. I've had to fight him on this as well as Violet and Willard, who think this is probably one of the greatest ideas he's ever had. They even think I'm jealous and want to hold Purdy back! Such a mad-house here!"*

Jessica paused, chewing on the end of her pen. She waited a moment, then bent over once again and began spilling out sentences in a rush.

"And you can't imagine how awful it is getting Violet to market (August sometimes lets her go, why I don't know). She takes the train and she simply won't get ready on time. August goes down to the stable, gets the horse ready, pulls the carriage in front of the house and loads Violet's stupendous trunk in it, then he waits for her. He waits maybe five minutes before he puts down the reins and comes inside. 'Damn it, Violet,' he says, 'will you get down here so we don't have to race for the train?'"

"And the funny thing is, Violet always makes it — just barely — but she makes it. She must lead a charmed life."

Now Jessica stopped writing, looked out over the quiet store: the hardwood floors gleaming, for August loved to swish the big mop about, moving customers aside as if they were pieces of furniture, dusting the wooden display counters, where yard goods, hats, lingerie, men's undershirts, and overalls were stacked. Below her she could see the grocery section where Lon sliced bacon for customers, ground coffee, weighed beans. It was peaceful here, Jessica decided, quieter than her home where Jake was likely to be playing some noisy game.

Sometimes people would walk by the window and stare in, not seeing her. She felt like a spy, seeing, but not being seen; she could look out, hidden, watch people engaged in their rare leisure pursuits, walking about town in their Sunday best.

Jessica picked up the pen again. *"I guess what bothers me about this awful slowness of Baby Purdy,"* she went on, *"is that it reminds me how fragile life is. It reminds me of my own, devastating, unforgettable loss."*

Jessica sighed: it was out.

"*Why is it that I cannot warm up to little Jake? I try sometimes — he looks up at me as if he wants to eat me up at times, yet I can only feel something for him when he isn't well.*"

Jessica leaned back. She could hear voices out on the street, people passing by, a few carriages traveling down the dusty main thorough-fare.

"*I feel as if he's an orphan, belongs to someone else.*"

What was wrong with her, Jessica wondered. She did not like feeling this way.

"*Sometimes I think my whole life here is a mistake, or a dream. I feel I mustn't love anybody — they'll die! I mustn't attach myself. I seem to be someone else, living my life. If I keep working, I don't notice it so much, but if I stop to think — if I take too much of a rest — these thoughts come rushing at me. They'll crush me, Elsie!*"

What Jessica *did*n't write was that August had suggested they sleep in separate bedrooms, that August had relented in his "lascivious" pursuit of her, and that it was only rarely she had to "subject" herself to his caresses. She also didn't note that she cared most for August when he was indif-ferent to her. There *was* something wrong with her! And once again she seemed to have been broken in two and she couldn't find the break, couldn't seem to mend it.

Jessica bent over the letter again.

"*Sorry to burden you with all this, Elsie, but I've felt unusually iso-lated lately. Perhaps it will all pass. I hope so. Anyway, my love, Jessica.*"

Well, Jessica thought as she sealed the letter, wrote the New York address she knew so well, she would just have to pull herself together. Enough people in the Lutz clan were always going to pieces — it wouldn't do for her to shatter as well.

And then she recalled another scene — on Elsie's last trip to Atlas City. She and Elsie had gone up to her bedroom and sat there on the bed. They had covered each other with powder, and then they had lain, hands behind their heads on the pillows, and plotted the wonderful things they would see and do.

"I'd like to paint," Jessica had once told Elsie, long ago.

"Oh I know you could, Jessie. I just know you could — you've got a good eye and I've *seen* you draw."

Jessica bent her head in unaccustomed humility. "My drawings are nothing compared to yours," she said.

"Oh but they are!" Elsie protested.

And then, without Jessica's really wanting it, Elsie got up and went over to the sketch pad — the only one — which Jessica had completed, black and white charcoals, of scenes in the town, on the farm. Elsie swore now that they showed talent.

"What you need to do," Elsie said, "is go to a school and study. Talent shrinks if you don't use it."

"Have you ever seen a farm wife who paints?" Jessica scoffed.

"What has that to do with it — talent can be anywhere."

"I don't mean that," Jessica said. "What I mean is — we work so hard here with the store, the farm. How could I possibly take time off to go to school? Impossible!"

"Well, you went to college."

"That was before."

"You could do it," Elsie said, "if you really set your mind to it."

"But August likes me here!"

"Of course." Elsie had smiled. "A man needs loving."

"Elsie!"

Well, Jessica thought now, that seemed a very long time ago. And she hadn't done anything about going to school. Sometimes she got the sketches out, looked at them, thought they weren't so bad. But she always rolled them up again, stashed them away.

Farm wives *didn't* have time to paint, Jessica told herself.

The cousins' reunion in August was always held at Sister Purdy's boardinghouse and Elsie McDonald was coming. Jessica was relieved that it wasn't at her house — in the first place, the Pratts always came and she would just as soon never have seen any of them again. They were such boobies! There were few of the Lutzes she cared about either, but they were superior — in Jessica's eyes — to her own clan, the Pratts. In college, she and Elsie had dubbed people either GG's (Great Gods or Goddesses) or MM's (Mere Mortals). If there had been a ranking below MM's, she would surely have put the Pratts in it!

Sister Purdy's boardinghouse sprouted signs all over the yard, just as Baby Purdy's would do years later. She had a sign which read, "*Professor Miss Purdy Pratt, Seer and Teacher. I cure Boils, Warts, Fevers,*

Blindness, Fits, all manner Disease, also Deaf and Dumbness. Tea readings. Seances."

Imagine asking the relatives to such a nuthouse! But Purdy always stuck the relatives out on her lawn — filled with all sorts of rotting, rusting junk — for Purdy would throw nothing out, instead went to all the auctions, farm sales, even funerals in the vicinity and asked the families if she could buy their "leftovers." She served the buffet from her "gazebo" a flimsy affair that Cousin Willard had helped her construct from warped, unsaleable lumber. Jessica refused to set foot in it. August had to bring her her plate when it was time to eat. Even then she only ate what she herself had brought. "You don't know how clean any of these people are," she told August. "I *know* I'm clean." She added, "And I'm not going to have that monstrous thing, that crazy gazebo come crashing down on my head."

Purdy had statues strung about her yard, which she'd collected from local graveyard monument dealers who'd made mistakes somewhere in the sculpting. A child might have two left hands, or a piece knocked off the nose; misspellings were common: "For Mither," the legend might say, or "Bother Still Lives With Us All."

"Why is it I get the idea I'm in Dante's *Inferno* whenever I'm at Purdy's?" Jessica once asked August.

He only sighed.

To make matters worse this year, Jessica was having doubts about having invited Elsie for the reunion. Actually, she hadn't really invited her; it was just that Elsie had said this was the only time she could come and Jessica couldn't bear to miss her. Now she would see all the clowns in the family. Well . . . she and Elsie would laugh about it later — they would arrange everyone in descending order — Sister Purdy, with her healing of Fits, Boils, Warts, at the very bottom. No, maybe Violet last.

Olie had not met Elsie and seemed to be curious. He had gone with Jessica in the buggy to fetch her from the train.

"She is good friend, eh?" he asked Jessica.

"Oh, my best. She is. . ." somehow she thought she could speak of this to Olie, he was so sincere, "she is re*fin*ed. She speaks French and paints!"

"Ah."

Olie rocked back on his heels as he stood beside Jessica, absorbing this.

"She is so accomplished, Olie. She makes me feel," and Jessica seemed to search the dry countryside beyond the train station, the dirty pieces of coal that had fallen from the tender lying beside the track gleaming in the sunlight, "she makes me feel so inadequate."

"But *no*!" Olie protested.

For a moment she thought he would seize her hands and wring them.

He didn't go on — the train whistle blasted the air, coming from Darby's Crossing; moments later they saw the black ink blots of smoke that accompanied the engine, smudging the sky and merging into one long, wavery line behind the smokestack. Then the train came chugging into the station, Oscar Smith, the elder, getting ready to hand the engineer some kind of message.

"I often wonder what they have to say," Jessica mused as she watched Oscar importantly snap the rubber bands holding up his sleeves, first one, then the other. "Hello? . . . Goodbye?"

But Olie didn't answer.

Behind them, Boots, the new chestnut August had bought for the buggy — he had to buy something, for Coalie wouldn't be coaxed into any kind of harness — stomped his white-socked feet and switched his tail. It was already getting hot and flies buzzed around the sweating gelding. Boots impatiently flicked his tail from side to side, occasionally turning his head to try to bite the insects tormenting him.

Why in the world, Jessica wondered, looking at the uncomfortable horse, would Elsie want to leave New York and come to boiling hot Kansas? Her parents, *yes* . . . but Atlas City? That was friendship, if that was the only reason she came!

But Jessica didn't care what Elsie's reasons were — she was coming, and even if it *was* reunion time, somehow they'd make the best of it.

Elsie came off the train looking magnificent — in a lime-green dress with handmade lace, a matching hat and ostrich feathers, dainty lime-toned shoes and purse. The soft color of the dress brought out the green of her eyes, played off the blonde hair, the fair coloring.

"Isn't she beautiful?" Jessica asked as she pointed out Elsie to Olie Olson.

"Ya," he said.

But Jessica saw he wasn't looking at Elsie. She blushed, flustered. She looked back at Olie and found, much to her consternation, that a little shiver of pleasure coursed through her as she gazed over his handsome face.

To cover her confusion, Jessica ran to clutch her friend, pulling her close in a wild embrace. "Elsie! Oh my dear Elsie, you're here!"

It seemed as if all the boredom, all the wretchedness of the hot summer and the harvest and Violet and all had slipped away, and Jessica was once again the carefree young college woman.

"Jessie!" Elsie said, returning the embrace and then bursting into happy tears. "Oh my sweet Jessie!"

Olie stood looking at his feet as the women greeted each other, then, remembering, Jessica pulled back and beckoned to him, introducing him to Elsie as "Our boarder and helper, Olie Olson. He's like us, Elsie — *cultured*!"

Olie blushed, extended his hand to Elsie, who looked him over mock-solemnly. "Really, Jessie? Like us?"

"Yes. Just like us!"

Olie moved to take down the steamer trunk from the baggage cart; it had to be Elsie's — no one else was getting off in Atlas City.

Plastered on the sides of the trunk were stickers from France, Italy, Switzerland, and England.

"You visit there?" Olie asked, now interested. "You see Sweden?"

Jessica supposed he'd felt a wave of homesickness.

"To your first question, not yet," Elsie replied. "As for your second question, no, I haven't seen Sweden. But all those stickers are there to encourage me to make an honest woman of myself."

Olie didn't understand.

"Well, you see," Elsie said as they began to swing up into the buggy behind Boots, the buggy shifting beneath their weight, "if I put those stickers on and haven't been there, I'm not honest. But I want to go and those stickers will remind me I have to."

"Oh, Elsie," Jessica said, laughing. "You think of everything!"

"Indeed," Elsie agreed.

As they proceeded through the town behind Boot's smart trot, the townspeople treated Elsie to their usual bald stares. Her plumes waved in the wind like Boot's long tail and Jessica felt a sudden pride and peace with Elsie McDonald beside her and Olie driving them — a kind of truce with Atlas City and its demoralizing commonness. Perhaps she could survive after all, she thought, if she just had a few moments like this!

"And August?" Elsie inquired — rather diffidently, Jessica thought.

"Oh, fine. Crazy as always. But at least he and Cousin Willard aren't inventing things!"

Elsie laughed. "You can't keep a good man down."

"Who said August was good?"

And they both whooped again like young girls, Olie flushing, for he apparently didn't understand that Jessica was only joking.

Jessica's and Elsie's laughter shook the buggy as it drew up in front of the house, Boots taking the bit in his teeth and yanking his head up and down as he stopped as if to say, "See, here we are."

"Oh — one thing," Jessica said to Elsie then, her face serious now, and Elsie looked at her as if she expected bad news.

"The cousins' reunion is at my sister Purdy's. You know how *that* is."

"Is that all?" Elsie asked. "Goodness! The way you looked I thought someone had died."

"Well, you know how Purdy — and the Pratts — are."

Elsie looked startled. Jessica supposed it surprised her to hear Jessica say things like this; she had been a Pratt after all. But Jessica liked shocking her.

"Well, Jessie," Elsie said as Olie helped her down from the buggy, "there wouldn't be a real world without problems. And there wouldn't be GG's without MM's!"

Jessica laughed. "I guess you're right." She brightened, "We'll have fun anyway, won't we? We can have fun even if there *are* Pratts all over the place."

As Olie stood at the front door of the stone homestead, August came bursting out of the house.

"Elsie," he said, clasping her hand boisterously so that Jessica feared he might break the delicate bones, "welcome to Atlas City!"

"I bring the luggage," Olie offered as the three of them left Olie to drag in Elsie's enormous steamer trunk and then to take care of Boots.

No one looked back to see Olie pensively tracing his fingers over the stickers adhering to the black sides of the trunk.

Chapter Thirteen

OLIE LAY ON HIS COT in Jake's old room, but found it hard to relax and get to sleep this night. Memories of Sweden — tall fir forests blotting the sky, winds sweeping snow before them, lakes frozen and blue with cold, the sea, cold, but relentlessly washing against the shore . . . Ollie was trying hard to turn his mind to his beloved Sweden, but the sight of Jessica was beginning to disturb him more and more.

When Elsie had arrived, Olie knew that the ache in his heart was not going to stop, that the way he caught his breath every time he saw Jessica's flaming hair, her tiny waist, her deep blue eyes, that this momentary suspension of breathing would never cease. He tried not to think of her, but in not thinking, he *was*, and the smell of her starched clothes, her soap, her perfume would overwhelm him. She seemed to rise before him, daring him to forget her.

Jessica had been kind to him. In the strange household, surrounded by a language he barely knew, he often was overcome by remembrances of his homeland, and homesickness. His parents were dead, but it was just that there had been a short while there, in Sweden, when they were still with him and he recalled that as a happy time.

Olie stirred, putting his hands behind him on the pillow, propping himself up slightly. He could hear August's snores across the hall, and he could imagine Jessica in bed beside him. He flung himself over and pushed his face into the pillow, as though he would smother the thought. Then, forced to breathe, he rolled over again and stared once more at the ceiling.

He remembered his father taking his hand one night and telling him they were going to go "far, far away." He remembered the words because they were imprinted on a letter he later received from one of his aunts. That was after his father, his mother, and he himself had boarded the ship that would take them to the "New Land," and to the opportunities they were certain, his aunt had written, awaited them.

But on the ship going over, his mother caught pneumonia and died. He could barely remember seeing her white-encased body slipping into the sea. His father had pressed his hand and told him his mother was now with God. Later Olie wondered why God had let her slide into the sea instead of curing her.

When they reached the New Land, America, his father had to fill out many papers in a huge building, which made Olie feel weak and small. A welter of languages swirled around him, and he could not understand them. When his father spoke in the new foreign tongue, Olie also could not understand and he clutched his father's hand even more tightly.

They lived in New York for a time, and then — now Olie stirred on the bed, a breeze from the window briefly cooling him — then one day a stranger came to Olie and said that his father had been killed. He had been working in a factory, Olie later learned, and he had gotten caught in some machinery.

Olie turned his head again, once more not wanting to think, but somehow being compelled to remember. He found himself on a train going west, with other strangers and children like him, nametags attached to their clothes, going far away from New York.

The train seemed to expel the children here and there and at last, Olie too was taken off, met by a grim-faced family who took his belongings in their buggy but made him walk behind.

For five years he stayed with this family, working on their farm, seldom getting to rest, never to share their table or their children's affections, never getting a gift at Christmas. He remembered this particularly, for in the idyllic years of Sweden, there had been presents under the tree for him, kisses, hugs.

He had run away.

Again Olie heard August's snores rising on the air; they seemed to reassure him that everyone was there, that he was still surrounded by a kind of family.

He heard someone in the hall outside his bedroom then. A little cough, the shuffle of a slipper on the stair.

Looking out his door, he saw Elsie, making her way down the stairs. Seeing him, she put her finger to her lips, then whispered, "Can't sleep with that racket. I'm going to go downstairs for awhile."

Olie nodded.

He was glad Jessica had a friend. Sometimes, strangely, she seemed very lonely, and he could understand this feeling. It was the same isolation he had had with the farm family: he was there, but he was not a part of anything.

Shutting the door behind him, Olie returned to the bed. The springs squawked in protest a moment as he crawled in, then all was quiet.

Olie had made his way from one job to another: making sandwiches for harvesting crews, later being a part of one crew himself, and at last, making himself go into the Lutz Store, seek August out, and ask for a job. He never thought he would get one.

Afterward, having seen Jessica and sensing her warmth toward him, he was torn between happiness and being stricken at the thought that he might actually be falling in love with the wife of his employer. He often thought of August as his savior — a kind of earthly savior, for Olie had turned to the Bible when he was with the farm family, and it had comforted him. The Swedish New Testament was the one thing he still had from his father, and Olie would have died rather than give up the book if anyone had tried to take it from him.

He knew he must try to control his feelings for Jessica, however. Surely he could turn his senses away from her and learn new ways of avoiding his emotions.

But Olie was wrong.

Jessica's friend, Elsie, had suggested they go to Purdy's before the reunion and have a seance, or play the parlor game, "Rise, Table, Rise."

Olie didn't know what it was, but he had heard of a seance, and he thought it was probably contrary to Biblical law and somewhat frightening.

"Olie must come too," Elsie declared. She winked at Jessica.

"Well — " Jessica hesitated.

"It'll be fun," Elsie insisted. "And who knows what spirits we may dig up?"

Elsie and Jessica laughed.

Olie shivered.

But Elsie and Jessica were firm in their wanting him to join them, and so the three made their way, behind Boots, to Purdy's.

"Well," Purdy said when she saw them draw up at her twisted iron gate, "well, well. The reunion's not until tomorrow."

Jessica had already started up the walk, removing her hat and wiping her forehead with a lace handkerchief.

"We know that, Purdy," Jessica said. "But we wanted to play 'Rise, Table, Rise' and maybe even have a seance."

"Well, well," Purdy repeated, her voice lilting at the end. "I think we can do that in my sweet little parlor."

Jessica and Elsie smiled at each other, and each took one of Olie's arms and led him up the walk. He thought he would faint with Jessica's nearness.

When they reached Purdy's parlor, the darkness and the coolness seemed to wrap itself around Olie. There was an old piano in one corner, with a rag doll sitting on top of it, legs hanging over as though the doll were performing, preparing to sing.

Olie looked around. Purdy seemed to have quilts, throws, pieces of loose material over everything. Protective antimacassars were on top of all.

"Let's use this," Purdy said then, directing them to a rather spindly table in the center of the room. "It's lighter. It'll be easier for us to work with."

Elsie giggled.

Olie didn't know what the game was, or what the point was, but Purdy was pulling chairs up to the table for them, and placing her hand on the cloth that covered it.

Purdy ordered everyone to sit down.

Olie helped seat Jessica and Elsie but Purdy was already in place when he got around to her. He was to sit opposite her, she said, surrounded by Elsie and Jessica.

"Now," Purdy said, "we must all close our eyes."

Olie looked at Jessica, saw she was doing as Purdy ordered, so he closed his eyes. His head was spinning, for he didn't know what lay ahead in this game.

"Now let's all say, 'Rise, table, rise.' . . . Ready, set, go!"

Olie was mumbling, but Elsie, Jessica, and Purdy fairly shouted the words.

Nothing happened.

Olie wanted to ask what was supposed to take place, but he didn't wish to break the spell. He could hear Jessica breathing, caught a faint whiff of her perfume, felt her hand brush his accidentally, slowly pull away.

"Rise, table, rise," Purdy said, chanting.

"Rise, table, rise," they all repeated.

And then, to Olie's great surprise and consternation, he felt the table actually begin to shift. He squinted through half-opened eyes, looking at the others, seeing them still with closed lids as though in a trance.

While Olie almost started from his seat, the table — on Elsie's side — actually began to rise in the air.

"I can feel it!" Purdy said then. "We're doing it!"

And then Olie saw they had all opened their eyes and were staring at the table, which indeed had risen from its original position. On Elsie's side, it was off the floor, slanting toward Jessica.

As they all looked at it, the table began to tremble and then went down with a bang on its legs.

"We did it!" Jessica said. "I knew we could. What fun!"

Olie studied the table, as though he were certain someone had lifted it. Yet their hands — as he had seen through his half-closed lids — had all remained on top.

"I can do a seance," Purdy said then. "We all work well together."

"And who is your spirit guide?" Elsie inquired with a smile.

"Daniel Boone," Purdy pronounced.

They all laughed.

"But it has to be at night," Purdy said.

"I — I think have to work," Olie stammered.

Jessica laughed.

"Don't worry, Olie," she said, putting her hand over his so that he felt himself redden. "We'll protect you."

Later that same day, Olie found himself once again at Purdy's parlor. If Jessica had not insisted, he would surely have refused, somehow, to go; but she had urged and he wanted to be with her.

Purdy now had her head wrapped in a turban, with one big, blue jewel in the center front, and she was wearing a large flowered gown.

They again sat at the table where they had played the earlier game. Olie blushed when Purdy said, "Now let's all clasp hands," and felt Jessica encircle his fingers. He knew Elsie had taken his other hand, but it was as if the hand Elsie held simply didn't exist; all the feeling was in the one Jessica clasped.

"We must be quiet," Purdy said, scolding them unnecessarily.

Jessica and Elsie smiled at each other, Olie saw, but they did not talk. When he looked over at Purdy, he saw she had thrown her head back, her eyes tightly closed. She seemed to be asleep.

Suddenly Purdy sat forward. Eyes still closed, she said, in a deep voice, which sounded like a man, "I am your guide through the underworld. I am your spirit control. I am Daniel."

Then Purdy's voice said, "Daniel? Are you Daniel Boone?"

Again the male voice responded. "Yes."

Jessica and Elsie snickered and Purdy said, harshly: "Hush."

"Can you guide us through your spirit world? Have you messages for us?"

And the voice replied, "Yes. I have messages."

Olie looked at Jessica, then at Elsie. They had suddenly become very serious. They seemed as impressed by the deep voice they heard, as he had been.

"What are the messages?" Purdy said then in her own voice.

"Trouble," Daniel said.

There was silence for a moment, then Purdy asked, "For whom?"

"For all," the voice said.

Purdy cleared her throat, but did not move from her position.

"What is this trouble?" she asked.

Olie, fearing now that there must be something to this seance, that perhaps Purdy really had contacted the dead, began to shiver. Though he had loved his parents, he did not want to contact them. He did not want to contact anyone dead at all.

"Cloudy, disturbing clouds," the voice said.

"Can you see?"

"I see — I see," and Olie found himself leaning forward as though to somehow confront Purdy's spirit voice, turn it aside. He felt certain it was going to reveal he was in love with Jessica.

"I can't get it," Purdy said after a moment. "He's going away. Daniel —" she called. "Come back. You must tell us."

"*Death*," Daniel said. "*Much sadness.*"

Olie felt Jessica jerk his hand as though she would seize it and carry it — and him — away from the table.

"I don't want to contact anyone," Jessica said.

When Olie looked at her, he saw she had turned pale.

"Oh, Jess," Elsie said, evidently also thinking the messages were just for her.

"There is special message," the deep voice said. "For *him*." Purdy's control grew silent. "I know he had bad foster family."

Olie thought he surely would be betrayed. How could Purdy know about his foster family? Did she really have a contact in the other world and did this contact know his other secret?

But Daniel's voice said, "I cannot talk more now. Later."

There was a pause and a wind seemed to whip through the room. The piano keys suddenly sounded and Olie, starting, thought that the spirit had begun to play.

Looking over, however, he saw that the doll had fallen onto the keys. He saw Jessica and Elsie staring at the piano, not laughing, simply staring.

Purdy's voice cut through the silence. "Keep the circle, everyone," she warned. "Daniel knows all and we mustn't offend him."

While Olie watched, frozen at the table, Purdy leaned forward and said, "*Trouble. Only trouble.*"

Then Purdy's head went back; she seemed to have fainted.

Disengaging his hands from Jessica and Elsie, Olie ran to Purdy, took her head in his hands. He lifted her eyelids, one by one.

"She all right," he said at last.

As if responding to his voice and returning from a great distance, Purdy raised her head, shook it. For a moment, neither Jessica nor Elsie seemed to be able to say a word. Then Jessica stirred and, running a hand through her hair, told them: "It's just for fun, really. Just for fun. . . . Daniel Boone! *Purdy, really!*"

But Olie felt as if someone had searched his soul and branded it.

Chapter
Fourteen

"TEA READINGS, ANYONE?" Elsie asked with a sidewise wink at Jessica.

They were standing outside Purdy's gazebo, watching the "passing parade," as Jessica termed it; both women wore their gold college pins conspicuously on their lapels. "These people won't know what they are," Jessica told Elsie, "but *we* will."

Anyone in the neighborhood would have known that Purdy Pratt was having some kind of "do." Buggies lined the street in front of the boardinghouse, the horses shifting from foot to foot as they waited for their masters, some with feedbags attached as the owners took advantage of a quiet moment in the festivities to attend to their animals.

Behind Jessie and Elsie, freshly plowed wheat fields stretched almost endlessly into the horizon, a line of osage orange trees miles away the only vertical intrusion. "This is the view that gets to me," Jessica told Elsie as they stood there. "Nothing to make a background, nothing to stop the eye."

Elsie didn't answer; in front of them, children played with hoops, rolling them as far and as long as they could until they toppled over, a croquet game going on to one side, and all around red-faced farmers, their wives in print dresses and bonnets, the children as fresh-faced and sunburned as the parents.

"The kids are cute," Elsie observed. "Maybe I'll paint some."

Jessica snorted. "For free, I hope. These people don't appreciate art."

Suddenly Elsie said, "May I paint a portrait for someone?"

Silly Violet, who had edged up to the two friends, seized on the idea. "Indeed you can," she said.

Violet had always tried to make a friend of Elsie — Jessica thought she wanted to pump her about their college days, for Violet seemed certain that Jessica had been "wild" while away at school. "Willard would love it," she went on.

Elsie got out her sketchbook and began drawing.

"Put her beside the mulberry tree," Jessica whispered. "And then cover her face with the branches!"

Obligingly, Elsie asked Violet to please assume a pose leaning against the mulberry tree — her favorite tree, Elsie explained when Violet seemed reluctant.

"Well, if you really think so."

"Oh, yes, my dear," Elsie said, winking again at Jessica. "The leaves are a natural background for your lovely black hair."

Violet blushed with pleasure.

"Shall we put the baby in too?" Elsie asked — ostensibly of Violet, but actually of Jessica.

Jessica shook her head no. She didn't want to tell Violet that Baby Purdy would not add to the picture. Baby Purdy had been accidentally scarred by a horse during one of the Fourth of July celebrations in town, and the indentation, right above her forehead, was most unattractive. The poor child had always been nervous and crotchety and the unfortunate incident only added to her troubles.

"I'll hold her," Jessica offered.

It was little enough to do; Elsie — the dear one — took a great deal of time arranging Violet against the tree, politely attaching Violet's hand upward on the trunk, then pressing her face against it.

"Oh, dear," Violet said. "You know, Elsie, I think I may be allergic . . ." she began, but stopped.

"Nonsense, darling," Elsie said. "I won't be a minute and your white skin looks so perfect there."

"Well — if you insist."

Moments later Violet began itching. But Elsie was quick at sketching and had already outlined her work and was ready to put the finishing touches on it when Violet lunged away from the tree, gasped, put her hand to her face where giant red blotches were appearing, her face swelling up as though it were rising dough.

"My face, my face!" Violet screamed.

She began to run, until she collided with Sister Purdy, bearing a huge crock of potato salad. While the two schemers watched, surprised and fascinated, potato salad upended and oozed down on poor Violet's head until her face seemed to be covered by gigantic welts, pickles, pieces of egg, and mayonnaise.

Sobbing, Violet ran for the house.

Willard came up to take Baby Purdy from Jessica. He looked at her questioningly — suspiciously — and said, "Did you do something, Jessica?"

But for once, Jessica was innocent. She hadn't known Violet was allergic and she hadn't expected such a dramatic turn of events.

"Of course not!" Jessica snorted. "But your baby *is* doing things! You'd better go change her."

Purdy's bottom was soaking; Jessica watched, relieved, as Willard made his way with the wet child through the startled Lutzes and Pratts and various married kin to the sanctuary of Purdy's boardinghouse. Purdy's round, somber face stared at Jessica over Willard's shoulder, as though she were representing Violet, silently accusing Jessica of something.

Violet did not return to eat at the buffet and August gave Jessica a calculating look when Willard announced that Violet was suffering from an allergic reaction. Jessica then asked one of the distant cousins, Otto Lutz, who had journeyed from Missouri, to sing "The Battle Hymn of the Republic." It seemed to be the only tune Otto knew; he would render it, in a trembly tenor, at every reunion.

"You see what I mean?" Jessica whispered to Elsie as Otto struggled to keep the truth marching on.

"I dream of leaving this town," Jessica was saying languidly as Elsie massaged her back while she lay beneath the huge walnut headboard on her bed. "It's only when you come that I feel really . . . well, in touch with civilization."

Elsie pressed sympathetically on Jessica's fine, strong shoulders. "It's in the mind, Jessie, dear," Elsie said. "You can conquer everything with your mind."

Elsie was a bit platitudinous, Jessica had always thought, though still she appreciated her interest.

"I don't know about that," Jessica said. "Some things are dependent on other people and you can't control that."

Elsie didn't answer.

Now Jessica rolled over to face Elsie; both of them were stripped to their chemises, Jessica lying with one foot tapping aimlessly into the air while she studied the ceiling of her room.

"When I'm here, in my room," she went on in the dream-like voice, "I can almost forget I'm in Atlas City. I can even believe," she looked up at Elsie suddenly, who was studying her nails, "that I'm in New York with you."

"Sweet Jessie," Elsie said.

But she, too, seemed preoccupied; perhaps it was the warm afternoon, the breeze that reached lazily into the room and swung about them, the quiet after the noisy reunion they'd attended the day before.

"I'm actually sorry about Violet," Jessica said then. "I'm sorry she broke out. I honestly didn't know." She thought a moment, and, when Elsie still didn't speak, went on, "But it *was* funny when she hit Purdy and Purdy spilled the potato salad all over her. Silly Violet. She has more trouble!"

"She's still red. I saw her when I looked out the window this morning," Elsie said. "I feel a bit guilty."

"Well, you didn't know either," Jessica said. "And we were just trying to have a bit of fun. Goodness knows, I don't get many good times here." Jessica looked angry then. "And Willard accusing me!"

Her eyes flashed and she shook her red hair until it fell about her face, long, thick. "Oh, Jessie," Elsie laughed then, looking at Jessica and pulling up one strand of the vibrant red hair, "you *are* a wildcat. Just like August says. Tell me — are you a wildcat in bed too?"

"Elsie!" Elsie McDonald had never asked such a thing before and Jessica's eyes darkened in irritation. "None of your damn business!"

"I take it you're not," Elsie said, apparently rebuffed.

For answer, Jessica reached across the bed, grabbed her hair brush, began vigorously brushing Elsie's long, blonde hair.

"Ouch!" Elsie said, putting up a hand to defend her head. "Jessica, you don't have to get mad about it!"

As quickly as she'd gotten angry, her pique left. "I'm sorry," Jessica said.

"If you're not, you should be," Elsie insisted.

Jessica didn't know if she meant she should be a wildcat in bed, or sorry.

Jessica got up then, began stalking about the room. She went over to the window, pulled the curtain aside. "I can see Willard out with the baby, pushing it around in its buggy as if it's really something to see. Honestly, that child is the ugliest . . ." Jessica stopped, inwardly chagrined. Baby Purdy couldn't help it if Violet had been so careless that the baby was permanently scarred.

"Jessie?" It was August's voice.

To Jessica's consternation, she turned to face her husband: he was staring from one to the other, looking rather fixedly at Elsie, who, Jessica thought, seemed very hesitant to grasp and pull up the coverlet so that her round bosom was discreetly hidden.

"Oh, I'm sorry . . ."

August, flushing as furiously as Olie, backed awkwardly from the room. "Sorry, sorry," he muttered, closing the door on his apologies.

"Damn fool," Jessica said sourly.

"Jessie!"

"Well, he should know I always rest after lunch. He's seen me do it often enough."

Now Elsie seemed playful again. "I'll *bet* he has. Is that when . . .?"

"Elsie! I won't have you prying about in our private affairs."

Elsie puckered her lips, defiantly facing Jessica as she seldom did. "I wouldn't let a man like August wait while I napped," she said.

"You're not married to him," Jessica said, as if that explained everything.

"Does that make a difference?"

Now Jessica gave Elsie a hard look; she still held the brush in her hand and she advanced on Elsie as though she were once again going to punish her with it.

"Oh no, you don't," Elsie said, retreating on the bed. Suddenly she tittered. "I was just kidding!"

"It's just that some things are better not discussed," Jessica said.

But Elsie apparently wasn't quite ready to concede total defeat. "Oh, I don't agree," she said. Then: "Well, anyway, I'll tell *you* about my artist friend."

"Oh?"

Now Jessica was interested; she adored gossip . . . about someone else.

"He's promised that he'll marry me one of these days," Elsie said. "And he says then we can do great things in art together. It helps to have support, you know. He says he'll establish me in the art world."

Both women had propped themselves once again on their stomachs, chins in hands, elbows on the bed. They sank into the soft down and regarded each other.

"He *is* a wildcat," Elsie said. "What he likes to do best I can't tell you!"

But she did tell Jessica, and Jessica was properly shocked. Elsie had a streak of animal in her, Jessica decided that afternoon, but as long as it was Elsie, it was all right. She was an artist, an intellectual, and could do as she pleased.

It always seemed to Jessica that the days passed so much more quickly when Elsie was in Atlas City; all too soon it was time for Elsie to go home.

Jessica waved at the train that was bearing her dearest friend away from her until it pulled out of sight; when she turned back to Olie and the horse and carriage, her eyes were wet.

"I sorry, Jessica," Olie said softly. "I know you miss the friend."

Elsie wrote Jessica a long letter when she got back to New York. It was convoluted, went through the exhibits and art shows she'd been to and the mention of a painting she'd completed and sold, and then Elsie said, the handwriting suddenly jerky, as if she hated to write what she was writing, "*My artist friend here says I must concentrate on my painting if I am to succeed. And I can't really say I care for Atlas City, Jessie, even with you there. But our friendship is so precious to me that I hope you will want to come to NYC and visit me. There is more to do here anyway, and I know you'd like to get away from Atlas City. So please don't feel I'm abandoning you, dear. Come. Come.*"

When Jessica read the letter, she hugged it to her chest. Would she ever see Elsie again?

Chapter Fifteen

LOW-HANGING CLOUDS and cold winds began early in December, and August protested he didn't want to go out in the pasture and cut the Christmas tree. Olie, who had not had money enough to return to Sweden for Christmas with the other Swedes in Atlas City, offered.

"Ya," he said. "I will get it."

Olie took the axe and went out.

"You could have gone with him," Jessica scolded August after Olie had left. "You *do* take advantage of his goodness, you know."

"Ya," August mimicked. "But he's got a good yob."

Hmmph.

Jessica didn't add that she would have missed Olie had he gone to Sweden. She didn't want to admit even to herself how important he was becoming to her, how attractive he was.

Jessica was making mountains of Christmas cakes and cookies, both Swedish and German delicacies — the Swedish not only to make Olie feel at home, but because Jessica was proud of the portion of Swedish blood she bore. "It makes me less hard-headed," she told August, who promptly collapsed into laughter. "It modifies the German side."

Lutfisk, bruna boner, potatis Korv, lingonberry jam, ost-kaka were being made in Jessica's kitchen or were already stored in the cellar. And she had made the German pfeffernuesse, Schuken, Kranz Kuchen, and Schnitz brodt, all tucked in crocks or lining pantry shelves. Jessica was careful to set out three ears of corn for Santa's reindeer — they represented the three wise men, she explained to Jake. Jake himself was ecstatic with the preparations and kept asking Jessica when St. Nickolas would be coming and when he would be getting presents. Even Herman Lutz, who seemed to be slipping into the past and a sleepy silence more and more, was stimulated by the festive atmosphere.

"I got big one," Olie told them that afternoon when, after much searching, he had found a huge cedar, loaded it on the wagon, and brought it home.

"We'll set it up in the parlor," Jessica said.

The tree filled one corner, sending the odor of cedar throughout the house; perfectly shaped, there were tiny blue berries on the cold limbs, as if Nature had already done part of the decorating. Jake, Henrietta, and Olie, and sometimes even Herman, made cranberry strings and hung them on the tree. Oranges, apples, and nuts were added, as were tiny white candles, which Jessica warned were not to be ignited until Christmas Eve. She would play "Stille Nacht, Helige Nacht," on the old upright piano in the parlor while everyone sat on the horsehair sofa and chairs and listened, and then, and only then, would they all help light the candles on the tree. She *did* allow them to light the advent candles on the dining table.

The day before Christmas, August brought a sprig of mistletoe back to the house. Playfully, he hung it over Henrietta as she was serving supper that night and announced, "Now Olie has to kiss her."

Henrietta and Olie both blushed, but though Olie stared impassively at the table, Henrietta inclined her cheek and closed her eyes in preparation. Herman Lutz, the big head nodding, smiled vaguely at the end of the table where he sat. Jessica gave August a withering look.

"That's nonsense," she said. She dug her fork into the slaw she'd made that afternoon and went on, "Sit down, August. Stop that foolishness!"

But August wouldn't stop. Giving the mistletoe to Henrietta, who obligingly held it over her own head, August went to Olie and seized him by the shoulders. "Come on, Olie," he urged. "You're not going to embarrass us all by not performing your duty?"

Reluctantly, with a sidewise glance at Jessica, who had pursed her lips in anger, Olie pushed his chair back, strode over to Henrietta, and gave her cheek a tentative brush with his lips. Henrietta smiled — idiotically, Jessica thought — and went on simpering around the dining table with the cold, sliced beef left from that day's dinner.

"And now Jessica," August said.

He had darted behind Jessica's chair and was extending the mistletoe over her head; Olie blushed violently again, his face almost matching the intensity of her hair.

Jessica snapped, "Sit down you idiot! Why don't you just have him kiss everyone — starting with your own father!"

Herman Lutz seemed to brighten as the faces turned toward him, and Jake giggled. Henrietta stood as if rooted to the spot.

"Come on . . . afraid?" August taunted.

"You damn fool," Jessica said.

She jumped up, grabbed the mistletoe from August's hand, and went over to Olie. Holding it over his head, she stood on tiptoe and placed a soft kiss directly on Olie's lips. She could feel the heat of his face as she pulled back, and suddenly she flushed too, for his lips felt soft and cool beneath hers and she was acutely aware of his body close to her.

"Merry Christmas, Olie," she said.

Olie was so overcome he couldn't speak; abruptly he turned and fled from the room.

"Now," Jessica said, recovering her composure and turning to the rather startled August, "I hope you're satisfied! Or do you want to go running about the town kissing every man, woman, child, and dog who shows up?"

"Well," August said, rubbing his moustache as he did whenever he couldn't think of anything to say. "Well, well."

The dinner passed in silence, though Herman Lutz once started, "In Colorado . . . ," which was usually the beginning of a long, boring story; but then, inexplicably, he became mute.

That night Jessica heard Olie praying in his room. She knew he was religious and that saying his prayers in Swedish no doubt eased his loneliness in this foreign place. He would be fingering his well-worn New Testament and must be reminiscing, Jessica thought, over whatever friends and family he still had back in Sweden. Jessica supposed it was hardest to be away from family and familiar surroundings at Christmas time, and to experience everything in what remained a foreign language to him.

Jessica could understand his feelings of alienation because she, too, sometimes felt she was in a foreign country. It didn't matter that this was where she was born; she had never fit in, and she didn't suppose she ever would. She and Olie had left everything behind in this country; they had that in common.

That night, at midnight, Jessica crept down to the parlor and placed her presents under the tree. She guessed that little Jake had already been there before her; some of the presents, left by the others, though still wrapped, were in different places from where she had last seen them.

She remembered how she too had crept down early in the morning when she was a child, and how she would shake the few presents, trying to determine what might be inside. Usually she was disappointed in the gifts because they were always practical. She had dreamed of a beautiful doll at one time, with a satin dress, perhaps, and a gold brooch. Instead, she had gotten a rag doll, handmade, with a plain, round face and freckles, not at all what she'd hoped for.

Now, however, she understood the need for practicality; there was never enough money to buy what wasn't useful. And she had never tried to tell Jake that there was a real St. Nickolas — though August had — because she remembered her own abject feeling of betrayal when she had learned that the story was only myth. Adults shouldn't tell lies, she had thought. Life was hard enough without that!

At five in the morning, just as Jessica was getting up to go down to the kitchen and start roasting the chickens, she heard Jake sneaking downstairs. He no doubt wanted to see if there were more presents under the tree. Silently, she followed him. Jessica could hear Herman Lutz snoring as Jake had not closed the door behind him, but Olie was quiet, and Henrietta, who slept off the pantry downstairs, was apparently sound asleep too.

It was dark and Jake had been resourceful: he had taken the kerosene lantern off the hook in the hallway and carried it into the parlor, where he had lighted it. As the wick caught hold, the light sank like water into the room, flooding it, the thick, oily odor of kerosene staining the air and the horsehair furniture, the rugs, the heavy damask drapes at the tall, narrow windows. The light shone on the family portraits in their severe, ancient wooden frames and gave the little-used area a warm glow, the room itself a sharp contrast to the plain, workaday kitchen with its cold water pump, wood stove, plain white wooden cupboards.

Under the Christmas tree, Jake must have seen the extra presents, for he suddenly squealed, put the lantern down, and raced to the packages.

Spying on him from the hallway, Jessica smiled as he counted the gifts: four! Besides those for the members of the family and Olie and Henrietta, she could see that he had counted four for himself!

But Jessica frowned then as Jake suddenly tore into the packages. She had hoped to play St. Nickolas later — even if she didn't believe in it — and hand out the packages so that everyone could see the presents at once.

"Jake!" she said.

Startled, Jake turned around.

"Jake, you should have waited until everyone was up," Jessica said. "We're supposed to open the packages together."

Jake hung his head. "But I couldn't wait, Momma," he said, low. "I just had to see."

"See what?" Jessica asked.

She hoped it was the beautifully knit cap she'd made for him. She had worked so hard — and so furtively — on that!

"The soldier," Jake said. "Daddy promised me a soldier."

So that was it! Jessica was both disappointed and angry. She had told August not to encourage warlike feelings in the boy, but August kept regaling Jake with tales of Teddy Roosevelt and the Rough Riders and all that business down in Cuba in 1898, and Jessica was sick of it.

"I don't know why August always wants war toys," Jessica said. "War is not fun."

"Well, can I?" Jake pleaded. "Can I open his present?"

The packages he held in his hand were simply wrapped, with yarn and pieces of string over fabric and paper coverings from the store; Jessica saw his hands were trembling with eagerness.

"Oh, all right," she said, relenting. "But then you have to wrap them up again so we can open them all together and you'll have to act surprised."

"Oh, I can do that," Jake said. "That's easy."

And he proceeded to rip off the yarn from the first package. Jessica saw his face fall as he pulled out the knit cap, but she had to admit he recovered quickly and he ran to her and hugged her. "Thanks, Momma," he said.

Then he tore into the other packages: a hand-carved whistle from Olie, which Olie was later to confess he'd made himself, an apple from Henrietta, which, she said, she had carefully saved from the fall, and the last one, the best one, Jessica could see by Jake's face, the metal soldier from August.

Jake immediately forgot his mother's presence and put the other gifts aside. He began to stomp the soldier about the floor.

Sighing, Jessica, went into the kitchen and started building the wood fire in the stove so that she could roast the chickens. One of the farmers who couldn't bring his bill current at the Lutz Store had given them chickens and a ham, but Jessica was saving the ham to cook for New Year's.

As the kitchen began to heat up from the warmth of the stove, Henrietta finally appeared to help with the Christmas breakfast. She made the coffee while Jessica went back to the parlor to see what Jake was doing there for so long.

It was cold in the parlor; they hadn't lighted the fire.

"Jake!" Jessica protested. She'd assumed he had gone back to his room to play with the soldier. "You'll catch your death of cold!"

She could see Jake's breath in the frigid room as he said, "I'm all right."

But he seemed to be shivering now and there were cold drafts in the room, the wind creeping under the sill and circling about so that the lantern wick wavered.

Suddenly Jessica was beside herself. Another such terrible scene was penetrating her thoughts.

"Jake!" she said, distraught. "Come here this instant!"

She took Jake by the hand and led him to the kitchen. "Here," she said, pulling up a chair by the stove. "I'll get August to light the coal for the furnace."

Jake seemed flushed, and he didn't protest.

Jessica made hot chocolate for him, even gave him a piece of the Kranz Kuchen she'd been saving for Christmas dinner. The Kranz Kuchen was her sister Purdy's favorite — and she would be there later, garrulous, trying to steal the show.

But Jake didn't get to eat Christmas dinner. Later that morning, after they'd all had some breakfast and Jake had gone outside to play with the whistle Olie'd made, he grew sick. He began to vomit, his head throbbing, he told Jessica. "My chest hurts too, Momma," he said, putting a hand on his wool shirt as if that would help.

Jessica felt his forehead and cheeks; they were burning. She ran to the washroom off the kitchen, opened the medicine cabinet, and got the mercury thermometer there. When she pulled it out of Jake's mouth, she gasped: it read 104!

"Oh my God," Jessica said, and began to tremble. "Oh my God."

Jessica promptly asked Olie to let Jake have his old room back while he was ill, putting a cot in the hallway for Olie. Then she told August to go get Doc Harvey — Clarence — who was close to the family and knew Jake well, as his son, Will, was Jake's best friend.

When Clarence came, he took one look at Jake — and at the assemblage of people in the room — Olie, Henrietta, Jessica, August, even the elder Purdy — and said, "All of you but Jessica clear out. We don't need an audience."

Clarence Harvey turned back to Jake, looked at the thermometer reading, pulled out his stethoscope, and pressed it to Jake's chest. Jake winced and coughed — a rattling interminable hacking, which seemed to cause Jake even more pain, as he began to cry. Doc Harvey frowned. Then, to Jessica: "Keep him warm if he chills." When there was no response, he looked over at Jessica. She was cowering in a chair as though she knew she would be going through another terrible death. "Jessica," he said, curtly. "I need your help. It's pneumonia. You can't help Jake by crying."

Slowly Jessica got up, walked over to Doc Harvey. She didn't look down at Jake, who was tossing feverishly in the bed.

She felt Clarence Harvey's hands on her shoulders. He seemed to be pressing in. "Try to bring down his fever with cold cloths," he said. "Force him to drink fluids. You've got to be strong; Jake's counting on you. We'll know how he's doing in a few days — hopefully the fever will break."

When Jessica looked down and saw little Jake with his eyes closed as though he were already dying, she realized she wanted him to live more than anything.

"And pray," Harvey said.

Jake was struggling with the bedclothes, delirious. "Chest hurts," he said, wildly turning again as Jessica tried to hold him still. "Hurts." His eyes flung open briefly. "See ol' Whitey," he said. "Grampa and I see Whitey."

Now Jessica turned and went back to Jake's room and got the presents he'd been given that morning. She lined them up on the bed beside him and then, sighing, began to tend to him.

"Olie," she called to the hallway. He had stationed himself just outside the door, as though he sensed she might need him. She felt a rush of gratitude for his faithfulness and sensitivity. August, as usual, had disappeared; he hated sickness. No doubt he was into the Christmas brandy, already avoiding thinking about Jake by downing his glass as fast as he could. "Tell August to get a bucket of cold water, and Henrietta to get some clean cloths. Bring them here immediately!"

When Olie returned with the water and cloths, he stood beside the bed for a moment and then, reaching into his pocket, pulled out his small Swedish New Testament. He began reading in Swedish.

Jessica kept replacing the cloths; they seemed to get warm so fast.

Jessica asked herself: would Jake, too, be taken from her? Was this outrageous land determined to make her suffer even more?

Jessica didn't know when Henrietta took the almost burned chickens out of the oven, nor if anyone was fed that day, nor what had happened to their Christmas plans. She stayed in Jake's room all that night, the next day and night, and again the following day. She was exhausted.

At about eight the evening of the third day, Doc Harvey came back. Jessica was dozing in the rocker she had stationed beside Jake's bed. When Doc Harvey saw Jake, he said, again putting a hand on Jessica's shoulder but the touch gentle now, "He's going to be okay, Jessica. I can see his fever's down. Thank God — and you — the boy will be all right!"

Jessica quietly began to sob with relief.

"Why are you crying, Momma?" Jake asked then.

It was the first time he'd spoken since he fell ill.

"I'm happy, dear," she replied.

But Jake was already asleep again.

Jessica could hear August blowing his nose, loudly, just outside the door.

It was a Christmas none of them would forget.

Chapter Sixteen

*J*AKE WAS LATER TO remember that all through his childhood, he thought of his mother as "touchy." It wasn't simply that she seldom wanted to hug him — just when he was ill — but she seemed to withdraw from close contact with anyone. With anyone, he corrected himself, but Olie and — perhaps — Elsie McDonald.

He remembered that, shortly before he got pneumonia, he had overheard his mother and Olie in the kitchen. Olie was trying to help Jessica prepare the Christmas dinner by storing some of the homemade food on the shelves of the pantry. He remembered thinking that when his mother spoke to Olie, her voice was very soft, almost gentle.

"Put that one over there," he heard his mother say.

Peering into the kitchen through the dining room door, he watched as Olie obediently took a crock of something or other and put it on one of the pantry shelves.

"And that one." Leaning further into the kitchen, Jake could see his mother was pointing to yet another covered dish. "Put that one just beside it."

"Ya," Olie said.

Sometimes Jake found himself feeling almost jealous of Olie; he knew that Olie worked hard, so he certainly deserved some pity, but his mother seemed to care what Olie felt and thought almost more than anybody.

When Jake felt lonely, as he did now, he usually went up to the room he and his Grandfather Herman shared to listen to his Grampa's tall tales.

"They can talk," he told himself, "but I have things to do too!"

Jake could hear their voices as he wound his way up the stairs, then he shut the door behind him, cutting off the voices.

His grandfather was lying on the bed, fast asleep.

"Grampa," Jake said, shaking him by the shoulders. "Gramp, I want you to tell me about Whitey."

Usually Jake was tired of hearing the same old stories, but this one he loved. It was a way of bringing him close to his Grandfather Herman again, because now, even though they stayed in the same room, there were barriers between them. For one thing, Jake was tired of waking up to the smell of urine — or feces — and then listening to his mother's futile scoldings of the old man. And Jake had to admit that, nice as Olie was, he resented him for causing him to be moved out of his room.

But when his grandfather told this story about Old Whitey, Herman seemed to come alive, his mind to clear, his senses to sharpen — the way he used to be.

"Go on, Grampa," Jake said, like a fan urging on his hero. "Tell it just like you always do."

And Jake settled himself on the foot of the bed while Herman propped himself up on his pillow and began to recite: "Well, my dog Whitey must have gone off to search out a female."

Here, Jake knew, his grampa always gave a little cackle. "He was quite a ladies' man, that dog was, old Whitey," and Jake waited for his grampa to smack his lips as he always did. "Well, anyhow, off he went when I wasn't looking. There were wolves and mountain lions in these parts then — I was out a-working in Colorado — and I knew damn well they would've enjoyed making a snack of little ol' Whitey. So I set out."

Jake rocked back on his heels, waiting. He could almost tell the story himself, he knew it so well.

"Bears, too."

A smack.

"Well," and Grampa Lutz began rocking too now, the bed moving as they seemed to time themselves together, "my friends tried to warn me it was too late in the afternoon to go looking for Whitey. It was still winter, there were storm clouds in the sky, at least three feet of snow on the ground, more to come it looked like. But I just couldn't let ol' Whitey freeze to death or get et by a bear, though Mr. Bear was likely to be a-hibernating. No sir."

Jake shook his head just as his grandfather did.

"So I set out like a damn young fool."

Again the cackle, a flash of light in the eyes as Herman Lutz pictured that young man once more.

"'Course I got caught by the darkness."

Jake pinched his lips together, caught his lower lip in his teeth and waited. "Go on, Grampa," he said.

Herman Lutz swallowed, gripped the rocker arms a bit more firmly. "I saw I was going to have to make-do for the night. Warn't smart to be wanderin' around in the open; might fall off a cliff" — a giant laugh here — "get my *self* et by a wolf or lion or anything. So I come across a kind of den. Hmm, I says to myself, could be there's company in there. I mean — it was the kind of place a sleepy bear would admire to lay hisself down in and get a nap. But it was warmer inside the cave and the wind was coming up something fierce, so I just swallowed and pushed myself in."

Jake was now rocking so fast he nearly fell off the bed. Pushing back on his heels, he unwound himself and got up from the bed, sat on the floor, never taking his eyes off his grampa for he didn't want the story to end before it should.

"I would've built a fire but by now it was snowing — hard — and I didn't want to chance losing my way in the blizzard and not getting back to the cave. So I just forgot getting firewood and plunked myself down against one hard rock wall and it warn't long 'fore I was asleep. . . . Well."

Jake heard his mother's footsteps outside the door then. She must be listening, he thought. But instead of scolding Herman for telling this "tall tale," as she called it, Jake heard her sigh and her footsteps go on down the hall to her own room.

Jake knew that the pause his Grampa made now was the longest one, and there was no point in trying to hurry him over it. Herman began pawing at his suspenders, pulling them away from his scrawny chest, looking at them intently — and Jake was afraid he might focus on them, as he sometimes did, and forget the story.

"Go on, Gramp," Jake urged.

His grandfather looked up at him then as if just seeing him, dropped the suspenders, and began, "I would've built a fire — "

But Jake interrupted him. "No, Gramp," he said. "You were in the cave and you went to sleep."

"Oh."

Grampa Herman's eyes looked searchingly at Jake for a moment, as though trying to determine if Jake was right. At last he sighed and went on, "I heard wolves howl that night and you can believe I pulled back against that wall as far as I could. Once I even thought one poked his head into the cave opening, but the wind was carrying on so I couldn't be sure. When I woke in the morning, the opening of that cave was about tight shut with blown snow. It had stopped coming down and a weak sun sorta lay light just at the top of that drift. I rubbed my eyes," Herman did it again, Jake following, "and next thing you knew I began looking around my hotel room."

Jake laughed, knowing his grampa would laugh too.

"My legs and hands were near froze, and I began moving them a bit to get the blood runnin' again. I can tell *you* that when I got that blood circulating it damned near shut off all over again when I saw something in the back of the cave — just a-lyin' there. It wasn't Whitey. Oh, no."

Jake shook his head, bit his lip again, repeating, "It wasn't Whitey!"

"Huddled up there in a big black heap was the biggest ol' bear I'd ever seen!"

Jake giggled nervously. "Go on, Gramp!"

"I mean to tell you I was scared. Oh my!"

"Go on, Gramp! Go on!"

Now Herman Lutz scratched his head and chuckled. "Well, that ol' bear just kinda woke up then and looked at me. Like he hadn't noticed nothing before and was as surprised as I was. He just sorta leaned up and looked square at me. Boy, I thought! Here it comes. It ain't ol' Whitey gonna be food for some animal, it's gonna be Herman Lutz!"

Jake squealed, the sound peeling out in the room.

"But I'll be damned if that ol' bear didn't act like he didn't care for the likes of me. Like I didn't look good enough to eat! He just took one look at me, sighed, and I swear to God he turned his back to me and went back to sleep. *Huh!*"

Jake, delighted again, his teeth clenched tightly. "Then what'd you do, Gramp?"

Jake knew, but it was part of the game to pretend he didn't; he liked to hear the words from his grandfather. He knew his gramp loved to tell the story.

"Well," his grandfather said, "I kinda snuck out of there, I did. I said to myself, better not wait any longer because ol' Mr. Bear *might* decide he would like to take a taste of me. So I snuck out."

Now Jake tossed his head back and said aloud with his grandfather, "Never *did* find Whitey!"

"I saw 'em panning for gold, too," Grandfather Lutz was about to start another story, but Jake was still lost in the first and he did not want to listen to a second.

"Never *did* find ol' Whitey," Jake said. "Never did!"

And before his grandfather could start another tale, Jake turned and went out of the room. Grampa Lutz didn't seem to know he'd left, however, for Jake heard his voice winding down the stairs as Jake descended.

"Don't listen to that stuff," his mother said then, her head appearing at the top of the stairs. "He just likes to tell yarns."

"I know, Momma," Jake said. "But I like to listen to some of them."

And then Olie Olson came out from the kitchen, looked up at Jessica and said, "I am through here now."

"Go on, Olie," Jessica said. "You've worked long enough."

Olie turned to go . . . Jake looked up at his mother, who was watching Olie.

Chapter
Seventeen

*T*HE DAY AFTER Jake's miraculous recovery, Jessica insisted August stay with Jake while she and Olie took the sleigh and went out to the cemetery.

"For God's sake, Jessica," August protested. "It's cold outside. Are you out of your mind?"

"I know it's cold," Jessica said. "But we have the fur throw and there's no wind today and I want to go!"

"Well," August said, scratching his head pensively. "Well, be sure and not stay long. One pneumonia in the family is enough!"

"Don't tell *me*," Jessica said. "You're the one who had to fortify himself."

August didn't speak, merely combed his moustache with his fingers.

Jessica and Olie both bundled up in their fur hats and coats, pulled on heavy gloves, and turned up the coat collars to protect their faces as the sleigh moved through the crusted snow on the road to the cemetery. Boots seemed happy to be able to be out and about; he trotted smartly, the bells on his harness keeping time with the crunch of his hooves.

Jessica had fashioned a small wreath of cedar from some of the branches Olie had cut from the giant Christmas tree in the parlor. With the small blue berries still intact, and with a red cloth bow, the wreath was pretty. It would give a spot of color to a drab, unhappy site.

The day was clear and bright, the air prickling with cold. The bells seemed to shatter the stillness, as though the whole world were ice and only sound could penetrate it. The fenceposts and the bare trees in the pastures flashed by as Boots pulled them along; Jessica could see Boots' flanks working, first one, then the other, the skin no longer shiny as his coat now was heavy and thick. As they trotted toward the cemetery, he worked his ears back and forth and pulled against the bit.

"He want to run," Olie said, laughing. "The cold make him pep."

"Keep him reined in," Jessica warned. "We don't want him to get over-heated."

"Ya," Olie said. "He a good horse."

When they turned into the cemetery, Boots slowed, as the snow was thicker where no one had been. Drifts piled up against the stone posts on either side of the narrow road and lay in folds against the gravestones. The sky seemed far away, a clean blue cover over them. A row of cedars to the north was iced with snow, the branches glassy in the sunlight. Yet the sun was pallid and low in the winter sky, and no warmth reached them. Still, Jessica was not cold. The fur throw over their legs was heavy and snug.

Olie stopped Boots at the Lutz graves. He got out of the sleigh and walked up to take the bridle, Boots again shaking his head up and down as if to say, "Why are we stopping?" But then he seemed to accept the delay and began to try to nose something out of the snow to eat.

Bunches of dry prairie grass took his attention briefly, and he pulled at them, chewing what few morsels he could wrench from the frozen ground. Then he shook himself again, the bells jingling loudly, and settled down to stand, shifting from one foot to the other as Olie and Jessica went to the graves and placed the wreath upon the center stone. She saw that fingers of fungus had worked over the words on the grave marker, "Sleep On, Little Babes," as if something were trying to pull the stone back into the earth and to the heart of things.

Jessica stood for a moment, her face lined with sadness, tracing a finger over the stone that stood sentinel over her babies' graves. "*Why?*" she asked.

There was no answer.

Then she turned and, digging her heels into the snow, jumped back in the sleigh, and grabbed the reins, holding Boots, for he had felt her weight in the sleigh and was ready to bolt.

As Olie climbed in and took the reins from her, Jessica looked out to the side. A small field mouse emerged near one gravestone, sprung out of his cover of stiff grasses, and now stood as if paralyzed, his sides furiously beating in and out. Had they frightened him so much?

"We mean you no harm, little one," she said as he sniffed the air for danger.

Then Jessica saw the reason for his fear. Spreading on the ground, moving over it like a black hand, was the shadow of a hawk. Jessica heard it cry, a wild, ringing call. For some reason, she said to Olie, "That's a soul, Olie." She shaded her eyes so she could follow the sweep of the hawk as he swung in the sky.

"Ya?" Olie asked.

Clearly he had not understood what she'd just said. "I was babbling," Jessica said. "Let's go."

She gave Boots a smart crack with the whip they kept on the floor of the sleigh. Startled, Boots jerked and began to trot in the wrong direction until Olie stopped him, turned him, and they went back down the cemetery road to town.

"That is a poor little mouse," Olie said in his staccato voice. "He be food soon."

"What?" Jessica asked absently. Then: "Oh, the hawk. Yes — I suppose so."

It gave Jessica a shiver to think of it — death, always death.

As they trotted along, the sun struck the golden-red strands of Jessica's hair that had fallen out from beneath the fox hat. Her blue eyes were piercing in the cold, crisp air. She was aware that Olie was looking at her.

Flustered, she pulled her hat further over her eyes.

"Is wrong, Jessica?" Olie asked then.

He had finally learned to call her "Jessica," but his innate shyness kept him from saying the word very often. Jessica turned to look at him: he was so handsome! His eyes were as blue as hers, his hair still blonde, though darker without the summer sun.

Sensing her approving gaze, Olie flushed. He was more at ease with her than with August, perhaps because August teased him unmercifully, and though he was at least ten years younger than she, they seemed contemporaries.

And she knew he was devoted to her. It had occurred to her recently that he might even be more than devoted.

"You're very sweet, Olie," she said then.

He flushed again, and gave Boots a touch with the reins so that he began to trot even faster, the sleigh gliding over the ruts in the road. The bells seemed insistent, timing their movements.

"Is like Sweden," Olie said. "The bells."

"I'd like to go to Sweden," Jessica said then.

"Ya," Olie said. "You like Sweden. Is a beautiful land."

They were silent briefly, listening to the crackle of the runners on the snow. Jessica felt the cold wind against her face and she pulled the coat collar up closer around her. She could almost pretend as if she and Olie were the only two people in the world and that this moment would go on forever. She did not want to end it.

"Tell me about Sweden," she said.

"Ya?" Olie asked. He must have been surprised because Jessica — no one really — had asked him about his native country.

"Like Elsie, I would like to go there," Jessica said. And, as she said it, it became true. She could see it: she and Olie with another horse-drawn sleigh, tucked in against the cold and setting out into the cedar and firs of that northern land. And she thought of something else: those forebears of hers who had come to the New Land and settled, first, in Vermont and Michigan and then pushed on to yet another frontier of this vast space. How strange it must have seemed to them when they first glimpsed the barren, tallgrass prairie! What must her maternal grandmother have thought?

"You know, I have — well, had — a Swedish grandmother." She felt proud to tell Olie more about herself. "She used to say 'Cheets' instead of 'sheets.' We used to laugh at her. She would say, 'I must wash the cheets.' And we thought her so cute and funny." Jessica paused, the words taking her back to her own childhood, when things had seemed simpler, though she had always wanted, fiercely, to grow up and make her own decisions. Well, she had. Jessica frowned. "She made cardamon cookies and she was so clean — everything had to be clean!"

"Ya, ya," Olie said eagerly. "Swedish housewives always clean. Good cooks! She make ost-kaka too?"

"Of course."

"Ah," Olie said.

"So you see," Jessica went on, "I'm practically Swedish."

She knew that Olie was aware this was not true; most of the blood that coursed through her veins came from the German side of the family and there was only a portion that was Swedish. Yet she clung to the idea as if that blood made all the difference.

"Swedish girls very beautiful," Olie said then. He looked over at Jessica as though he were linking her with the young girls of his native land. "I tell you have Swedish blood, Jessica."

And then he blushed again as he always did when he blurted out something personal.

Suddenly Jessica frowned. She looked over at Olie and said, "Why didn't you ever find someone in Sweden, Olie?"

The question took Olie by surprise apparently, as he jerked on the reins and pulled Boots to a halt. He touched the reins to his cheek thoughtfully and then lifted them again and urged Boots on, though now at a walk. "You remember I go five years ago?"

Jessica nodded. He had told them, though they hadn't known him at that time.

"You remember I go two years ago?"

"Yes."

"I don't have family in Sweden now. All die." He sighed. "I a foster child. I not like people who raise me — they treat bad." Olie's face grew sad. "I run away."

"I'm sorry."

"But love Sweden. Love my country."

"Yes," Jessica said.

"Five years ago I look for someone but not find. Two years ago — " and now Olie looked earnestly at Jessica. "Swedish girls beautiful, but it not work."

"Why?"

Now Olie turned away from her and looked out at the sun which was sliding down into a pocket of clouds, the day coming to an end. "I try to forget something there."

"What?"

When Olie didn't answer, Jessica decided to change the subject. She sucked in her breath then blew it out in a cloud of fog. "Well," she said, "you don't have to tell me. But did you have trouble learning English, Olie?" She realized she had never given it a thought. "Learning a foreign language is always hard."

"Ya," he said.

Olie still had a sing-song in his voice, a soft lilt which intrigued Jessica. Usually he didn't say much, certainly he didn't speak in protracted sentences, but now his voice seemed soothing and charming. It had always soothed her, she realized; she smiled at him.

Again he blushed. Finally he said, "I get headaches then. All the time English and no Swedish and I try follow and I get headaches. So much."

"Yes," Jessica said. "It must seem as if one is under water and can't breathe — almost. I mean, words just swirling around like a current."

Olie looked at her. "You good person, Jessica."

She didn't blush, but it was her turn to bend her head. "That's undeserved praise," she said. "I'm afraid I didn't understand at all how it must have been for you. I'm sorry. It must have been very lonely for you those days."

"Ya," Olie said.

"And here we were so absorbed with our own lives that we didn't give you . . ." she didn't want to say "a thought." Surely that was too cruel. She didn't finish the sentence. "I'm sorry," she said lamely.

Olie looked puzzled.

But Jessica didn't go on. She looked out at the sky where the hawk was still wheeling, saw him suddenly dive to the ground. She felt as if talons had seized her and were about to carry her off.

She shivered.

Misunderstanding, Olie pulled the fur throw closer to her, tucking it around her. She could feel him so near her; it seemed that the aura he carried with him surrounded her and she felt something she had not felt for a long time — maybe never: she felt safe and protected.

"If I tell you something, Olie," she said, turning to him then, "will you promise me never to say anything to anyone else or to interrupt me?"

Olie nodded.

"My dead children," she began. "I miss them so much!"

She turned from his face, looked at the ground, a few black patches of earth sticking out from where the snow had been swept into drifts as if by some giant housekeeper. She felt her own face tighten and, to her consternation and surprise, huge tears sprang from her eyes and raced down her cheeks, tears streaming down her face like miniature rivers.

"They're dead, Olie, they're dead. And I may never see them again. I don't know if I believe in all that the minister says about resurrection. All I know is that my babies are gone."

And then, not quite knowing when or how it happened, she realized Olie was holding her in his arms and that he was kissing her. She felt his cold lips on hers and then she felt his body shudder as she returned his kiss.

When he broke away, he told her, his voice anguished, "Oh, Jessica, I love you. I always love you."

"Olie . . . ," she began.

But he shook his head. "I not help it. I try but I love."

Jessica could not stop herself; she sank more deeply into Olie's arms, the warmth, the safety. She was unable to tear herself away from him.

"I want you to hold me, Olie," she said. "Please, please, hold me!"

Later that night, August again drinking up his worries and having collapsed into bed, Jessica went to Olie's room. He was lying with his hands behind his head, staring up at the ceiling.

He didn't say anything when she came to him, but he got up from the bed, lifted her white nightgown over her head, and looked at her. He held open the covers for her and she slipped in while he undressed and lowered himself beside her. She felt his warm, strong hands on her and thought she would burst.

She had never known such gentleness, such kindness.

"Always I love, Jessica," Olie told her.

"And I — I love you," Jessica said.

And once more she shivered, for she realized that she had never been in love, not in this way, in her entire life.

Still later that night, unable to sleep, Jessica wrote a letter to Elsie. She was in her room — in bed — the writing paper propped on a book on her knees. As she began, it seemed to her that Elsie appeared before her, her head inclined thoughtfully as Jessica poured out her thoughts. Jessica pressed more and more firmly onto the white paper as she wrote, half-excited, half-dismayed.

"*My dear Elsie,*" Jessica began, "*I really don't know how to begin this letter. Something happened today which I suppose I had known would happen sooner or later but which, as time went on, I imagined would take on another form. That is, I thought there would be more control . . . well . . . I won't go into details . . .*" and now Jessica paused, pen in air, looking out into the space of her bedroom and into the dark beyond the window, "*but Olie has at last declared himself. I don't know whether to feel relieved or terrified.*"

But she did know: she was terrified!

For one of the few times in her life, perhaps the only time — except for her wedding day — or when someone was ill, Jessica was afraid. She knew that things set in motion were not so easily stopped.

"*Now that Olie and I are in a different relationship . . . ,*" and, in spite of herself, Jessica thought once again of Olie's arms about her, and, again in spite of herself, shivered with pleasure, "*I don't quite know how to handle it.*"

Again Jessica paused, searching the room as if an answer might appear before her. She listened for August, but he apparently was still sleeping it off; all was quiet. She heard the creakings of the old wood in the interior of the house, the startled squawk of a bird outside, roused from its sleep. Then quiet once more descended, and she could hear only the slightest rustle of the tree outside her window, sawing the breeze.

"*Obviously Olie and I have to be together.*" But as soon as Jessica had written it, she scratched it out. She bit on the end of the pen. "*August doesn't really love me . . .*" she began, but scratched that out too. "*I just don't know what to do. I don't think I can be around Olie without wanting to be with him — you know what I mean.*" And then Jessica thought: her mother once said something strange: "*The woman can enjoy it too,*" not explaining the "it" but not having to. But her mother hadn't explained that men were different and that some men could call forth feelings in a woman that others could not.

"*I always thought one married for life. I married for life.*"

Jessica, looking at the paper, was rather surprised to read her own words. But it was true, wasn't it? She had always thought that once married, she would never leave. It was not so much a matter of the marriage vows — like any restrictions, Jessica accepted only what she herself wanted — it was a matter of sticking with what she had chosen. And she *had* chosen August.

"So, Elsie, what do I do? I can't pretend to love August when I don't. And I can't pretend to not love Olie when I do. And I know Olie. He'll be so ashamed. And I don't want him to feel that. He shouldn't be. It just happened!"

And she thought again of how Elsie had encouraged her to invite Olie to the seance and the table game. Had she seen their attraction?

Then she thought she wouldn't mail the letter. But she had to write it.

She went on: *"I have to speak to Olie again. We have to work something out. All I know is that I can't bear not to be with him. Perhaps we will have to run away. But then, there's Jake. Oh, God, Elsie, what do I do?"*

Jessica felt as if her head were going to burst. Quickly she wadded up the paper and threw it as far as she could. She knew she would have to talk to Olie and perhaps he would find a way for them.

Yes, she thought. *Olie will find a way . . . he had to.*

Chapter Eighteen

*J*ESSICA'S TALK WITH Olie took a very different course from what she'd planned. August came into the parlor that very day and told her she would "have to talk to Olie."

At first Jessica was astounded. How had August found out? Surely Olie had not confessed?

August set her speculations to rest.

"There's a problem at the store," he told Jessica. "And I thought you should consult Olie. See what he has to say."

"What problem?" she asked.

She had built a fire in the stove in the parlor and heat was flowing around her. She stirred the wood with a poker that had been a commemorative item for the store. The engraving on it read, "1885-1900. The Lutz Store." Then the partners were listed: August, Jessica Lutz, Willard Pratt.

"Why did we have to put Willard's name on this?" Jessica asked, looking at the poker. She thrust it into the fire as though she were burning Willard himself.

"Jessie! He has capital invested, you know."

"Barely! They withdraw more than they put in."

August didn't argue.

Jessica noted that Olie's name had not been engraved on the poker; he hadn't been a real partner, apparently was never meant to be. But, Jessica thought now, she would see that she and Olie were treated fairly in regard to the partnership; if August thought he could get out of giving them their fair share, he was wrong! That is, if she and Olie . . . oh, dear. When *would* it be settled?

"I don't understand something," August was saying, interrupting her thoughts.

"What?"

"The inventory. We're missing some items, but there's no accounting for it."

"Were they sold?"

"Couldn't have been. They would have had to show up on the books somewhere."

"I'll do the auditing from now on," Jessica said without pursuing August's statement. "You don't like figures and you don't keep track of things!"

"Oh, pshaw," August said, pulling at his moustache. "I do the best I can."

"And *when* you can," Jessica said sourly. "You are hardly a regular auditor."

"Well —"

"I'll see what I can find out," Jessica said then.

Without knowing, Jessica suspected Willard — or Violet. She knew she had a habit of putting blame on them, but often she was correct. Yet, in spite of Willard, the Lutz Store was prospering, had outlasted two other grocery stores in Atlas City and two other hardware stores, all of which had tried to hire away Olie Olson.

Olie, she thought. It was a perfect excuse to see him. Then she and Olie would have to plan.

"If you would talk to Olie, Jessie," August said then. "He likes you — trusts you."

Suddenly Jessica's face flamed; she turned away from August.

"Jessie?"

August's voice was startled, questioning — Jessica didn't usually act this way.

Quickly Jessica recovered herself, said, her voice starched, "I'll talk to him, August. But surely you don't think that he —"

"I don't think anything, Jessie," August said. "That's what I want you to find out."

"I'll talk to him," Jessica said again. "Now leave me alone for a moment so I can think."

Olie had been at the store and when he later came in the front door, Jessica called to him. He approached her in her chair in the parlor, and as Jessica looked at him, his face ignited. He looked down at his feet.

"You want talk to me, Jessica?" he asked at last. He looked up and his blue eyes searched hers, his manner intense, but his glance soft and loving.

"The store," Jessica said, keeping her voice calm. "Won't you sit down?"

Olie twisted the hat he had just removed, finally used it to point at the horsehair sofa. "There?" he asked.

"There," Jessica said.

He was seated opposite her, and he looked at her again, blushed.

"Olie," Jessica said, "I want to ask you some thing."

"Ya?" he asked.

He waited while she rearranged her skirts on the parlor chair, then he moved forward on the sofa, hat in hand, as if at any moment he would bolt out of the room, race out the front door. He seemed not to want to look at her and he studied his hands with great care.

"Relax, Olie," Jessica said then. "It'll be all right. Everything's all right."

She felt a warmth when he was near; it was as if the fire had reached out and infused her, but without harming her.

She saw Olie was still blushing. "Ya," he said, not too convincingly.

"I wanted to talk to you about a matter at the store." If he had really expected something else, Olie gave no indication. "You know that my brother, Willard, is not a good farm manager."

Olie hated to criticize, but at last he said, "Ya."

"And you know that Violet," Jessica couldn't keep the contempt out of her voice and Olie looked at the floor, "is even worse."

Olie didn't say anything, so Jessica prompted: "Is that right?"

Olie studied his hands. "Ya," he said.

Jessica leaned back in the chair. How to talk to him — how to reach him beyond the words she was having to say to him now? She had to be careful — August might come in at any time.

"Something does not seem to be right at the store," Jessica finally said.

If she had thought she was controlling things, she was not prepared for the anxiety her words caused in Olie. He leaped up from the sofa, threw his hat back on it, came rushing over to her, grabbed both of her hands in his and said, anguished, "But I should have telling you!"

Jessica stared at him. "Should have told me?" she said.

Olie dashed out of the room. She heard his pounding footsteps on the stair and then he appeared back in the parlor, clutching something in his hand. He was holding it out to her. "Take," he said.

In Olie's trembling fingers was a beautiful wooden carving.

"Take," he said again haltingly. "I meant for Christmas, but I afraid to give."

Jessica was completely bewildered. "I don't understand," Jessica said.

But she took the carving, felt the smoothness of its sides, the wood warm from Olie's encircling hands.

"Is snow goose," Olie said then, the furious blushing beginning again. "Tulip wood. I order — for you. I carve for you. Is snow goose. You know? The snow goose mate for life."

His face looked as if he were about to explode. Reaching for him, Jessica tried to guide him back onto the sofa. But Olie was so embarrassed and agitated that she could not get him to sit down. He began pacing about the parlor, looking, in manner, exactly like August.

"Olie," Jessica said. "The store! What does this have to do with the store?"

"Oh, yes," Olie said, almost irritated, as if that problem were the least of his worries.

He scratched his head, cleared his throat.

Violet — she taking things," he said at last. I not know what do — I afraid you not believe me."

"Oh!" Jessica said now, "I'd believe you all right. I *knew* it. I just *knew* it!"

"I should have telling you. But I thinking . . . maybe she stop, maybe thinking she pay for things. I should have telling August and you."

"Well," Jessica said, leaning back in the chair. "At least we've solved *that* problem. August and I will handle this from now on. Thank you for your honesty, Olie. But please tell us immediately if she does it again."

She realized they had said nothing about their own complication. And her voice, now, was droning on as if everything would be the same. But it couldn't be!

Olie pointed then to the snow goose, his mind obviously on something else. "You not understand?"

He was looking at her with such shame, and yet with such devotion, such abject and hopeless ardor, that she could think of nothing to say, could only turn the snow goose over and over in her fingers, rubbing it as if her life depended on it.

"It never be," Olie said, as if to himself.

"Oh, Olie —" Jessica began, but stopped herself. She turned from him, but Olie apparently was caught up in his own agony for he went on without looking at her.

"You have been so good to me. You — and August."

"Olie!"

She had begun to suspect what he was going to say and she wanted to stop him. She didn't know how.

"You take me in home, you give yob," he looked up at her as if pleading. "You care."

"Olie!" She realized suddenly he was not talking solely of his love for her, their mutual guilt. "What are you trying to say?"

There was a long pause. Olie shifted on the sofa, spun the hat around in his hands, then looked at her and said, "I ask Henrietta if she marry me."

If he had said he thought the moon was made of cheese, Jessica would not have been more startled. She couldn't speak, her throat was so tight.

"She good. She have trouble now. She say she have baby."

Jessica seemed to have been paralyzed. Her eyes widened.

"The people — they talk. I know about baby with no name. All baby should have name."

Still Jessica could not speak.

Jessica felt frozen.

"I not want child having bad life. We not —"

Now Jessica found her voice: small and strangled. "Olie, I love you," she said.

Olie blushed, looked down at his hands.

"That is reason I marry Henrietta," he said. "It is not right I love. That wrong thing."

She was astonished. All her plans had never taken notice of anything like this. She was completely unprepared for what Olie was saying.

"But Olie —" she protested.

"No," he said firmly, assuming again the role of parent. "August, Jake. You have duty."

"Duty!" Jessica exploded. "*Duty!*"

Olie ignored her. "I want blessing," he said then. "I want you understand."

"I'll never understand it," Jessica swore. "*Never!*"

"I sorry, Jessica," he said.

Henrietta! Jessica felt her mind whirling even as she saw Olie was preparing to leave. Henrietta and Olie. Why should that plain, stupid girl get the man she loved? Who was the father of her baby, if indeed Henrietta was really pregnant? Oh, God, she wished she were a million miles away.

"Keep snow goose," Olie was saying as he edged from the room. "Please keep always."

It was hot now in the parlor, or so it seemed to Jessica. She felt she would faint if Olie didn't leave.

"Goodbye, Jessica," Olie said. "I dream different . . ." But he didn't finish his sentence and his voice, strained, faded to silence.

When Jessica heard the door close behind him she turned to the fire and, taking the snow goose in her hands, threw it as far into the flames as she could.

Chapter
Nineteen

*I*N THE WEEKS following Olie's and Henrietta's wedding, Jessica waited for the announcement of a birth. But as though life itself wanted to thwart her, it turned out that Henrietta was *not* pregnant, and there *was* no baby.

Jessica wrote Elsie: "*I don't know if Henrietta is clever enough to fool everyone — including Olie and myself — or if she is just as stupid about the 'facts of life' as she is everything else. I suspected her of 'playing around' with some of the harvesting crews — she would be easy to flatter, easy to seduce — but she has made fools of us all.*"

Jessica didn't add that she knew Olie would have married Henrietta anyway; he would not have wanted to cause a scandal nor to hurt his employer — but it seemed a terrible twist. She remembered her sister Purdy and the seance they had held; her "spirit guide" had prophesied trouble for them all. Perhaps this was it.

"*Violet, however,*" Jessica went on, "*<u>has</u> given birth: to a child with a head of red hair just as bright as mine used to be! That infuriates me! He has no right to it!*"

Of course, Jessica thought to herself, Doc Harvey had to use forceps and it caused Willard, Jr., to stutter as he was growing up.

"It is thought," Jessica wrote, *"that he will outgrow it. We'll see."*

It was quiet in the house — Jessica in her bedroom — and she could marshal her thoughts with ease. She loved writing Elsie — what in the world would she do without her?

She bent over the paper again. *"Sometimes Violet brings little Willard over to play, but even small as he is, he doesn't seem to want to "play" as Jake used to. He's fascinated by electrical gadgets and devices, and always wants to know how to take things apart. He's not so good about putting them back together! August seems to be regarding him as a possible partner when he grows up. Heaven forbid!"*

Jessica leaned her head back, closed her eyes.

"August's father has died. You remember Herman, of course. Always telling the boring stories. And August's Aunt Hermina too — of a stroke, I guess. Since Hermina never married, some of her friends boxed up her personal things and sent them to us — most items I would never have purchased! I don't need a bunch of Greek vases and decorative table ware. I would much rather have had some extra cash!"

The cash was a sore point for Jessica at the moment: August had, without consulting her, bought a large herd of cattle. He had tried to persuade her that since they had pasture land, and since he had just acquired some adjacent land, again without consulting her, that they needed cattle to put on the grass. He was certain they would make barrels of money.

"I told him," Jessica wrote, *"that it was idiotic not to concentrate on the Lutz Store and import things for Christmas and other holidays. We could give the store a bit of class. We could bring people in from neighboring counties. Maybe you would even be tempted to return to Atlas City just to see the <u>improvement</u>!"*

Of course, Jessica thought, Elsie would never come. Her parents had died and there was no longer a reason for her to come to the Midwest.

"August should remember," Jessica wrote now, *"that some of this land came from <u>my</u> side of the family, and that my work in the store has contributed to the profits he keeps taking and putting into land and cattle. He'd better be right!"*

Jessica didn't tell Elsie that she had asked August to put Olie to work on the pasture land and with the crops and cattle. She didn't tell her how she still remembered the night she and Olie had made love, how he had held her, and how deeply she had fallen in love. She would remember how he had kissed her and she thought that the pain of losing her children was nothing compared to the pain of losing Olie. At least there had been a reason to mourn her babies; with Olie, she could only bury her grief.

Jessica *had* confided to Elsie that there had once been someone else in her life, but she didn't say when. And she did not say they had consummated their desire for each other, nor did she reveal who it was. *"I loved somebody, Elsie,"* she said. *"And he loved me. But it wasn't to be. It wasn't to be."*

At last Jessica quit writing about it. Elsie never answered anyway; she was busy traveling over the countryside and in Europe with her artist friend, and though the friend was making something of a reputation for himself, Elsie seemed to have quit drawing. Her letters never mentioned her own work now, and there seemed to be a note of pessimism in Elsie's vision of the future. *"I don't know when we'll marry,"* she told Jessica. *"But I wish we would go ahead and do it. This traveling around without the benefit of being husband and wife is beginning to tell on me. At first it was fun — very modern, very shocking, and I liked that. You would have too, Jessica — I know you! But now I would really like to get married. It's been long enough and my life is invested in my friend. Alfred seems not to worry about it, and he changes the subject when I mention it, but really, I'm not getting any younger!"*

Jessica thought, *And she won't inherit anything either if he should die before she marries him.*

Nevertheless, she tried to cheer Elsie up by writing, *"I'm sure it will happen one of these days, Elsie. At least Alfred has never made a move to leave you, and I'm sure he wants to marry you too."*

But Jessica wondered about that. She, too, had always thought Elsie very modern and daring to be living as she was without the benefit of marriage; now she wondered if Elsie were a bit of a fool. Why would Alfred marry her if he already had had the benefit of her love, her money, her time?

Still Jessica continued the correspondence: it was her lifeline.

In the spring of 1915 Jessica informed Elsie: *"Henrietta has given birth to a little girl. She's named her Ilse. I don't really want to see the child and I've refused to be the godparent. Henrietta asked me if I would do that. I told her it would require too much time.*

"But I <u>do</u> see her sometimes — a beautiful, happy child, I have to admit,

with a gay laugh. Henrietta often brings her into the Lutz Store; she's made a point of showing her off to me.

"'Here is your godmother, Ilse,' Henrietta says, then corrects herself. 'Well, your almost godmother.'

"And Ilse truly beams at me.

"'Yes, yes,' I say, trying to sound distracted. 'But Henrietta, I really can't visit. Working hours, you know.'

"'Oh, sure,' Henrietta replies.

"I think, Elsie, that I may have underestimated Henrietta. She may have an animal instinct about her. She seems to know exactly how to wound me."

Jessica swore the child intuitively knew something; little Ilse had a way of staring back at Jessica over Henrietta's shoulder, impaling Jessica with a grown-up, sober glance.

The child looked so like Olie — the blonde curls, the blue eyes. But most of all she had Olie's quiet, measuring look, a look that always cut Jessica in two.

She had never written Elsie about Olie and herself, but she knew that from this letter Elsie would surely guess. Well, it was all right. Elsie would not condemn her.

What she had to do, Jessica thought now, is plan her future. Perhaps she should simply pick up and leave — Jake was grown up now, did not need her — go to New York City, see if Elsie would move out of Alfred's quarters and into an apartment they could share. Perhaps they could both study art.

And, Jessica thought, perhaps she could somehow persuade Olie to leave his family too. They could go to Sweden, Jessica thought. They could start a new life. She knew he still loved her; she could tell by the way he looked at her when he had to come into the Lutz Store for supplies.

They had to seize life, Jessica thought. They could not wait for life to work things out for them.

But for Jessica there were other events looming on the horizon.

On May 7, 1915, the *Lusitania* was sunk.

Though an avowed pacifist, Secretary of State William Jennings Bryan wrote a formal protest to the U.S. Ambassador in Germany, requesting he pass on the note to the German foreign affairs minister:

> In view of recent acts of the German authorities in violation of American right on the high seas which culminated in the torpedoing and sinking of the British steamship *Lusitania* . . . by which over 100 American citizens lost their lives, it is clearly wise and desirable that the government of the United States and the Imperial German government should come to a clear and full understanding as to the grave situation which has resulted.

"I met him!" August exulted when he read Bryan's statement in the paper. "He sat in my rocker!"

Bryan had made a campaign sweep years ago when he ran for president; August had indeed met him, and bragged about it endlessly!

Though the German government declared in May 1916 that her submarine warfare would be conducted according to international law, in December of that year Germany proclaimed outright submarine aggression. When the United States entered the conflict in Europe on April 6, 1917, Will Harvey and Jake both enlisted. They were inducted into the 89th, which was completing training at Camp Funston, Kansas, with General Wood as the Division Commander, General Pershing head of the American Expeditionary Force.

"This is insane," Jessica said when Jake proudly told her he and Will had enlisted.

"I had to," Jake said. "Don't you know how suspect all Americans of German ancestry are? Don't you know that the townspeople think we have a picture of the Kaiser down at the church and that we all worship him?"

Jessica didn't bother to point out that Jake did not spend a great deal of time in the German church.

"Hmmph," Jessica said. "We have Swedish blood too. What do they think about *that*?"

But Jake was not mollified.

In September 1917, Jessica wrote Elsie: "*You may not be aware there in New York City, how German-sounding names have aroused an angry patriotism. Can you believe that even Teddy Roosevelt has joined the fray, saying, 'The crucible must melt all who are cast in it; it must turn them out in one American mold.' I thought he was fairer than that!*

"And then to see that Americans, prominent persons, of foreign descent would have to sign that humiliating document which asserts once and for all that they are <u>American</u> citizens and loyal to its government!

"You probably don't understand, Elsie, since you are of Scottish origin. It's the Germans they're after. Me. Us. I can't believe that some people have actually stopped coming in the Lutz Store and buying from us. We've been here for fifty years and yet nothing seems to matter to some of these people. I know they think we are German sympathizers, and nothing could be further from the truth!

"I suppose they think our price codes are war messages," Jessica wrote. *"And our salesmen are couriers."*

"Of course, Jake doesn't think as I do. He always takes the opposite tack — just like August — gives everyone the benefit of the doubt. But it makes me angry that they distrust us!"

"I don't know what they think," Jake had replied that day he told his mother he had enlisted. "I don't care. But I want to do my part and I will! Just think, T. E. Lawrence has stirred the Arabs to revolt and now Baghdad has fallen! We're going to win this war!"

"You *hope!*" Jessica said. "And why pay any attention to your wretched old mother!"

"But, Elsie," Jessica went on in her correspondence, *"it would be far better to send August and Willard with their inventions to Europe. That is, have them actually working for the Germans! The two of them are now working on a cannon which will shoot — they hope — crushed glass. This would be cheaper than cannonballs, they maintain, and it would have just as wide a range as ordinary ammunition! Can you imagine?*

"Well, anyway, Jake and Will have enlisted and Jake has written that they are both part of the 353rd all-Kansas regiment. Jake swears that because of their former outdoor life, they are both far better able to handle the rugged basic training than some of the clerks and bank assistants that they see. They go on marches of miles and miles and battles among the soldiers themselves."

Jake told Jessica that they practiced digging trenches, ducking real gas and flares, throwing grenades, knifing dummy pickets, scouting "enemy" positions. They learned to assemble rifles and machine guns blindfolded and to distinguish the hollow pounding of the three- and five-inch guns from the bark of the one-pounders.

"He's actually <u>proud</u> of all this war game stuff," Jessica wrote.

And then, the war games stopped. Will and Jake went over, still togeth-er.

"*I can't make plans now,*" Jessica wrote Elsie. "*I will have to wait until all this nonsense has ceased.*"

Chapter Twenty

*J*AKE AND WILL were seasick on the troop ship that took them to the coast of France, dodging enemy submarines on the way. Jake wrote his parents, but he could not say where he was. In fact, once they'd landed in France, he didn't know.

"Somewhere in France," he wrote.

He and Will were amazed at the chaos of the landing; tanks and artillery rolled off the ships, troops marched to the shore, officers shouted orders above the din of the unloading.

But when Jake wrote, he mentioned other issues.

"There is a peculiar kind of heroism here, or perhaps I should call it folly. Men will go over the edges of the trenches, rush an enemy position, when they know damn well they'll be cut down. And I've seen men panic — or be cruel, whichever it is — when German soldiers whose dugout has been reached will surrender, raise their hands up, and someone will bayonet them like an animal. I can't understand it! I'm proud to be a part of what President Wilson calls our struggle to 'make the world safe for democracy,' but I find things very confusing here. I can't see enough . . . I can only see the action as it is played around me, I know

nothing of what the generals are planning or their German counterparts, I just do what I have to.

"Will is fine, though like me, he finds things confusing. And the mud! It seems to rain constantly and when we have to move, the horses get bogged down in the mud and we have to push the cannons and the wagons loaded with ammunition until we reach a drier spot. And it's so hard to move the wounded. The stretcher bearers struggle to carry the soldiers — they don't want to injure them or cause them pain — yet they have to wade in knee-deep mud! I wish this damn war were over!"

Jake wrote that the American Expeditionary Forces were singing "Over There" and "Hinky-Dinky-Parley-Voo." He even sent back the lyrics of a song entitled, "Would You Rather Be a Colonel with an Eagle on Your Shoulder, or Private with a Chicken on Your Knee?":

> *I'd rather be a private than a colonel in the army.*
> *A private has more fun*
> *When his day's work is done.*
> *And when he goes on hikes,*
> *In every town he strikes,*
> *Girls discover him, and just smother him*
> *With things he likes. . . .*

Jake knew the words would cause Jessica to explode: "Oh, those French tarts! Out to entrap our innocent boys!"

But Jessica wrote letters to Jake too, nearly every day. Jake appreciated them — things were dull in camp at times, though Jake couldn't say he preferred to be fighting! Jake supposed his mother was writing because she probably was able to express herself at a distance in a way she could not do when he was near.

She wrote that she had been reading the papers, and though she didn't know where Jake was, she knew it was terrible. There had been quite an article in the Atlas City *Gazette* about the German U-boats and how the Allies were gradually reducing their numbers. She had read about the trenches and how enemy soldiers sometimes crawled forward at night and threw grenades into them. She so hoped Jake wasn't in the front lines; yet, concerned as she was, she knew other mothers felt as she did and when one Atlas City woman received notice that her son had been killed, Jessica went to see her, even though they were strangers. Jessica had put her arms about the weeping woman and had told her, "It can be no comfort, my dear, but your son was noble and honorable. He served his country in its time of need."

Jake knew that the Army was preparing for some kind of assault; word was it involved the Argonne Forest and that General Pershing was going to have to use some of his less seasoned men — like Will and Jake. Jake wondered what would be in store for them if that were really true. He had seen artillery and tanks slowly moving into the area where they had encamped; the tanks could penetrate the hedgerows and forests. But again, Jake was not able to see the whole picture, he could only guess.

Sometimes Jake wrote to his father alone. When he was expressing some of the fears he had, some of the anticipation in opposition to those fears, he felt his mother would not understand. She had never wanted him in dangerous situations, he knew, and she would not like it if she learned he was probably going to be in the thick of battle in a very short time.

And Jake didn't want to write Jessica of the French villages they some-times went through — the houses with the roofs gone, the walls shaken. He especially didn't want her to know that they, indeed, did see some French girls at times and that they had offered the men some of their local wines. They couldn't understand each other, but the girls often knew a bit of English, and those that were determined to "fraternize" didn't need the language. But Will and Jake stayed away from such encounters: *"I'm going to marry some nice girl when I get home,"* he'd written his father. *"I'm going to have children and make myself a secure future."*

At this time in his life, Jake knew, he had to keep on hoping for good times, good things. He knew the mention of marriage would no doubt frighten his mother, so he didn't write about that in letters to her.

Jessica's own letters spoke of the mundane affairs of Atlas City. Jake didn't know if she actually thought he'd be interested, or if she too was "editing" what she said.

"I tried to start a literary club here in Atlas City," she wrote. *"But none of the women would read the books!"* And: *"The city has decided — again — not to create a memorial park to commemorate the fallen veterans of this and other wars. Can you imagine?"*

Usually Jake would pause while reading his mother's letters, and look around him at the camp. Tents were everywhere and men were aimlessly walking about, as though they were back in the States and there were no war. But Jake could hear the booming of the distant artillery, and could see the wounded being brought back to camp for first aid.

Sometimes a horse was killed by a shell, and then the men had meat for rations. It tasted good, but Jake was sorry that a valued animal had to die to furnish them a better meal.

Jake wondered if Jessica wasn't writing about her own fears, because she had always had the notion that if she imagined something, it would happen — the family curse, Jessica had once declared. The only way to prevent other disasters was to refuse to think about them.

But in one letter, Jessica confided: "*The Germans will probably win this wretched war and then we'll all be slaves. They <u>do</u> know how to fight wars!*"

Sometimes his mother would write of sickness. "*Mrs. Kunzler claims she is dying again. One of these days, the old biddy actually <u>will</u> die and then we won't know what to think!*"

But one of the funniest letters, Jake had to show Will.

"You'll get a kick out of this," he told him. "You know my crazy family!"

His mother had written, "*Your father and Cousin Willard are trying to invent things for the war, even though we know here it's almost over. Isn't it? I do hope so. Anyway, one of the most outrageous ideas these two nuts have had the temerity to write the war department about is a bandage with stays in it like a corset! They think this will prove effective in cases of broken arms — splints, you see. I can't imagine where these two get their inspirations, but if one of them ever came up with something useful I'd faint!*"

Usually his mother's letters were uncharacteristically upbeat. But Jake was surprised one day to receive a letter from her which said, "*I know you've been writing your father letters, excluding me! I found them. Why in the world are you keeping things from me? You've told him a lot that you never revealed to me. Why??? You know I care!*"

In one of those now-discovered letters, he had written, "*Will almost got shot, Dad, and I just about got hit by a shell two months ago. I got shell fragments in my leg, and haven't been on the front now for some time. I can't say I'm sorry about that, but I do have a curiosity about what's going on. I hear rumors — you know how that goes — but I can't verify anything.*

"*One of my best buddies got bayonetted on a charge. It leaves you feeling very strange — one moment, you have a friend who is living and breathing beside you, and the next moment, he is gone. I wish this world could learn to live without war!"*

"*I put my hand to my heart then,*" Jessica wrote. "*I crushed the letter to my chest! I wanted to tear it up, pretend it wasn't true . . . not only that you had gotten wounded, but that you and August were keeping things from me.*"

Jake did not know exactly what to say to his mother about the letters, so he said nothing. But he could see how she could feel that the two of them were shutting her out.

All Jake knew was that his mother's letters were "vintage Jessica": "*Your father has quit smoking. Thank God! Having that part-time maniac smoking those long, black cigars was about as safe as leaving a convict in charge of the jailhouse!*

"*And Willard has joined the Catholic Church! Can you imagine! I know Violet has been nagging him for years, wanting all the children brought up Catholic — you know how they are — and don't just say I'm prejudiced! I wouldn't belong to any group that tried to control me like that!*

"*And now Willard has finally done it! I swear! Can't you just see Willard genuflecting and muttering all that rubbish? How could he do it? But of course, Willard and your father are <u>different</u> to say the least, and now I have to listen to the two of them arguing.*"

His father continued to write him occasionally, and Jake welcomed those letters, even if August went off in strange directions. His father wrote that Olie Olson had not had to go to war because he was farming; Olie wanted to enlist, but the Army wouldn't take him, feeling it was more important for him to stay on the farm and raise the crops the military needed. August said he was trying to think of some super crop Olie could raise that would feed thousands with just a few bites: "*Sorta like the miracle of the fishes, Jake. But so far we haven't found anything.*"

August also wrote that Henrietta was telling everyone that Olie was a "hero," and just the backup the entire nation needed.

"*I don't know why your mother avoids him,*" he confided in a letter. "*Henrietta brings their little girl, Ilse, here when she cleans and Jessica always leave the house. I suppose she gets tired of Henrietta's prattling.*"

Jake could not continue reading. Will had run up to him, hastily adjusting his helmet as though he were ready then to do battle: "It's the Argonne, Jake. We're going in."

There were no more letters for a time. Will and Jake learned that there had been an attack in Flanders, led by King Albert of the Belgians, and that they had succeeded in capturing the whole crescent of heights around Ypres in three days! The war seemed to be going well for the Allies, but there was yet another scourge to be faced: influenza was now taking a toll on the troops.

Jake knew it was widespread: his mother had written that Olie Olson had come down with it and had nearly died. "*Henrietta wanted me to nurse him,*" she wrote, "*but I refused. I couldn't see it.*"

Jake was a bit surprised. His mother had always seemed to relish the role of savior — it seemed to quiet her constant fears of disaster when she was actually trying to stop one or another. Yet Jake also felt a familiar twinge of jealousy when she mentioned she might have nursed Olie Olson to health. He knew it was petty, but there it was.

When Jessica wrote again, however, she was back on her familiar monologues: "*Willard is so Papist, he might as well be Pope. He crosses himself every other move, just to show off, I think, and August gets furious then and they start shouting at each other and throwing things. At least August and I share that particular point of view — you know — about the Catholics. And one of these days, if they ever get that blasted crushed glass cannon actually made, they'll probably use it on each other! Did I write you about that?*"

She hadn't, but Jake guessed what it would have looked like: a missile with an explosive that flew everywhere. He could see Willard and his father sweating over the drawings, imagining that they would receive some kind of medal from the President for their service to the country.

We are the craziest family, Jake decided. Even when there were global conflicts, the Lutz family stayed true to their attitudes, as if they were glued together by their differences.

Jake didn't know Jessica had a moment of great pain when Olie came down with the flu that was raging all about. He didn't know that his mother could not imagine a world without Olie Olson.

He did know, however, that his Aunt Purdy had come down with the flu and that his mother and August and Clarence Harvey were trying to keep from getting it while still taking care of Purdy.

Later, his mother wrote that Olie was better and that he had come into the Lutz Store. *"He was getting some harness for the farm,"* his mother wrote. *"I thought he looked pale and thin, when I saw him. But he made it through."*

She added that she hoped her sister Purdy would do as well as Olie had.

Purdy, however, was not so lucky.

Just before the war ended and Jake and Will Harvey finally got to come home, Jessica wrote one last letter: *"Your Aunt Purdy died a few days ago. Flu. I can't really believe she's gone — we tried so hard to keep her going — but her sickness came on quickly, worsened, and there was nothing Doc Harvey could do to save her. Mrs. Kunzler died of the flu also. It seems to be everywhere."*

Jake knew he would miss his funny old Aunt Purdy. With her seances and "spells," she was one of the family characters. He knew he had lost a very special person.

Just before the Armistice, August wrote that Jessica had told the townspeople, *"I'm going to ring the church bell when Jake comes home."*

And she did.

Chapter
Twenty-One

*B*UT JESSICA HAD NOT written Jake everything when he was overseas: she had gotten a heartbreaking letter the summer of 1918, a few months before the November 11th Armistice was signed and before Jake and Will had returned to Atlas City. Jessica simply couldn't tell anyone about it.

The letter had tersely said, *"Elsie died today. I found her lying on the bed, a pill bottle open and empty beside her. She was dead when I got there. I thought you should know."*

The letter was signed by Elsie's artist friend.

Jessica had noted the handwriting on the envelope was not Elsie's, and that the return was the artist's address. Even before she read the letter's content, she began to be afraid, a premonition rising within her.

When finally she had ripped the envelope open and read the ghastly message, her hands began to shake. Surely, she thought, she'd read wrong. She read the note again. The same thing: *"Elsie died today."*

For a moment, Jessica felt as if a huge fist had seized her heart and were strangling it. She moaned and collapsed on the bed in her room.

"Something wrong?" August had called from the other room.

"*No!*" she shouted back, terror striking her. "Don't come in!"

August mumbled something, but Jessica didn't hear. She went over to her door, turned the key. She couldn't bear to see anyone — not just yet.

When she walked back to her bed, she sat on the edge, the letter falling from her hands. Elsie dead. *Elsie died today.*

Oh, Elsie. Jessica flung herself onto the bed, but she didn't cry. She didn't cry anymore.

Jessica remembered how she and Elsie had sat in this room and covered each other with powder, how they had lain, hands behind their heads on the pillows, and plotted the wonderful things they would see and do.

She remembered how she had once told Elsie that she wanted to paint.

"You can, Jessica, you can," Elsie had said.

She had been such a wonderful friend!

What had happened to Elsie to make her do such a terrible thing?

And, suddenly, Jessica felt guilty — she had been so concerned with her own problems, with the war, with Jake, with Olie — *still!* — that she'd almost ignored the pain in Elsie's recent letters. She had kept the letters; she'd saved them.

Jessica went over to her dresser, opened the top drawer, and pulled the letters out. Now, as she read them, the tears welled. Why had she been so blind?

"*Albert hasn't done as he promised — he hasn't introduced me to the people he told me he would. He told me he would help me in my <u>own</u> career, but he hasn't done that.*"

There was another letter, which caused even more ambivalent feelings in Jessica: "*Albert has a beautiful young model. He looks at her with such affection. She is young and gorgeous and fully aware of her power over him and her defeat of me. Yes, Jessica, I feel defeated! Where are the joys I used to feel? What has happened to my talent? Do you remember that I told you how talent shrinks if it isn't used? Well, mine seems to be gone. I haven't had an idea for a painting in weeks, and the canvases of my old works have long been dry.*"

Jessica realized that she had responded to Elsie in the same kind of innocuous, half-listening tones in which Elsie had once replied to her own letters of discouragement about the farm. Could they not have seen each other's wounds?

And suddenly Jessica felt dismayed: why had she allowed Elsie to banish herself from Atlas City? Why didn't she insist Elsie visit? Why hadn't she traveled to New York to see Elsie, as she had once thought she would? Little by little, she had allowed their friendship to give in to attrition; little by little, she had destroyed one of the few relationships she'd ever had that had promised her understanding. And there was no one to understand her now — Elsie was gone.

Jessica went over to her door again and turned the key. She didn't want to chance August's coming in, but she was certain that he would respect her privacy. She did not want to have to repeat to him what she had learned that day, but she had thought of a way to ease the pain. August would never find out.

That night, Jessica wrote the first of the letters to an Elsie who would never respond. As she began, it seemed to her that Elsie was resurrected before her, that the person she addressed was not dead, ashes flung on water, but alive and awaiting news from her best friend. Jessica's pen began to press more and more firmly onto the white paper as she wrote Elsie, her grief, if not entirely assuaged, buried as she had buried so many other hurtful feelings in her life.

"*My dear Elsie,*" Jessica began. "*I really don't know how to begin this letter. But I am awaiting Jake's return from the war and I have found out some things since he's been gone.*

"*He and August were writing each other and not including me. It wasn't the first time I suspected they were shutting me out of something, but it was the first time I was able to prove it to myself.*

"*You are my one true friend, Elsie, the one I can tell everything to.*" Now Jessica put her pen to her lip a moment, thinking that it wasn't quite true — she remembered how she had edited earlier letters or torn them up if they were too revealing — but it was how she wanted to view the relationship.

"*Jake will be coming home soon, and I can hardly wait. I'm going to try to mend whatever it is that is wrong with us, see if we can't have a better mother-son communication. I can see now that I'll have some work ahead of me!"*

Then Jessica told Elsie how she would ring the church bell; she told Elsie how grateful she was that Jake wasn't killed.

She signed her letter as usual, *"Love, Jessica."*

"I've met someone I want you to meet," Jake told Jessica not too long after he had returned from the war.

"What? How could you?" Jessica asked, as if it would take awhile to meet anyone anywhere, much less anyone in Atlas City.

"Mother, I'm not dead! I like to go out. I met someone, that's all!"

Always defensive, Jessica thought.

Nevertheless, she had a small tremor, a small feeling of imminent threat.

"Who is this 'someone,' as you call it?" Jessica asked then.

"Her name is Louise Swenson."

"Swenson, Swenson. Which Swenson?"

There were so many Swensons in Atlas City, and Jessica was trying to think who might have a daughter named Louise.

"She doesn't live in Atlas City, Mother," Jake said. "I met her at the Legion Hall in Center."

"Oh."

That meant, Jessica thought to herself, she would have to do some snooping. She would want to know what the kinfolk were like, where they came from.

"Well, then," Jessica said. "I hope she comes from good stock."

"She's not a prize Hereford, Mother," Jake said in that infuriatingly superior way he had — just like August — of making it sound as though she were being unreasonable. "But Louise is a nice girl."

Jessica sniffed.

She decided to "inspect" this Louise Swenson, however, at Sunday dinner. Jake, of course, questioned her motives.

"Are you intending to be nice to her, Mother? Or are you going to quiz her and make her feel miserable?"

"Well, the idea! Just let me try to do something nice — I thought you would like her to meet your family. But perhaps you're ashamed of us!"

Suddenly Jake laughed. "Welcome home, son," he muttered.

Again, Jessica sniffed. "Really," she said.

"I'll bring her over," Jake said then. "But you and Dad better be on your best behavior and all or I'll never forgive you!"

"Well! Don't you issue ultimatums to me, young man! You're not so high and mighty with the Lutz enterprises you know."

Jessica dangled the prospect of inheritance before Jake like a carrot bobbing in front of a donkey. She couldn't believe he didn't really care, but he certainly acted otherwise.

"Then I'll go to work for *her* father!" Jake shot back, stomping angrily out of the room.

Louise Swenson, Louise Swenson, Jessica thought. *Now you are the one who will try to keep Jake and me apart. First August, now you.*

"He's just like his father," Jessica told the walls. "Exactly like his hard-headed father!"

Jessica had not changed her mind about Louise being an obstacle to her bettering her relationship with Jake, but the Sunday dinner began auspiciously enough. Jessica had told Violet and her family preemptorily to stay away, she was entertaining that day. She had no intention of Willard giving some Catholic prayer at the dinner table, trying to convert them all in the privacy of their own home! He could save souls for the "Romans," as Jessica termed them, on his own territory!

And then there was the suspicious fact that this Louise Swenson was beautiful: blonde, blue-eyed, with a slender figure and long, lithe legs. The idea!

"She's so pale," Jessica said as she sighted Louise, pulling Jake into the parlor and shutting the door. "And she doesn't look as if she ever says anything!"

"Oh, she's quiet, all right," Jake admitted. "But I like that in a woman."

And he gave Jessica a calculating, again amused, glance.

"You don't need to worry, Mother. She won't challenge you or Dad for the conversational lead."

Indeed!

Opening the parlor door again, Jessica led the way into the dining room, where the table, already grandly appointed with Hermina's silver and her own mother's china, was groaning with the spectacular dinner she'd prepared — baked chicken with dressing, a special Virginia ham, a choice of baked sweet potatoes or mashed potatoes, green beans, corn, relish, rolls and butter. Jessica had outdone herself and she smiled as she saw what a splendid repast she had laid before this rival of hers.

She probably can't cook, Jessica told herself. And Jake *does* like to eat.

But Jake seemed entranced with Louise. He pulled her chair out, carefully seated her, as though he thought she might break. August, too, seemed enchanted.

At once, August began a long dissertation on his latest invention: a giant spool for a sewing machine which would almost never require changing. Louise, Jessica observed, faked attention very well, even asking a few polite questions, allowing August to expand.

"This girl can absorb things," August then said to Jake. He scratched his head and smiled at Jake, then back at Louise. "She's got a mind like mine. A steel trap."

"In your case," Jessica said sourly, "the trap's been sprung."

"Hmmph," August said.

Louise looked a little startled at Jessica's observation, but Jake put his hand over hers and said, "Mother and Father have their little jokes."

August dominated the conversation during dinner, as usual. If Jessica ever tried to pontificate, it was during dessert, when August began to get sleepy because he'd eaten so much. And so well!

Now Jessica got up — it was sometimes necessary to prod Henrietta — and hovered about the table, providing extra dishes of the crisp, baked chicken and the ham, and more of the homemade hot rolls. She kept staring at Louise surreptitiously, as if expecting to catch her in some charade.

But Louise was passive; she listened, absorbed, smiled. She seemed to want to be an observer, not a participant. Jake, Jessica thought, evidently thought she was magnificent for he kept smiling at her idiotically.

Finally Jessica sat down. Henrietta served the elaborate chocolate cake Jessica had made for dessert, and as everyone *oohed* and *aahed* over its beauty, Jessica began her offensive.

She fired: "And what do you plan to do with *your* life, Louise?" she asked.

Louise was caught off-guard. She hesitated a moment, looked at Jake, then back at Jessica. "I want a family," she said.

"I see." Jessica drew herself up. "Well, most people do make plans for their life. I don't agree with this male-manufactured philosophy which dictates that women should just stay in the home and vegetate, popping out children all the time. I take an active interest in the Lutz Store you know, bookkeeper-manager and all."

"Yes," Louise said, flushing. "I think that's wonderful."

"*Mo*ther!" Jake said testily.

"And I hope you agree that women are entitled to vote," Jessica pursued.

"Well, I —"

"I want to tell you more about this spool, Louise," August inserted then, apparently trying also to head Jessica off.

But Jessica was adamant. "You know, in certain states — Wyoming, for instance," Jessica paused, giving August a steely glance, as though he were personally responsible for the lack of women's vote in Kansas, "they've voted for years. It's coming — and high time too!"

"Well, yes," Louise said. She seemed to be floundering. She looked helplessly down at her chocolate cake, as though searching for some answer there. She apparently did not want to challenge Jessica. "I guess I really haven't thought about it."

"You haven't thought about it!"

Jessica's emphasis was bitter and she pounced on the words.

Suddenly Jake pushed back his chair and propelled himself to his feet. "Thank you for a delicious — and informative — dinner, Mother," he said evenly. "Louise and I must go. We're meeting friends."

"For a dance?" Jessica asked innocently. "On Sunday?"

Though she certainly wasn't religious, she didn't mind using religion if it served her purpose.

"No, Mother," Jake replied as he helped the flustered Louise from her chair. "Not a dance. I hope we don't disappoint you. We're going for a ride in Will Harvey's new car."

"I see."

Jessica made it sound as if that too, were forbidden on Sunday. It *did* seem to her that Will had made an unnecessary purchase, even for one who was planning to study medicine. His father had managed without a car; Will could have too, she thought.

Jessica innately understood what having a car meant — distance and mobility. And she was certain this was a further obstacle to forging closeness with Jake.

"Nice to meet you," August called as he stood up, watched Louise and Jake prepare to leave.

Jessica kept her head down, ostensibly much concerned with the texture of her cake.

"Thank you, Mrs. Lutz," Louise stammered then, flushing once more. "I really enjoyed meeting you."

Jessica didn't answer.

Jake took Louise's elbow, edged her from the room.

That girl was going to ruin everything, Jessica thought.

Chapter
Twenty-Two

*J*AKE AND LOUISE were married, in spite of Old Jessica's objections. By 1926, two children had been born: little Jessie, and Fred. Though they shared the same house, it was as though Old Jess and her son lived under different roofs; except for a closeness that seemed to develop between Fred and his grandmother, it was a kind of "live and let live."

Jessica grew accustomed to ignoring them.

When she lay in her wonderful little bedroom, Jessica thought, she could almost forget the cares of the day, and imagine she was back in happier times. She could dream that Elsie McDonald was still alive, that few changes had been made in her life. Her south-west room had a constant breeze from the pastures that lay beyond the house and the bluff above the creek where the bulls liked to stand. In fact, lying in her bed, she could sometimes see one of the huge Hereford bulls surveying his domain; he seemed so power-ful and so confident in his purpose. When she opened the win-dows in the summer, the curtains would blow in, swelling out like a pregnant woman. The earth was bearing its fruit — the wheat was ripe and the men were ready to cut it. The bulls in the pastures had impregnated the cows and they too were bloated with unborn calves.

Jessica wrote Elsie that she had learned to "*appreciate*" the rural atmosphere, but she still felt she did not belong to it. She enjoyed the rare times when she could go to Chicago to market — for they now carried furniture in the Lutz Store and it was there that it was principally merchandised. Jessica did the buying; she was overwhelmed at first, by the floor after floor of furniture in the Chicago Mart, but she learned to spend her energies searching for items that would sell in the store, not items which *she* necessarily liked.

It was a lesson she had learned from buying clothing for the store; her taste was far different — perhaps of necessity — from the farm women she served, and their practicality called for few frills. She learned to purchase sturdy, washable dresses for the most part, though she had a few of the "Sunday best" styles for the churchgoers.

Jessica sighed. When she had looked out the window moments before, she had seen the threshing machines ready to go out into the fields and cut. She had finally persuaded August to buy his own equipment and it was proving profitable. Olie did most of the cutting; she had seen his blonde head disappearing down the road that led to the fields.

Henrietta was working downstairs, with Ilse helping. Jessica usually kept out of their way by either working on the books at the store or coming up to her preserve, her bedroom.

Jessica guessed she must have fallen asleep in the languid air; she was disoriented for a moment when she heard someone shouting. Suddenly Henrietta burst into the room.

"Jessica, Jessica! There's been an accident!"

"What?"

Jessica sat up in bed, brushed sleep from her eyes. She tried to focus on Henrietta, who was now pulling at her, trying to force her out of the bed.

"Come, come!" she said.

"Henrietta, please! What in God's name is wrong?"

Now Henrietta looked straight at Jessica.

"If only he'd stayed working in the store," she said, looking in an accusing way at Jessica. "This would never have happened!"

Jessica was fully awake and irritated. She grasped Henrietta by the arms, made her face her. "Don't be stupid, Henrietta," she said. "What is wrong?"

"Olie," Henrietta said then. "There's been an accident."

Jessica felt her heart constrict. "What kind of an accident?" She realized she was trembling. When Henrietta only stared at her, she snapped, "You fool! What *kind* of an accident?"

"The tractor," Henrietta mumbled. "The tractor pulling the combine overturned."

"And?"

"Olie was under it! He's been badly hurt! He's lying out in the field — they're afraid to move him. They've gone for Clarence or Will Harvey."

Jessica put her hand to her chest, pressed in, as though that gesture would stop her heart from pounding. Oh no, she thought. Not Olie. Her children were gone, Jake too, she felt, Elsie was gone, but not Olie!

"Come," Henrietta said. "Olie asked for you."

And then the pounding stopped. Jessica thought her heart might never start again.

Olie was lying beside the tractor, still pinned under it. Someone had shut off the motor. The combine had not quite turned over and was now at an angle, the wheels on one side in the air. The men were trying to unhitch it and set it upright. At last, they succeeded and the huge machine groaned like an animal, crashed down on all wheels.

There was blood all over Olie, his face grimaced in pain. Jessica knew he was dying — she had seen that look before and it was unmistakable.

She rushed to Olie, leaned over him, cradled his head in her hands. "Olie," she said, tears starting. "Oh, Olie!"

She felt his hand take hers, blood running along his arm and leaking over on her fingers. She could see Henrietta standing with her fists to her mouth, frozen in helplessness — as usual, Jessica thought.

"I want you keep snow goose," Olie said to Jessica. "I want you keep always."

"Don't talk, Olie," Jessica said. She pressed his hand. "You'll be all right."

Olie moved his lips but she couldn't hear what he was saying. She bent over to catch the words.

"I still love, Jessica," Olie said, coughing. Blood gushed out of his mouth. "I always love. Keep snow goose. Remember."

The weight of the tractor had crushed his chest. He groaned.

"Where's the doctor?" Jessica asked wildly, looking about. "Where is that idiot doctor?"

But it was already too late. With his hand tightly holding hers, Olie closed his eyes. He said it again, "I love you, Jessica."

Jessica thought she could never let go of his fingers.

When they made her take her hand from his, led her away, she wanted to tell everyone there that she loved Olie too, had always loved him. She was guilty! She had put Olie out on the farm because she didn't want to have to see him in the store! She herself had exposed him to all the dangers and now, once again, fate had made her pay for it.

If only she hadn't destroyed the snow goose!

It seemed whenever she tried to hurt other people she hurt herself most — with her actions, her inactions — August, Jake, Elsie. And now they seemed to confront her as insurmountable barriers.

She had the rest of her life to spend with this agony; it would never go away.

The funeral was simple; the service in the church was full of people who had come to pay their last respects to Olie, for he was so kind that the townspeople loved him. Sprays of flowers were bursting into color at the front of the church, and the congregation was hushed. Jessica looked over at Henrietta and Ilse; Ilse was staring back at her, but the gaze was not hostile, merely curious. Did she know of her father's devotion to Jessica? Surely not.

"Then shall this corruptible put on incorruption," the minister was saying.

It was hot in the church; though windows were open, the breeze seemed to have vanished this day and Jessica saw August running a finger around his coat collar, his winter suit too heavy for the heat. She plucked a fan from the holder on the back of the pew before her and fanned him. August put a finger to his lips as though she had spoken.

She looked out the window beside her as the minister spoke. She could see the trees near the river that flowed by the church, their tops bending in the wind. The hot breeze stirred the papers on the podium and the minister reached to hold them down, momentarily lost his place. His voice droned on, rising and falling on the air like the wind: "And he showed me a river of life, clear as crystal, proceeding out of the throne of God and of the Lamb. In the midst of the street of it, and on either side of the river, was there the tree of life, which bare twelve manner of fruits, and yielded her fruit every month: and the leaves of the tree were for the healing of the nations. And there shall be no more curse: but the throne of God and of the Lamb shall be in it and His servants shall serve Him: and they shall see his face . . ."

Jessica cleared her throat, once more moving the fan to try to cool August and herself.

". . . and His name shall be in their foreheads. And there shall be no night there; and they need no candle, neither light of the sun — for the Lord God giveth them light: and they shall reign forever and ever."

Jessica let her eyes drift to the front of the church where the open casket with Olie stood on its catafalque. Henrietta had asked her what suit Olie should wear, and Jessica had not been able to answer. She didn't know what Henrietta had chosen and she was not going to look. Though it was the custom to "admire" the body in this rural community, she would refuse to do that; she wanted to remember Olie as he was on that long-ago, joyous night.

Someone was singing, "The Old Rugged Cross," and people were stirring as though they knew the service was almost over. Louise, Jake, and the children sat behind Jessica, and Jessica heard Fred asking, "Can we go now, Momma? Please?"

Jessica turned to smile at him, but pursed her lips to indicate he should be silent. Louise had put a hand over Freddie's.

"Ashes to ashes, dust to dust," the minister said when the song was over.

People got up, the family left, and the rows filed by the casket. When August took her arm to lead her by Olie, she shook her head. She made her way, alone, to the back of the church and out into the torrid afternoon.

Jessica had saddled up her mare and, much to August's surprise, had taken off at a gallop for the creek. She didn't ride much anymore — she was in her sixties and thought it inappropriate, but she wanted to be alone, wanted to feel the wind on her face, hear the water of the creek as they poured over the rounded stones beneath it.

The creek was where, years ago, she had come to gather watercress and morel mushrooms. Both places were secretly guarded; no one wanted to share his special spot for collecting these delicacies.

Now, as her mare tore off the long grasses beside the creek, sucked them in, chewing contentedly, Jessica thought this creek was almost as wonderful as her bedroom. She felt safe here too, hidden from view; she could smell the leather of the saddle — an odor she had learned to like — and the bright fresh wildflowers that grew in the darkness of the thick cottonwoods.

She sat on the edge of the creek and took off her shoes; gingerly, she put her feet in the running water to cool them. The water felt marvelous. In this creek, though farther down in a natural pond, her mother and father had been baptized. They were not Baptists, but they had both wanted to be immersed, as though that were the only way to be sure one had God's grace. "The river of life," Jessica thought, remembering the words from Olie's funeral. "*And he showed me a river of life, clear as crystal, proceeding out of the throne of God. . . .*"

Perhaps, Jessica thought, they had read this Biblical verse and dreamed of being immersed in it. Suddenly, sitting there, almost mesmerized by the heat filtering through the leaves of the cottonwoods and the steady crunch of her mare's jaws, Jessica wondered what it would be like simply to slip into the river, slide over the rocks, let the waters wash over her. It seemed as if then her pain would be over; she could sleep forever.

But she shook her head. Was it true that there was a resurrection? Would she really see the throne of God, be reunited with all those who had gone before her?

And then Jessica pictured herself seeking her children, those little lost ones, the ones she had mourned all her life. She saw herself with her mother and father, with Elsie, with Olie. Youth had not prepared her for growing older, she thought; in youth, everything is in the future, in old age, it is all past.

The mare neighed then, and rubbed her head against Jessica. Jessica got up, pulled on her shoes and socks, put her arms around the horse and hugged her. She reached behind her ears and scratched her while the mare tossed her head in ecstasy.

The river of life, Jessica thought.

Jessie

1927 ... 1946

Chapter
Twenty-Three

"STAY OUT OF THE water, Louise," Old Jessica said before the family took off for the Ozarks. "You know you don't swim well."

"Oh, I'll protect her," Jake said, flinging an arm around Louise and pulling her to him. "I'm a good swimmer."

"*Hmmph!*" Jessica shot back at him.

"*I* swim," Fred announced to his grandmother.

Jessie, standing quietly beside her mother, smirked. "Oh, sure you do," she said.

Old Jessica ignored Jessie, patting Fred on his head. "Of course you do," she said. "You do everything well."

"See," Fred said, sticking out his tongue at Jessie.

"Well I swim really well," Jessie said, going over to Old Jessica and standing in front of her. "I can dive too."

"That's interesting," Old Jess said, but she turned away from Jessie and Jessie felt she had tossed the remark behind her like a crumb.

"Come on, children," Jake said then. "We'd better be on our way."

Jake had rented a boat.

"Will we go out very far?" Fred asked him, fearful.

"Of course not, silly," Jessie said. "You're always so afraid of things! What's there to be afraid of?"

"Jessie!" her mother said, pulling Fred to her. "Shh!"

They stepped into the boat from the dock, the boat dipping as they each got in and found a seat; then Jake started the motor and out they went.

Jake and Louise sat in the stern near the engine, and Jessie and Fred straddled the plank across the bow of the boat. As the engine caught, the bow had tipped up and Jessie enjoyed the wind and spray in her face. Fred had screwed up his face in distaste.

Jessie reached out to touch Fred's hand. "It's okay, Fred," she said.

In spite of how angry she got at him sometimes, she felt protective of him. He was afraid of so many things!

Jake jerked the boat around, maneuvering it out into the open water.

Her mother leaned her head back, seemingly liking the way the breeze struck her, just as Jessie did. The oak trees on the shore created a canopy of green, silent and mysterious, fencing the land from the water.

Other boats crisscrossed with theirs and Jake moved to one side as another craft — its driver gesturing boisterously and obviously drinking — came close to them then sped away.

"Gotcha!" he called back, waving a beer.

"Damn fool!" Jake said.

"Poppa," Jessie pleaded then. "Go faster!"

"You're a speed demon, Jessie," her father said. But he laughed and turned up the motor.

They seemed to be swallowing the water, taking it in, spitting it out behind them in a white wave that spread in a "V" behind them, then dissipated. Fred was gripping the plank beneath him with white knuckles when her mother said, "Let's slow down, honey. Couldn't we just drift awhile? My head is spinning!"

Immediately Jake cut the engine, the motor gasping into silence. The only sound was from the engine of the other boater, far down the lake, tearing back and forth somewhere like an angry bee.

"Is this better?" Jake asked Louise.

"Yes," she said.

She put a hand to her eyes to look out over the water and into the thicket of trees lining the lake. The sun beat down on them. "It *is* hot," she added.

"I'm going swimming," Jessie announced.

She stood up, the boat tipping. Fred squealed.

"You are *not!*" her father said. "Sit down, Jessie."

And she did, quickly, for she could see her father was furious with her just at the thought.

"If you're hot," her father went on then, "just dip your fingers in the water and splash it on you. That'll help."

Jessie frowned, but she turned to lean over the side of the boat, again tipping it.

"Daddy, Daddy!" Fred shrieked. "Jessie's gonna drown us!"

"Phooey," Jessie said. "Scaredy-cat!"

But she pulled her hand in, then sat with both hands folded in her lap and turned back to glare at her father briefly.

"Are we going to sit here all day?" she asked.

She was always in some kind of motion; it was very boring not to be.

"We'll sit here as long as I say so," Jake said firmly.

Her mother trailed her hand in the water briefly. She put a few drops on her forehead. "It's cool," she said. "That feels better."

"Why is the water so dirty, Daddy?" Fred asked then.

He too had put a hand in the water and Jessie saw that it had almost disappeared, turning that peculiar yellow.

"When the rivers pouring into it come through farmland," her father explained, "it's going to be muddy. I suppose, years ago, when Kansas was just grassland and Missouri was unplowed too, the rivers and lakes were clear."

"Well, anyway," Fred said in his somber way, "it's wet."

"Yes, dear," her mother said.

Jessie sighed again, putting her head in her hands and her elbows on her knees and studied the far shore as if now yearning for it. How long was this going to last? It was so dull!

Just then the purr of an approaching motor rolled over the water to them, shortly becoming a roar, getting louder and louder until the boat of the man they'd seen before began bearing down on them.

"Oh, God," Jake said. "That damn fool wants to scare us again."

"He *is* scaring me," Louise said. She grasped the plank she was seated on with both hands. "Let's get out of here."

Her father pulled the cord and the motor sputtered, died.

"Hang on," Jake said. "I'll get it in a minute."

He tried again and this time the engine caught for a few seconds longer, then died again. Jessie could see her father was getting nervous, but trying not to show it.

"Jake!" Louise said then, her voice trembling uncertainly. "What'll we do?"

"I'll get it, Louise," her father said testily. "Just a minute."

But the boat was hurtling toward them. Jake could see the man standing, waving at them to get out of the way. He seemed completely unaware of the fact they were not moving.

"Jake!" Louise screamed.

The white boat shot around them, motor screaming, missing them by just a few feet, the wash behind slamming into their own boat where Louise and Jessie and Fred sat huddled. With a great heave, the boat pitched over. Jessie, Fred, Jake, Louise were thrown into the water.

Seconds later, Jessie and Fred bobbed up to the surface, and then Jake's head appeared. But there was no sight of Louise.

"Daddy!" Jessie screamed, paddling for the boat while Fred grabbed at her. "Mommy's drowning!"

Hesitating a moment, seeing that Jessie was pulling Fred onto the upturned boat, her father plunged under the surface of the water again.

Jessie sat watching where her father had disappeared, her hands pulled into fists and placed over her mouth. The water looked impenetrable, dirty and sinister.

Her father's head popped up again; he was coughing and spitting out water.

"Daddy!" Jessie yelled, just as he went under again.

This time, he must have dived even deeper, the dark water folding him in and out of Jessie's sight. She stared into the lake as if trying to see down to the bottom, a hundred feet or more, hoping to see her mother's head pop up somewhere near.

But there was nothing.

At last her father came up again, gasping for air. He faced the agonized look on Jessie's face; Fred was sobbing.

"Mommy! Where's my Mommy?" Fred cried.

Her father began to retch.

When Doc Harvey came, he and her father sat at the edge of the lake where they'd watched the dredging boats and the divers, searching for her mother's body. Jessie saw the doctor put his hand on her father's shoulder and say, "It's not your fault, Jake. You couldn't help it."

The horrible hooks had sunk into the lake over and over again and when they finally were through, there was nothing to do but get a coffin, seal it, and return the body to Atlas City for burial.

Jake had not spoken all the time they had searched for Louise's body. He stood, jaws working, looking out at the water that had taken his wife.

When Will Harvey told him that they had found the other boat abandoned, didn't know who it belonged to, Jake only sighed. There were no words for his grief — or his anger.

Will again put his hand on Jake's shoulder. "I know how you feel, Jake," he said. "I lost my mother so early, you know."

Jake shook his head back and forth. "No," he said. "No one knows how I feel."

Jessie, standing behind him, her legs shaking, said to herself, *I do, Poppa. I do.*

For two months after her mother's funeral, her father went out on his horse early in the morning, not taking Jessie with him, staying out until dusk. Louise's parents had died several years before, so there was no one for Jessie to turn to except her father and Old Jessica. And Jessie had never been close to her grandmother.

When Jake would return to the house, he'd go up to his room, close the door behind him, not speaking to Fred or Jessie or Old Jessica. It was as if he hadn't seen them.

Jessie began to feel her father had died too. Hadn't he promised she could watch this fall when they branded and castrated the calves?

"Poppa," Jessie said to him one day after he'd come in early from a ride. "Please let me in."

She'd been standing outside his bedroom door, which he had left slightly ajar, and could see that her father looked startled upon hearing her.

"What?" he said.

"Please, Poppa," she said.

Jessie began to push the door into the room, little by little because she didn't want him to feel she was insisting.

At last he sighed and said, "Come in, Jessie."

When she walked into the room, she saw he was sitting in his rocker by the window, looking out. She looked too, as though she could focus on *whatever it was* he was focusing on, but all she could see were the bright colors of the oaks her grandmother had planted in the yard years before. The leaves were ochre, scarlet, the hues so stark against the sky that they seemed to flash as the wind shook them. Jessie could see the horses in the corral; they sensed colder weather coming, sniffing the air. Their energy — nipping at each other, bucking — was such a contrast to her father's silence.

Jessie didn't know quite what to say; even Old Jessica had had enough of Jake's seeming absentmindedness: she had wrapped her arms about Fred and told Jessie, "You're old enough to take care of yourself, Jessie. But Freddie needs me."

"I'm only ten," Jessie had countered.

"*Indeed.*"

Now Jessie pushed the door fully in, saw her father was not moving in the rocker, not looking at her.

"Poppa?" she began.

Jake looked up. Again, he seemed startled. "What?" he asked.

"Poppa," Jessie went on. "I have to talk to you."

He was all she had, Jessie thought, and she wouldn't let him go!

"Please, Poppa."

He was going back and forth in the rocker now; it seemed to calm him, for she had heard the rocker when she was downstairs in the kitchen the other night — ceaselessly rocking.

Jessie straightened her back and marched into the room. Her grandmother had told her she would have to manage for herself, so she would!

She took a seat on the soft down bed, the feather-tick collapsing beneath her as she struggled to stay upright. Still her father looked out the window, not at her.

"Poppa," she began again. "What do you *do* out there?"

Jake kept looking out the window, his glance sweeping over the hills and the cliff above the creek as though he were searching for something, as if something were certain to appear to him at any moment.

When he didn't answer, she repeated, "What do you do out there, Poppa?"

He didn't answer.

Jessie swallowed. Clearing her throat, she thrust her own hands in her lap, then turned her clear, brown eyes on her father and stated, "I'm here, Poppa."

Again, she didn't think he'd heard her. His eyes were looking at her, she saw, but the glance seemed to be going right through her, right through to the brown, walnut backboard behind her. Was he seeing something else in his mind?

She tried again. "I'm doing well in school, Poppa. The teacher says I'm bright!"

She'd never bragged this way but she felt she had to to break through her father's terrible, frozen look.

She went on: "I'm in a play, too. I didn't get the lead — I'm not pretty enough Old Jessica says — but I'm one of what the teachers say is a 'character' part. I play an old woman. Like Grandmother."

There, Jessie thought. That serves Old Jessica right.

Still her father said nothing; had his gaze deepened or was it clearing? Again the hand brushing at his eyes — was he wiping the haze away?

Jessie cleared her throat again. "Freddie has Grandmother, Poppa, but I don't have anyone."

She was surprised she had said that; but now that it was out, she was glad. She sighed, her ribs heaving up.

"Poppa!" she said then, sharply.

Suddenly she leapt off the bed, ran to where her father sat in the old rocker, seized his face in her hands. She turned it to her. "Poppa, I need you. I need you *here!*"

"Jessie?" he said then, as if he'd just recognized her, realized there was someone in the room. "Oh, my dear Jessie!"

There was a moan then, and Jessie saw the look she'd hated slip off her father's face as if it had only been a mask all along. He turned his eyes full on her, took her shoulders, and pulled her close to him.

"Darling Jessie," he said. "What have I been doing to you?"

That fall, just before the roundup, her father gave her a pony.

"Now you won't have to ride Goldie anymore," her father had said, knowing the big tame mare was no longer a challenge for Jessie.

Goldie had been a part of the ranch for as long as Jessie could remember. She didn't even know how old Goldie was, but she was so gentle anyone could slip off her, walk behind her, pull her tail, her ears, and Goldie wouldn't flick a hair. Jessie could do anything with her — even managed to urge her into a slow trot from time to time. She was the only horse Fred was not afraid of, though he didn't want to ride her. "That's dumb," he always said when Jake asked him to come riding with him and Jessie. "I'll stay home with Grandma."

The pony her father bought her was not — thank God — a Shetland. She'd ridden those before and they were often bad-tempered, always rough-riding with their spindly little legs. This was a real horse, though a small one, bred by one of the tenant farmers Jake had on land he'd bought out in Western Kansas. Blaze was a chestnut gelding, with four white stockings and a splash of white on his face. If he had been sorrel instead of chestnut he would have looked like a relative of the Herefords that grazed the same pastures he did. He was a strong, well-formed, fast horse and Jessie loved him.

"Oh, Poppa," she cried when she first saw Blaze. "I love him. I love you!" And she threw her arms around her father, then turned to hug the horse too.

Blaze jerked his neck around in surprise and nuzzled her. From the first, they got along.

She and her father took to riding almost every day. As they left the corral, Fred would appear at the kitchen door.

"You'll get thrown off," he'd taunt Jessie. "You'll break a leg."

There was a kind of desperation in his voice, as if he wished Jessie *would* fall off, though she never hurt herself in a fall.

"Why doesn't Fred like to ride?" she asked her father once.

"Damned if I know," Jake replied, shaking his head. He looked very sad for a moment. "Maybe he will later."

But Fred never did.

From the moment that Jess got home from school until dusk, she would be out with Blaze. She would dash up the stairs, take off the loathsome long, black stockings Old Jessica made her wear and the print dress, pull on her bluejeans and plaid shirt and boots. Clanking down the stairs — her father had given her spurs but she never used them on Blaze, they were for "show" — she raced to the stable. Blaze would snort and run up to the corral rails when he saw her small figure dart out of the house. Then she would saddle and bridle him and they would flash by the gate, the gelding wheeling and rearing as Jess pulled him in to get off, shut the corral gate.

Once she almost ran over Fred, who had inexplicably followed her to the barn and had hidden in the shadows of the hay pile watching her.

"Look out," he screamed as she and Blaze lurched past him.

"Watch out yourself!" Jessie screamed back while Blaze hurled himself into a canter. "I didn't even know you were there!"

Of course Old Jessica — at dinner that night — had to mention the incident to her father.

"Jake," she said, not looking at Jessie but smiling over at Fred, "I'm afraid your daughter . . ." the *your daughter* bothering Jessie because Old Jess had begun referring to her this way instead of by her name, "your daughter is getting very careless with her horse. She nearly killed poor Freddie today."

Of course, Jessie thought, *Fred tattletaled.*

Fred, smirking across the table at Jessie, stuck out his tongue. Naturally, no one saw that.

"Is this true, Jessie?" Jake asked her, his eyes pinning her down in her chair.

Jessie pushed the mashed potatoes Old Jess had made around and around the plate.

"And don't play with your food!" her grandmother ordered.

Fred, as if to emphasize his own good behavior, took a slow, careful bite of his own potatoes. Jessie made a face at him.

"I wouldn't do that if I were you," Old Jessica warned then, having seen the gesture. "Since you are not to be known for your beauty, I fear . . ."

"Mother!" Jake shouted, flinging down his fork. "There is no call for that. Now what in hell are you trying to tell me?"

Old Jess withdrew, sulking. Primly aligning her silverware across the plate she said, "I'm trying to tell you that your daughter risked Fred's life this afternoon when she went charging out of the barn on her horse and nearly ran over him."

"Is this true, Jessie?" her father asked.

Now no one was eating. Old Jessica had seen to that; a deathly hush had fallen over the table.

"Fred hid himself in the hay," Jessie replied. "If he had jumped out at Blaze and me — which is what I think he wanted to do — Blaze might have thrown me."

"I didn't do that, I didn't do that," Fred shrieked.

"Hush, children," Old Jess said then.

She looked with her piercing eyes straight at Jessie. "But you *did* almost hit Fred with your horse, didn't you?"

Numbly, Jessie nodded. "But I didn't mean to. Blaze and I didn't even see him."

"I think Fred had better stay out of the barn," Jake said, picking up his fork to begin his meal again. "I know Jessie wouldn't deliberately threaten Fred with her horse — and I hope — expect — that Fred did not mean any harm either. Let's drop it, shall we?"

Pinching her lips together, Old Jessica also took up her fork and began to pick at the roast beef she had made for their evening meal. "I don't always want to be a referee between Jessie and Fred, son," she said.

Jake frowned. "No one has asked you to do that," he said firmly.

"Um-mm," Jessica murmured, in the way she had of saying "yes" while leaving the distinct impression she was really saying the opposite.

That night, Jessie went to her father's room, removed the paper from his hands, and crawled into his lap. "Why doesn't Grandmother like me, Poppa?" she asked.

For a moment her father didn't answer. Then he took her hands in his and said, "I'm sure she loves you, Jessie. But perhaps you remind her of the way she was herself at a certain age and she can't bear to remember that. Life seems to have failed your Grandmother somehow."

Jessie didn't know what he meant. She thought a moment.

"But everyone says that Grandmother was beautiful. She was lucky!"

"Yes, in a way she was," her father said. Jake pressed her to his chest, his large hand cupping her. "Yes, your grandmother *was* a beautiful woman — is still striking."

He paused a moment, went on, "There's been a lot of pain in her life too. Her brother Willard taking his life —"

"I thought everyone told me it was an accident," Jessie protested. She remembered hearing the family talk about it — Violet weeping — she remembered them saying that he had lost most of his money in the crash. Later she found out the "crash" they spoke of was the stock market, not a car wreck or anything. And Violet seemed to be crying as much over the money as over her Great Uncle Willard.

"Well, it was a kind of accident," her father said now.

Jessie was solemn. "Well," she said, "I'm not beautiful so I can't play princesses or anything like that, I have to be characters. You can't play princesses if you're not pretty."

Now Jake pulled her away from his chest and looked at her.

"You're my princess, honey," he said. "You always will be."

But was that enough?

Jessie wasn't sure.

Chapter
Twenty-Four

WILLARD . . . her father.

As Purdy moved about her kitchen, put the tea-kettle on to boil the water, she thought about her father and that awful day when Old Jessica had called her at the boardinghouse.

"Purdy," she'd said. "There's bad news here."

"What?"

But Old Jessica wouldn't tell her.

Purdy had gone running to the house next to Old Jessica's, the one where she'd been taken when the horse had kicked her and she lapsed into a coma, the one where she had played on the porch when she was very little.

When she went into the dim parlor where Old Jessica stood, waiting for her, she asked, "What, Auntie?"

Old Jessica took her hands. "He's dead, Purdy."

Purdy felt a cold draft, right on the back of her neck. Though she was afraid, she asked, "Who?"

"Your father. Willard has killed himself."

"Oh, no!" Purdy had not seen that there was another figure

there in the dark room. It was her mother. Now Violet repeated her protest. "He didn't kill himself. The gun went off accidentally!"

"Nonsense, Violet," Old Jessica said, turning to face Purdy's mother. "My brother took pains to end it all — elaborate pains it seems — but it's no good denying it. I don't want to admit it either, but it doesn't help to say it was not deliberate."

Now Purdy paused, took the kettle from the stove and poured the boiling water over her coffee grounds. She would let the mixture steep, then strain it into her cup. As she waited for the coffee to brew, she remembered that Old Jessica had seemed very pale in spite of her controlled voice. Her hands had been shaking, and her face ashen.

Purdy had begun to cry.

Old Jessica had put an arm about Purdy's shoulders in a vain attempt to comfort her. "Why would he do this to us?" she asked of no one in particular.

Purdy was not allowed upstairs into the bedroom where the terrible incident took place. Clarence Harvey came down the stairs, his face stricken.

"Don't go up," he said to the women who faced him, almost as if they expected him to refute the evidence.

"I'll call the funeral parlor," Jessica said then, filling the silence that had followed Harvey's words. "Emmett Carter can pick him up."

"I already have," Harvey said. He cleared his throat, went on, "And I have given some medication to August — over his objections of course. But finding Willard . . ." He stopped, turned to survey the women in the room, bent his head in recollection. "Do you want any sedatives?" he asked, as though in a daze himself. "People will be coming, but you will need to rest."

"I won't be doped," Jessica said firmly.

"I will," Violet said. "Oh, yes! I want to sleep!"

Clarence Harvey portioned out some pills, extended a few in his hand to Purdy, but she shook her head.

"I'll stay with you tonight, Violet," Old Jessica said. "And you can stay here too, Purdy, if you want."

Purdy was grateful to her, but she felt an awful urge to get out of the house, into the fresh air, away from this place. She tried to forget that when Clarence Harvey had reached out his hand to her, he still had some blood in his palm.

Later, however, Purdy sneaked back into the house and up to the room where her father had died. It seemed necessary somehow, to see the scene, if only to convince herself he was really dead.

    When Purdy opened the door to the room, she stepped back in horror, stuffing her fist in her mouth: there was blood all over the back of the rocker where her father had been sitting. Behind the rocker, on the wall, blood bloomed in spots like obscene red flowers.

    Purdy burst into tears.

    Doc Harvey had been right, she realized. She would never forget the look of this room and she had been terribly wrong to come here.

    Purdy remembered playing at her Aunt Purdy's as a child, hiding behind marble statues which had been moved there in the hopes of selling them for cemetery monuments, picking weeds to put in the white wicker baskets that lined the front porch. Purdy had been fascinated by the sign her aunt had made about curing "all manner disease." (The "Jesus Saves" had been her own idea.) She used to trace her fingers over the letters, imagining she was obliterating boils, warts, just by running her fingers over the words.

    When she was grown up, and after her father had killed himself, Purdy was sorry that her aunt had made no claims for raising the dead.

    Her father.

    It was strange, Purdy thought now as she strained the coffee from the bottom of the pot into her cup, how she considered this house where she had played so often as a child, and the house where she grew up, as secondary places. The house where Old Jessica ruled — the stone one — was the center of all their lives. She didn't know exactly how she got this impression, but Violet and Willard seemed to defer to Old Jess, would talk, their heads nodding toward the stone place, their voices hushed, as if they feared Old Jessica would stalk out and assault them for their conversation. Was that it? Or was it simply that Old Jessica was always formulating some plan and the rest of the family was supposed to follow placidly?

    The fact that Purdy never again got to see her father after that terrible day only added to her sorrow; when they held the funeral, for the family only, the coffin was closed. As Purdy sat in one of the awkward, folding chairs at the funeral parlor, she tried to imagine her father alive, tried to erase the image of the room she'd seen, imagined her father wanting to breathe, yet suffocating in the coffin. Open the lid, open the lid, she wanted to shout. But when she stirred in her chair, her mother put her hand over hers and said, "Quiet, child."

She wasn't a child, of course. But her mother had always thought of her that way and Purdy knew it wasn't going to change.

The loss of her father left Purdy feeling there was a part of her missing — like an arm — or a leg — and she would be crippled forever. She hadn't really been close to her mother, and when Violet decided to move away from Atlas City — out to California, she said — Purdy opted to stay near her aunt, Jessica, live in the boardinghouse she was to inherit, try to reconcile the conflicting feelings within her.

Purdy sipped her coffee. It was quiet in the boardinghouse — she had only Ned and Lars as tenants at the moment. She sighed. She was going to have to see if the county couldn't supply her with more of the elderly and the disabled to take care of. There were plenty of rooms after all, and tending to her "people" kept her from worrying about herself.

Purdy had been told many things about Jessica, but remembered little of the conversations. She did remember, however, that Old Jessica had taken care of her when the horse had stepped on her. She remembered Jessica's face leaning over and the raucous voice ordering people about. "Will her face be permanently scarred?" she heard her ask Doc Harvey. She had asked the question right in front of Purdy, as though she didn't exist or was deaf.

It was Will Harvey who was taking care of her. He had gone into practice with his father after the First World War and he had been the first one on the scene.

"She'll be fine and healthy," he had said.

He'd glanced at her as if to gauge the effect of Jessica's careless words.

Purdy knew then that she would never look like other children; she was what they would term "plain." Her mother, Violet, was pretty, and Old Jessica was beautiful, they said, and perhaps that was why Old Jess seemed to be contemptuous of her: the disdain and the guilt of the handsome for the less-than-perfect.

Ned came into the kitchen.

"Coffee?" Purdy asked, lifting her cup.

He nodded.

Purdy got up, took another cup from the cabinet near the stove, poured out a brown stream for Ned.

"You good, Purdy," Ned said, and sucked up the coffee, almost burning his lips.

"Careful!" Purdy warned. "Now sit you down, Ned, and be company."

She liked having Ned and Lars in the house; people are not meant to be alone, she declared, and since she'd never married, having two bachelors — platonic of course — was the next best thing.

"You know," Purdy went on to Ned now as if he would be interested, "I gave up the Catholic Church so my old aunt Jessica would be pleased with me. And she was!" Purdy exclaimed.

"I like trains," Ned said.

"But of course I didn't adopt Old Jessica's religion — I don't even know what it is, except I'm sure she's the head of it!"

And Purdy laughed.

Ned took a sip of coffee. "Good," he said, pointing to the cup. "I like coffee."

"I'm glad," Purdy said.

Ned didn't comment, so Purdy got up, filled her cup again, sank back into the chair.

"I remember I used to like to stand before that stove," she said to Ned. "When I was little and would come here to see my Aunt Purdy, I would stand there, holding out my cold hands to the heat. Then I would turn — like a roast on a spit. I would say, 'Me hot, me cold,' because whatever side was toward the heat was warm and the rest of me was not."

Ned looked at her as if she were speaking a foreign language.

"Well, you know, Ned. You face the heat and you're hot, but the other side, facing *away* from the heat, is cold."

Still Ned stared at her. "Coffee good," he said.

"Oh, *dear*."

Purdy could hear Lars stirring in his room above the kitchen; no doubt he had been "guarding" the landscape with his senile eyes, looking to see if his cattle were still there. Of course they were long gone. Purdy just hoped she wouldn't have to go out after him.

Why was it, Purdy thought then, looking at Ned and then past him to the little white kitchen pump as if it would give her the answer, she had grown up expecting everyone important in her life to always be there? Sometimes she had wished they weren't — Old Jessica for instance, when she was on a "tear" — but when dire events actually took people away from her, she was stricken. It was safer to put one's faith in things, she'd decided: little white pumps for example, signs saying, "Jesus Saves."

"Do you know, Ned, that once my Aunt Purdy rented rooms to some actors? And was my dear ol' Aunt Jessica furious!"

Ned put down his coffee cup. The word "actors," seemed to have some meaning for him.

"Circus?" he said.

"No, no," Purdy said, putting out a hand to touch him, trying to pin him to the table. She didn't want him running about the back yard, swinging in the trees just because she'd said a word he knew. "They were with a troupe. They were staying here because it was cheaper than in Harper. And were they something!"

Purdy rolled her eyes. "Old Jessica said, 'Men and women should not travel together. And they certainly shouldn't stay under the same roof!'"

"Well, they can't camp out, dear sister," Aunt Purdy had told her.

Purdy had watched them carefully. The women wore great quantities of makeup, which Purdy found fascinating. Their hair dyed the darkest black, their eyes lined with kohl, extending upward toward the temples and making them look faintly Oriental. These women wore heavy perfume and moved about in her Aunt Purdy's parlor with a practiced grace. Their clothes were exotic too — bright oranges, purples — Purdy wondered if one of them was really Aunt Purdy's "spirit guide," changed into a woman and prowling about in the familiar room.

"I was very aware they were beautiful," Purdy said then to Ned, as though he would understand.

Ned raised his brows.

"I knew I was not." She sipped thoughtfully for a moment. "But August told me I was beautiful on the inside and that . . . that is where it counts."

Ned's brow was furrowed. "I like trains," he finally said.

Now Purdy heard Lars descending the stairs. *Oh dear*, she thought. *He's going out looking for his cattle and I've got to stop him.*

"Finish your coffee, Ned," Purdy told him kindly. "We'll talk later."

She had a crazy kind of life, she decided. But it was much happier than she'd ever thought possible. With her tenants, she had a place in this world and it didn't matter that Old Jessica took no notice of her. Little Jessie, even Fred, liked to come see her once in awhile, sometimes even have a play "seance," and Jake had always cared for her.

She was sorry for Jake now that Louise was gone; but she was glad that he had Ilse to help him. She was a fine, Swedish girl and she would take good care of the entire family. And that was what mattered in the end: taking care of people.

Chapter
Twenty-Five

*T*HOUGH JESSIE didn't really understand her Grand-mother Jessica, she felt close to August and Jake. They were the buffers against a world she perceived as hostile — or at best indifferent — and she was happy when they asked her to join them on land- and cattle-buying expeditions.

Actually, as August's Big Chief Tablet later recorded (like the earlier Willard, August felt he would make a diary of the events of the Lutz family — the yellow, lined pages of tablet after tablet being the repository of his literary jottings), Jessie and Jake and he made the best threesome for judging the worth of both animals and farms. *"We are extraordinarily adept,"* he confided to his journal one day in 1934, *"at detecting the slightest flaw in pasture or bottom land, or in the bulls, steers and heifers we wish to buy. I,"* he went on immodestly, *"am no doubt the leader of the group, but Jake offers something and even little Jessie seems to know when the farm is not what it was written up as or if the cattle are inferior."*

It was true; Jessie seemed to have a sixth sense even as a very young girl, and her father seemed partial to her fancies. She liked nothing better than to pull on the faded bluejeans — she no longer wore the spurs, not even for "show" — and head off with her father and grandfather in the old dark blue pickup.

She liked to bounce between the two men as they jolted themselves over country lanes, pastures, creek bottoms, and into the farmyards of various land holdings just to view a bull or a piece of property, or perhaps even a horse to herd the cattle. She liked to listen to the men talk — and wrangle — as they discussed the price of something Jake and August were interested in. Then Jessie would draw very near the men, edge up against the warmth of her father so that he would put an arm about her, and gaze up at the faces of those who were arguing so vehemently with her relatives.

Later, in a way Jessie never quite understood, with signals not apparent to her, her father and the farmer would arrive at an agreement and then they were both all smiles, August beaming, shaking hands, and maybe the farmer's wife would lean over Jessie and say, "Now she's a fine young girl, she is. And you're doing a good job — without her own mother, you know."

At the comment, Jake's face would cloud over and he would turn his eyes down.

He wouldn't linger long then. He would pull Jessie with him to the pickup and in seconds they would be rattling back down the lane they'd just come up, August letting one hand trail out the window.

"Stop," he might order Jake.

And Jake would. Then August would climb out of the pickup, step off the running board, go to the edge of the road and crawl under the barbed-wire fence. He would take up a handful of dirt, let it sift through his fingers. "Okay," he would say, "okay. We made a good buy. I just wanted to feel it again."

Sometimes her grandfather would stop by a stream and drink from it, leaning over and sipping like an Indian. "Grampa!" Jessie would exclaim, "You mustn't drink from streams just like that. You might get poisoned!"

Old Jessica had warned of such things — cattle polluting streams.

"Naw," August would say. "I've drunk from 'em all my life and I haven't been sick yet."

It was true: he never had.

"We want to find those bulls that have Domino in their line," Jake explained one day. "He's the greatest Hereford in these parts and it's worth what you have to pay to get a bull calf out of him. You get exactly what you pay for in this business, no more, no less."

Gradually the land holdings, the cattle herds built up; the homeplace became five sections and grazed some 600 head; soon there was land even in Western Kansas, where Blaze had come from, great wheat fields which Jessie and Jake and August drove through in the pickup one July just after harvest. It seemed to Jessie that she was in the middle of a yellow ocean, a sea that stretched so far she could not detect the end of it.

"Are we lost?" she asked her father, joking.

Jake laughed. "If we are," he said, "we're in the best place in the world to be lost in."

They discovered oil, too — an unexpected bonus.

"Well," Old Jessica finally admitted, "I guess you did right after all. You spendthrifts finally hit it."

"It wasn't the oil we were after," Jake told her.

"You hang onto that," Old Jessica warned. "When your wheat lands give out, when they have to lie fallow, you'll still see those pumps moving."

"Well," Jake said, scratching his head and laughing. "Guess you're right."

Jake had plans for her, Jessie knew. Without saying so, he seemed to be looking to her to carry on the ranching when he was no longer able.

"I think it's time you had a calf to raise for yourself," Jake told Jessie one early spring day. "It's time you learned how to take care of it, what's involved. And it's time you learn that you have to part with them too."

Now Jake looked sternly at her — she was always attached to horses, dogs, cats that would slink around the farm, not really belonging to anybody, but a constant feature of the landscape. The cats kept the mice controlled and Nature somehow controlled the cats so that the population — though they bred easily and readily — mostly stayed within boundaries.

"But that damn caterwauling when they're making love," August complained to Jake once, shaking his head. "Damn they make me mad then. Threw my boot at them once and then the damn dog hauled it off to the pasture and I never *did* find it!"

Jake laughed. "Serves you right," he said. "Cats gotta have love too, you know."

Jessie was intrigued by the ritual of the cat's "lovemaking" — and the results of it. She fed the kittens in the evening, watching them come and rub up against her, mewing. And their mothers in turn watched Jessie's every movement as she steadied the pan of food on her way to the barn; then tails stiff, they clotted around her, waiting for the moment to pounce on the pan, or on *her* should she threaten any of the offspring. She always fed the little ones to the side so the bigger ones wouldn't crowd them away, once taking special pains with a blind kitten who could only direct itself by smell, and was constantly abused by others around it. But in spite of her efforts, the kitten eventually died.

"Nature has a way," August told Jessie when she found it in the barn. "Don't grieve, Jessie. That's the way things are."

"Then I don't like the way things are," Jessie replied.

August said, "Not liking it doesn't change it. You'll have to learn to take it, Jessie."

The steer they finally found for her was a beauty; strong, with the Hereford red and white distinctive markings and sturdy legs, the calf liked to follow Jessie around the barnyard.

"Feed it corn," Jake told her. "It's best for putting on weight."

Jessie got the calf a halter, to lead it down the lane and back, and she named it "Rummy."

"Why 'Rummy?'" her father had asked.

"Because he has Domino for an ancestor and Dominoes is a game and . . . "

Jake smiled at her.

"But I don't think I want another calf," Jessie said then.

Already the time was nearing when she would have to send it off with the others in the truck. It had gained as much as her father would allow — he was almost nine hundred pounds — and he would have to go.

"They don't put on weight fast enough after that," Jake told her. "It's better to ship them after the summer pasturing and buy again in the spring. Then we won't have so many to winter."

The day the cattle truck pulled up in the barnyard, Jessie ran into the house calling for Jake.

"It's time, Jessie," Jake told her kindly.

Jessie begged to keep him over the winter. "He won't eat much. I don't want him to go to market. I don't want him to be killed!"

"Jessie." Jake took her chin in his hand.

They were in the dining room, sitting at the empty table with the hand-crocheted cloth that Old Jessica always kept covering the table, removed only when she served the food.

Jessie put her hands up and brushed off her father's fingers.

"Why do we have to do this?" she asked.

"We eat meat in this country, Jessie. And that's the way — or one of the ways — our family makes money. We have to learn not to get too attached to these animals because the time comes when they have to go. Remember, I warned you. You have to learn to be detached if you're going to run a ranch."

It sounded terrible to Jessie. But she trusted her father and, looking up at him, putting her elbows on the table and her chin in her hands, she told him, "I don't want to raise another calf for myself, Poppa. I don't ever want to do that again."

"I understand, Jessie," he said.

Rummy seemed to be looking at her out of the slats of the truck after he was loaded with the other yearlings. He was on his way to the stockyard in Kansas City. Jessie imagined that his eyes were still rolling at her as they drove down the path to the highway and out of her sight.

Fred said, "So much for your little honey, Jessie," and Jessie turned on him so fast, hit him so hard with her fist that she blackened his eye.

Old Jessica raced to help Fred and rebuke Jessie, but Jake headed her off. "Don't you ever do that again, Fred. You know how Jessie feels. Or you should!"

And later, when Fred told her he was sorry, tried to make up with her, Jessie said, "Okay, Fred. But you're going to have to face the world without Grandmother someday. Will you be ready for that?"

Fred simply stared at her, uncomprehending.

Jake kept his promise to Jessie: he let her go on the roundup.

August was excited. "Oh, God," he said as he mounted his horse, "I can't wait to get up in those pastures and go."

Jessie was riding Blaze.

"He knows what to do," Jake told her as they left the barnyard corral. "Just give him his head."

Jessie nodded.

Sandy, the new foreman, and some of the neighbors who helped with the roundup were already in the high pastures, getting the stragglers together, moving them out to the holding pens. As they rode along, Jessie looked at her grandfather. August had never liked farming, but he enjoyed the roundups; he liked driving the cattle back down to the pens so they could be dipped, branded, and the young male calves castrated. Cattle that were going to be sold would be separated, and the whole scene, riding on the trail with the herd, cattle bawling, calves tripping alongside their mothers, cowboys yapping and cracking their whips, throwing their ropes at the laggards to urge them on, dust rising beneath the herd's hooves, all this inspired August and he had told it all to Jessie so many times that she too was eager to go.

Even Blaze seemed to sense her excitement, tossing his head up and down as though he wanted to run; but she held him in. Jake had told her to follow him and to do what he did; this was not a day for riding, it was for herding.

Jessie looked at her father. He seemed so handsome as he rode along, his left hand holding the reins lightly, his right hand on his hip. She could hear the saddle creak as they moved, his chaps brushing against the side of the saddle. He looked the picture of the cowboy, silent, confident.

Jessie knew her grandmother had always wanted the city; she didn't know how her grandmother could have lived on the ranch and not loved it. How could she look out over the smooth rounded hills, the winking ponds, the brush along the creeks and not adore it?

To Jessie, it was heaven itself just to be out in the open air, smell the fading grasses, see the trees with their golden leaves flashing in the sun. And, with Blaze beneath her, feeling her legs curve around his warm body, hearing him snort with impatience, smelling the leather of the bridle and the saddle — there couldn't possibly be a better place on earth.

Now her father turned around, putting one hand on his horse's haunch.

"When we get up to the pastures where the herd is, Jessie," he said, "just pull in behind me. Blaze will follow. And whatever you do, don't go shooting off away from the herd. Keep close, watch what I do."

"Okay, Poppa," Jessie said.

She knew her father liked being out as she did, but she also knew that he had done this many times, and that helping neighbors with their cattle day after day, plus doing his own, made it all somewhat less enchanting.

This land had been grassland since pre-history, August had told her. "It's land that's fed cattle driven up from Texas and it's land that's never been broke. Beneath the surface of the grass is flint. Whenever a road is cut through — and, thank God, there are few roads — you can see the teeth of the rock. Six inches down from the topsoil, there it is. This is God's country, Jessie."

Jessie could imagine Indians racing over this ground on their ponies; they must have stood on the crests of the hills and looked at it, loving it, as she did.

"The cattle will be nervous," Jake told Jessie now. "They seem to know we do this every spring and fall, and even the little calves, the new ones, seem to sense what's coming."

That was one of the things Jessie didn't want to think about: the sharp knife that would turn them from bulls into steers, the hot brand that would be awaiting them.

"It's hot, dusty, exhausting, dirty work, and I hate having to do it, but it's a part of ranch life. It's got to be done."

Though her father would be involved in the castration and the branding, August did not do much besides help them drive the herd into the pens. His horse, another Coalie, liked to work the cattle and would turn with eagerness to the task as soon as August had saddled her.

"I don't know what this old mare will do when she can't work anymore," August told Jessie once. "She's got cow sense in her blood and she won't give it up until she dies."

Like Blaze, Coalie could sort the cattle easily. She would turn and spin, following the movements of the calf her rider had selected, and she would not allow the calf to go back to the herd. All August had to do was let the reins fall loose and move with her.

Jake's horse was a chestnut with four white stockings, named for the earlier Boots — another good cow pony. She looked forward to the drives, along with their cattle dog, the collie-shepherd mix, Lady, who trembled with eagerness when the horses were saddled and who would run back and forth in the corral, whining. Boots would perk up her ears, twitch them, over and over, one then the other, and then set out methodically and steadily up the path to the pasture.

When Jessie had saddled Blaze that morning, Lady had thrust her moist nose in her palm urging her on. But instead of following the riders to the herd, Lady set off on her own to the pens where she knew the cattle were headed. There she would wait for them, excited and tense. She knew that she would receive the offerings — the testicles — of the poor calves.

"Can I help sort?" Jessie asked now.

"Just wait and see," Jake said. "You sit on Blaze and wait. If we need you, we'll let you know."

Jessie frowned. She had hoped for a more active part, even though she knew she was lucky to be allowed to come along.

Sandy and the other men worked in teams in the pastures, driving about 150 of the cattle to points on the trails leading to the pens and, once the entire herd was together, taking up positions on both sides, banking the herd, a few cowboys in the back, driving them on. Leaders of the herd — either a heifer or a steer — were no longer kept from year to year as they had been in August's day. "In those days," August told Jessie, "the cattle had to be driven clear to the stockyards at the railroad station, and the cowboys needed one of the herd to show them the way. Like the 'Judas goat,' the leader of the herd would go out in front, and the herd would follow."

"What's the 'Judas goat'?" Jessie asked.

"Well," August told her, "that's the one that led the others to slaughter."

"Oh."

Jessie was silent, thinking. Then suddenly she saw dust rising ahead of her.

"They're here, Grampa," she said, pointing. "They're here!"

August followed her pointing finger. "You're right, Jessie," he said. "Just over that rise."

It had been dry over the summer and huge mounds of dust rose into the sky. Soon she would hear them — the constant bawling, the complaints of the calves — August had told her all about this many times too.

Years ago, August said, he did the castrating. Now Jake would have to do it.

Coming over the swell of the land, Jessie saw the herd in front of them. One of the cowboys turned and waved. Now she could hear what August was talking about: a constant roar accompanied the herd, the calves trotting beside their mothers, voicing their protests over the whole affair. One of the calves had stopped walking as if in defiance, with feet apart, his wet nose pointed upwards in the air, his neck outstretched as he cried.

Jessie had only noticed him when Jake rode up on Boots and turned the calf back into the herd and on its way.

Lady, too, did her part: the pens were close and Lady had heard the commotion; automatically, she joined the roundup. Whenever a calf tried to lag behind, Lady sneaked up and nipped it on the heels. The calf soon trotted back to the herd and went on.

Jessie wanted to get closer. She began to urge Blaze forward and then her father, impatient, called to her: "I said to stay behind, Jessie. Don't spook 'em."

"Okay, Poppa," she said.

She never liked to encourage a scolding; she always wanted to please her father, to be the one he looked to for support.

She settled back in the saddle, sighing. Blaze, too, seemed to sense they were to play a minor role in this roundup, his head stopped nodding impatiently as it had been doing, his teeth not taking the bit. He snorted.

"It's okay, fella," Jessie said, stroking his neck. "We'll get to do something I'm sure."

When they reached the pens, she saw the railroad tracks that would take the cattle to the market. Now her father sat on Boots, waiting to the rear of the herd, watching Sandy and the others as they worked to sort the animals. The bulls to be sold were already in an adjoining water lot, and now Sandy worked to cut the cows from their calves — "stripping" as they called it. The little calves didn't want to leave their mothers, and tried to get back to them, but always there was a horseman — or Lady — who prevented it. The men were careful to take only those cows whose calves were large enough to live without them, and cows over ten years old.

August had pulled up beside Jessie. He seemed to know he would be a spectator too. "They sell the bulls at eight, Jessie," he said, pointing to the milling cattle in the other pen. "They shoot too many blanks, if you know what I mean."

Jessie flushed.

Being raised on a ranch, she knew she probably had had more experience in "life" than city kids did. But it embarrassed her sometimes when the men in the family were so explicit.

"You stay with your grandfather," Jake told Jessie now. "I'm going to go help Sandy and the others."

Jessie and August reined in their horses and sat patiently as they watched the others do the sorting.

One by one, the calves were weeded out, herded over to one side of the pen so they could be driven down the alley and into other pens, the little heifers in one, the soon-to-be steers in another.

Lady helped with the sorting — nipping at the heifers' heels when they tried to trot back into the herd, driving the calves away from their mothers.

Sandy, an old hand who had worked more cattle than Jake ever would, rode up to them. "They got a sharp knife, I hope," he said, "and a hot iron."

"They better," August said. "They gonna de-horn this time?"

"No. No muling today . . . the calves are too small," Sandy said. "They can't even find the knobs."

At last the initial sorting was done and they were ready for the next. Jessie watched while the cattle were driven into the first of four corrals, three to hold them while the calves were again separated from the remaining heifers, which were to stay with the herd. All the corrals opened onto the alley, where the feeder calves would be driven to be weighed and loaded onto the stock cars. Later the alley would be used to separate heifers and steers, and still later, to dip all the remaining herd, except for the newly castrated calves.

"Some of the men can't get over your dad and me using a truck to take the new steers back to the pasture," Sandy said then to Jake.

"They've been through enough," Jake said. "And I'm going to do just as he did."

Sandy looked again at Jake. "How long do you think this will last, Jake? The world doesn't stand still, does it?"

"It'll last as long as we can make it last," Jake said.

Jessie was amazed by the noise from the cows and calves when they became separated, more even than they'd made on the trail.

"Look at that little one," August said, pointing out a Hereford, barely a month old, whose upturned face looked sad, his mouth constantly opened in a long, drawn-out protest.

On their side of the fence, the cows answered, bawling and milling about in the corral, going up to the wooden slats and nudging them, trying to break away and get back with their calves.

"Okay," Sandy called then. As foreman of the ranch, he directed the whole operation. "Let's get the steers and heifers now."

Three men worked the gates — two in the corrals, one farther down in the alley, who opened the gate for the large calves that were to be sold. The cows had been returned to the water lot while the calves were sorted once more.

"Steer," Sandy called to the man waiting at the first gate.

"Heifer."

Working with whips and shouts and prods, the men swung the gates of each corral open and shut again as the young steers and heifers were herded through into their respective quarters.

Three other men had gone with the already sold old bulls and cows to help load them into a waiting stock car.

"Okay," Jake said. "Let's get these calves loaded and get to the branding and castration."

The gates were swung open to admit the little calves into the side pen where Sandy's son had been tending the wood fire in which the branding iron was heating. Jessie could smell the burning wood, the stench of hot metal.

Jake took out the long bladed, razor-sharp knife. "Okay, got him," one of the men yelled to Jake as they took a steer, threw him on the ground — one man, the "header," on his front legs, the other man, the "heeler," forcing apart his rear legs to expose the genitals.

With one expert maneuver, Jake pulled the testicles away from the body and sliced them off. Seconds later, Sandy's son took the branding iron, held it to the steer's left leg, flames shooting up as the hair burned, some steers bawling in surprise and pain, others stoic, remaining quiet. The odor of singed flesh and hair stung the air, then the calf was dabbed with screwworm ointment on the wound left by the castration. In an instant, the calf was up off his back and trotting over to the side. Somewhat dazed, the steers milled about at the far side of the corral, some — the smallest ones — sinking down to rest after their ordeal.

Jessie bent her head, pitying them.

One by one the steers were taken, the men moving in swift, orderly precision. On the truck in the corral, which had transported the branding materials, Lady stood, panting and whining in anticipation, for she knew that soon Sandy's son would gather up the testicles and throw them to her. When he did, she fell upon them eagerly.

Jake looked at the black, scabbing hide of the branded steers: "O–O" it said — "O Bar O."

Walking over to Jessie as she sat on her horse, Jake told her, "The day's over for those little fellas. They'll be trucked back to the pasture where their mothers are waiting. Seeing them greet each other after all this is the only good thing about the day."

"Poppa," Jessie said then. "Is this something else I've got to learn about ranching?"

". . . 'Fraid so," Jake said.

The men had shared a beer before the castration and branding, Jessie had seen, and now they shared another. When the herd was back in the pasture, August had told her, they would have yet another.

Then it was Sandy's wife's turn to feed them, and Dorothy always had enough food for three trail teams — fried chicken or roast, mashed potatoes, cole slaw, biscuits, and hot berry pies.

"That Dorothy's a damn good cook," August always said.

"You bet she is," Sandy agreed.

Jake especially enjoyed the cooking at roundup time. "I could eat my fill here any time," he said. And Jessie saw that he did.

Jessie could hear the distant bellowing of the cows whose calves had been sent off; their udders full, there would be no relief for them until time had dried them up once again. The sound was always plaintive — a lament for which there was no cure.

In an instant Jessie thought: *I don't want to go on the roundup again. And if I'm ever in charge of the ranch, the cattle won't be branded.*

Chapter
Twenty-Six

*I*N 1939, FRANCE fell to the Nazis. Jessie had heard August and Jake talk about a coming war, and heard her grandmother begging Jake not to enlist.

"You probably won't be drafted at your age," she advised. "Please don't get all patriotic again and feel you alone can solve the world's problems."

"If I have something to offer," she heard her father reply, "I'll do it."

Her father *did* enlist, and he became a part of Army Intelligence. She knew he worked with codes, but she didn't know exactly what he did. She also knew he was out of the country — she heard Mexico City once, London, Lisbon. But she didn't know where and he of course couldn't tell them.

It was six months after her father enlisted that August discovered he had cancer.

Clarence Harvey told them all after he received the biopsy reports. "I'm afraid it's not good," he said.

They were in the living room of Jake's home, with August. He had wanted to be open about it, not try to hide the bad news.

"Most people don't want to admit they have cancer," Doc Harvey said. "It's a death sentence to them."

"It's a death sentence to *me*," August said, pulling at his moustache.

Jessie ran over to him, took his cold hand in hers.

"There are things we can do," Clarence Harvey said. "Will, being younger than I am, has studied some of those things. We'll do the best we can."

"I know," August said then. "But I also know my chances."

Old Jessica went over to him then, put her arm around his shoulders. "We'll fight this," she stated — almost an order.

August smiled. "We'll try."

It was lung cancer. They operated and he took some cobalt treatments, but at last he told them to stop trying — he knew he was going to die.

As if he didn't wish to drag things on, the cancer seemed to race through him.

Jessie thought that death was everywhere in Atlas City; her mother, the grandparents she'd never known, the dead children Old Jess had had, her Great Uncle Willard, and now her grandfather. And he was so dear!

Death was like the Nazis. It entered where it wanted, snuffed out resistance, took everything over.

Toward the end, August's pain became unbearable. It was summer, and the plains had come alive with a sudden storm. Jessie heard thunder as she went up to August's room, saw lightning string itself across the black flesh of the sky. There was moisture in the air and the horses milled around in the corral, nervously awaiting the lash of rain. Coalie was there — looking toward the house as though expecting August to come, saddle her, ride out the storm.

When the rain did come, Jessie held onto August's hand. He was moaning, tossing the covers back, then pulling them up over himself again. Will Harvey had taken over his care — Clarence said he was too close to August to see all this.

Will gave him morphine, the injections coming closer and closer until it seemed August would be drugged from this life, slip into death unawares.

Sometimes, however, August insisted on no drugs because he wanted to be clear-headed; then pain would grip him like an adversary and he would fling curses at the world and everyone in it.

"Ah little Jessie," August said this day when she came into his room.

"Why do you want to see this old wreck? I'm a goner, thanks to God — or the Devil. It doesn't matter which — one is as far away from me now as the other."

"I came, Grampa," Jessie said, "because I love you."

August *hmmphed*, reminding Jessie of her grandmother, then he studied Jessie momentarily with a bit of his old, sly, calculating glance, the one that always said to Jessie that life was a charade, that it was all crazy. In an instant August sat bolt upright in the bed as if he'd been stabbed. Leaning over, he snatched at the covers, tore the sheet with his hands, began to rip it.

"Goddammit, god*damm*it!" he yelled. "When will I die? I want to die!"

Old Jessica came rushing in then. Jessie had to admit that her grandmother took wonderful care of August — they still fought about things when August was able to argue, but Old Jessica treated him carefully and tenderly.

"Why don't you leave, Jessie," her grandmother said then, not unkindly. "I don't think he's up to company."

"No!" August shouted. "Let her stay!"

"I'll get Doc Harvey then," Old Jessica persisted. "You need a shot."

"No!" August shouted. "Leave me be. I want to talk to Jessie."

Old Jessica left the room, throwing a long, quizzical glance at Jessie, pulling the door shut behind her. August breathed out almost as if expiring. Jessie went over to the bed, rubbed her hand over his briefly. To her surprise, August snatched at it.

"Purdy," he said, his voice suddenly soft. "Little Purdy."

"Oh, no, Grampa," Jessie said. "It's me. Jessie."

Purdy, as if she thought she could heal August, had begun visiting him. But of course Purdy could not heal him.

"Jessie," August said now, smiling. "I'm glad you're here."

"Yes," Jessie said.

She couldn't confess the lump in her throat, the terrible sadness she felt in looking at August. He was obviously suffering; would it be better for him to die?

And yet, she couldn't imagine her family without him.

"Jessie," August went on then, his eyes seeking hers, his gaze suddenly pinning her down, "I'm dying aren't I? . . . "

Jessie had never lied to August; she didn't want to now. She chose not to respond, merely bent her head.

"Ah, yes," August said. He dropped her hand. "You were always honest, so you can't lie to me. Why is it, Jessie, that just when things begin to get good on the farm I have to die? . . . Jake needs me."

It wasn't true about Jake needing him — or was it? — but Jessie didn't say anything. She knew her father felt as she did, that August had been the bulwark against Old Jessica, that in his off-hand, non-conformist way, he had always supported his son. But he really didn't need him on the ranch — *she* was there.

"And if America gets into the war, well then . . ." But August's voice drifted off, and her grandfather turned his face to the window and looked out. "All the young men will go. Jake may need me more than ever. I said I wanted to die but I don't! No . . . *I don't!*"

"Rest," Jessie said. "Don't think."

"Freddie may have to go," August said then. "They'll take everybody."

Jessie hadn't thought of that. She couldn't see Fred in the armed services, could imagine that Jessica would shoot the Draft Board if they tried to take him. His work on the farm would surely prevent that!

"I don't think they'll take Fred," Jessie said then. "He can say he's needed on the ranch. He *will* be needed."

"But Freddie on the ranch," August said then, laughing. "He'll be sitting on horseback adding columns!"

Jessie had to laugh too. "Grampa," she said, her voice thick with the moment. "You're awful!"

For a moment, August's face again had the sly look of old.

"Why couldn't Purdy heal me?" her grandfather asked Jessie then.

"Rest," Jessie repeated. She didn't know. She took his hand, kneaded it. "Purdy is not a doctor," Jessie said.

"Well, the doctors can't heal me either," August said. "So I don't know what's so wonderful about being a doctor."

"Purdy heals people's mind sometimes," Jessie said then, thoughtfully. "I mean, she says the body follows the mind . . . but there are some things. . . "

"There are some things," August went on for her, "that are beyond anyone's skills. God has made it that way."

God, Jessie thought. She didn't know what to think about God.

"Are you afraid, Grampa?" Jessie asked at last.

She felt as if she were very little again, very insecure, looking for some adult in her world to help her.

"Yes," August said.

He stared at her, his face suddenly writhed in pain. "Wait," he gasped. "Wait till it passes."

Moments later, his face relaxed and he sighed. Jessie saw his hand was stroking the bedcovers, trying to put the sheet back together where he had ripped it, folding it over the blankets.

"You're a maverick like me, Jessie," August said at last. Again he sighed. "And the whole world — almost — is afraid of mavericks. Don't be afraid to be yourself, my dear. Don't ever be afraid to be that."

"I won't, Grampa," Jessie said.

"Sometimes," her grandfather went on then, "in the night, I'm afraid to die. Late in the night has always been the time for me to have terrors. I would lie in this bed, years ago, Jessica beside me, and be sure that the most awful things would happen. Jessica never knew any of this of course . . . But I was afraid Jake would die, or run off and leave the farm, Jessica might leave me — I was afraid someday you might get involved with the wrong man, Fred with the wrong woman — all these things over which I had no control. Nightmares would come and I couldn't seem to let go."

"I understand," Jessie said, knowing that she still had terrors of her own.

"My late forties and fifties were the worse — I spent many nights tossing and turning, trying to refute the seeming logic of doom. I think I feared my own mortality. When I finally got to sleep on these worrisome nights, if I rested well, the dreadful fears of those early hours would be gone and reason would have reasserted itself. I have always thought that if there is a Devil — and that presumes a God of course — those early morning hours belong to him."

"I know," Jessie said. Now she pulled a chair up beside the bed, took August's hand in hers again. She could sense little jerks in his hand from time to time, but he seemed happy to have her there. "I used to have dreams," Jessie said.

She thought of the terrible nights after her mother died, when she would wake up, certain she was in water and unable to breathe. She remembered one dream in which her mother came back and said to her, "I'm all right, Jessie."

Then the dreams stopped.

"On lonely nights," August said, "and night is always the loneliest time, you know, fears creep back. They are not so strong, not so haunting — because there *is* the pain you know, and release from it seems full of promise — but the fear is still there."

"Yes," Jessie nodded.

"I wish I believed in God," August said then. "It might be a comfort."

"Yes," Jessie almost whispered. Then, pressing his hand to her cheek, she asked, "Could you make believe, Grampa?"

"Maybe so," August said.

He sighed.

One night, Old Jessica came into Jessie's bedroom after August had finally fallen into a restless sleep. Jessie was surprised to see her — it was Fred who was her confidante. But her grandmother sank into a chair opposite Jessie's bed as if this were routine; Jessie herself sat propped up on pillows reading *Vanity Fair* for her Literature class.

"You know," Old Jessica said dreamily, as if speaking to the air, "August was never boring."

Jessie put down her book. She didn't comment.

Leaning her head back, putting her hand over her eyes, Old Jess went on, "I had a choice of young men, and most people were certain I would choose someone else, but I chose August."

She took the hand away from her eyes and looked over at Jessie, as if expecting her to respond. Still, Jessie was quiet.

"It was a strange wedding," she said.

Jessie didn't know if she meant the ceremony was strange, or if the whole idea was strange.

"August and I were never thought to be serious. And the wedding night! Oh goodness! What a charade!"

Her grandmother laughed, the sound loud in the room. Then she sobered.

"We lost two children in those hard days," her grandmother said.

"I know."

"It wasn't like today, where you have all the modern conveniences."

"I know."

"Still, it bound people together, those hardships."

If she meant herself and August, her grandmother didn't elaborate.

"There are times," Old Jessica went on, "when you think you may take a different path and then something happens —"

She abruptly stopped the recitation.

"No," she went on then, as if deliberating something in her mind, "he was always surprising me. It can make life difficult, surprises," Old Jessica went on, again putting the hand across her eyes as if to shut out anything that might interfere with her view of the past, "but in the end, you count on them. Predictability is not necessarily a virtue."

"I suppose not," Jessie said. Then: "Grampa was quite an inventor, wasn't he?"

She meant it more as a statement, but her grandmother took it as a question.

"Yes," she said. She laughed. "But he never made a single invention that was worth anything. He used to take Jake —" now her grandmother was wryly smiling to herself, "and I thought sure he would blow him up with the darn contraptions he was working on. He used to work out in the barn — I wasn't about to let him in the house, let him set *that* on fire — and I worried that he'd blow himself and your father up in some stupid invention. But," she went on, her voice lower, tired, "he never did. And your father followed him around as though he were a god."

Her voice seemed to have had an edge of bitterness in it, but she lost it as she went on with her recital, "We've been through a lot, August and I," she said.

Old Jessica let out a long deep breath, again took the hand away from her eyes, looked over at Jessie. "You've got a lot of August in you, my girl," she said.

So that was why Old Jessica had chosen her for her revelations!

Yet Jessie wasn't certain if her grandmother had said it with a certain pride or not. But as Jessie looked over at Old Jess, she saw the strain of the nights of tending to August and the certainty of the end of his illness reflected in the lines of her face. She looked suddenly old.

"Oh, Grandmother," she said.

She wanted to reach out to Old Jess somehow, but her grandmother had never seemed to want people touching her, binding her with their affection.

"I wish I believed in God," Old Jess said then, just as August had.

"I know," Jessie said. "Sometimes I do — I really do."

"Yes — at moments so do I. But they never last."

"No."

"Aren't we a mess, though," her grandmother said, getting up from the chair and going to the door. "We get smart when it's too late."

And then Old Jessica left the room and shut the door.

Shortly after that, August got worse. The cancer had gone to his brain, and the grandfather she knew did not exist any longer. He cursed at everyone, shouting that the bedcovers were hurting him, that his brain was on fire. The shots no longer seemed to help, even though Will Harvey had shown Old Jess how to give them so they didn't have to wait on the doctor. Jessie prayed that he would be taken soon.

One night, August curled up into a ball — like a fetus — and died.

She had never seen her grandmother cry, but when she realized August was dead, Old Jessica sobbed in a way Jessie could never have imagined. She *did* love him, after all, Jessie thought.

Chapter
Twenty-Seven

*O*N DECEMBER 7, 1941, Jessie and her friend, Olga Benson, were at the movies in Harper. They were watching Laurel and Hardy when suddenly the film flicked off and the lights came on.

"What? . . . " Jessie asked.

The owner of the theater walked on the stage. His eyes squinting out over the audience, the man turned to them and announced, "We have just received a terrible message. The Japanese have attacked *Pearl Harbor.*"

Jessie couldn't take it in. Pearl Harbor? But the Japanese ambassador had just been in Washington! What was going on?

"We will discontinue the movie today," the owner was saying. "We must all go home and listen to the radio for further news."

For a moment the audience sat silently, stunned.

Then, one by one, murmuring amongst themselves, they filed out. Jessie turned to see the man still on the stage, as if he could not summon the energy to move. She felt her chest tighten. Good Lord, what did it mean?

Jessie and Olga went out into the street, screwing up their eyes against the bright light. It all seemed unreal.

Olga took Jessie's hand in hers, holding it tight, "Oh, Jessie, are we going to be bombed?"

"Olga, don't be silly," Jessie said.

She tried to remain calm, but she could feel her heart pounding. Her father was going to war, *she knew it!*

Atlas City was near a big Army base and perhaps it, too, would be bombed without warning. Maybe the Japanese were already on their way. They didn't abide by normal declarations of war apparently; what if they were able to strike again so quickly that they would take over the country? What would happen to women like Olga and herself — would they be captured — raped, kept as slaves?

Jessie tried to stop the wild thoughts; it would do no good to panic; she would have to control herself.

"What does it mean? What does it *mean?*" Olga kept asking, following Jessie as she strode quickly away from the theater down Harper's main street. In the bright sunshine, in the quiet of the Sunday afternoon, it seemed impossible that the announcement could be true: *Pearl Harbor had been bombed!*

"I'm going to join the Army today," Jessie heard someone say behind her.

"Your son can go," another voice said then, "but you're a little over the age."

"Yes, but I'm not in an old-age home yet! I'm not going to just sit this thing out — we're going to need everyone we have. Why just think — the Germans are taking over Europe and now those dirty Japs are trying to take *us* over!"

Jessie turned to see if she knew the speakers, but they were strangers. Both men seemed way past the age of enlistment to her.

"Your son can do the fighting," the voice repeated.

"Like hell he can! I lost my brother in the last war and I'm not going to lose my son in this one!"

The war fever — the patriotism — was afire once more with the outright, unexpected attack on Pearl Harbor. Jessie knew all the young men would rush to enlist and though she herself had once wanted to be in the Women's Army Corps, what did they really do? Anyway, she and the family had been through this, hadn't they, when her father had enlisted, and she knew she wasn't likely to encounter a change of heart in Old Jessica *or* Jake.

The next day, they all listened to Roosevelt's address to the joint session of Congress, his well-modulated voice carrying throughout the hushed chamber: *"Yesterday, December 7, 1941 — a date which will live in infamy — the United States of America was suddenly and deliberately attacked by naval and air forces of the Empire of Japan. . . ."*

It was true then, Jessie thought. It wasn't a bad dream.

". . . It will be recorded that the distance of Hawaii from Japan makes it obvious that the attack was deliberately planned many days or even weeks ago. . . ."

Moments later, the President asked the Congress to declare war on the Japanese Empire.

Later, in a "fireside chat," the President insisted he had insufficient information on the damage inflicted at Pearl Harbor to tell the people about it. He didn't list the losses then in Hawaii; he didn't mention the ships that had gone down with all hands on board, nor the terrible destruction the Japanese Air Force had inflicted on the men, planes, and ships in Oahu. Jessie knew that morale was important, and the nation would learn fully about the devastation at another time.

"He's lying," Old Jessica said as she listened to the talk. "He *knows* we've lost everything."

"We couldn't have lost everything, Grandmother," Fred said then. "He wouldn't be talking to us like this if we had."

"War, war!" Old Jess said then, throwing up her hands. "Why is it we keep fighting wars to keep us *out* of wars?"

"Will *I* have to enlist?" Fred asked then, his voice thin.

"Nonsense, angel," Old Jess replied. "You have to stay and work on the farm. We have to eat, you know. Even armies do."

"Since Poppa is already in," Jessie pointed out, "I expect we *will* need you here. And I don't suppose they meant women to be drafted so I'll be here too."

Fred sighed with relief. "Yes," he said. "I'm needed here."

Expansive, safe, Fred went on: "I'd like to take those little yellow-bellies by the . . ." he stopped, looked at his grandmother, "by the neck and strangle them. I wish I could. I wish I *could*!"

"You'll get your chance," Jessie said with sarcasm. "That is, if we're invaded, they'll take *everyone* no matter what he's doing!"

Fred paled.

"You stop it, Jessie," Old Jessica snapped. "America hasn't lost a war yet."

Jessie didn't argue with her. She also didn't say anything about her father already being in England. It had never seemed safe there for him; it was less so now. Old Jessica seemed to be staring at her, as if she had read her mind.

"I just hope we don't have to knit things and make bandages all over again," Old Jess was muttering.

"I doubt that'll be necessary, Grandmother," Jessie said.

"*God oh God*, why can't men stop making wars?" Old Jessica said, her voice trembling. "Do they like it that much?"

"Well, Grandmother," Jessie said, "they run everything right now and they won't let us women really do anything. Maybe there'll come a time when we'll have a chance to take part."

"I won't let them take Freddie," Old Jessica said then, as if she hadn't heard Jessie. "No, indeed!"

The next few weeks there was nothing but talk of the war. And it was going badly for the Americans: on January 2, 1942, Manila had fallen to the advancing Japanese. The American troops, under the command of General Douglas MacArthur, withdrew to the Bataan peninsula. Jessie read how MacArthur, without replenishing of supplies, was holding out.

"They can't last," Old Jessica said. "They just can't last."

And then they read that Bataan too had fallen — April 9, 1942 — and the tired, ragged remnants of the American forces had retreated to Corregidor. General MacArthur was ordered to Australia and General Wainwright had taken over command of the fighting men.

Corregidor was ready to fall. The Japanese seemed to loom everywhere, and everywhere they went they wreaked destruction; there were even rumors of submarines lurking in California waters. Jessie wondered what would happen to the men who tried so hard to keep the Japanese from taking Corregidor.

And then — in May, Corregidor was lost too.

"*We must be brave,*" Jake wrote from somewhere in England. "*We will win this war, but it will not be easy.*"

But Jessie wasn't certain; the possibility of losing all they had worked for — or perhaps being put to death — remained in her mind. She grieved for those people in Atlas City who had already learned their sons were dead. Two families had sons in the Navy and they had gone down with the *Arizona*.

Signs went up around the nearby Army post : "Loose Lips Sink Ships." Troop trains passed through now on the Atlas City tracks, trains that sped on without stopping and from which pale young faces stared out.

Songs like the British Children's Prayer were heard:

> *If I should die before I wake*
> *I pray the Lord my soul to take.*
> *I pray the Lord that I may be*
> *Not safe, oh Lord, not safe, but free.*

And over the radio, the haunting melody, "There'll Be Bluebirds Over the White Cliffs of Dover. . . ."

It wasn't until the Battle of Midway that the tide of war began to change.

It was June, and Jessie had moved fully into control on the ranch. It was Jessie who had bought the cattle to put on the pastures, it was Jessie who had overlooked the births of the new calves that were now frisking beside their mothers in the upland grass. Sandy — who helped with the roundups — had not been called to military service as he was past the age and had a bad leg. Now he helped Jessie supervise the planting on the bottom land, and he would help with the harvest. The Lutz ranch was the proud owner of two combines, and Jessie and Sandy could each run one, pile the grain in the truck, make Fred haul it to the elevator.

Jessie read about the Battle of Midway in the Atlas City *Gazette*: on June 3-6, 1942, the U.S. Navy and the navy of Japan had engaged in a carrier-based battle. Although the U.S. suffered some losses, the Navy inflicted heavy casualties on the Japanese and now everyone was saying the U.S. *could* win the war, that the Empire of Japan had been stopped.

"Well," Old Jess said, "we'll see. Those Japs are sly — they could be planning something."

"I hope the paper's right," Jessie said.

Scrap-iron drives all over the country had been started, and Atlas City had proudly donated several tons to the government that would be turned into new battleships and destroyers, some already under way to the

Pacific. The assembly line was going strong, shift after shift keeping the plants running day and night in a way Jessie would never have thought possible! If only the country had been that effective *before* the war, she thought.

"We've got a letter from your father," Old Jessica said one night at dinner.

Jessie felt a sharp pang. She didn't like the idea of her father writing her grandmother and not her.

"It's for all the family," Old Jess said then, as if sensing her discomfort, extending the letter to Jessie.

Jessie snatched at it, noticing the way her father had addressed his letter: Mrs. August Lutz *and Family.*

So she was just included as "Family," Jessie thought. She was the only one who was writing regularly. Her grandmother did at times, but she didn't write as often as Jessie did. And Fred didn't write at all.

Jake's letter was vague about everything. He only said he was well and hoped that they remained so. He added, "I know Ilse's taking good care of you."

He apparently didn't know that Ilse had returned to her mother's home some months ago, only doing odd jobs now and then.

Jessie felt like wadding up the letter, but instead she placed it beside her plate on the table, pushed back her chair, and left the room.

Jessie knew her grandmother was keeping Jake's letters in the top drawer of the dining room buffet and she quietly entered the room, pulled the letters from the drawer. Seating herself at the dining room table, she began to read.

"*England, June 25, 1942: I went to town last night. There was an Army band playing in the park and I sat down to listen. It was wonderful! And you wouldn't believe all the gold braid that was there! There were four generals and a couple of admirals. I kept expecting the King to appear!*

"*You can't believe how brave these English people are. We walk past bomb craters and rubble as if it were normal and the English do the same. They are very polite and often even ask us in for tea.*

"*I'm beginning to think we are making some contribution in this war, that is, my unit. Everyday we make a little progress and that is all you can ask.*

"*Had a letter from Grady Manning's boy; he's in the Pacific and says he's seen some action. Since we fooled the Japs at Midway, maybe we can do it more and more and finally get this whole ghastly business over.*

"*The thing is, I got the letter only three weeks from the time he sent it. In a world torn up by war, I think that's remarkable!*

"*I suppose Jessie's got Sandy to help her with the crops and the cattle. How I would like to see our place again. And thinking of that, if we had all our land over here, we would probably be Dukes or Lords!*

"*Well, I'd better end for now. I want to get some sack time. Take care of everyone, Mother, as you always do.*

"*Love, Jake.*"

. . . So he was thinking about her. She just wished he would send *her* a letter — to her alone — not just included with the others. . . .

But then Jessie was ashamed. Her father was in danger there in England — *some*where — and she was fussing about his writing her *alone*. He had done so well to write as much as he had . . . she really couldn't complain.

Putting the letters back in the rubber band that had bound them, Jessie tiptoed out and up to her room. She would read them all again another time — it was a way of being close to her father.

Olga and Jessie had been recruited by the USO in Harper. Installed in the old American Legion building there — the one where her father had met her mother — the USO was dedicated to entertaining the servicemen. They held dances and other events for the men from the nearby Army post, and they welcomed the men on leave or special duty who happened to be in the area.

Jessie and Olga had gone to many dances, had made cookies and brought coffee, had even taken part in a musical some Army wife had written and for which she had recruited everyone in the surrounding countryside. Jessie, too shy to sing, which was what Mrs. Root had wanted her to do, helped with the sets and the staging. It was a homely affair, but the boys seemed to appreciate it.

This night, Jessie looked into the mirror over her dresser before she went down to get out the car and drive over to pick up Olga. She was tall she realized — taller certainly than her grandmother who had once looked into this mirror. Jessie looked at the girl staring back at her as though she were a stranger. Then with a sudden shock, she realized she *was* pretty! She wasn't just a "character" anymore, she thought — but, just as she had prayed, she had grown into a very attractive young woman!

Squatting down before the mirror so that she could study her torso, Jessie noted her lean boy's body fit nicely into her casual dress, and that her small round breasts emphasized the slimness of her waist. She had always known she had long legs, well-shaped, but she had paid so little attention to herself as a whole that now she was truly surprised.

Her skin had always been good, and tanned almost black in the summer sun. It was now a coffee color, and her dark-brown eyes looked bright and large in her rather angular face. On an impulse, Jessie picked up the eye-pencil liner she had never used — it was a gift from Olga — and carefully outlined each eye. Her hand was a little unsteady as she had never practiced the art of makeup, but she soon caught on and smudged out the errors. It was the first makeup, other than lipstick, she had used since the debacle of the eyeshadow Ilse had encouraged her to wear.

Leaning back then to study herself, she regarded her image. Slowly she adjusted to the fact that she looked different, that she was pretty, that her hair, long and full, a deep reddish brown, framed her face and made it noticeable. She wasn't as attractive as her grandmother had been probably, Jessie decided, but just as Olga had said, "You're not bad, Jessie, truly."

As carefully as she had put on the eyeliner, Jessie reached down, picked up the "Eve's Apple" lipstick Fred had given her for Christmas, and painted a dark-red, delicious cream over her lips. She finished with a dab of perfume — Tabu — the local favorite. It was something she rarely used because, as she'd once explained to Jake, "Horses don't like it."

Jake had roared. "But *men* do, honey," he'd told her.

"Oh?" she'd asked, as if that had never occurred to her.

But, at that time, she'd far rather have pleased the horses than any man she knew!

Feeling very adventurous, Jessie walked down the stairs to confront Fred, who was working on the books for the store and the farm. He always seemed happy when he was surrounded by papers and ledgers — he seemed natural in that setting.

Fred, who never wanted anything to do with entertainment for servicemen because he *had* tried to enlist and was turned down because of flat feet, looked up at her. He frowned. Anything connected with servicemen was suspect with him — the rejection had confirmed his feeling, apparently, that the whole world was plotting against him.

"Well, have a wonderful time at your orgy," Fred said as Jessie swept past him. Then: "You smell as if you're heading for a tryst with a Roman senator."

"Oh, shut up, Fred," Jessie said. "You can spend your life with those damn books if you want to, but I prefer people."

"Don't get in trouble," Fred warned.

"What kind?" Jessie snorted. "Anyway, what would you know about it? You've got your head in ledgers all the time!"

"All the same," Fred said, smiling in the way he had of not really smiling at all, "You know how soldiers are. They only want one thing."

"In that case," Jessie retorted, sliding past him and out the door, banging the screen, "I only have one thing to worry about and I can handle *that*."

"Says you," Fred called after her.

Jessie got into the car angrily, turned the ignition, jerked the gear into reverse and backed out. She supposed she should feel sorry for Fred — she knew he didn't want to serve in the military, but he didn't really want to be rejected either. He had probably seen himself as an officer, decorated, girls falling helplessly in love as he walked down the streets of Atlas City.

Ah, well. Fred had always been a problem of sorts.

The orchestra they'd assembled from local musicians wasn't bad; they were playing "Long Ago and Far Away" and "String of Pearls." When they went into "There'll Be Bluebirds Over the White Cliffs of Dover," Jessie felt her stomach muscles tighten. Her father was there — wasn't he? — and she wondered what he was doing at this precise moment; then she remembered the time difference and decided he was probably trying to sleep. Was he as frightened for himself as she was?

Jessie followed Olga into the room. Olga, always more assertive in social affairs, soon went off on the arm of a soldier while Jessie leaned back against the wall. She listened to the plaintive lyrics the young, inexperienced male singer was delivering and she wondered if all war songs were the same — nostalgic, sadly hopeful, assuming that whoever was listening *would* come home and that there would be someone waiting. Even as she thought this, the orchestra went into "Now is the Hour" and Jessie heard the singer almost sighing the words, "Now is the Hour, When we must say goodbye . . ."

Jessie shivered. She was glad she didn't have someone to say goodbye to. One of the girls she knew had already had the fateful visit from the War Department emissary, the letter that said, "We regret to inform you. . . ." She was six months pregnant and now she was a widow. At twenty-three.

Again Jessie shivered.

There was another, less empathetic side to the war: young women, whose men were gone to fight, dancing closely and intimately with soldiers who came to the center. She had seen these same women leave with the men, somehow acting as if there were no loyalties or morality to follow anymore, as if nothing mattered. Perhaps it shouldn't matter, Jessie decided, but it was something she could never have done.

Each Saturday night, these girls came to the center and would wait hopefully, patiently, for another man to dance with, flirt with, go home with. And each Saturday night they found one.

Perhaps, Jessie thought, she was judging them too harshly; perhaps they covered up their terror with a passing romance. But surely there were other, better ways to forget for a time.

Jessie was standing on the sidelines still, watching the men and women move about, jitterbugging on the fast tunes, cheek to cheek on the slow ones, when she felt someone beside her. More than that, a haze of cigarette smoke seemed to be oozing around her, an aura preceding whomever it was at her elbow.

Jessie turned to see a blonde, blue-eyed, very tall and slender young Army officer — a Second Lieutenant — regarding her quizzically, the cigarette dangling from his lips.

"Hi," he greeted her. "You look lost."

He spoke with the cigarette still in his mouth, the cylinder jerking up and down as he shaped the words. It was like a baton, almost exactly in time with the music, punctuating his words.

"I'm not lost," Jessie said, startled.

He laughed. "Well, you're found now anyway. By me. Want to dance?"

He removed the cigarette, stomped it out on the tile floor, and began to move toward her as he held up his arms. Jessie had the ludicrous feeling that if she merely stepped aside, he would continue forward, dancing by himself.

As she felt his arms curve about her, she got a strong scent of whiskey, interlaced with the tobacco.

"You're drunk," she accused, pushing him away as he lurched around the dance floor.

"No, I'm not," he said. "I'm getting sober."

"You're drunk," she repeated.

But she found herself smiling at him. There was something very child-like about this boy — man — he was charming, even if he *wasn't* sober.

"Where's your mother?" she taunted him then. "I think you need a keeper. I think you're out too late."

"I need you," he said. "You're my kind of woman." And he grinned at her, launching another cloud of bourbon towards her.

He pulled at her elbow, directing her to a set of chairs in the corner. "Let's go sit down. I think I may — I think I may get sick."

She looked at him, his face very pale. He put a hand to his stomach and then to his forehead. "Hey," he said, "I *am* sick."

Holding his hands to his mouth suddenly, he dashed from her, down the steps into the basement, to the restrooms.

Jessie supposed he would not come back, and she leaned against the chairs so she could watch the couples dancing; she liked to observe, not partake, she thought. She hoped no one would ask her to dance again.

In a moment, the soldier returned. He still looked pale, but better. He managed a weak smile. "Am I a little less green?" he asked her.

Laughing, she nodded. Then: "I'm sorry. I know it isn't fun to get sick — not even if you *are* responsible for it!"

He grinned. "How's that for a classy introduction?" he asked then. "I want to impress you, I get sick. You gotta admit it's a new gimmick."

"Not too many use it, that's true," Jessie said. "It may have something to do with the fact that it's not exactly flattering."

"Why?"

Now the young man seemed genuinely puzzled.

"Well," Jessie countered, smiling at him even as she scolded him, "would you like a woman who is obviously drunk to tell you you are the man of her dreams?"

"Am I?" he asked with a grin. He turned his pallid face back to her and looked into her eyes. He leaned forward, squinted, as if he saw something far back in them. "Am I the man of your dreams?"

When she didn't answer, just folded her arms and looked at him, he answered himself. "Good! Because you are the woman of mine. My dreams, I mean. There isn't a song about that, is there?"

Jessie laughed. "No. Not that I know of. But probably there should be. But I didn't say . . ." She looked at him, fumbling with his shirt buttons, as if he were going to take off his clothes. "What're you doing?"

"It's hot in here," the lieutenant said. "Let's go outside."

"I think that's a very good idea," Jessie agreed. She studied him, his short-cropped, hair showing perspiration drops at the roots.

"I have a feeling," Jessie said, having taken his elbow and steering him as quickly as she could out the door, "that you may be sick again. Fresh air should help."

"I won't be sick," the soldier protested, stumbling, leaning on her, flinging an arm impulsively around her shoulder.

"I hope not," Jessie told him as they moved down the steps, and onto the hot pavement of Harper.

"Whew!" he said. "It's just as hot out here as inside."

"Not quite. There's a breeze." She took his arm, this time led him to her parked car. "We can sit in the car until you sober up."

"Hey . . ." the young officer said then, trying to wink at her but the gesture going askew so that it looked more like a grimace, "are you making a pass at me? My mother told me to watch out for strange girls. Can I trust myself with you?"

Now Jessie was almost irritated. She put her hands on her hips, pushed the door shut behind him, watching his head loll back against the seat, "Probably more than you'd like to," she said. "I'm not a pickup."

Instantly he got serious. "I know," he said. "I wouldn't have wanted to meet you if you had been."

"All right." Jessie got in the driver's side, put her arms on the steering wheel, facing forward. "Now that we have that straight."

"You're a nice girl," he went on, then he yawned. "You're a nice girl even if you *do* talk to strangers."

"*Hmmph,*" Jessie said.

She opened the door as if she would get out, changed her mind, banged it shut. Instantly the young man grabbed his head.

"Ouch!" he said. "I have a tender head."

"You're going to have an even worse one in the morning," Jessie mused. "And you deserve it!"

She looked over at him, now huddled up as though he were sulking from being punished. "I don't envy you getting up tomorrow."

"Maybe I won't," he said. "Maybe I'll just stay in bed all during the rest of the war. I'd like to, that's for sure."

"Yes," Jessie said, sobering. She thought of her father and all the other men who had to face death.

Again she looked at the young lieutenant, his face outlined by a street light nearby and, in spite of herself, she felt an unaccustomed wrench. Here was this young man — as millions of young men — being sent somewhere to seek out other young men and kill them. And so many would never come back, or if they did, they might be horribly mangled, their lives changed forever. Was it true that wars were declared only by old men, but fought by the young? *Would it never end?*

Jessie looked over at the officer, feeling an empathy for him. No wonder he drank! She saw he was asleep, his head beginning to slide toward her. He looked terribly vulnerable.

Adjusting herself as his head fell on her shoulder, she heard him sigh, smacking his lips happily, as if he were having a pleasant dream. Some wonderful, youthful dream, before all this madness had begun.

Well, Jessie thought, let him sleep.

Chapter
Twenty-Eight

SHE DIDN'T KNOW how long they had been there; she was stiff when she finally woke up.

"Oh," he groaned, reaching for his head. "My God, what time is it?"

Olga had come a hour ago, looked into the car, laughed, and had gone home with another girl and a serviceman she'd picked up rather than wait for Jessie. At least, Jessie *thought* it was an hour ago.

She looked at her watch: two o'clock! The dance had been over at twelve.

She remembered Olga had asked, "Will you be all right?" and somehow Jessie was certain she would. But she'd smiled and said, "Take one look at him, Olga, and tell me."

Olga had smiled. "I think you're safe."

"You can't say I'm not doing my part for the war," Jessie told her.

She looked at her watch again as if to verify the time.

"Two o'clock," she told the young man now.

Her wristwatch, her first one, was a gold Elgin. It had been a gift from her father the past Christmas.

She held it out for the young man to see. "It's from my poppa," she told him.

"Poppa?" he asked, frowning, then grimacing because the gesture hurt. "What kinda word is that?"

"I don't know," Jessie admitted. "It's just what I've always called my father. Even now that I'm grown up."

The lieutenant looked at her. Jessie turned away as she saw his glance sweep appraisingly over her. "Well, you have grown up," he said.

She flushed, put her hands on the steering wheel. "I expect I should be getting home," she said.

The lieutenant looked so unhappy when she turned to him that once more Jessie's stomach wrenched. She had never felt such an attraction before. Even his hands — strong, well-shaped — sent a shiver down her spine. What in the world was wrong with her?

"Well," she said, softening her tone a bit, "maybe I can drop you off somewhere."

"No," he said.

"What?" She was puzzled. "Are you meeting someone who'll take you back to the fort? The last bus may be gone."

"No."

"I can't take you home with me," she stated, almost in question. "I mean — well — don't you have any place to stay?"

He looked distressed for a moment. "No," he said. Then he looked over at her. "Well, yes I do, that's a lie. But," now he seemed to be pleading with her, "I don't want to be alone."

Jessie knew she didn't want to be alone either.

"Poppa isn't home," she said, starting up the car. "But my grandmother is, and you can come. You can have my room and I'll sleep in Poppa's."

"You're sure Poppa won't mind?"

She knew he was teasing her, but she didn't care.

"Poppa is overseas," she said, starting up the car.

"Oh."

When she glanced over at him as she drove home, she saw he was smiling. He winked — broadly and good-naturedly — completing the gesture this time.

"Glad to see you got your wink back," Jessie said.

He laughed. "You don't have a German Shepherd killer dog, do you?"

Jessie eased the car into the driveway in front of the old farmhouse. The lights swung across it, then she turned them off and shut off the ignition. Darkness washed around them.

"I have a brother who sometimes acts like one," Jessie told him.

His laugh, spontaneous and full, made Jessie feel warm and secure in a way she hadn't since her father left. What would Old Jessica say when she saw him in the morning? What would Fred, when he came over as usual? Ilse, she told herself fiercely, would be there then, but she didn't matter.

Suddenly Jessie laughed. The whole situation was just too funny!

She realized she and the soldier hadn't exchanged names yet, but as she turned to ask the lieutenant what to call him, his head once again fell on her shoulder. He nuzzled into the curve of it contentedly and in moments, was once again fast asleep.

"You have to get up and go in," Jessie said, prodding him awake.

The officer yawned, then reluctantly opened his door and got out. He almost fell for a moment, but Jessie raced around the car to his side and propped him up.

When she left him in her room, he fell across the top of the bed without pulling the covers down. Jessie got an extra blanket out of the hall closet, brought it in, flung it over him. Again he smacked his lips as if that were all he was waiting for.

In the morning, the lieutenant awakened with the head she had predicted — even worse than he'd had in the car. For a moment, after she had come in to check on him, he looked disoriented in the strange room. She saw him eying the horse pictures on the wall, the polished leather boots near one chair, jeans hanging on a nail on the closet door and the dresser, which must have looked almost masculine to him, so bare of cosmetics as to belie it was the room of a woman.

"Hi," she said, moving to open the curtains, smiling.

"Oh, don't, please," he said, motioning her not to let the blessed dimness disappear. "You were right — my head is a balloon! An aching balloon."

"A balloon, huh?" Jessie said. "Well, I've got some hot coffee and rolls for you downstairs — juice — bacon, eggs — whatever you want, and we'll make a new man of you in minutes. But first —" now she looked at him as he modestly pulled the sheet up across his chest, "you've got to tell me your name. I mean, if you spend the night in my bed, I'm entitled to that, right?"

Across the room from her, the lieutenant blushed. Sober, he was much less aggressive, almost shy. "I can tell you my name, rank and serial number," he said, relaxing at last and sinking back against the tall walnut headboard. "And if this is a prison camp, I don't mind it at all."

He looked at her, smiled broadly. "I'm Peter Johnson. Lieutenant Peter Johnson. Pete. I don't think you even want to know my serial number."

"You're right," Jessie said. "But Pete, I'm happy to meet you."

She strode across the room, her bluejeaned legs thrust into dirty workboots, a hand-tooled leather belt with a silver and turquoise clasp at the waist. She stuck out her hand.

"I'm Jessica Lutz," she said. "But my friends call me Jess or Jessie."

"Jessie," he said, as if tasting the word.

And Pete Johnson took her hand, held it, turning it over to look at the hardened flesh on the palms. It wasn't a lady's hand, Jessie knew, but Pete seemed to like it.

"Working hands," Jessie said, smiling at him as if she'd read his thoughts. "You don't work on a ranch like a man without taking on some of the attributes."

Once more Pete looked at her and Jessie felt the same odd stir, the same awkwardness before his glance.

"You haven't taken on *all* the attributes of a man I'm happy to say," he told her.

Without answering, Jessie beckoned him to follow her downstairs. She stopped at the door, put her head back in the room. "My family is going to be *very* surprised."

In the bed, she heard the lieutenant laugh.

"Would you like to see some of the ranch?" Jessie asked Pete when he'd finished what he could of the more than ample breakfast. Coffee and one roll and a small glass of juice was all he could manage.

He stubbed out his third cigarette of the morning.

"Sure," he said. "It might be good for the head to give it some air."

Ilse had offered to wash and iron Pete's Army shirt and pants, to press his coat, brush his military hat — in fact, Jessie was grateful to her for her help and her understanding. Old Jessica had been far less solicitous.

"Hmmph!" she'd said, upon hearing the story of why the lieutenant had come home with Jessie. "Your grandfather had a taste for liquor," she sniffed, "and it didn't do *him* any good either."

But she'd supplied Pete with some of August's old jeans and a shirt, jacket, clean socks, and underwear.

Fred had come into the kitchen, done a double take, then recovered and shook hands with Pete as though this were an ordinary practice with Jessie, bringing young men home to stay the night. Then he'd disappeared.

Jessie thought Fred probably didn't relish the idea of Pete talking to him about the military and perhaps asking what *he* was doing as a civilian.

"Do you want to ride?" Jessie asked. "I have several good horses."

"I might fall off," Pete said. "I'm not in the cavalry, you know."

"Okay," Jessie said. "Walk it is."

They set off down the lane that led to the creek bottom crossing, the fields looking bare, for the wheat had been harvested, the raw ends jutting up on the scalp of the earth like the cropped hair of the young soldiers. Little by little the trees thickened as they approached the creek and the coolness began. Jessie said, "You can smell it, can't you? The water?"

"Umm," Pete said.

He seemed to be absorbing the land, the time with Jessie; it seemed to be a kind of release to him that he had not thought possible.

"You know, Jess," he said, taking her hand for a moment to stop her from wading into the shallow water and going to the other side, "I've been through Atlas City but I never thought to stop. I didn't know places like this existed in Kansas."

"What places?" Jessie asked, shading her eyes as she looked up at him.

Sunlight patched through the trees, a slight breeze moving them so that the shade was like lace, rippling across Pete's face. She saw tiny drops of perspiration on his forehead, for the day was already beginning to heat up.

"Beautiful, green places. You don't see this from a car. You don't see it unless you walk here. . . . You love this place, don't you?"

Pete studied her face as she answered. "Yes. I do. Poppa and I —"

Again he teased softly, "Poppa."

She jerked up her chin. "Yes, Poppa! I told you — it's my name for him. And I'm not going to apologize for it."

He seemed to like her sudden anger. He hadn't dropped her hand and now he squeezed it softly. "I know," he said. Then: "Where is he? Can you say?"

She shook her head. "I don't know for sure," she said. "He's working for the government, but he's not in the military. He's overseas, but I don't know where. I worry about him."

"Of course," Pete said.

He released her hand for a moment. "Do you want to wade across? Let's take off our shoes — more fun."

Jessie nodded.

Like teenagers, they removed shoes and socks, squealed as the cool creek water washed about their toes, poked into the crevices between them, the soft mud oozing up.

"I think I felt a crayfish," Jessie said, jumping.

Pete laughed. "Not in shallow water surely."

"Well, something touched me."

And then as the water splashed upon them, Jessie turned to Pete.

"What . . . Jessie?" he asked.

They had reached the far bank now and Jessie sat down, pulled her knees to her, staring up at the sky. She said, "My mother drowned. Water scares me sometimes."

"Oh, Jess," he said, "I'm sorry."

"I've gotten used to it I guess," Jessie said. "But sometimes — like now — I'm reminded of that day. . . . And I miss her."

Jessie felt as if she'd known Pete Johnson forever. It seemed safe — and right — to confess things to him she'd never told anyone before, not even her father.

"It's natural that you miss her," Pete said.

"It's too bad people have to —" she started to say "die," found she couldn't use the word. Shielding her eyes from the sun, she stared over at Pete, his clean, borrowed clothes already getting smudged from branches brushing against him and the soft mud of bank. She didn't want Pete — she didn't want *any*one — to die!

"It's sad there have to be wars," she said at last.

"Yes."

"I wonder why?"

"I don't know."

Pete's voice had become quieter, deeper; then she was aware he was standing very close to her — she could hear his quick shallow breathing.

She watched Pete's face as he bent over her. Gently he took her head in his hands, looked at her, softly put his lips on hers. For a moment, he kissed her lightly, brushing his lips back and forth over hers; abruptly, his arms tightened about her, she smelled the starch Old Jessica had used on August's clothes, keeping them clean for some unknown reason, she smelled the cigarettes he'd smoked that morning, she smelled the toothpaste he'd evidently used to try to mask the tobacco. She could feel his tongue in her mouth, exploring. Together they eased to the ground.

She leaned back on the cool earth with him and returned his kiss as eagerly as he gave it.

That next week, Pete and Jessie talked on the phone every day and planned again for the weekend.

"There's something funny about your young man," Old Jessica said the next day, accosting Jessie in the kitchen.

"He's *not* my young man!" Jessie retorted hotly.

"Whose is he?" Fred stuck in then.

"Fred," Jessie said, her voice thin and harsh. "You just stay out of this."

"Well, I'd be careful, all the same," Old Jessica went on. "You never can tell about things in wartime. People act strangely."

"People act strangely around this house all the time," Jessie said, flouncing out of the room.

The next Saturday night, after Pete got leave, he came to take Jessie to a movie. Old Jessica and Fred had stationed themselves at the front bay windows, behind the lace curtains, and they watched Pete walk up to the door, appraising him.

"He *is* good looking," Old Jessica admitted.

"Somewhat," Fred said.

Jessie was sure Fred couldn't give any serviceman too much credit.

"Everyone looks good in a uniform," Fred went on. "I would have too."

Abruptly his face fell and he hastily released the lace curtain he'd pulled back from the parlor window.

"I *would* have," he went on, as if someone had disputed him.

Old Jess leaned over. "Of course," she said, patting him on the shoulder.

"But you mustn't worry about that. You're doing your duty here on the home front."

Fred sniffed. "Some duty! Working on the books all day and trying to get people to run the ranch. We can't even have the normal amount of cattle what with everyone gone to war."

"It's bound to get better," Old Jessica said. "Things will get better."

But Fred was not moved. "I doubt it. War means sacrifice and the war isn't over yet."

"Still, Fred," Old Jess said, apparently remembering another war and another time, "it's necessary. We really can't have the Germans — and the Japs — running over us. I don't want to be serving tea in clogs to some barbarian captors!"

"Hardly!" Fred said.

The handle on the front doorbell turned, sending a *burring* of sound through the old stone house.

"I'll get it," Jessie called breathlessly as she ran down the steps, "let me get it!"

"Be my guest, eager one," Fred said sourly. "But — " he smiled slyly, "don't you think you should play a little harder to get?"

"Go to hell," Jessie said.

But she was so happy she said it with a lilt in her voice, not meaning it.

Fred turned and disappeared into the kitchen.

"When will you be home?" Old Jessica asked Jessie before she opened the door.

"Really, Grandmother! I'm 21, you know."

But her grandmother was firm. "And living at home. So when will you be home?"

"Midnight — I — I don't know."

Again the bell sounded. But Old Jessica had stepped in front of the door. "Eleven-thirty," she bargained.

"One," Jessie said. Then: "Well, maybe before. She moved to one side of Old Jessica, swinging the door open to greet Pete, who stood there smiling at her now, looking handsome, a bouquet of red roses in his hands.

He thrust them at Jessie. "Not exactly sweets to the sweet," he said, "but something of that sort."

"Hmmph," Old Jess said, retreating backwards a few steps and crossing her arms, leveling another appraising glance at Pete Johnson.

"Oh, thank you!" Jessie said, taking the bouquet, lifting it to her nose and sniffing. "Oh, Pete," she said, taking in the aroma, "they're lovely!"

"*Hmmph,*" Old Jess said again.

Pete swept his hat off as he caught sight of Old Jessica, bowed to her slightly. "Hello," he said. "I'm Pete Johnson."

He extended his hand but Old Jessica didn't take it. Instead, she turned to Jessie and said, "One o'clock at the *lat*est, Jessie. Beyond that, I call the police."

She cast another look at Pete, snorted, and turned to leave.

"I'll see that she's in, Mrs. Lutz," Pete offered then, smiling.

"Hmmph," Old Jessica said, and retreated down the hall and to the kitchen where, Jessie thought, she and Fred would no doubt spend the next hours discussing her and her young man, enthusiastically dissecting them.

"And *that* is Grandmother," Jessie explained as Old Jess disappeared behind the kitchen door. "Usually we keep her leashed."

But she grinned.

"She just cares about you," Pete said, sobering. He twirled his officer's hat in his hand for a moment. "It's natural." Then, smiling broadly, "Maybe I'll grow on her."

Jessie returned the smile. "Don't count on it," she said, "but — even Grandmother is human so maybe you will. Anyway, I'll get a vase for your lovely flowers and then we'll go."

She left Pete briefly, went into the kitchen, ignored the stares and muffled coughs of both Old Jess and Fred, opened the bottom cupboard by the stove, extracted a vase, and poured water into it. She arranged the roses quickly, then picked the vase up again and returned to Pete. She set the roses down on the hall table, their color igniting the room, brightening the dull gray of the wallpaper, the dark varnish which still remained as it had been in her grandmother's day.

"They're really lovely, Pete," she said. "Thank you so much."

"*You're* lovely," Pete said. And, quickly, he leaned over to kiss her. "Umm," he said then. "You smell good."

"I stole some of Grandmother's Chanel," Jessie admitted with a smile.

"Well, then, thanks to Grandmother because I like it!"

"Uh-huh," she said. "But we better get out of here before Grandmother comes after us with a broom."

Pete put his hat on as they walked off the porch, adjusting it at a rakish angle over one eye. Holding the door open to a dark blue Chevy, he helped Jessie into the seat.

"I borrowed the car from a buddy," he explained. "I didn't want you to have to drive again."

"Be good then," Jessie teased.

"Of course," Pete said. He looked back at the house as he walked around the car. "I see we're being watched," he told Jessie.

Jessie turned too, saw Old Jessica and Fred were again at the window, spying on them.

"I think you have *two* German Shepherds," Pete said as he twisted the ignition to a start.

Jessie laughed. "And their bite *is* as bad as their bark," she added.

Jessie noticed the car had an "A" sticker for gas. They wouldn't be driving it far, because the "A" provided little gas per week. But Pete was lucky to have gotten any transportation.

"Out of sight, out of mind," Pete said, as he pulled away.

"Oh, forget it," Jessie told him. "Grandmother will keep us in mind, don't you worry about that."

Pete laughed.

The movie was a war film on the fall of Bataan and Corregidor and it was just too grim to take. "I want to be entertained if I can," Pete said. "I don't want to think about the war anymore than I have to."

"A mistake even going," Jessie admitted.

"Where do the kids park around here?" Pete said lightly then. "We can talk, you know." He winked at her. "That is, if we don't find better things to do."

Jessie felt the shiver going through her again. "Top of the World. It's very near one of our pastures. In fact, right across from it is where one of the big bull always stands, looking over his domain."

"Then Top of the World it is," Pete said. "If it's good enough for one of your bulls, it's surely —" but abruptly he flushed, not finishing his sentence.

Jessie noticed that the leg makeup she'd put on was coming off on the car seat. She preferred the makeup to the awful-looking rayon hose she could still buy, the silk ones having long gone to the war effort.

"Oh, dear," she told Pete then. "I hope I haven't ruined your friend's upholstery. This darn leg makeup —"

"We'll wash it off," Pete said. "When we get home. He won't mind."

Winding up the road past their farmhouse, Jessie looked out, half expecting to see her Grandmother following them in her old battered pickup. Having learned to drive with a stick shift, Old Jessica insisted that anything other than that really wasn't a *car*, much less a truck, and she would continue driving the way she had learned, *thank you very much!*

But the house was dark, except for one light still on the living room, where Old Jessica was no doubt asleep on the couch, awaiting Jessie. Fred would have gone back to the house he and Molly shared, as he was an early-to-bed, early-to-riser, and indeed looked with suspicion on anyone who did not also have that habit.

The breeze coming in the car's open windows was cool and Jessie was grateful for it; this July had been so hot! She couldn't help but think of the soldiers fighting in overgrown, steaming jungles so many miles away and the fact that no matter what they did, they couldn't get away from it.

When Pete pulled to a stop on the summit, there were no other cars. In the moonlight they could see for miles across the pastures.

Pete put his hands on the steering wheel, staring straight ahead. He cleared his throat. "Jessie," he began, "I have something I have to tell you."

"Oh?"

Jessie felt a tightening in her stomach, wondering if he were going to tell her his unit was pulling out. But of course, she reasoned, he couldn't tell her that.

Then Pete sighed. He brushed his hand across his forehead, reached across the seat and took her hand in his.

"I don't quite know how to begin," he said.

Jessie swallowed. When Pete didn't speak, she said, "I have something to tell you too, Pete."

She turned to him, saw moonlight lining his face, felt again the wash of emotion whenever she heard his voice or saw his face. "I've — I've fallen in love with you, Pete."

She had never said that before, but it seemed to release something within her. "I didn't know one could fall in love this fast, and I certainly didn't plan to — or want to — but I have."

"Oh, *Jessie* . . ." Pete said.

His voice sounded pained. But then he turned to her. "I knew I loved you the moment I saw you."

"It's not a good time for lovers, is it?" Jessie said then.

She thought of the women she knew who had already been widowed, some of them losing husbands in the very first battles of the war, some of them having lost husbands at Pearl Harbor.

"No," Pete said. "It's not a good time."

She saw that he had put one hand to his head as if to support it.

"I shouldn't have let it happen, Jess," he said finally.

"Why? Are you going away?"

"I will before long, I'm sure. But it's not that. It's —"

Again, his words seemed to choke him.

"Oh, Pete," Jessie said, "let's not talk about bad things. We have enough bad things in our lives. Let's just live."

When he turned to face her he took her chin in his hands and gently kissed her. "I love you, Jessie," he said.

Jessie returned his kiss as though it were the last they would ever share.

"Jessie . . ." The words seemed almost like a cry; but Jessie pressed herself into him, felt his hands begin to explore her, and she did not want to express anything to Pete Johnson but the way she loved him.

Chapter
Twenty-Nine

*T*HE LATE NOVEMBER blizzard was early for such a fierce storm. Jessie and Sandy had let the cattle stay up in the pastures, and though most of the pregnant heifers were in the corral, a few had straggled. They both had thought there would be time to get the animals in before they calved, before the weather changed.

Now they were riding up to the high pastures, hoping to find those heifers, because the snow had started early in the day and showed no signs of letting up.

As they rode through the creek bottom, Jessie saw the cedars straining under the wet, heavy snow, their branches bending to the ground. Ice had formed on the edges of the creek, and the horses stumbled as they drove their way up the bank and onto the trail which was rapidly disappearing under its cover of white.

Jessie was riding Redbird, a new, dark sorrel gelding who was big and smart. Sandy was on his old Appaloosa, a breed Sandy swore by because it was descended from the Indian ponies the Spanish explorers had given the Native Americans.

"She wants to go," he'd explained when Jessie wondered if the older horse were really up to it. Making their way through drifting snow would be hard.

She and Sandy didn't speak; the snow hit their faces like little pieces of glass, and Jessie pulled her cowboy hat further down over her face and ears. Redbird issued little puffs of air as he pushed through the thickening snow, and Jessie could hear the stiff saddle creaking under her weight.

"Down in the timber," Sandy said. "We'll find them there I'm sure."

As they went across the broad back of the hills, they could see the ravine that cut the land in two a quarter of a mile away. The timber there was thick and dark, bare limbs reaching into the gloomy sky as though scratching its gray belly.

"Hope the coyotes haven't gotten the calves if the heifers have already birthed," Sandy said.

Sandy's spotted horse shook its head, trying to detach the snow tangled in its mane; Sandy reached out, brushed the snow off, then shook his head as more fell onto the hair.

The whole horizon was getting whiter, as though they were riding inside one of those glass balls people sometimes gave as Christmas presents: shake it, and snow fell over the scene. But they weren't inside a ball, Jessie told herself as she shivered, pulled her jacket tighter. Already her feet and hands were cold, her face seemed frozen.

As they went down the steep sides of the hill around the ravine, Sandy pointed: "There's one," he said. "Can't see if she's calved or not."

They came close and soon could see the small form lying in the snow. At first they thought it was dead, but then the calf rolled its eyes at them, still clinging to life.

Sandy offered to take it. "I can carry it on the saddle."

Just then they caught sight of the other missing heifer, standing over something almost buried in the snow. As Jessie rode up, she could tell the calf was dead. Whether it had survived the birth, she didn't know, but the poor thing was cold and stiff, the mother milling helplessly over it. Jessie felt her heart tighten as she looked at the little body; she never had gotten accustomed to the death that lurked constantly in ranch life.

"Take it, Jessie," Sandy said. "They'll follow us if we have the calves."

Jessie leaped off Redbird, letting the rains trail in the frosted snow. He wouldn't move — he'd been trained too well for that.

She struggled to detach the calf from his catafalque of ice, his eyes closed, his red fur frozen and hard. He may have been alive for awhile, Jessie thought; they just hadn't gotten to him in time.

She leaned the calf against Redbird's side as she pushed him up and over the withers, the legs protruding stiffly, lifelessly. Redbird snorted as he caught the scent of the dead animal, and swung his head around in protest, but Jessie rubbed his forehead, told him, "It's okay, fella," and he turned back, shook impatiently, stood still.

She swung into the saddle, put her hand on the calf to steady it, jerked the reins.

As they made their way back through the pasture, the wind came up, whipping the snow and hurling it into their faces. Jessie could hardly see. She watched the snow piling up on the dead calf, as though Nature wanted to disguise what it had done, cover up.

"We got to this one just in time," Sandy said, stroking the fur of the calf that lay across his horse's shoulder. "He seems to know he'll be alright — he hasn't moved."

The mothers trailed their calves and Sandy and Jessie held tightly to their burdens as they went down the hill once more and over the creek. In the valley, the wind was less but the temperature was steadily falling. Jessie wondered if she and Sandy would be frostbitten.

At last they reached the corral, opened the gate, and put the cows and the one calf inside. When the other calf did not follow, the mother gave a long bellow and tried to get out of the corral to follow Sandy and Jess.

"We'll skin him," Sandy said. "We'll buy a calf and put the hide on it and hope she'll nurse it. Otherwise we'll have to get her milk and freeze it for some cow who can't produce."

Jessie didn't answer.

She let Sandy take the calf into the barn, saw him getting out the knife, and then she said: "Sandy, do you mind if I don't watch?"

He smiled at her. "No, Jessie. No point in putting yourself through anything more than you have to."

Later that day Sandy took the hide when they discovered that one of the neighbors had lost a cow. They bought the calf, then Sandy tied the dead calf's hide over it and put the newcomer in the stall with the mother. At first she looked as if she wouldn't accept it; he had tried to nurse and she stepped aside. Then she swung her head around and began to sniff. After a time, she stood still while the orphan reached in under her belly and began to suck. The two began to bond, just as Jessie and Sandy had hoped.

"I guess mothers are the same all over," Jessie murmured. "They feel a loss, and even if they're fooled, they don't know it and everyone's happy."

"Well, we were lucky," Sandy said, rubbing a hand over his forehead. "It doesn't always work out."

Jessie and Sandy made their way back to the house. Jessie could hear him humming: it had been a good day.

But the day — the night — that she and Olga had decided to take in the movies at Harper, the night Pete didn't have leave, was not good.

"I have to tell you something," Olga said.

Jessie put her hand over her stomach — something she found she was doing lately whenever she was afraid. But what was there to be afraid of?

"*He's married*," Olga said. "Pete Johnson is married."

Jessie inhaled what sounded like an *Oh* — almost a moan — felt her heart leaping in her chest, thumping against her ribcage.

"Pete Johnson has a wife, Jessie."

Again Jessie felt the constriction in her chest; tears seemed to want to push from her eyes but she bit her lip, turned her head away from Olga and fought them back.

They were in Jessie's car; Jessie had been saving her gas coupons for weeks so she would have enough to take them to Harper and back.

"I thought it was just that he was going to be shipped overseas," Jessie said, as if to herself.

"What?"

"He tried to tell me something."

"He *should* have," Olga said, her voice firm.

"Yes."

Jessie felt she was throttling the steering wheel; she couldn't seem to keep from pressing her fingers into it.

"I didn't want to tell you like this," Olga was saying from the other side of the front seat, facing forward as though looking at Jessie would be too painful. "But I thought you should know."

"Yes."

And Jessie released one hand again to press against her stomach, then put it back on the steering wheel. She supposed it was a kind of protective movement: the warrior shielding his spleen, the duelist hiding his heart.

Jessie tightened her grip on the wheel again, slowed down.

"How do you know this?" she asked at last, her voice seeking steadiness.

"Jessie," Olga said softly then, reaching across the seat to touch Jessie's shoulder briefly, "I know it hurts. But I'm a friend. And sometimes friends have to hurt."

"Yes," Jessie said again.

They drove in silence for a few moments, the blacktop road like a pencil line, narrowing as it stretched before them, pressing between a grove of trees as it traced itself over the horizon. Cold seemed to rise from the macadam, oozing through the floorboards; although the sun had not yet gone down, it was low in the sky. A chill hung in the air.

"Old Jessica knew it," Jessie said then, as if she were completely detached now from what she was saying. "I don't know how she knew it, but she has a sixth sense for disaster. She said, 'There's something wrong with your soldier, Jessie.' *My* soldier! God, how I hate her sometimes!"

Olga didn't say anything for a moment. Then: "Of course it's not your grandmother's fault that she was right."

"No."

"And I'm sure she cares about you."

Jessie sniffed, but didn't answer.

Suddenly Jessie swung the car over to the side of the road. The motor coughed, died, shaking them as it did so. Jessie put her head in her hands, resting them against the wheel. She felt Olga's hand on her back, rubbing silently.

"What do I do now?" she asked.

"I don't know," Olga said.

Once more they didn't speak, each seeming lost in her own thoughts. Then Jessie said, not looking at Olga, "How did you find out?"

"You remember I went home with someone else the night you and Pete first met?"

"Yes."

"I went home with a friend of Pete's — another soldier. When I told him where Pete was — he hadn't seen him leave — he asked, 'Does your friend know Pete is married?'"

Now Jessie's head bumped against the wheel; then she turned and lay her face on her tensed knuckles.

"I don't know what to do about all this, Jessie," Olga continued. "But now you know."

"Yes. *Now I know.*"

"Jessie? Have you fallen in love with him?"

Jessie drew in a breath, expelled it. "Yes."

"Damn."

Moments later, Jessie raised her head from her hands and pierced Olga with a glance. "You know something I don't believe?" she asked with a slight laugh. "That old adage about it's being better to have loved and lost than not to have loved at all. The *hell* it is!"

Jessie abruptly turned the key in the ignition, jerked the car into a U-turn on the highway, sped back toward Atlas City.

"I wish I'd never met him," she said bitterly.

"I asked if Pete were in the process of getting a divorce," Olga said in the silence that followed Jessie's change of direction. He said no. Then I asked him if Pete were *going* to get a divorce. He said no. And in the end I asked him what in the hell Pete was doing with another woman — a good woman — in that case."

"And?"

"He told me — you sure you want this?"

Jessie bit her lip, frowned, "Yes."

Olga gathered her hands in her lap, straightened, facing ahead and said, "Pete's wife is insane." Olga paused, looked over at Jessie.

Jessie turned briefly, stared at her friend. She turned back to the road.

"I mean, *really* insane. She's in the state hospital now, receiving some kind of treatment, which I think means mostly taking experimental drugs they're using on her. She's been classified as a paranoid schizophrenic."

If Jessie had felt stabbed before, she now had the sensation that her whole abdomen was being ripped apart. "*Oh my God.*"

"I gather Pete feels it isn't fair to her to get a divorce — I'm not even sure he *can* — but the doctors seem to think she's hopeless. The outlook is bleak to say the least. And she's young. She could live — if you call that living — for a long time."

"I see."

"Jessie," Olga cried out then. "I hated to tell you."

"You had to, Olga," Jessie said. "And you're a friend for doing it."

"What will you do?"

"God," Jessie said, "I don't know."

But she did know. She confronted Pete the next day.

"All right," Pete said, hanging his head as they sat disconsolately in Jessie's car, which was once again parked at Top of the World. "I was wrong — terribly wrong. But Jessie," now he looked helplessly at her as though begging understanding, "you can't know how it is."

"No," she said.

"All the same," and now Pete hung his head, "I'm ashamed. It wasn't fair — I know that."

"No."

"Jessie —" Pete stopped abruptly, stared at her, reached for her hand, let his own clasp hers tightly as though she might pull it away, "I'm a louse. I did a lousy thing."

"I know you didn't mean to," Jessie said, looking out of the window at the pastures still covered with snow.

"But I hurt you and that was the last thing in the world I wanted to do!"

Jessie didn't speak, stirred on the seat beside him, staring out into the dusk filtering over the land. She put her hand over her stomach.

"I'm sorry," he said. "I'm so sorry."

Still Jessie was silent, biting her lip.

"Can you forgive me?"

"I don't know."

"No reason why you should," he said with resignation.

Pete had driven and now he put his hands on the steering wheel, inadvertently honking the horn. Both of them started, the sound echoing in the cold.

They sat in miserable silence for a moment and then Jessie asked. "Is it true what Olga said? That your wife — that she's unwell."

Pete sucked in his breath, expelled it with a sigh, the windshield clouding over with its warmth and moisture. Pete turned from Jessie and stared out over the pastures rolling away from them, the snow glazed with ice. On the opposite hill, where the great bull stood in summer, his tail twitching from time to time, the heavy head slowly turning as he looked first right, then left, there was nothing. It seemed the whole world had left them, and they were irretrievably alone.

Finally Pete turned, again taking Jessie's hand. "Yes," he said. "It's true."

Jessie was silent. She saw a hawk soaring on the drafts of air, gliding with ease over the frozen landscape, looking for the unlucky field mouse that would provide him his dinner.

Pete released her hand then put his head on the steering wheel. Jessie saw the hawk fly off, dipping and soaring as though it were ladling air.

"I don't know what to do, Jessie," he said at last.

". . . Neither do I."

"It was selfish — I've fallen in love with you."

". . . Yes."

Pete pulled her desperately to him. "God, Jessie, I'm sorry. I was so lonely. I just thought — I wanted to tell you."

"You would have," Jessie said then. She let her arms fall to her sides then lifted them up again to hug Pete against her, as if she was consoling a child. He began to sob into her heavy jacket.

"It's awful," he said, "seeing them just disintegrate before you. Sometimes she wouldn't even speak to me. I would go into a room and she would be standing where I'd left her fifteen minutes before. Maybe she'd been dressing, pulling on a slip or something, and she would be suspended in action as though she were frozen. Her mind was rolled back in time, going over something I knew nothing about.

"Sometimes I would come down for breakfast, say 'hello' and she would answer 'hello.' I was having to do most of the work by this time — she never seemed to know what to do — I would fry the eggs and bacon, make the coffee, wash up. I would ask her, 'Do you want coffee?' and she would turn her head and say, 'Do you?' I would say, 'Yes.' Then she would say, 'So do I.' I would ask her if she wanted cream in her coffee and she would ask, 'Do you?' I would say, 'Yes.' Then she would say, 'So do I.' Every goddamn thing had to come from someone else — it was as if she were an empty shell, the wind blowing through her."

"I know . . . it's terrible," Jessie said. She had been staring out the window trying to sort out her feelings. She loved him. What he'd said didn't change that. "Perhaps you shouldn't think about it now," she said finally.

"Oh, no, Jessie — " Pete jerked up his head and looked at her, tears in his eyes, "it's time I thought about it. It's gotten so I think of her as a distant relative — someone I once knew well but whom I haven't seen in a long time. She's been in the hospital for three years now. She says she feels safe there, she never wants to leave. I don't know what to do.

"She was so pretty. I used to have a picture —" He fumbled briefly in his trouser pockets, gave up. "It doesn't matter. Why should I inflict that on you anyway? It only makes it worse."

Jessie didn't answer.

"When I would go to visit her — I haven't gone much recently — she seemed so distant. She said her head had noises in it, felt 'asleep.' Can you imagine how terrible that must be for her? Asleep? She said she tried to wake it up by shaking it sometimes, but she couldn't manage. She laughed once and said, 'Let's elope.' I thought she was going off again and I asked, 'What?' She said, 'Elope. That's what they call it when you run away from the ya-ya house.' I could still hear her laughing when they told her it was time to leave, when they shut the door that led to the locked quarters and took her away."

Now Jessie stroked Pete's back as she pulled him a little tighter to her.

She thought how awful it must be for both of them: Pete's wife shut up in her craziness, Pete lost too.

"I'm sorry, Pete," she told him. "I'm sorry for everything."

"Better for you if you'd never met me," he answered, sliding back behind the wheel, curling his fingers around it.

"No, Pete," Jessie said. "I was hurt and angry of course. I wish to God it weren't like this. But — I love you. And all that's happened doesn't change that. What we *will* do however, is decide where we go from here."

"I think we shouldn't see each other anymore," he answered. "It's too unfair to you."

Jessie absorbed this for a moment. "I don't think I want that, Pete," she said. Now she bent her head, studying her hands, which were kneading themselves in her lap. "I don't think I could stand that."

"Jessie," Pete said, leaning over her suddenly, his mouth seeking hers, pressing hard, "Jessie . . . I do love you!"

When she and Pete made love again Jessie thought, it wasn't right and it wasn't really good, but it was all they had. War didn't leave people time to sort things out.

Chapter
Thirty

B Y JANUARY 1943 the war had been going better for the Allies: the Red Army had broken through a line held by Hungarian troops on the southern Soviet front and had pushed toward Kharkov. Farther south, the Soviets pressed their attempt to cut off Germans withdrawing from the Caucasus. U.S. troops had landed on Amchitka Island in Alaska's Aleutian chain, while Australian soldiers and tanks attacked the Japanese outside Gona on New Guinea. In spite of the surprise attack on Pearl Harbor, the U.S. was gaining in the South Pacific and was hammering the Germans in Northern Europe with a pattern of strategic bombing. It began to look as though the Allies might overcome the Axis.

But though the war was going better, Jessie was absorbed in her own dilemma: she had discovered she was pregnant. She also knew that Pete had shipped out and she had only an APO address in New York. She never wrote.

She *did* write her father — but not about Pete and herself. She kept the letters as brisk and cheerful as she could, detailing work on the ranch, trying to picture it for him.

"The grass will be tall and full this spring," she had written

earlier. *"I can take Red and trot out to the herd, get off and see the tiny, thick sprouts ready to push up into the air. We've had a warm January. I can see why they used to bring cattle up from Texas to feed on this bluestem; there's nothing like it."*

It was the one subject that was always safe for Jessie and Jake — the love of the land. Unlike Old Jessica and Fred, the endless space didn't frighten them, it thrilled them. "We have eons of time and acres of space here," Jake once asserted. "The day is coming when both of those will be in short supply."

"In short supply?" Jessie questioned.

"Well," her father had told her, "we're going to become more urbanized. It's bound to happen. And the war we're in will only make it worse. It's already started — the move from the farm. And have you ever known a city person who didn't feel somewhat lost here — no noise, few outside interruptions, a pace of life so slow compared to theirs?"

Jessie thought a moment. Molly — who had once lived in Denver, which seemed citylike to Jessie — was a good example. "I guess you're right," she said. "Molly's like a fish out of water."

"It's going to get greater, the difference," Jake prophesied. "It's going to come to where city folks will be interested in this land, but only as investment. They won't know the damnest thing about it and they may — if we let them — destroy it."

"But why?" Jessie asked. "Why, if they ever come here, would they want to destroy it?"

"Oh, they won't want to necessarily," Jake said. "They just won't know any better. You can't take someone who's grown up on city streets, played all his life on pavement, someone who's had to wrestle against other people to get ahead, and put him in a place where there is so much space it terrifies him, where the things you have to watch out for are mostly from Nature, not other people. And there's something else as ominous as the space and slow-moving time. . . . Whims of Nature — floods, tornadoes, lack of rain, all of it."

He didn't go on then, didn't expand, but sometimes, as when Jessie simply rode out over the pastures on a Sunday, not working — though her eye was always checking fence, it was automatic — she thought of what her father had said: "Nature."

So she kept the letters she wrote her father while he was overseas in the safe, philosophical vein of the discussions they'd once had.

"*I suppose a farm person can somehow blend into the city,*" Jessie wrote one day, bending over the white paper in the kitchen, wetting the end of the pencil absently with her tongue, "*but I'm afraid that something would always be missing for this person. He would feel compressed, uncertain. He would miss the expansiveness of the prairie, the animal life, even the vagaries of the weather. There's a kind of feel in the country that would always be missing.*"

And Jake wrote: "*Yes, Jessie. You see it in you and you see it in Fred. Fred is like Old Jessica, has never been able to adapt, has always wanted something different. And Molly doesn't even try. But you and I, Jessie, and my father, August, we let this land take us over and we'll be in it no matter what happens with the rest of our lives.*"

Jessie felt a pang then. At one point, before she knew Pete Johnson, she had thought she might leave and try life elsewhere. Sometimes she felt swallowed by the Lutz land, the Lutz enterprises, as if Jessie Lutz lay buried in a great mass of flesh called Lutz.

But since Pete Johnson had entered her life, everything was somehow different.

This day, as she worked on a letter once again in the kitchen, Old Jessica approached her. Antenna seeming to tremble, searching her out, her grandmother said, "Jessie, what's troubling you?"

Jessie reached out to cover her stomach, the slight swell there, the swell that was growing daily, the swell she could no longer deny. It seemed to press back against her hand as she rubbed her abdomen.

Then, with Old Jess's penchant for the quick jab, her grandmother said, "Are you pregnant, Jessie?"

Jessie, astounded, didn't answer.

"Molly's pregnant," her grandmother said. Then, again: "Are you?"

So that was why Molly had been taking on extra weight. Because she was already big, Jessie had thought she was simply gaining weight from eating too much.

The pencil fell from Jessie's hand and went rolling away across the table. Her grandmother reached out, grabbed it before it went over the edge. Jessie turned her head away.

"Are you?" her grandmother persisted.

Numbly, Jessie shook her head up and down.

"*Oh, my God,*" Old Jessica said.

They were silent a few moments, then Old Jess slid into a chair beside

Jessie. She took her hand and pulled Jessie's face back so she was facing her grandmother.

With the way she had of adapting to disaster, Jessie thought, her grandmother now said, as if it were simply a matter of recognizing the problem, "Well, what shall we do about it? I suppose it's your soldier."

"Yes, goddammit, Grandmother, yes, it's my soldier!" Jessie shrieked. "He wanted a roll in the hay — is that what you want me to say? That you knew it all along? You could *sniff* it on him?"

Once attacked, Old Jessica felt secure. She always suspected a flanking motion it seemed, so that when it came, she knew how to meet it.

"Let's don't get emotional," she said. "That isn't going to help any of us."

But there was an undercurrent of gentleness in her voice, Jessie realized, a tenderness she hadn't felt before.

"All right," Jessie said at last. "Let's try not to get emotional. Is that better?"

But Old Jessica didn't answer.

Jessie couldn't help but press her further. "You don't need to get emotional I guess, Grandmother," she said. "You seem to be made of stone. Have you ever truly cared about anything in your entire life?"

Again: silence. When Jessie turned to confront her, carry on the assault, she was surprised to see that her grandmother suddenly looked vulnerable, defenseless. But Old Jess apparently recovered, for just as quickly as she had shown Jessie a side of her Jessie never suspected, she stiffened.

"Let's not get personal," Old Jessica said, moving about the kitchen, picking up plates, setting them down — for the dinner dishes still were couched in the drying rack in the sink. Old Jessica was *still* doing the cooking, the cleaning, for Molly was constantly "under the weather," or nauseous, or something.

"I think I can help you, Jessie," her grandmother said then, "if you will let me."

The offer of help from a source Jessie would never have imagined, threw her off balance for a moment. She almost felt as though she would cry, she was so desperate.

"What can I do?" Jessie asked.

"Well, first," now Old Jessica seated herself opposite Jessie at the kitchen table, glanced around to be certain they were alone — Molly liked to spy on them, always trying to hear things not meant for her ears — "first we have to decide if you want to get married."

"I *can't* get married," Jessie stated baldly.

"Oh?"

"Pete is already married."

Now her grandmother's face fell. "Beautiful," she said.

Neither of them spoke for a moment, then finally Old Jess said, "Well, none of that matters. I was afraid —" but she cut herself off. "No use my getting emotional — in spite of the fact you think there is no feeling in this old body."

The air in the room began to clear. They seemed co-conspirators suddenly, not antagonists. Jessie marveled: she and Old Jess had *never* been on the same side before, at least as far as she could remember. What was happening?

"If you can't get married to Pete," her grandmother said, musing, her voice once more impersonal, matter-of-fact, "do you see any other prospects?"

"Hardly."

"Scratch that then," Old Jessica said, in the way she had of picking up younger people's phrases, using them so that they came out awkward and unreal. "We'll have to think of something else."

Her grandmother looked out the window — staring out at the corral and then past it to the cliff that rose by the creek and then up at the high pastures as if it were not a vista she'd hated all her life — as if the whole scene were simply a place she'd one day found herself in.

"I won't have an abortion," Jessie said. "I want this baby."

"Ah."

The point touched, Old Jessica rebounded off it. "You're sure?"

"Yes."

"Well," her grandmother said then, "I would be scared if you did. The methods —" She did not finish.

"Yes," Jessie said.

She knew. The horror stories of women with botched abortions circulated among young females like fire: coathooks used to start the bleeding, infections that raced through the body and ate the young mothers up.

"Yes, I'd be afraid too," Old Jessica said again.

So, Jessie thought, her feeling of the moments before surging back: there *were* fragile places in her grandmother. There was some warm blood in those veins, though it seemed to have been buried so long that it took a real crisis to bring it back to the surface.

"You'll have to go somewhere," Old Jess said, sighing.

"Not easy," Jessie said. "There's work —"

"You will have to go somewhere," her grandmother repeated firmly. "Sandy can find someone to help him."

"Well, we'll see." Jessie returned the sigh.

Suddenly Fred bounded into the room. Eyes alight, he said, "I heard it all. I just *knew* it!"

Old Jessica, her voice level, said, "Knew *what*, Fred?"

Because Fred and Molly *had* to get married — Fred told his grandmother that things had "gotten out of hand" — Jessie knew he wasn't one who could speak in judgment. To Fred's credit, Jessie knew it was Fred himself who suggested that they get married. He had always tried to pretend that he really wanted to. And, Jessie thought now, perhaps he had.

"I knew Jessie was in love with Pete," he finished weakly.

"We have a problem," Old Jess said, going on to include Fred in the discussion, "because Pete is married."

"I'll kill him," Fred said protectively, putting an arm about Jessie, another unusual happening.

"No," Jessie said. "I knew what I was getting into — I mean, Pete told me."

"You *knew*?"

Old Jessica was incredulous.

"Not at first. But I knew early enough that I should have been more careful. And you can't kill him, Fred. He's shipped out."

Fred seemed disappointed and relieved at the same time. "Shipped *out*?"

Fred looked over at Jessie and suddenly she saw his face grow red and tighten. She saw him ball up his fist.

"I'll kill the son of a bitch," he said.

Without warning, Fred struck out.

Later Jessie wondered if he were trying to strike the table; instead, he whirled toward her. The fist he perhaps meant to plunge into Pete Johnson did not hit the table; with great force, Jessie felt it drive into her swollen stomach. Pain spread through her like a bullet.

"*Oh, God,*" she groaned.

"Fred —" Old Jessica began.

But it was too late.

The blow was heavy and it was only seconds before Jessie felt blood running down her legs.

"Oh, my God," she said, bending over in pain.

She put her hands between her legs, trying to stop the flow that now raced down her thighs. She felt herself growing faint as Fred and Old Jessica watched her, then her vision blurred and she lost consciousness.

Jake wasn't told until he came back from the war. And then he was told that Jessie had had a miscarriage.

It was true that Jessie had not completely aborted the fetus; it was necessary to do a dilation and curettage.

Jessie lay in the hospital, looking out at the bleak winter sky; she put her hand on her stomach. She had painkillers now so she didn't feel — physically — the loss of the child. But she felt there was a great empty place in her, something she had lost forever.

Will Harvey talked to her, held her hand, told her it was better this way.

Jessie couldn't talk, began to cry. She turned her face to the wall.

"It's better for the child," Doc Harvey said.

Still she didn't answer.

"And I won't tell Jake."

They didn't speak for a moment, then Jessie said, "Could you tell — was it a boy or a girl?"

The question hung on the air. Will Harvey cleared his throat. "I don't know," he said.

But Jessie always thought he *did* know.

Jake seemed so tired when he returned from the war. And though Jessie finally found the courage to tell him what had happened to her, he seemed strangely abstracted, as if he were going through the death of Louise all over again.

But it was a different kind of abstraction, she realized. He couldn't really relate the things that had happened to him, he couldn't share the experience with anyone close to him. Doc Harvey, of course, had not gone to war again. The war seemed to have convinced Jake that there were far greater horrors than an unexpected child or one that had been somehow aborted.

Then one day after Jake was home again, and after life had tried to return to some normalcy, Jessie was poking around in an old desk in the cellar, trying to gather some rummage for the local high school. She found a Swedish Bible. It looked well-worn. When Jessie opened the frontispiece, she saw the name, Olie Olson.

She remembered the name — she vaguely remembered Olie. She knew he had died tragically.

She held the Bible to her and wondered: her grandmother refused to talk about the accident, or about Olie. She always got a stricken look on her face when the name came into a conversation.

The ink was blurred, as if a hand had wiped it when it was wet or as if rain — or perhaps tears — had fallen on it.

The Lutz family trials were not to be over. In 1945, just before the end of the war, when the two hydrogen bombs had been dropped on Nakasaki and Hiroshima, the family experienced another tragedy. Violet's son, Willard, Jr., and his wife, Hazel, were killed in a car that had failed to make a sharp turn on a country road, about five miles from Atlas City. They were headed to the cousins' reunion. Their little boy, adopted, Jamie Pratt, was the lone survivor.

"It's a curse," Jessie's Aunt Purdy said when she took her nephew in. "The Lutz family is cursed."

"*Hmmph,*" Old Jessica said.

Jamie
1946...1957

Chapter
Thirty-One

*J*AMIE HAD TWO recollections of the events surrounding the deaths of his parents, Willard and Hazel
Pratt: tire wheels aimlessly spinning on the overturned
car while he stared at them from the roadside, and a
face hanging out of the window at his Aunt Purdy
Pratt's after she had clasped hands with Jamie at his parents'
funeral and took him home, telling him he was going to live with
her. Jamie remembered walking up Purdy's tilting sidewalk, past
the almost unhinged wrought iron gate, past the signs springing up
like demons in the yard, signs saying "Jesus Saves," and, farther
back, a badly weatherbeaten one reading, "Professor Miss Purdy
Pratt, Seer and Teacher. I Cure Boils, Warts, Fevers, Blindness,
Fits, All Manner Disease. Also Deaf and Dumbness. Tea readings.
Seances."

The yard was overflowing with discarded items — even then he
felt he somehow belonged there: iron pots, rusting bathtubs,
wooden windmills spinning, *like the tires*! And a peeling-paint
wooden duck poking its bill straight into the ground, having been
blown over and never uprighted.

But the thing that chilled Jamie the most about the first sight of his Aunt Purdy's ravaged boardinghouse was the glimpse of Old Jessica, shrouded in black, like a witch, in the upstairs window. Even at five, he could sense she regarded him with a kind of horror, as if he were bringing a plague into the house.

As she watched Purdy lead him in, Jamie's gaze locking with hers, Old Jessica suddenly reached out and slammed the window down.

The sound snapped then shuddered through the air, Purdy sensing Jamie trembling, as if the action had set off a corresponding reaction in himself. As Jamie put one foot on the first step leading to the rotting porch, she told him, "Oh, that be your great-grandmother, my Old Aunt Jessica. You pay her no never mind. She doesn't like *any*body!"

Still Jamie paused, looking into the well of darkness that was the porch, past the empty white wicker flower baskets, which stood on the dusty boards, pieces broken out, staring at the sagging porch swing and the crumbling shutters on the ancient narrow windows.

Jamie was ready to go in the screen door with Purdy, the sreen screeching as she pulled it, when he saw there was someone sitting in the old swing — a huge hulk which blotted out the background. Suddenly a voice issued from the dimness. "I talk to trains," it said.

"Oh, hush, old Ned, you'll frighten the child," Purdy scolded then as she dragged Jamie in the door. "You keep your nonsense to yourself."

Though Jamie didn't say anything, it was Ned's voice, low and soothing, confidential, that kept the disparate pieces of Jamie Pratt from being blown apart that day, and it was crazy old Ned alone who brought Jamie a kind of comfort in the aching days that were to follow his advent at the Jesus Saves Boardinghouse.

"I talk to trains," the voice said, and Jamie was certain he did.

"Now you eat your egg, boy, put some fat on those ribs!"

Purdy soon established her routine with young Jamie; breakfast was served in the kitchen, at the white enamel table, precisely at seven o'clock each morning. Attendance was required.

Jamie thought at first that Purdy's kitchen was in the process of being put in: his parents had had a modern stove in Kansas City, and a refrigerator, and he thought no one lived like Purdy did on purpose. No one, he thought, had a wooden chopping block for meat, a white pump in the corner that pumped out only cold "cistern" water, and no one did the dishes in two pans on the kitchen table with water boiled on the stove. He was even more surprised to see that Purdy then took the dishpans and flung the water out the back door, the reason for the spot of dampness next to the porch, where the dirty water sank in.

Purdy cooked on the wood-burning stove, and she cooked with the heat so high that the eggs sizzled and splattered in the hot skillet, always frying too hard.

Now Purdy slammed the plate with the tortured egg on it under Jamie's nose.

"Eat," she ordered.

To Jamie, the egg possessed one giant, malevolent eye — like that of Old Jessica — which stared up at him. He took his fork and punched it in the middle. Take that, he thought, and that and *that*.

But he didn't eat.

Minutes later, after gulping down her own cement-like egg, Purdy looked over at Jamie. "Jamie Pratt," she said, exasperated, "are you letting that egg freeze to death again?"

It was to become a ritual question; years later Purdy was still saying it. Purdy always exaggerated. She never said, "Your egg will get cold." Even in the middle of summer, when it was hotter than hell, Jamie thought — Purdy would have washed out his mouth with soap had he spoken that aloud — when it was impossibly *impossible* to freeze anything, she always said, "You letting that egg freeze to death?"

"No, I'm eating it and it's harder than a rock!" Jamie almost hollered back.

"Now don't you go a-criticizing, young man! Time was people were fighting over eggs like that. I can remember my dear old Daddy saying . . ." she paused, swallowed, some memory of her own causing pain Jamie guessed, ". . . 'waste not, want not.' I've never forgotten that."

It didn't take Jamie long after his arrival at Cousin Purdy's to sense that Purdy, though of kind demeanor, was nailed to the past. She was as much of an antique as the aging things she collected, her mind as flawed as they were with the vicissitudes of time.

"We're cursed, this family, we're cursed," Purdy Pratt often told the wide-eyed Jamie. "God has singled us out — the Pratts and the Lutzes for His most terrible vengeance!"

To Jamie, it seemed horrifying at first; later, as he grew accustomed to the curses and doom-sayings of his aunt, he tried to ignore them, concluding they were assumptions of a demented mind. But there was a part of little Jamie that somehow felt maybe his Aunt Purdy was right: maybe the animosity of Old Jessica was proof of that.

By the time Jamie was eleven, he was eating most of his meals at Jake's and Jessie's; it was a habit whose beginnings were gradual but progressive, and, like Ned, Jake and Jessie gave him feelings of warmth and happiness.

Old Jessica, of course, disapproved. "Molly and Fred have Wilbur there, you know," she told Jamie. "They don't need other young people."

"If the boy wants to go, let him go, Auntie," Purdy put in. "No telling what trouble he'll get into here."

And Old Jessica stomped out, cane lacerating the floor.

"I swear I don't understand my sweet old Auntie!" Purdy countered. "I just don't get that woman at all!"

Jamie went, still feeling the negative vibrations of Old Jessica, as if she were the healer and dispenser of curses around the boardinghouse, as if she had singled him out for a lifelong curse.

But as soon as Jamie was out of the boardinghouse, his attitude changed. Freer, he could enjoy the walk across town to Jake's and Jessie's, could spring upon the whining floorboards of the wooden porch in front of their home and swing through the door as if he were in a different world. In fact, he was. Except for Molly and Fred, who were suspicious like Old Jessica, and weasel-faced Wilbur, the atmosphere was pleasant.

"Come in, come in," Jessie said this day as Jamie walked down the hallway to the living room — no longer called the "parlor" as in Old Jessica's day, and freely used. Jessie gave him a hug and said, "Good to see you."

"Well, Jamie," Jake's deep voice said then. "How're you?"

"Fine, sir," Jamie said, grinning.

He looked at Jake — tall, and very handsome, Jamie thought, the brown hair beginning to gray at the temples but the lean body staying muscled and sleek. Jamie was awed by Jake — would he, with his too-large eyeglasses and weak eyes, his pale brown hair, would he ever grow up to be so impressive? Not likely! But then, he contented himself with the comparison, neither would Wilbur.

"We'll eat and then we'll go for a ride," Jake promised. "Cannibal's waiting."

"Really? I can ride Cannibal?"

"If you think you can, you can." Wilbur's dry, sarcastic voice reached them then.

Reclining across the Victorian sofa was Cousin Wilbur, languidly studying a *Vogue* magazine, pointing out to his mother various clothes she should wear.

"It's amazing how Wilbur knows my tastes," Molly was telling Fred now. Indirectly she included Jake, Jessie, Jamie. "He can pick something out for me that's exactly right."

"A tent," Jake whispered to Jamie and Jamie giggled.

At the sound, Molly turned her calculating, slitted eyes on Jamie. "What *are* you snickering at?"

"Nothing," Jamie said, flushing.

"I should imagine that nothing is what you're usually occupied with."

"You should know," Jake put in hotly. "That's all *you*'re ever worrying about!"

Molly snorted, went over to the sofa and sat beside Wilbur, running her fingers through Wilbur's lank hair while the two of them turned the pages of the magazine and fantasized about turning Molly into a ravishing society matron.

"Hey Dad," Fred called to his father then, tracking after Jake and Jamie and Jessie as they fled to the kitchen, "I'd like to go over some figures for the store with you."

If it was an attempt to smooth things over — as Fred always tried to do, or an attempt to ingratiate himself with his father, which was usual, it failed.

"That's *your* line," Jake said, not even turning to face Fred. "I hate all that stuff."

Fred stopped, watched them retreating.

"As soon as dinner is over, we'll go," Jake went on. "I'll shorten the stirrups on Jessie's saddle for you because she can use Fred's — he never does."

Jamie was so excited at the prospect of being allowed to ride the high-spirited Cannibal, the Sunday roast dinner Jessie had prepared held little interest for him. Like her grandmother, Jessie could do many things with ease — work the ranch, cook, even sew and knit when she found time. Unlike Old Jessica, however, Jessie was calm of temperament, seldom became enraged like her grandmother; when Jessie *did* get angry, though, she was formidable.

"When Jessie's mad," Jake once told Jamie with admiration, "she hits her target. I've felt it at times!" And he laughed. "When my *mother* gets angry, she just loads the shotgun and shoots in all directions!"

Again the laugh.

Jamie, at the mention of Jessica, was uncomfortable.

When they rode out of the barn that day, Jamie leaned over the saddle and patted Cannibal's strong, black neck. A purebred quarter horse, Cannibal had the strong haunches of the breed, the stamina, the ability to turn quickly and shortly. He was a perfect work horse, instinctively knowing when the cattle would turn so that he could head them off, able to work a herd with the smoothness of the professional. In fact, Cannibal *was* a professional; Jake and he had won many trophies at rodeos around Kansas and the neighboring states. He just had to be the best horse in the world, Jamie thought.

Jake had said he was going to have a colt by Cannibal and give it to Jamie. Then he would geld him, to make him more dependable.

The day was warm — May — and the wheat in the Lutz fields was tall and green, waving like water when the wind caressed it. Jamie glanced back at the corn in the bottom land near the river, as they ascended the steep bank up to the scaly hills with their long bluestem.

"Race you," Jake called to Jamie.

Off they went, Jamie afraid at first because of the power with which Cannibal set off; ears back, he would let no horse pass him. Jake, on Jessie's sorrel, could only come up to Cannibal's rear legs before the horse would put his ears even farther back and gallop still faster — which was how Cannibal had earned him his name. Jessie had christened him thus because he seemed to *eat* the competition.

"I swear that horse would burst his heart before he'd quit," Jamie marveled after he had won the race and Cannibal stood panting, sweat pouring down his legs. "He's something, this horse is."

"You'll have a colt," Jake promised again.

Three months later, however, before Jake could breed him, Cannibal broke his leg.

Jake was riding him across the backs of the hills when a coyote broke out from behind a bush. Cannibal shied, stepping into a prairie dog hole. Jake was thrown off — breaking *his* leg too, because Cannibal had rolled over on it. The two lay in the pasture for hours until Jamie, searching and calling, found them. Cannibal raised his head to Jamie as though he knew, understood, what was coming.

"Get my rifle," Jake had told him.

Cannibal was buried near where he had fallen, a softer area of ground that had allowed the ranch hands to dig a deep grave. Jamie remembered looking up into Jake's moist eyes when they had put the last shovelful of dirt over Cannibal. Jamie was crying too; it seemed he could still hear the echo of the shot in the canyons near the hills, resounding as though it would go on forever.

Afterward, Jake lay in his upstairs bedroom for weeks; Jamie sometimes kept him company, even staying overnight there, though Ned missed him then and begged him to stay home at Purdy's.

"Will Harvey put me in this damn thing," Jake complained regularly to Jamie, "and now he won't let me out!"

The cast covered him from ankle to thigh, his broken leg lying on the bed like a marble pillar. Jamie knew that Jake hated the way it slowed him down.

"I may take a hammer to it myself," Jake told him. "I want to get out of here!"

"Don't do that, Jake . . . sir," Jamie said.

Sometimes Jamie read to Jake, books from Jake's attic. They read Montaigne's *Essays*, though Jamie couldn't follow a lot of it, couldn't even pronounce some of the words. But he swore to himself that he would read them when he was older and could understand them. He read Shakespeare's plays.

"I just wish he'd written plain English," Jamie confessed to Jake one day while struggling with *King Lear*.

"But that's the point, Jamie," Jake said, laughing. "It's part of the whole thing. You'll understand when you're older. You're still a youngster."

"I am not!" Jamie burst out uncharacteristically. "I'm almost twelve!"

"My, my."

Jake leaned up to appraise him then.

Jamie knew what he was thinking: it was true Jamie was helping with the haying and feeding the cattle, that he was already much better than

Fred, for Fred was still hopelessly ineffective when it came to livestock. But, to Jake, Jamie knew, he seemed young.

"So read me something *you* like," Jake finally said.

Jamie didn't want to read him the comic books from the drugstore, or the books he got at the school library, so he said, "I'd rather you'd tell me about the war. What you did."

Jake frowned, the corners of his mouth drooping. This was to be his look the rest of his life whenever anyone mentioned the war, or Cannibal, or Louise.

"I can't really tell you about that," Jake said, turning his face away.

"But Jess saved some of my letters," Jake said then, his voice softer, as if he knew he had suddenly shut Jamie out. "They're in the bureau. Help yourself — they may give you an idea of the times." And he waved an arm toward the cherry dresser.

Jamie pulled open the top drawer, took out a bundle of letters, held together with a rubber band.

"These?" he asked.

Jake nodded.

Jamie thrust them in his shirt pocket.

"Thank you, sir," he said. "Thanks a lot."

Jamie cleared his throat, adjusted his glasses on his nose. "Well then, sir," Jamie said, "I think I'd better go. Ned will want me to go with him to see the train."

Jake was silent for a moment, his eyes falling back on Jamie. "You still thinking about leaving town on that train some day?"

"How did you know that?" Jamie blurted.

"I see the signs," Jake said, rather solemnly. "Young people always want to go someplace else — the grass is greener. Once I even thought for awhile about leaving the Lutz Store and all."

"Really?"

Jamie found it hard to believe.

"Louise, my wife — " the words came out of Jake with great effort, "Louise once wanted me to leave the store and farm. Maybe if I had. . . Of course, I left the store eventually, but not before she died."

Now Jake's eyes searched the ceiling and Jamie had the feeling Jake had forgotten he was there.

"Maybe it would have been better," Jake said at last. "I don't know. One never knows."

"No," Jamie said.

He didn't understand what Jake was trying to say. He knew about Louise, but he didn't know what Jake meant when he said he might have left the ranch. He couldn't see Jake anywhere else.

"Well," Jake said then, dismissing him, "you run along. You see your train and enjoy it. Just don't get on it — not yet! I'd miss you too much."

He smiled at Jamie, Jamie basking in the warmth.

As Jamie went down the stairs and out the door, he told himself: *Old Jess may not like me, but Jake and Jessie do!*

It was a lifesaving thought.

After Jamie and Ned returned from the train station, Jamie went up to his room, shut the door, extracted the packet of letters from his shirt pocket and began to read.

The first one, to Jessie, was dated March 12, 1943.

"*Dear Jess,*

"*We're settled for awhile now and all cleaned up after our voyage. Our trip wasn't so enjoyable but everyone endured it and it was uneventful.*

"*We'll be assigned soon — or I will — to my work and I will no doubt be moved again. I can say that our food here is unexpectedly good, a lot better than anticipated and now I'm glad that I happened to be sent here.*

"*I don't think it would be telling a military secret that we're somewhere in England. The countryside is really wonderful in its ways and most typical. It is interesting to talk to the English people although you do have to be careful what you say. The people are kinda touchy.*

"*You can really appreciate being an American and having luxuries they never dream of.*

"*I imagine things are about the same at home. I suppose it will be hard to get pumps for the oil wells now. I saw a lot of that equipment on railroad cars when I was enroute to the east coast. Maybe Fred can manage.*

"*Well, I'm going to turn in now. I hope things are going well at home. I hope Mother is all right, Ilse, everyone.*

"*Will write again soon.*

"*Love, Dad.*"

Jamie held the letter on his lap for a moment; he wondered exactly who Ilse was. No one had mentioned her before except for old Purdy, who told Jamie she had taken care of Fred and Jessie when their mother died.

"And did my dear old Aunt Jessica detest Ilse!" Purdy had told him.

This interested Jamie: if there were anyone Old Jess disliked, it seemed to form a bond with him.

Jamie opened another letter and began to read again.

It was dated September 16, 1944, when Jake was still in England. But there was something interesting about the letter: something Jake had said had caused the censor to neatly clip out several sentences. He wondered if Jake would remember what they were.

"*Dear Mother and all,*" the letter began. "*Thanks for the money order! I never thought I'd be getting money from my kids, but I appreciate it! Don't know exactly where I will go on my leave, but I will get as much out of the money you sent as possible. I'll also take lots of pictures!*

"*A hundred dollars is equivalent to 25 pounds, but at the extremely high prices over here, one spends a pound like it was a dollar bill. Girls over here would love to have this money, as they pay anywhere from $2.00 to $4.00 for cheap cosmetics. And luxury tax is 100% over here. They never get oranges and American cigarettes and gum seems to overjoy these English people. Kids always spot the "Yanks" in a crowd and come up with the rather irritating phrase, 'Any gum, chum?' You've probably heard that already.*

"*Tonight we set our clocks back so we'll get an extra hour of sack time. I wish I could fill you in on everything, but of course I can't.*

"*The war now is likely to end at anytime and that of course suits me all right. We've all worked hard and steady, so maybe a little boat ride or flight would rest us up.*

"*I suppose I may get to see the Mediterranean, Suez and the Red Sea, that is, everything on the way to the South Pacific. But that won't last long either if Patton's men get on Tojo's back!*

"*Well, all of you, thanks a million. Wish I could spend my leave with you in Chicago, or even make it back to Atlas City, but that will have to wait.*

"*Write often. Love, Jake.*"

It took Jamie a moment to come back to reality. Reading through the letters made him think of Jake in a very different way. He seemed much younger, and certainly vulnerable. He wondered how it would feel to be in a situation where your life could be ended.

Jake was a hero, all right, Jamie thought. He had learned from Jessie that Jake had worked primarily as a decoder, mostly in London, though he had moved about and spent some time in Gibraltar.

Someday he would go back to every place Jake had been, Jamie thought. He would retrace every step he took in that war!

Chapter
Thirty-Two

*P*URDY HAD LOVED the Jesus Saves Boarding-house long before she had inherited it from her aunt — her father's sister Purdy Pratt. She had loved the chaos of the place, and after acquiring it, had added her own peculiar possessions to its confines. She knew that Jamie thought she was eccentric — and perhaps she was — but her old things made her feel safe in what she deemed to be a very unpredictable world.

Her father had killed himself, after all.

Purdy had wrapped herself in the people who stayed with her; they needed her, she needed them. Except for Old Jessica of course. Purdy laughed. She had inherited Old Jessica too!

Purdy was moving about the kitchen in her slow, rocking walk. She liked to touch her little water pump, her faithful stove, her countertops. It all reassured her that at least *this* had not changed.

Nellie Nameless was taking a nap upstairs, her snores coming in waves. Ned was wandering about overhead, no doubt waiting for Jamie to come so they could go see the train. Lars was probably looking out the window, searching the area for his "cattle."

"That boy should go," Purdy heard someone say then.

Startled, she turned around to see that Old Jessica had crept up on her.

"Well I swan," Purdy said.

"May I sit down?" Old Jessica asked.

Typically, she had already seated herself at the kitchen table. Purdy sat down too, looking over at her aunt, thinking that Jessica, in her customary black, looked like a figure in a reverse negative against the white of the kitchen. Or perhaps she looked more like a "spirit guide," as her old Aunt Purdy used to call her mentors.

Purdy had told Jamie that Old Jessica seldom "favored" her with a visit, and that when she did, it was almost certain that she was up to something. "My mother warned me about Old Jessica," Purdy confessed to Jamie. "She warned me about *her* years ago."

Old Jessica seemed to straighten her spine and pull in her chin even tighter than usual. "Do you think this is the proper place for young Jamie to be?" she dropped the question like a rock hitting water.

"I don't know what you mean," Purdy answered.

Purdy got up, lurched aimlessly about the kitchen, pushing the handle on the little white pump, sweeping invisible crumbs off the white enamel table. It was her way of putting people off; though Purdy was quite sure she was more than a match for her Aunt Jessica.

"Well," Jessica said, leaning forward then as if to pin Purdy in one place, "what I mean is, I don't think this is any place to raise a child."

"Well, for goodness sakes, why not?" Purdy shot back.

She placed both hands on her hips, as she did when was taking a "stance." No one was going to bully *her*: she could be as hot under the collar as anyone!

"I provide food and shelter and enough loving for any child!" Purdy went on. "Something *you* might not know so much about!"

So there! she thought. *Take that.*

Old Jessica reared back in the chair. Purdy was certain she would attack again, but apparently Old Jess had decided she would take a different angle. "What I meant," she said smoothly, running a finger over the surface of the table, then lifting the finger up as if she had felt dust, "is that the other people in this boardinghouse — Nellie, Lars, Ned — can you regard them as fit company for a growing boy? An im*press*ionable young man?"

As if to reinforce what Old Jessica had said, Nellie Nameless let out a prolonged snore and Ned began to stomp his feet overhead. He was impatient for Jamie to come to his room.

"Well!" Purdy said. "They's part of the world. I don't see why they can't be fit company."

"Purdy," Jessica said, in the voice that Purdy knew meant she definitely had something in mind, "I just thought that another home — a place away from us Lutzes and Pratts — might be better. Here Jamie is always going to have to compare himself with little Wilbur, and we must be realistic — Wilbur is the legal heir to the Lutz estate. . . ."

"Jessica Lutz! I don't see what that has to do with anything! Far as I know, no one's ever brought up inheriting anything, and you know as well as I do that Jake Lutz is as healthy as they come. He might even remarry!"

"God forbid!" Jessica exploded.

"Well, he's a healthy man," Purdy insisted, "and not old. Jake and I, you know, are contemporaries."

"Yes," Jessica said drily, "I'm aware of that." She cleared her throat. "If Jamie were only old enough to serve in the Army," Old Jessica went on now, "he might have gone to Korea. At any rate, he could have a chance to develop on his own. That would have solved things."

"For who?" Purdy shouted. "You?"

When her aunt didn't answer, Purdy said, "Yes, Jake might remarry. He's just in his fifties — though edging up — has a good setup. It must get lonesome."

"He has Jessie."

"Oh, Aunt Jessica! Now a daughter can't be a wife, can she? You know men. They like . . ."

"Never mind," Jessica cut in, and Purdy saw her shove her chair back from the table, heard her cane suddenly pound the floor, as though she had stabbed the wood in place of Purdy. "I don't want to hear the gory details."

Purdy laughed as she listened to Old Jess stomp up the stairs to her room; she slipped into the hallway and stared at her Aunt Jessica's back as she made her way up.

It had never been a secret, she thought now, that Old Jessica did not care for Jamie, but she was beginning to think she knew why: he stood in the way of her dear Wilbur. Jake thought the world of Jamie. And Old Jessica would do anything to see that her great-grandson came out ahead of Jamie.

"... But not if I have anything to do with it," Purdy vowed. "Jamie has had enough pain in his life."

Purdy began to spy on Old Jessica. It seemed necessary somehow to try to determine what she was up to. It was also rather fun for Purdy who imagined she could be a spy — just like the ones in World War II. She could be a *decoder*, as Jake had been.

One day, peering again through the slit in the door, she saw Old Jess writing a letter. She seemed to sign her name, then thrust the letter into a little box on her dresser, not bothering to address an envelope.

Purdy knew the box had been there for a long time; Jessica had brought it with her when she fled the family homestead.

When Old Jess went down for her lunch that day, Purdy crept upstairs and into Jessica's room. Old Jessica seemed pleased Purdy would not be "watching her digest," as she used to put it.

Purdy half expected her aunt to have hidden herself behind the door, to feel her cane strike her across the back. She was *so sly*, Purdy wouldn't put anything past her!

But the room was empty.

Purdy looked around at the furnishings, Victorian things Old Jess had taken from Jake's house when she left. They seemed to give her room the air of museum. Of course, Purdy thought, she herself loved museums, old things . . . but these bore the aura of someone else — Purdy believed all things had a spirit and an aura. Her aunt's possessions therefore were — if not openly hostile to her — at least unfriendly. She had better be careful!

The dresser was walnut, with a pink marble top and brass drawer pulls. On top were her many perfume bottles and, to one side, the little box Purdy'd seen her put the letter in.

Looking around again to be sure she was alone, Purdy reached for the box, saw that it was labeled "History of Chinese Agriculture." *What?*

Inside, neatly stacked, were dozens of letters. Pulling a bunch out, Purdy saw they were all addressed to Jessica's old roommate, Elsie McDonald. The dates were very old, some dating back to the '20s and '30s.

Purdy remembered Elsie from her childhood; at one of the cousins' reunions, Purdy remembered her mother had gotten sick from posing for Elsie McDonald under a mulberry tree. And then Elsie never returned to Atlas City, whether it was because of that or not, Purdy didn't know.

Looking at the letters, almost feeling a tingling sensation arising from the ink, Purdy put them all back except the one her aunt just finished writing, dated that very day.

"*Dear Elsie,*" she read.

She ran her fingers over the letter, smoothing it out, feeling the indentations of the pen on the back of the paper.

"*You know what a cross I have to bear living here with Purdy, and you know why I'm so anxious to get rid of Jamie Pratt.*"

Well! Purdy thought. Some gratitude! And Jamie? What in the world was her problem with *him*?

Purdy held the letter at her side, clutching it tightly as though it were a grenade with the pin pulled out; she walked to the door and listened to be certain her old auntie was not climbing back up the stairs. She wouldn't want to be caught snooping in Old Jessica's room!

But all was quiet in the kitchen. Evidently Old Jess was enjoying her lunch for once.

Turning back to the letter, she began again.

"*I have a feeling Jake is getting rather too fond of Jamie, and he treats Wilbur like a leper! I know he was never very close to Fred, but Wilbur is his grandson, after all.*

"*Having someone 'alien' in the house makes me understand, a bit, you know, what Hitler was after in his campaign, though I have no sympathy for that horrendous idea — all that 'final solution' nonsense. But with crazy old Ned in the house, you begin to wonder if he was all wrong about sterilizing mental 'defectives.' I'd hate to think of more Neds in the world. And like does seem to perpetuate like. Somehow the breeding of the human race could stand improvement. Ministers like to tell you that there has always been evil, and that it is the will of God. Some even tell you that Satan got his power from God! But then, doesn't that make God responsible for evil? I can't get it organized in my mind so I usually just shut it away and say, 'Yes, I believe, but I don't know why.'*"

Purdy paused, looked up. She knew Old Jessica didn't like Ned — she didn't like *anyone* in the boardinghouse. But Ned had been, still was, a good friend. It didn't matter that he didn't act smart, he was loving and good.

Turning back to the letter, Purdy read: *"Of course Purdy finally gave up all that catechism and rosary bit."*

Oh really! Purdy thought.

"But it hasn't changed her much — she's so superstitious! Always talking about our family being 'cursed,' though I must say, looking at her and that intruder, Jamie, that I wonder. But there's no way to get ahead in this world, always crying about the past. Purdy seems to be set in it, like cement.

"What about this cold war? I just <u>knew</u> the Russians would turn against us — they're Orientals, aren't they? Or Slavs? Devious stock, at any rate. Why did we allow them to get into Berlin? I blame Eisenhower for this — I <u>don't</u> like Ike — and of course sick Roosevelt and 'Pendergast' Truman, who is also on my list for discharging MacArthur. I don't know why we don't just drop a bomb on them all before it's too late. Though of course, perhaps it is al<u>ready</u> too late, thanks to the Rosenbergs and Greenglass. I hope they execute them! To think they would betray our country and its nuclear secrets. That's gratitude for all America has done for them!

"Elsie, I don't know what has happened to us here in this country. We send money, machines, troops and tanks, experts in all fields to help the very countries we defeated! You mark my words, we'll end up paying through the nose for this. Germany and Japan will rise on our very backs, to say nothing of our 'ally' Russia. Well, I never trusted those foreigners anyway. What do they know but to drink Vodka and sing the Volga Boat Song? I wish someone would give them the old 'heave-ho!'"

Again Purdy put down the letter. She could hear sounds in the kitchen and no one on the stairs, so evidently Old Jessica was still there. No doubt she was making herself a cup of tea, for she declared Purdy's coffee to be "lethal." Purdy turned back to the letter, her hands beginning to shake for the next words were again about Jamie, her ward.

"Here at Purdy's, there are crises enough it seems. I tried to get Purdy to listen to reason today about Jamie, and get him out of here before there's real trouble in the family. I can sense it's coming, and it's tied to that boy. Yet I can't get Jake or Jessie to do anything about it — they <u>adore</u> the boy — possibly because I <u>don't</u> . . . "

Purdy took in a deep breath. She let it out slowly. What had Jamie ever done to Old Jess to make her dislike him so?

"Molly and Fred are such nincompoops when it comes to doing anything effectual. Molly lies around looking at magazines, tethered to the

sofa like a giant hydrogen balloon at anchor. I just wish someone would slip the rope and Molly would float up and out of our lives!

"Fred works like a demon at the store and then comes back to the old homestead to do the books. If I didn't call him every day, I wouldn't hear anything from him! He doesn't come to see me often any more, though Jake does. Oh, I wish I could think of some way to get back in that house and settle things! Believe me, I would soon have everything in working order there and the first thing I'd do would be to plant Jamie and that moron Ned on the first train going out of here."

Purdy drew herself up, put her hands on her hips, crumpling the letter in her hand. Quickly she straightened it out. She knew Old Jessica was not Jamie's friend, but she really hadn't thought she was such a determined enemy! Purdy began to tremble with anger as she went on reading, *"Thank God Jessie didn't leave any kinfolk dangling around — God took care of that mess handily."*

Purdy found herself puzzled: something must have happened — and not too long ago. Something had happened to Jessie. . . . Maybe her Aunt Purdy's spirit guide was right; Purdy knew that her aunt had once stated they all had trouble before them, that she had heard that from her Daniel. Maybe they all *were* cursed.

"Well, Elsie, I'd better quit for now. I can hear Purdy banging around in the kitchen so I suppose she'll soon be calling me for lunch. We'll have some poisonous garbage she calls food as she likes to use pink and green food coloring for everything. Pink noodles are not my idea of gourmet food!

"But I must put on my black dress and go down, as I try to instill some manners and sense of decency in the lunatics who congregate below. It seems to be a hopeless struggle.

"Take care and I'll write again soon. Love, Jessica."

Thrusting the letter back in the box as if it were a snake being forced back into its hole, Purdy turned to leave the room.

She would never reveal to Old Jessica that she had discovered the letters; when Purdy seals her lips, she vowed, no one can pry them apart.

But she would warn Jamie to be careful: "You need to watch yourself, boy," she told him later.

She saw Jamie shudder.

Chapter
Thirty-Three

LARS HAD DIED — the very day after Purdy had told Jamie about Old Jess and how he needed to watch himself. Lars had gotten away from Purdy the night before and though Jamie and Ned and Purdy had searched through the fields for him, calling, "Lars, Lars!" until the sound doubled back on them and was lost in the dark, they couldn't find him. At last they came upon him, near the county bridge, his body washing up against the shore, face downward in the water. "He was looking for them blasted cattle!" Purdy said. "He musta fell in."

Jamie couldn't forget the way Lars' face was smiling when they turned the body over to remove it from the water; it was as if, at last, his search was complete. Jamie turned on his heel and ran back to Purdy's alone.

It seemed to Jamie as if the summer were a great weight pressing on him; there was Old Jessica and her "witchhunt" — and now there was the loss of Lars, who, if not a close friend, like Ned, at least shared the boardinghouse as a home and whom Jamie had always liked. And there was the rather hollow feeling that came over him at times when he wondered who he was and where he had come from. Why didn't his birth parents want him?

Images clustered in his mind, shaking against each other. Sometimes he thought his parents must have been very good, but poor, and so they let him be adopted by Willard and Hazel. At other times, mostly when Old Jessica had been ranting about him, he wondered if he had come from someone like Ned and Nellie Nameless, someone whom the authorities would not let keep a child.

And now Ned had gone off again . . . probably roused by Lars' death. This very morning he had been swinging up in the trees in Purdy's back-yard.

"Ned Antrim!" Purdy shouted. "You come down outta that tree, ya hear?"

His body blocking the sun, Ned swung from branch to branch in the old tree, his huge shape amazingly agile, his feet propelling him as he swung them backward and forward.

Purdy's hands were grinding together. "Ned, you fool! Get down outta there 'fore you crack your skull!"

But Ned only looked at her, grinned and said, "Circus, circus!" and swung again. From his position, Ned could see the blue mantle of sky, Jamie knew, and the fiery eye within it. He could see out across the high-way, could see down into the ravine that plunged beside Purdy's home and where, last night, they had searched for Lars.

Jamie didn't like the memory of finding Lars: he had to push it out, even though Lars had seemed happy. But Ned, Jamie knew, was very upset that Lars had died and this was the way he had to express it.

"Circus, circus!" he panted.

"I declare!" Purdy shook her head. "I'm gonna tell Jamie to get you down outta there!"

And she stomped into the house, banging the door shut.

Ned laughed suddenly, tossing his head back so that the sun struck his eyes and he had to close them; squinting, he tightened his grip on the tree branch. Jamie could tell, watching him out the window, that he felt good, that it was great to swing free. Ned's muscles, so little used now, seemed to stretch and grow resilient as Jamie watched him paw his way from branch to branch, his mind no doubt whirling with the images of his trapeze act in the circus.

His body cut through the air, defying gravity, liberated from the usual, Jamie thought. Ned had an ecstatic glow on his face, his smile wide, the pull on his arms apparently feeling wonderful. "Circus, circus!" he called again. "See the greatest aerialist in the world!"

"Ned? Hey, Ned!"

Ned stopped his swing, hung for a moment, his eyes trying to focus.

"It's me. Jamie! I'm in my room and I'm coming down. Purdy says you have to come down."

Jamie ran out of the room, down the stairs, out the back door, letting it bang behind him.

"Ned!" he said. "Come down!"

"Hee, hee!" Ned laughed, and, for answer, swung to still another branch, the limb crackling in protest, the sound disturbing a squirrel sitting near so that it chattered in fright and sped to the ground.

"It's the train, Ned. We gotta go see the train."

"Huh?"

Ned hung suspended again, his eyes slowly seeking the ground and the origin of the insistent voice that apparently he knew was asking something of him.

"The train," Jamie repeated.

Jamie could see Ned pause in thought. Suddenly he released his grip and fell to the ground, rolling over and then up on his feet, landing without harm directly before Jamie. He bowed.

Jamie clapped, winking: Ned had helped *him* forget too.

"Hey, Ned," Jamie said. "That was great!"

"The greatest aerialist . . . in . . . the . . . world!" The words came out slowly, as though Ned were trying to remember them. He pointed to his chest and grinned. "Me!"

"Yeah, hey, you were great." Jamie took his arm and pulled him over to sit on the stoop, the loose overall strap brushing against him for a moment. "Now, lookit, you're sweating. Better rest a minute."

Ned put a hand to his forehead, felt the great drops of perspiration there, reached in his pocket and pulled out a soiled white handkerchief, which he then brushed across his face. "Train, Jamie?"

"Yeah, soon. Not just yet. Maybe it won't come today."

Ned was silent a moment, then Jamie felt Ned's hand close around his arm slightly, Ned's face frowning into his. "You kid me, Jamie? Train will come?"

"Hey, cut it out!" Jamie said, trying to push Ned's hand away. "That hurts."

But Ned wouldn't let go. Jamie's arm was beginning to ache. "Train will come, Jamie?"

"Sure, sure. Now what the heck — lemme go!"

Abruptly Ned dropped his arm and Jamie put his hand up to massage the spot where Ned had clasped him. Examining, he saw the beginnings of a bruise, the flesh reddened.

"I was gonna try to teach you something today," Jamie told Ned, "but now I don't know."

"Teach me?"

"Yeah. You oughta know something besides trains and circuses."

"Trains and circuses."

"Oh, for cripes sake!" Jamie said, pushing a toe at the packed dirt of the backyard. "Quit mimicking me."

Ned was silent.

They sat there a moment, then Jamie cleared his throat, drawing his foot back in and propping his elbows on his knees, his chin in his hands. He squinted through his glasses.

"Okay," he said. "Now, do you know what that is?"

He pointed to the sun and Ned looked up, blinked, turned back to Jamie. "Sky?"

"No — the *hot* thing."

"Sun?"

"Right." He paused. "Now if you're gonna be in this world, you gotta learn a few things about how things are. What do you know about that sun?"

"Huh?"

Ned's brow was furrowed and he looked intently at Jamie: he seemed to be asking *what did Jamie want*?

"Huh?"

"Well, does it shine all the time, for instance?"

"Shine all the time." Ned ran a hand across his forehead, then let it rest on the back of his neck. "It —" he brightened, looked at Jamie, "it goes down!"

"Sure! Right!" Jamie reached over and patted Ned on the back. Ned straightened up and smiled.

"*It goes down!*" he said in his sing-song voice, proud. "Down, down!"

"Okay," Jamie drawled. "Don't make a big thing of it. It goes down. Now —" and he looked at Ned, whose face had become cautious again, "does the sun stay in one spot in the sky or does it move?"

Ned looked up at the sun, paused. "Not — moving."

"No, no," Jamie moistened his lips, pulled the chin back in his hands. "You can't see it moving now, but is it in the same place in the evening as it is in the morning?"

Ned waited a long moment, looking first at the sun, then at Jamie. He pointed up at the sun and said: "The sun, Jamie."

"Yeah. Now answer my question."

"The same place . . ." and Ned's face was a mask of bewilderment, brows raised, while he moved his hands from the place where he had seen the sun come up that morning to where he knew it would go down. Suddenly he saw. "It moves, Jamie! It moves!"

"Okay. Oh, boy!" Jamie shook his head. "This is gonna be harder than I thought!"

"I knew that, Jamie. I knew it."

"Yeah —" Jamie saw the hurt look on Ned's face, smiled at him. "You sure did. You knew that good. Okay." He paused, found a stick beside the steps and idly began drawing lines in the earth. A wandering bug found the indentation of one line, began following it, then hurried off on some unfathomable errand of its own.

"The sun is round," Jamie said.

"Huh?"

"Like an orange. An orange is round. See? I'll draw one." And he made a circle on the ground. "The earth is also round. Here —" and he began another circle, "here you have the earth. Now, here's the thing —" he looked up to see Ned watching him intently, studying him as if he were afraid he would miss a word, his body leaning toward Jamie and his mouth slightly open. "The earth goes around the sun. It also turns on its axis."

Ned's face went blank.

"Well, I mean," Jamie took up the stick again, "it's like the earth — here — was on a stick. And it turns on that stick. And it goes around the sun. That's what makes our days and nights and our year."

Ned was looking steadily at Jamie, as though he expected him to say something else, something that would make it clear. "The sun moves," he said.

"Oh, cripes!" Jamie exploded. "Yeah, it seems to move."

"You said it moved."

"Well, yeah —" Jamie scratched his head, "yeah, I guess I did. What I meant was — the earth turns around on its axis and that's what makes the sun *seem* to move and what makes day and night."

"You said it moved."

"Well it just *looks* like it. All the time the sun comes up and is going across the sky, the earth, this ground —" and Jamie impatiently stamped one bare foot on the ground, "all the time *we're* moving."

Ned put his head in his hands. "No," he said. "You said it moved."

"Christ!"

They were both quiet a moment, Ned not looking up, letting out a vast sigh.

Jamie took the stick he'd been working with and poked at the lines he'd drawn, crossing them out. He was about to take the stick and absently press the end of it down on a beetle making its way in the dirt when Ned said softly: "Don't hurt him, Jamie."

"Hurt what?"

Without speaking, Ned took the stick and threw it away, then reached down and scooped up the beetle, who proceeded to walk across the hills and valleys of Ned's huge palm just as though he were still on the ground.

"They don't hurt you," he went on.

Jamie remembered someone else saying that to him, a long time ago, a memory that caused a twinge of pain, because it had all been so different then, and yet — Jamie looked over at Ned, sitting with the overall strap hanging down beside him, his hands gently moving the beetle back into his palm when it started over the ridge of his cupped hand — the feeling was exactly like the one he had now. Here — in Atlas City — with Ned Antrim. Jamie looked with wonderment at the thick white hair and the furrowed face, the huge body swelling the overalls, the heavy feet thrust into the hard crusts of the shoes.

Ned had a smile on his face, just as Jamie's father had in that long-ago time. Jamie remembered it had been a kitten that he was unwittingly tormenting.

"Don't hurt him, Jamie." Willard showed Jamie how to softly stroke the kitten, how to hold him gently so that he wouldn't crush him. "Don't hurt him."

Something Jamie didn't quite understand began to unravel itself within him: something of the bewilderment of Ned at a much simpler thing, something that he could not take apart and really examine, nor draw on the ground to see. A feeling . . . maybe a connection . . . as though he were somehow part of an unfathomable whole, a something that had its roots in Atlas City. It seemed strange to Jamie for a split moment that he could ever have envied those sterile people on the train.

Jamie sat at the dining table in the same room where Old Jessica had once prepared her extravagant meals. In fact, Old Jess's silver tea service still sat on the buffet, reflected in the giant mirror above it; Old Jessica had left in such haste that she had forgotten many things. But she had never used the tea service; she just liked to polish it for show.

And now Jessie served the meals, the largest always at noontime, as there was so much work to be done on the ranch that they needed a big dinner. Sometimes, just as in Old Jessica's day, hired hands shared the meal. But with the harvest over, it was mostly only Jake and Jamie, and Molly, Fred, and Wilbur.

Molly, like Violet, didn't help much with the cooking — except when she took a notion to "surprise" everyone with one of her gourmet disasters. Jake exploded one day when she produced a chicken salad, set in gelatin, with some homemade rolls that resembled granite. He threw his napkin down and stomped out. "I'll go to the damn cafe where I can eat a meal, not an appetizer!"

But Molly never learned; and when she did prepare a dinner, it was always time for Jake — and Jamie — to leave.

This day, Jessie served meat loaf, mashed potatoes, fresh green peas from her garden, and announced she had apple pie and ice cream for dessert. There was a stack of fresh, homemade bread, with crabapple jelly, made last fall from the crabapple trees in the front yard, and butter. Sometimes Jamie took his apple pie with cream from a neighbor's Jersey cows; rich and thick, yellowish, this cream was more like already-whipped cream. He particularly liked Jessie's gooseberry pie, which Molly declared turned her "sour all over." With Jersey cream on it, Jamie thought, it was a dish that couldn't be equaled. The gooseberries were hand-picked on the ranch, down near the stream beside the bluff, where gooseberries and blueberries flourished. In spring, succulent watercress sprang up there so thick it looked like a carpet.

"We have everything we need right on this ranch," Jake was saying then to Jamie. Jamie knew that Jake seldom directed his conversation to Fred or Molly, and never to Wilbur. "If hard times come again as they did in the thirties, we'll make out."

"You did all right in the thirties," Wilbur pointed out. "Buying that land and all at Depression prices."

Jake went on as if Wilbur hadn't spoken. "I just wish we weren't giving away everything we've got in this country. Maybe Eisenhower will change things."

"Don't bet on it," Molly interjected then, her mouth full of mashed potatoes. "Speaking of giving things away, I must say I sympathize with Old Jessica when she tells Fred how much she hopes the Rosenbergs will be executed."

"I'm not so sure," Jake said. "It was a bad thing, that's for sure, letting the Russians get our secrets, but I'm not certain that the death penalty is the thing."

Wilbur, *his* mouth also full of food, mumbled "Why not?"

Again Jake ignored him. "And this witch-hunting of Senator McCarthy's! Seems to me he's just taking a roulette wheel and spinning it, then accusing whoever's name the ball lands on."

"You know there're columnists all over Washington," Molly continued, "just waiting to steal our secrets."

"*Col*umnists?" Jessie asked incredulously.

"Sure — from Russia. Columnist Party agents."

Jake roared; Jamie turned to look at him. "You mean *Comm*unists, Molly. *Col*umnists!"

Molly flushed. "A slip of the tongue," she declared, though of course it wasn't. She was always mispronouncing words — she would "wrench" the shampoo out of her hair, the Filipinos were "Fili*pop*inos."

"An error," Molly went on now. "It was a simple error, that's all."

"But what's left to steal, anyway?" Jessie asked then.

"There's a hell of a lot left," Fred said. "There's our technology for one. Those backward Russians would give their eyeteeth to know how we can produce so much here. Do you think they've improved their wheat strains as we have? Or have the harvesters we do?"

"That's right," Molly said. "We can feed the world, and it looks like we're goin' to. Free!"

"If I handled everything at the store like our government did after the war — destroying equipment, giving it away — to say nothing now of supplying the troops in Korea . . . why I'd end up broke!" Fred added.

"*We'd* end up broke," Jessie corrected him. "We're still in the store you know. Our capital is there."

"Well . . . yes," Molly said, reluctantly.

"A hell of a lot of capital!" Jake stormed. "You and Fred spend so damn much on your foolish clothes and magazines and Jessie and I work our tails off here and . . ." He was so agitated he couldn't continue.

Jessie leaned over and pressed his hand. "Take it easy, Poppa," she said. "Fred knows."

Fred, always willing to be martyred, looked at his fork, as if deciding where in his body to plunge it.

"Dad works hard at the store," Wilbur put in.

Molly nodded vigorously, hammering away at the assertion.

"And *we* work hard here at the ranch," Jessie said then, abruptly angry herself. "Just try lifting bales of hay and carrying feed sacks if you think we don't!"

"Now, now," Fred said then, putting down the fork and seeming to assume, once again, the role of pacifier.

Jamie felt as though he was watching a ping-pong game in the junior high school gym.

"Let's don't argue about it," Fred said finally. "We all work hard."

"Damn right we do!" Jake shouted.

"Poppa," Jessie said.

"If we weren't having apple pie," Jake said then, looking steadily at Molly, "I'd get up right now. The company here bothers me."

Jamie went on silently eating his food; the quarrels weren't unusual and he'd learned that Jake's temper — like Old Jessica's — was uncertain and flared easily. Unlike Old Jessica, however, Jake usually calmed down quickly.

"Let's eat in silence," Jake said then. "After dinner, Jamie, you and I will take the horses and go out. Maybe we'll just ride a bit."

"See what I mean?" Molly inquired innocently of her plate. "They get to play while we work."

"Goddammit," Jake said, starting to explode again, but swallowing it, stalking out to the kitchen, "I'll eat my dessert here where it's peaceful!"

"I don't understand that woman," Jake said later to Jamie as they lay on the bank of the river. "She gets my goat more than anybody I know. Even more than your Great Aunt Jessica."

They'd come to water the horses in the stream, had dismounted, the shade cool and inviting, so they'd dropped the reins on the horses and then stretched out to rest a moment.

At the mention of Old Jessica, Jamie shuddered. "*She* gets me," he confessed.

"Molly?"

"No." He couldn't even say her name, hated to criticize Jake's own mother. But he went on: "The other one."

"Oh." Jake laughed. "Mother. Yeah." He stood up, went over to stand beside the horses, watching them nuzzle the water with their noses, then drink, the water being sucked up and then visibly traveling down inside their long necks. He put out a hand and leaned on Duke for a moment. "Mother's a tiger, all right. But that Molly's sly."

Jamie didn't say that he thought Old Jessica was sly too, or that she always gave him the feeling she was plotting something — against *him*!

"I don't trust her," Jake went on. "You never know what Molly's thinking."

"Yeah," Jamie said. He didn't add that he still meant Old Jessica

"River's changed since I was a boy," Jake said then. He stretched away from Duke and pointed. "It used to cut in the other way." He paused, seeming lost in memories. "A lot has changed," he went on.

Now Jake was picking up the reins they'd let dangle, knowing the horses, trained, would not move with the reins on the ground, pulled them out of the water and placed the leather straps around Duke's neck, patting the horse. He said, "Yeah, I've been thinking. Gets lonely, Jamie. You don't know it, but when you're used to talking to somebody, kinda sharing things, you miss it when it's gone. I've been alone for years, but I can't get over that feeling."

"Well . . . I know, sir."

Jamie didn't tell him he too liked to share things with someone, that that was why Jake and Jessie and Ned were so important to him, why Old Jessica was so threatening because he knew she wanted him out of the way. But if Jake was talking of maybe getting married again, why the thought of Jake married — to a *stranger* — was almost too much.

Then suddenly Jake added, "She's a good looking woman. Young. Much younger than I am. Fifteen years or so. But I've kept in shape. . . ."

So he *was* seeing someone! Jamie had noted that Jake had been disappearing in the evenings of late, and that he had been giving his appearance an extra bit of care.

Jake turned to Jamie then, almost as if appealing to him for confirmation, for approval. Jamie studied him: as he'd thought before, he *was* handsome; he could see why a woman would want someone like Jake.

"Any woman would want to marry you," Jamie burst out then.

He couldn't face Jake, couldn't let him see his face, kept his glance on his feet. He began pushing dirt with the toe of his boot.

"And yet I don't know," Jake went on.

He was talking to himself, Jamie realized. Jamie picked up his horse's reins.

With some resignation, he offered, "Shall we go?"

He knew it was selfish of him, but he didn't want Jake to get married. He simply didn't see how it could help but change things between him and Jake and he couldn't bring himself to wish that. Not even if Jake wanted it.

"What do you think, Jamie?" Jake asked.

Jamie put the reins around his horse, put his foot in the saddle and swung up on Coalie, Jessie's horse. As he settled into the saddle, it groaned with his weight and Coalie turned to look at him as though he should be more careful.

"Jamie?" Jake prodded.

"Oh — fine, sir."

Still Jamie did not look at him.

"Don't lie to me, boy."

Jamie stared at the reins in his hands for a moment, pulled one over the other and placed them both in his left hand, then put his hand on the saddle, lifted his chin, looked Jake in the eye and said, "I think it would change things between us, sir."

"I see."

Jake didn't mount Duke yet; he seemed to be searching the river bank for something. "And if I said it wouldn't?" Jake's voice was low.

Jamie didn't answer.

Finally Jake swung up on Duke, pointed again to the dry channel where the river bed had been so many years ago and said, "Things change, and maybe a person should leave them that way."

Chapter Thirty-Four

*J*AKE HADN'T PUT Duke in the barn when he and Jamie returned from their ride; he'd said goodbye to Jamie and had taken off again toward the high pastures. He liked to think while he rode — the rhythm of Duke's hooves on the ground and the squeak of the leather saddle helped him organize his thoughts.

He was glad he had told Jamie about the woman in his life. He didn't like to keep secrets from him — or Jessie — but of course he hadn't told Jamie everything. That there had been another woman long ago besides his wife. Ilse. He hadn't told Jamie that he felt now he had really been in love with her all the time, but afraid to commit himself. . . . And then he had to return to England after he had gotten involved, and there was no time to do anything about it.

He had written Ilse when he got back to his duties in England, but his letter had gone unanswered. And she no longer was needed as a housekeeper. Jessie and Fred were both self-sufficient. But somehow Jake had assumed that Ilse would stay in the house anyway. She just seemed part of the family. Then he'd learned from Jessie that Ilse had gone back to her mother's house.

Jake leaned over Duke's neck, rubbed it. He took his hand and put one lock of Duke's stiff mane back on the same side as the rest. Duke's mane and tail were long and full; Duke liked to be combed and "fiddled with," as Jake put it.

"You're a good horse," Jake told Duke then.

Duke raised his head, seemed to nod in agreement.

Jake looked out over the pasture; some of the cattle were gathered in a ball under one of the trees near the pond. The scene was always comforting to Jake; it was people who caused the trouble, he thought then.

Perhaps even, he himself. Was he somehow responsible for Ilse's disappearance?

Ilse had left the household and he'd lost track of her. He had talked to Harvey about her, but Will didn't seem to know what had happened to her either; she seemed to have vanished.

The woman he was seeing now was a schoolteacher. Jake didn't feel the same thing he'd felt for either Louise or Ilse. It was more that she — like his pasture, the land — was comforting.

But perhaps that wasn't enough, Jake thought . . . not fair for a young attractive woman who could surely find someone closer to her age, some-one truly in love with her.

Jake patted Duke and the horse stretched out his neck, shook his head up and down and then from side to side. Duke was relaxed, Jake knew; he could sense that they were only out for a stroll, there was no business to take care of.

After he and Ilse had finally acted on their "mutual attraction," as Jake liked to think of it, she had said something strange.

"I hope you will never think I trapped you."

At the time, it seemed a casual comment. Later, when she did not respond to his letters, he began to wonder.

He knew that his mother and Jessie were both united in their opposition to Ilse, but he didn't know exactly why. With Jessie, he could suspect — as Ilse had once tried to tell him — that Jessie was afraid of losing him. Maybe it was the same with Old Jessica. He never knew what she really felt.

Now, as Jake eased back in the saddle, letting Duke pick his way across the pasture, he thought he would avail himself of his cousin, Purdy. He had always felt close to her, as he had to her namesake, the first Purdy. They were both "characters," and he liked that: they had the courage to be different.

Purdy would have seemed an odd choice for consultation about anything, let alone old memories of Ilse. But she might know more than she'd ever revealed about goings on in the family. People confided in her, because she was eccentric. They never thought she was intelligent enough to figure anything out.

Yes, Jake thought, as he turned Duke around in the pasture to head for home, he would go see Purdy.

"Well, Jacob Lutz, I declare," Purdy said when he walked up on her creaking porch and opened the ancient screen door. "Have you come to see your dear old mother?"

Jake swept off the ten-gallon hat, brushed it, laid it on an old walnut table near the door. He thought he remembered that his father had made that table years ago when August had attended the State Agricultural College and took woodworking. He must have given it to the first Purdy.

There was an odor of incense in Purdy's house and an overwhelming impression of darkness. Not a forbidding kind of dimness, but one that seemed conducive to Purdy's favorite pastimes: seances, table games.

Jake could hear trains running upstairs, knew that Ned — and perhaps Jamie — were there, playing with the train set. He could hear a humming, and turning, he saw Nellie Nameless coming down the stairs, sashaying from side to side as though she were a carnival dancer. Purdy followed his glance, cleared her throat, put her hands on her hips and said, firmly: "Don't you dare take anything off, my sweet Nellie."

Nellie giggled.

She brushed past Jake then, slyly pushing up against him, then past him. As she went down the hall and into the kitchen, she turned and waved.

"That Nellie," Purdy said.

But she laughed.

"And now what be you here for, Jake Lutz?" Purdy asked.

Jake hadn't seen Purdy for some time, but she never changed, he thought. Her corkscrew curls, the deep scar over her eye, her crazy-seamed dresses, all were as familiar as if he'd just visited her yesterday.

"Well," Jake said, "I came to see *you.*"

Purdy squinted her eyes, looked up at him.

"No reason," Jake felt compelled to add. "I just wanted to visit."

Purdy turned, signaled him to follow her, and went down the hall Nellie had just disappeared from, and into the kitchen.

Nellie was sitting at the table, sipping a glass of water.

"Upstairs, Nellie, for a moment," Purdy said then. "I'll call you when supper's ready."

Nellie giggled.

Again she sashayed past Jake, again brushing up against him as she passed.

"That Nellie," Purdy said. "She gets crazier every day."

"I wouldn't know," Jake said.

"Tea?" Purdy asked. "Coffee?"

"Coffee."

"You're not like your mother then," Purdy observed.

Jake watched her moving about the kitchen, her lurching walk, her brushing back the curls to stay out of her face as she filled the teakettle at her little white water pump, and he felt a peculiar kind of peace again, just as he had with Duke in the quiet of the high pasture.

"Your Purdy knows you have a reason to come, Jacob Lutz," Purdy said then, as she clanked the teakettle firmly down on her stove. A wood fire was already burning, and soon the kettle was humming and teetering on the burner, as the hard water had lined the bottom and made it unsteady.

Purdy folded her arms and looked at Jake. "Well?" she prompted.

Jake didn't know how to begin. He circled the cup she had given him with his hands, then lifted it up and took a sip. It was hot. "*God*," he said.

"Sorry," Purdy said. "Did you burn yourself?"

Jake laughed. "I don't think so, Purdy. But you sure can't be accused of serving your coffee cold!"

He studied her. He could imagine how she looked at people over the little table in her living room whenever she gave her readings — of tea, hands, whatever. Her eyes seemed to penetrate him, dislodging whatever protection he might have tried to employ.

"Well," Jake said, "this will seem stupid, but I've been wondering about Ilse. I can't figure out what's happened to her."

Purdy drew back, took in a long breath. "Well I swan," she said. She raised her eyebrows, the scar ascending up her forehead.

"It's not what you think, Purdy," Jake hastened to add. "I mean, I just wondered where she went. She left the house —" he really didn't know how to finish, "and . . . well, I just wondered. She took such good care of the family for so long."

"Uh-huh."

Purdy got up to walk about the room. She looked out the kitchen window for a moment, then turned back to Jake.

"Have you seen Henrietta?" she asked him.

"No."

"Seems to me that'd be the first step."

"Maybe."

They were both quiet for a moment; Jake wondered if he'd been wrong to come here, to talk to Purdy. But he trusted her not to reveal what he'd asked to his mother. Or to anyone. He knew Purdy could keep secrets.

"Why now?" Purdy asked.

She took up the teakettle, approached him to see if he wanted more hot water over the crystals she'd put in his cup. He shook his head now, covered the cup with his hand.

"And Jamie," Jake went on, surprising himself as much as Purdy.

Purdy returned the teakettle to the stove, put her hands on her hips, and looked at Jake.

Jake didn't tell her that he'd been thinking lately of adopting Jamie. He didn't tell Purdy that he'd regretted his inaction with Ilse and that perhaps he could prevent further regret if he acted on his affection for Jamie.

"Jamie? Ilse? Jake Lutz, you are a caution! Your cousin Purdy doesn't know what to think about you!"

"I know," Jake said, looking into his cup as if for an answer that would not be there.

Purdy sank into the chair opposite him.

"I guess I'm getting to the age when I start looking back on my life and seeing where I've gone wrong."

Purdy drew together her lips. "Wrong? With Ilse and Jamie?"

Jake blushed.

"I just wanted to thank Ilse for taking such good care of the family," he insisted. "And it's been such a long time ago. She never answered any of my letters."

Purdy looked at him, then up at the ceiling of the kitchen where the noise of trains penetrated. "They must be racing them things around the track," she observed.

"Yeah," Jake said.

But he didn't want to be distracted.

"And as for Jamie," Jake went on, "perhaps it would be better if he lived with me."

He looked over at Purdy to see how she would react. She seemed pained.

"Oh, Jake Lutz," Purdy said, again lurching up to stalk about the room, "everyone seems to want to take him from me."

"Oh, I didn't mean that!" Jake protested.

"Your mother wants him out of here," Purdy told him. "I just know she does. But Jamie is —"

Now Jake felt he had to get up, go to Purdy, put his arm about her shoulder. "I didn't know you cared so much about him, Purdy. I mean, I knew you were good to him, I just didn't know — well —" he stopped, not knowing how to finish.

Purdy picked up the skirt of her dress, wiped at her eyes.

"Whatever you want, Jake," she said. "Your friend Purdy doesn't want to be a stand-in-the-way."

Jake gave her a hug.

"We don't have to decide anything now, Purdy," he said softly. "You've been so good to all of us."

Purdy didn't answer, sat back down at the table and then Jake looked down at her. "And Ilse?" he asked. "No news?"

Purdy looked up at him, eyes squinting. "I don't know why you want to ask about Ilse, Jake," she said. "But she hasn't been around Atlas City — far as I know — for years. And her mother has gotten kinda — well, you know — confused. Far as I know, she's out there on that farm by herself and Ilse's gone."

"I see."

What did it matter, Jake thought now. But at least Purdy had decided something for him: she didn't know it of course, but she had decided for him that the business with the schoolteacher was all wrong and he would end it. He had enough obligations.

"Purdy," he said then, heading for the hallway and the table where his hat awaited him, "please don't say anything to Mother about our conversation."

Purdy swore, "My lips are sealed."

Chapter
Thirty-Five

*T*HOUGH JAMIE had once thought he would join the Armed Services when he was old enough, the war was not on when he had turned seventeen. Nothing, it seemed to him, was on, at least not in Atlas City.

Grace Kelly had married Prince Ranier: "I don't care if he *is* a prince," Old Jess had declared, "he's still a foreigner!" Three years earlier, desegregation had been ordered by the Supreme Court; the Rosenbergs had been executed, Stalin had died, Sputnik had startled the world. But in Atlas City, things hadn't changed.

It was still a ritual for the boys to gather in the dimly lit Parson's in the late afternoons and early evenings. Most of them, like Jamie, were bored, and most of them, like Jamie, didn't have cars in which to race back and forth, up and down the main street through town — the state highway, as some of the boys a year or two older did. Their part in this masculine strutting was to stand in front of Parson's and watch the cars spurt through town, mufflers roaring, tires screeching. Sometimes they were asked to ride along, and then they would sit beside the driver, who controlled the car and its symbol of maleness, projecting it down the street, feeling the wind on their faces, waving to the girls as they passed, feeling vastly superior.

Jamie and his friends — Ed Harvey, Will's boy, and Byron Smith, Oscar's boy — usually didn't get asked for rides so, demeaned, they boasted of conquests inside the cafe, jabbed the balls viciously around the pinball machines, drank beer in cups, pretending to hold Cokes — if Lila Hildenbrand, the waitress, was feeling good and ol' man Parsons was out of the way — smoked cigarettes behind the old outhouse back of Parson's. Then, smelling sufficiently of male prerogatives, they strolled back into the cafe to lay waste to all.

Lila was a great attraction in Parson's — a bosomy, luscious, Swede-blonde farm girl, not too bright, but reputedly able and willing. The old-timers declared her a takeover from the Lindstrom girl. It became a test of the young male's prowess to see if he could wangle a date with Lila. Half-frightened, half-silly with anticipation, the boys would pester her with cat-calls and admiring glances, asking her for dates, to which she always replied, "Pa'll take care of *you*."

The older boys, however, swore they *did* have dates with her, and the tales of her excellence in sexual matters was enough to cause fantasies in every boy in Atlas City.

But the younger boys, knowing her Pa would indeed take care of *them* if they laid a hand on Lila, always strategically backed off, saying they were only kidding.

Jamie had never actually gone so far as to ask Lila for a date; he'd been halfway terrified she might accept, and the idea of taking this fair prize on a stroll through Atlas City — for what else could they do — he had no car — was too much for him.

Nevertheless Lila, perhaps with the very rudimentary feminine sense of self-preservation, seemed to like Jamie.

"Take me out some night, Jamie," Lila would say, leaning over the counter to display her full breasts nestling in a low-cut white blouse so that Jamie would flush up to the roots of his hair, her voice low and strangely enticing. "Now, I'd go out with *you*."

And then the other boys, jealous, not knowing if she meant it or not, would jostle Jamie in the ribs and try to push him toward her. "Come on, Jamie," they'd say. "Show her what you can do."

Once one of the more boisterous boys had removed Jamie's glasses and pushed him toward Lila so that he caved against the magnificent mountains of her bosom. He had been stricken with apprehension, flailing sightlessly, until he realized he had clasped Lila about the waist, felt of her softness, inhaled the musk of her perfume, his out-of-focus eyes noticing the wet shine of her lips. It might have been a dream for one of the older boys; it was a nightmare for Jamie Pratt.

"Leave me alone!" he'd blurted, and fumbled for his glasses.

Byron had extracted the glasses from the floor where they'd fallen, and Ed put them back on Jamie's nose; the whole world suddenly appeared comprehensible.

Today he and Ed and Byron were going to plan another outing over at the old church at Darby's Crossing. Ed had made some grape wine in an old shed in the backyard in which Will Harvey had been told Ed was doing chemistry experiments. Byron was to furnish cigarettes, some stolen, one by one, from his father, others purchased mutually by the boys from money earned washing cars, windows, doing odd jobs in Atlas City. Last year, Jamie and Byron had worked on harvesting crews, Jamie helping Jake too, while Ed worked in the filling station on the highway. Ed couldn't do hard labor: he had an artificial leg. He had been in a train wreck. His father had taken him to Denver to a medical convention; on the return, the Golden Express had derailed near the Colorado border. Ed's leg was so damaged it had to be amputated.

The boys had earned enough money to supply them with contraband for many summers; consequently, like the fabled lazy grasshopper, they'd decided to live on their earnings as long as they could and just "goof off." Now, with the late summer hours stretching seemingly without end, Jamie almost wished he had gone back to work with Jake.

No one noticed him leaving Purdy's. Ned, coughing in his room, then clearing his throat and spitting on the floor — which always infuriated Purdy — didn't even raise his head as Jamie went by his open door. Old Jessica too, thank God, was nowhere to be seen. Purdy herself had the radio on and was listening to some gospel speaker, some hell-and-damnation fundamentalist who told his listeners they would be healed if they simply turned to the Lord, placed one hand on the radio and the other on whatever bodily spot was troubling them. Purdy, Jamie saw, was sitting in her chair with her hand on her heart; she was always certain she would die of heart trouble. "And don't forget to send in money so Reverend Flowers can pray for you and continue his mission, brethren and sistern," the voice was saying.

As Jamie went by Purdy's sewing room, he sneaked another glance: now Purdy was standing, one hand dutifully on the radio, the other on her back, as if some electric current were traveling between them and curling down her spine. "Jesus saves," she was mumbling, smiling upwards as if at God Himself.

Jamie shook his head and went out the back door. Heat swam around him. It was not only hot, but dry, the leaves of the trees coated with dust, curling from lack of moisture, the sky yellowish with dirt. A diesel truck passed him as Jamie reached the highway that went past Purdy's, the horn bleating so that Jamie jumped. "Damn fool!" he shouted at the truck's back as it sped through Atlas City, sucking litter behind it.

When Jamie opened the door to Parson's, a Miller's Hi-Life sign glowing like a Christmas wreath in the window, it took him a minute to adjust to the darkness, the dim outline of glowing beer signs surrounding him. Finally he sorted out images until at last he glimpsed Ed and Byron in a back booth. Byron was already smoking, the cigarette hanging from his lips, like some sort of movie hero.

"Hi," Lila called.

Jamie turned to see her, again in a low-neck dress, waving at him from the counter. The wave pulled the dress tight across her breasts and Jamie looked quickly at her, nodding curtly.

"What'll be?" she said, coming over to them.

"Ah . . . beer," Jamie said.

"You know I can't serve you beer."

Ol' man Parson's face hung in the window opening to the kitchen and Lila rolled her eyes in his direction.

"Worth a try, ain't it, Lila?" Ed said, smirking up at her, studying her body attentively.

Lila shrugged. "You guys want something or don't you?"

"Baby you bet we want something," Byron said, and winked at Jamie and Ed.

Lila rolled her eyes, chewing solemnly on her gum.

Burt Barton, the high school football star, ambled in then and, with an amazing display of controlled muscles lending depth and grace to his walk, hunched his shoulders slightly as he passed Lila and went to the counter. Lila put a hand to her hair.

"'Scuse me," she said.

"Some help they got here," Ed said.

For a moment they sat in silence while Burt ordered himself a beer and, with swashbuckling dash, downed it with one gulp.

"He doesn't train much, does he?" Jamie asked.

"He don't have to," Ed affirmed.

"Maybe not now," Jamie conceded, "but come fall he'd better. If we're gonna beat Prairie Heights, he'd damn well better."

Prairie Heights and Atlas City were locked in battle. First Prairie Heights would take the Central Valley Championship, then Atlas City. Secured behind an aging glass case in the high school were the trophies Atlas City had garnered — in 1942, 1947, 1949, nearly every other year up to 1955. There was a space, left ostensibly and hopefully, for the trophy of that fall.

Jamie didn't play on the first team, and Ed was water boy, but Byron was the fullback. And he was good — in fact, the glory of the other two lay on Byron's shoulders. In one deciding game with Prairie Heights, Byron had kicked a forty-yard field goal, winning the game for Atlas City. His prowess had also subtly changed his relationship to Ed and Jamie: seldom did they dictate to him now.

"You better train," Jamie muttered then. "We got to have you in top condition."

"Yeah."

Again they sat in silence, staring now out the windows and into the blazing sun. No one went past Parson's on foot, though they could hear the occasional sound of a car on the highway.

"What you gonna do when you graduate?" Ed asked Jamie.

Next year — Jamie in March — they would all be seventeen, and then the year after that, out of high school.

"Don't know. Maybe college, maybe the Army. I could get the GI bill if I went to one of the services first."

"Don't join the Air Force," Byron said. "Join the Navy and see the world."

It was safe to propose this — he was already consigned to be railroad agent.

"Yeah," Jamie said. "I know someone who did that and he ended up in Hutchinson!"

"Well," Byron said, "that's the world too."

Jamie laughed. "I'll still take the Army or Air Force. I can't swim that well!" He called to Lila. "Hey, give me a coke."

Burt Barton looked over at their booth briefly then, his eyes slightly red, his mouth frosted with the beer foam. "Hey there, Byron," he said, ignoring the other two.

Byron nodded.

"The son of a bitch," Ed said.

"Aw, he's all right. Just got a swell head," Byron said.

"Yeah — the way he wears that letter sweater of his all the time at school," Ed said. "You'd think he had a hole in his shirt."

"Who cares?" Jamie asked, though lately he'd noticed Ed seemed sensitive about everything.

Burt, having lent enough luster to Parson's for the moment, chucked Lila under the chin and said, "Be seeing you, honey." Then, repeating the rolling gait of his entrance, he slowly withdrew from the cafe.

"He thinks he's so much," Ed said.

Byron shrugged.

Jamie was preoccupied. What *was* he going to do when he graduated? He looked around at the wooden booths, carved and aged, at the oiled wood floor, at the casual splendor of the lit-up pinball machines.

"Okay," Ed said, "let's plan the wine party. Want to do it tonight?"

"Okay with me," Byron said.

"Jamie?"

Distractedly, Jamie nodded.

"You don't seem very interested," Byron said to Jamie.

"Huh?"

"Do you want to go or not?"

"Sure."

"Okay, then. Let's meet at the church at nine. It'll be dark and we can all sneak out. Let's get good and drunk tonight! I really want to tie one on!"

"Yeah, me too," Ed said. "I want to get all the good I can out of this summer. It may be one of my last in Atlas City."

"Yeah," Jamie said. "It may be for all of us."

The three were silent for a moment, then Ed said, "And Byron, like we agreed, you'll have to train this fall. You're no Burt Barton."

"So thanks," Byron said sourly.

Jamie downed his coke and got up. He flung a coin onto the table, the metal rolling on its edge briefly, then flopping down.

Jamie still helped Jake with the ranch. Now, winter, he and Jake had taken their two horses and were riding out across the pasture. "We'll check fence, see if the last snowstorm did anything, and we'll check the calves."

Jamie knew that in a few months they would be bringing the herd in, sorting out the calves for castration and the part of the herd that they were going to sell. Jamie liked riding along with Jake on Jessie's horse, a new Coalie. She had good cattle sense. Now both horses had a thick growth of hair to protect them from the cold and had lost the shiny coats they'd had last summer.

"That Coalie can turn a cow faster than any horse we've had," Jake was saying now, looking over at Jamie's horse, who seemed to be nodding her head in agreement. "She seems to know what way those stubborn creatures are gonna turn."

The morning was frigid, the grass stiff with cold, ice gleaming on the tips. Jamie could see across the pasture to the place where the cattle were gathering at one of the ponds, some standing at the edge where the ice was broken, and drinking, others seeking wind shelter by the lone cottonwood that rose up by the pond.

"You know," Jake said, "a person sometimes thinks the cow knows there's a gate you want to get her through or that the calf sees the riders and won't try to break through when you're separating them, but you can't figure on that. The cow probably *does*n't see the gate, and the calf *does* see the hole and you can't count on anything. But a good horse will always be steps ahead of the cow."

"Yeah," Jamie said, patting Coalie as though she'd earned the praise even without action.

Jamie inhaled the air. Though the pasture was free of snow, the smell of cold was all around them, Jamie's nose feeling dry, his cheeks red. Yesterday the trees had been glazed with ice, a bush near Purdy's frozen so that the big, stiff leaves looked like lollipops. But perhaps a thaw was already on the way — Gulf air, and it would bring an end to the cold weather, at least for a time.

That was the strange thing about Kansas, Jamie thought — about the plains, really. One day could be freezing, the next mild, even hot. Temperature spans of seventy degrees were not uncommon; it was a challenge to endure, always hard on the livestock.

Jamie remembered reading in one of Jake's books that there was an old story — like one of Sandy's — about the cold winters in Montana. A cowboy started to speak one day, and the words froze, and no one knew what he'd said until the spring thaw!

Well, it almost could be true, Jamie thought, the way things changed so suddenly.

"We've got to get those cedars," Jake noted then.

He pointed to some small starts growing in the pasture. They burned pastures in the fall, though some of the "experts" from the agricultural school nearby had tried to tell them that was old-fashioned. But Jake refused to stop; prairie fires had always been natural ways to keep brush and cedars down, and heaven help the pasture that let the cedars take over.

"It doesn't take long to have a pasture ruined by those things," Jake went on, pointing out two small cedars they would have to cut. "They look kinda pretty, and city-folk might think we should let them grow and keep 'em for Christmas trees, but they're mighty sneaky things. They can kill good grass, take over in no time. The birds eat the seeds and Nature takes its course and the seeds are spread all over."

Jamie didn't answer.

That was one of the most comfortable things about being with Jake: no need to comment or reply, everything seemed to be understood. Now Jamie let himself lean forward in the saddle, Coalie misinterpreting, thinking he wanted to run and setting off. Jamie reined her in.

"Sorry, ol' girl," he said. "Just stretching."

"Let's take a look at them," Jake said, wheeling Duke over to the cattle standing by the pond.

One by one, curious, the calves and cows turned their faces toward Jake and Jamie. The bulls were in a separate pasture, "resting up for spring," as Jake called it. They didn't want calving to occur at the wrong time; leaving the bulls in with the cows was too risky.

"These have all been branded," Jake observed.

Jamie looked at their ears — little notches cut out at the time of castration and branding, so that there was no need to trot along beside them and see the brand, saving time when riding the pasture.

The cattle stared at them all the while the horses walked past, keeping the riders in view — unconcernedly — until the two horsemen had passed out of sight over the next ridge.

"I can't get over how they always stare at you," Jamie said, grinning at

Jake. "They're like those women Purdy likes to gossip with on the telephone."

Jake laughed. "And Old Jessica likes to follow things too — I can just see her as the leader of the cows."

At the mention of Old Jess, Jamie sobered.

Jake didn't seem to notice his change of mood. "Purdy and my mother make quite a pair," he said then, shaking his head. "I never thought when I was growing up I'd live to see the two of them under one roof. Purdy maybe doesn't mind, but Mother? Huh!"

"Do you suppose she'll stay there forever?" Jamie asked then.

Why was it, he asked himself, that he could not rid himself of that face — of the image of that face — hanging out of Purdy's window?

Jake hesitated. "I don't know," he said at last. "Sometimes I wish she would come back," now Jake's face grew solemn, "and sometimes I think I couldn't stand to be under the same roof with her. Louise . . ."

Jake's voice abruptly dropped off. Though he seldom mentioned Louise to Jamie, he seemed to want to talk about her because he went on: "Louise seemed to get along all right with Mother. Mother badgered her — like she does everyone, but Louise never seemed to mind and she just went right on doing whatever it was she was doing and ignoring Mother. That's the only way to get along with her, I guess. It's something I never learned."

And then Jake wheeled Duke in so that both horses stopped. He leaned across the saddle horn, the reins bowing.

"It's funny how life is, isn't it?" Jake said. "You think of yourself as grown up, but darn it — you get back in the room with your mother, or whoever raised you . . ."

Jamie blushed, thinking of Purdy. Had *she* raised him? Had anybody?

"Well," Jake finished, "you become a little boy again. You say to yourself that you won't let that person get to you, you won't be put back in that impotent position you held as a child, and then, dammit, you face that person and there you are, thrust back into the past as though someone had balled you up and thrown you!"

It was the first time Jake had spoken of his childhood. Jamie, who always looked to Jake as a grownup, a model, couldn't picture him as impotent. Even the early war letters — World War I — that Jake had shared with him didn't give Jamie a real sense of a younger Jake — as, indeed, almost his own age. Jake seemed to have sprung up full-blown and powerful.

"But Old Jessica can make anyone feel helpless," Jake laughed then, pulling up the reins and touching his boot heel to Duke's ribs so that the horse started on, Coalie following. "She could always wither just about anyone I ever knew."

"Except your father?" Jamie asked.

Again Jake reined in his horse. A look of surprise crossed his face.

"By God," he said, "I believe you're right, Jamie. I used to think as a boy that Mother ran my Dad around, even though he fought with her, he gave in to her, but now that you mention it, I believe you're right!" He slapped the side of the saddle in glee and Duke shied, snorting in protest. "Dad was able to live his own life anyway — it was Mother who was reacting to Dad, not the other way around! *By God!*"

Jamie didn't know exactly why the revelation pleased Jake so much; could it be that he too had once been afraid of Old Jessica and to know that she had been defeated delighted him?

Possibly. But seeing Jake afraid of anyone was not an image Jamie could stay with long.

Jake interrupted his thoughts. "My grandfather Herman used to tell me stories," Jake went on then.

"Oh? Sandy tells Ed and Byron and me stories at the store. I remember you said your grandfather sang songs too, just like Sandy."

"The world needs storytellers," Jake said, looking over at Jamie carefully, studying him for a moment. "Even family storytellers are needed — weaving a people's history — which I guess is what Mother does except she distorts history to her own purposes."

"But don't you think everyone does?" Jamie asked. "I mean, even historians?"

He wasn't trying to defend Old Jessica, heaven forbid, he just had always thought history of necessity had to be slanted.

"I mean, don't historians become interested in certain parts of history and they study that pretty much exclusively, so doesn't that show they're distorting things a bit?"

"By God, Jamie," Jake exclaimed, looking at him again very closely, "you have a head on those shoulders. When did you figure all this out?"

Jamie basked in the praise. "Oh," he said, "I've got lots of time at Purdy's."

Now Jake frowned. "I'm sorry about that, Jamie," he said. "I mean, I'm sorry that Junior and Violet — well, you wouldn't be here though, would you? I mean, if they had lived?"

"No, sir."

But Jamie's voice had suddenly grown sad. He was happy to be with Jake, but he couldn't tell him that he felt he didn't really belong to anyone, any family. He couldn't tell him that ever since his parents had been killed, he felt he was "rented" out to Purdy, that even with Jake and Jessie, he didn't feel the connections he would like to have.

Jake seemed to have read his mind. "You miss them, don't you?"

Jamie nodded.

"Well," Jake said, and again dug his heel into Duke's side so that the horse once again plodded on, Jamie's horse moving with him, "loneliness — if that's what it is — isn't just because someone's family gets killed. You may not believe this, Jamie, but I was lonely as a child."

Jake seemed to be remembering something. But instead of continuing, he lit a cigarette, his hand cupping the match against the wind, the smoke spiraling out on the air. Abruptly, Jake began coughing — deeply, violently. "I can't. . . " he began, then was unable to finish.

"Sir?" Jamie inquired.

Jake's face grew red and Jamie drew Coalie alongside Duke.

"Can I help?" he asked.

He felt useless and unnerved; what should he do?

Reaching over, Jamie tried to pat Jake on the back, but Jake only doubled over further, then, suddenly, he reached into his pocket for his handkerchief.

Jamie watched while the white cloth, balled up to his mouth, became speckled with red.

"Oh sir!" he said, "you're ill! Really ill! You'd better go see Doc Harvey right away!"

"No!" Jake shouted back at him. He paused, removed the spotted handkerchief from his mouth. "No, I won't have it!" he said, almost as if to himself.

Jake's face was ashen, and Jamie thought: he's afraid, that's why he's so angry. He's not angry at me, but at something else.

By early summer, Jamie had almost forgotten the incident; Jake had not gone to Will Harvey, insisted he was all right. As if to prove it, he had offered to go to the Furniture Mart in Chicago to select pieces for the Lutz Store. It was a chore Fred detested — luckily, for his tastes seldom sold. He either bought furniture much too expensive for Atlas City, or so cheap that the farmers, though cost-conscious, knew it would never hold up to the years they intended to keep it in service.

"A car dealer can get by with a nick," Fred once complained to Jake, "but a farm housewife wants her furniture perfect."

"They see it at closer range and more frequently, I guess," Jake said. "They live with it and want it to be something they can be proud of."

Jake, however, did not have to be on hand when a customer returned a piece of furniture — obviously scratched from use in the buyer's home — and Fred had to make good on an exchange. He had always maintained that he had to decide quickly if he were going to return the customer's money or not; if he didn't, he'd lost a customer. If he *did* return it, but after a fuss, he'd also lost a customer. It was not an easy decision to make.

Jake was spared, he told Jamie now as they headed for Chicago on the Santa Fe out of Topeka; to be fair to Fred, he'd told him, Fred had to take a lot of abuse.

As the train had pulled out of Topeka, Jamie had had a tinge of remorse for leaving Ned behind; Ned never understood Jamie's not going to see the train, no matter what explanation Jamie gave him. But Jamie simply couldn't miss a chance to be with Jake and a chance to ride a train!

When they arrived in Chicago, they took a cab to a huge hotel — Jamie marveled at it — and checked in.

Jake wanted to go right over to the Furniture Mart. "This is something you'll never forget."

And he was right.

Jamie knew that Jake loved to shop the Mart, even though it was exhausting. "I've never seen anything like it," Jamie declared when he and Jake arrived at the enormous building housing floor after floor of furniture, display after display, lamps, tables, knick-knacks, everything — living room sets, dining room sets, bedroom sets, patio furniture — there wasn't anything, Jamie decided, that one couldn't buy at the market.

They had to get passes to get on the floors and Jamie thought the girl who checked their identification and their registration, a routine to be sure they really were furniture dealers, looked at Jake with interest. Jake *did* look good: twill Western trousers and polished leather boots, Stetson in hand. He looked handsome and distinguished. And he, Jamie, was his chosen companion! Jamie swelled with pride.

And then they were off, pacing up and down the marble floors, looking for some of the exhibits Jake had in mind. "You get so you buy from certain dealers," Jake explained. "If they're good lines, and in your price range — what you know you can sell to your customers — there's no point in shifting. It cuts down time to know just what and who you want."

But Jamie couldn't keep from swiveling his head to look at all the displays, so many that Jamie decided, after two hours of following Jake around, that if one didn't have firmly in mind what he wanted, he could easily get overwhelmed and never get anything done. And Jamie felt alien here for some reason; this was where he had thought he wanted to be — in a big town — somewhere besides Atlas City — but was this what was at the end of the rail?

At one wholesaler's, the salesman, a big, rotund man whom Jake seemed to like, asked, "Is this your son? The one who'll run that Lutz Store for you in the future?"

Jake looked at Jamie, who flushed. He was as much embarrassed by the attention as by the mistake.

Jake laughed, putting an arm around Jamie. "He might as well be," Jake said, "but actually he's a cousin."

"A fine boy," the salesman said.

Jamie knew no salesman would ever criticize a member of a buyer's family, but he felt pleased nonetheless.

When they got back to the hotel, Jake asked, "How about a drink, Jamie?"

"Sir?"

"You know," Jake teased, "firewater. Hootch. What you and Ed and Byron drink when you can somehow wangle it."

Jamie flushed again. "We only drink beer, sir," he said.

"Well then," Jake said, leading Jamie into the dimly lit bar on the first floor of the hotel, "it's time you had some of the real stuff. Learn to handle it."

So Jamie followed Jake in, and soon they were seated in a booth to one side, the cocktail waitress who appeared from the depths of the bar — wearing a very short skirt — smiling at Jake.

He did attract the ladies, Jamie thought. How nice that must be! He himself, now, he was far too ordinary to give more than a passing glance to. Someday perhaps, he would be as tall as Jake, as self-assured; then he might come back to Chicago and show them.

Behind the bar was an inset that contained a tropical scene — the bar's name, "The Tropics." Lightning flashed and water poured down, and sounds of distant thunder came from behind the bar; as the lightning struck and the water drenched the display, the waitress's face was ignited — kind of like, Jamie thought, the Miller's Hi-Life sign at Parson's when it went on and off, flickering on the customers. It wasn't so different, just more sophisticated.

Jake ordered two Scotch on the rocks. "You might as well learn to drink it neat," he said. He smiled then: "You know it's the mix that gives you the headache."

Jake didn't order them another, and Jamie was glad; his head was already swimming with just one. "This is sure more powerful than beer," Jamie said as he finished the last drop.

"Do you like it?" Jake asked.

"Well," Jamie said, and hesitated.

Jake laughed. "It's an acquired taste," he admitted. "But I think eventually you'll learn to. Not that you have to. No one has to drink to be a man."

"No," Jamie agreed.

"And don't forget that you don't ever need to feel you have to take more than you want. Set your own limits. One, two drinks is plenty. After that, it isn't the taste or the slight buzz you get — it all merges into one holy mess."

Jake bought a bottle and they took it up to the room with them. Jamie felt very sleepy and soon was stretched out on the bed; in seconds, he was asleep.

When he awoke, it was dark in the room; he felt cold and shook himself awake, got up, reached for the light switch. Jake was gone.

Stumbling over to the dresser, he saw a note. "Went out for a bit," the note said in Jake's forward-slanting script. "Be back in an hour or so."

There was no time on the note, so Jamie decided to wait by taking another drink from the bottle Jake had bought. Twisting the top open, he poured the Scotch into the glass sitting on a metal tray on the dresser.

Still Jake didn't return.

By the time Jake's key turned in the door lock, Jamie's head was spinning; he felt vaguely as he had the times he and Byron and Ed had gotten drunk, but he was beginning to feel much more nauseated.

When Jake came in, Jamie saw he had a streak of what looked like lipstick on the handkerchief he had put up to his mouth. Beside the streak was a long, red stain.

"Sir?" Jamie inquired. "Are you all right?"

Jake seemed to weave into the room — or was it that his own vision was aslant, Jamie wondered. He noticed a heavy odor of perfume on Jake's clothes as he approached.

"I'm sorry for leaving you alone," Jake said, not too clearly. "But sometimes . . . ," now Jake faced Jamie squarely, his eyes struggling to focus it seemed, "sometimes being with somebody," he paused, stumbled on, "helps."

Jamie didn't say anything. He felt awkward at the confession — almost as if he were being asked to understand the rules of a fraternity he didn't belong to. And for some inexplicable reason he also felt betrayed.

"You'll have a girl someday, won't you Jamie?" It was almost a statement, as Jake dropped himself full-length onto his bed. "Then you'll understand."

"I guess so," Jamie said.

But he wondered: was it really that good?

He meant to find out.

It was only later that Jamie realized he had not asked about the blood on the handkerchief, nor had Jake offered any explanation.

Chapter
Thirty-Six

*I*T DIDN'T TAKE Jamie long to find himself in a "situation" with a girl.

"I'll give you a beer in a coffee cup," Lila said to Jamie the very next day after he had returned from Chicago, "but you mustn't tell anyone."

Jamie had come to Parson's, seated himself at the dim counter. Ed was sulking in the back booth — Jamie had missed a drunk with them to go to Chicago — and, as at "The Tropics" in Chicago, light — this time from the Miller's sign — was imprinting itself, on and off, on his forehead. Ed refused to speak to Jamie.

Byron wasn't there — no doubt home with an ice-pack on his head, his mother insisting he had the summer "flu" and wanting to call the doctor. No matter. They'd forgive him soon enough — he was the only one with very much money still saved from their last summer's work.

"I won't tell," Jamie told Lila now. "Make it fast."

"Remember," Lila almost whispered, "not a word. Let me know when you want a refill."

Ed's eyes glared from the booth, but Jamie didn't even nod. He tossed back his head and, as Burt Barton had done, downed the beer with one gulp. Lila took a look into the cup and was surprised when Jamie pointed to it and said, "Refill."

Once again she turned and surreptitiously poured beer from the can under the counter. "You'll have to pay me for the beer," she said under her breath, "because ol' man Parson always checks."

"Will do."

Again Jamie gulped it down. And again he asked for a refill.

"Look," Lila said, "give me a minute to mop this counter, will you?"

But she grinned at him, her teeth starkly white against the red of her lips. Jamie, emboldened, stared at her blouse front. She flushed and turned away.

He sat there looking into the bottom of the white enamel cup for a moment; then it was taken from him and set again before him, this time brimming with beer. He drank it. "Refill," he said.

"Look, Jamie," Lila said.

"Refill. . . ."

Shaking her head, Lila opened another can and filled the cup, then another, and still another.

"Look, honey," Lila said then, her voice low, looking back over her shoulder toward the kitchen, where old man Parson was throwing together the noon meal, "look, don't you think you ought to take it easy?"

"I won't quit until you promise me you'll have a date with me tonight," Jamie said, amazed at himself.

"Honey . . ."

"No ifs, ands, or buts," Jamie said firmly, waving his hands around and raising his voice. "No ifs, ands, or buts!"

"Okay, okay," Lila said, "now take it easy." Then: "Come by the cafe, seven o'clock," she went on.

"Righto," Jamie said, and proceeded out of the cafe at an angle.

Behind him, he could hear Ed snort.

By seven that night, Jamie Pratt lay on his bed, stricken. What in God's name had possessed him? Now he would have to go down the main street, head thudding, and pick Lila up in front of all the leering eyes of the old men at the Manor, the working men of the town, the boys who hung out at Parson's. He could just imagine what they would think!

He rolled over. Could he have Purdy call and say he was sick? *Oh God, no.* That would make him a laughing stock. And Purdy would tell everyone that Jamie had asked Lila for a date!

There was just nothing to do but go and face her, walk her around town a bit, and then dodge her somehow.

Jamie got up from the bed and tucked his white T-shirt into his jeans. He had cut off the sleeves of his shirt, and he regarded himself in the mirror: his hair needed cutting — and combing — his glasses were sliding off his nose in the heat, his eyes were red-rimmed and swollen-looking. Flexing his muscles, sadly noting there was not a great deal of muscle to flex, he told himself he would just have to get through the evening somehow.

He was lucky. Parson's was empty, but for Grundy Ralston, who sat mumbling to himself in the booth where Ed had been that morning. Old man Parson, however, was sitting behind the cash register on the counter, smoking a cigarette, inhaling deeply, letting the smoke drift out his nostrils like a dragon. Was Jamie simply feeling guilty, or did the old man suspect something? He seemed to be watching Jamie with a peculiar, steely intensity.

"You be good now, hear?" he said.

His eyes narrowed at the "hear?" — was it for Jamie? Lila? Both?

"Yes, sir," Jamie said.

Lila swung out from a door beside the kitchen — looking fresh and really beautiful in a blue summer dress. She had on white sandals, and Jamie saw her feet were small and well-shaped, with tiny daubs of red polish where the toenails protruded from the leather straps. There was a glorious aura of perfume about her. She smiled.

"Shall we go?" she asked.

"Uh — sure."

Outside it had gotten cooler; Jamie pushed the glasses back up on the bridge of his nose, jammed his hands into his pockets, stared off toward the Manor, where a man in a rocker raised his cane at them and shouted, "Bang!"

"Uh — what'll we do?" Jamie asked then.

"Oh, I don't care." Lila seemed strangely quiet, subdued. She tossed her head. "Want to walk by the river? It would be cool."

"Okay."

His plans to abandon her early had dissolved; she seemed to expect nothing from him.

Jamie took Lila's arm with bravado and started down the street, now hurrying for he realized that Ned would be coming to see the train and Jamie earlier had to tell him he wouldn't go with him again. Ned's face grew sad.

"Bang!" the old man called again, and then, "Hee, hee!"

"Poor old things," Lila said.

"Yeah," Jamie said, and then looked at her because somehow he hadn't supposed Lila would think things like that.

Moments later they were at the county bridge, the wooden planks vibrating slightly as they walked over, Jamie stamping suddenly up and down to make them move, when the train whistle sounded.

It made him think, of Ned — and leaving.

"Lila, for heaven's sake, what are you doing here?" Jamie asked suddenly.

"Here?" She laughed. "I'm walking with you, silly!"

"No, I mean here in Atlas City. You could leave, you know."

She was nineteen and he had no doubt she could have gone to Harper and married someone, or even caught one of the truckdrivers who came through town and ended up heaven knows where — Los Angeles, maybe, or Chicago, or even New York.

Lila gave a long sigh and frowned. "I don't know," she said.

They were edging off the road and Jamie said, "Let's go sit by the river, on the bank."

Wordlessly, they pressed through the thicket of bushes and scrub brush until they came to the tall cottonwoods near the water. Magnificent, the crown of the great trees seemed to be holding up the sky like pillars. Dropping from one branch, like a limp snake, was the rope he and Byron and Ed used when they came swimming.

"It'll be dark soon," Jamie murmured.

It seemed so different, being here with a girl.

Lila didn't answer.

Jamie helped Lila down beside the tall, clay bank, and Lila, leaning back against it, adjusted her skirt over her legs. Jamie sat down, pursing his lips, watching her. A fish leaped up, flashing in the dimming light, sinking back into the fold of the waters.

"It's nice here," Lila said.

"Yes."

He felt, briefly, like confessing the love he had for this land, which was somehow separate from the contempt he felt for Atlas City itself. Here there was beauty, there . . . there was only banality.

"I wonder what this town was like when Jacob Lutz was young," Lila said then, surprising Jamie.

Her question made him think that Jake really was growing old, and of the red-stained handkerchief he had failed to ask Jake about. He shrugged. "I don't know," he said. "Maybe better."

Lila's eyes were closed, her face soft and relaxed; she seemed ready to fall asleep.

Her question had also made Jamie remember that Jake obviously had been with a woman there in Chicago, though he didn't know what had happened between them. The strange feeling he'd had when Jake had confided his own loneliness again came over him.

Jamie began, "I'm going to get out of here," he said, then added, so she wouldn't think he meant right away, ". . . someday."

Lila didn't comment.

"I'm gonna get on that train and leave this stupid town and never come back!"

But at the same time, he thought: would he really leave Jake?

He wasn't sure.

Jamie realized Lila had reached for his hand. "Don't keep talking all the time," she said, her voice low and strange. "Come here."

A wild pulse was beating in him and Jamie thought surely Lila must detect it; he felt excited — and scared.

"Don't you want to kiss me?" she asked.

"Well, I — yes . . . yes I do."

If *her* voice had sounded bizarre to him, his belonged to someone else, a detached self that hovered foolishly about.

She moved closer and he nearly fell on her, pressing his lips to hers, feeling them part, the flick of her tongue startling him as it insistently became alive in his mouth. He rolled on his side, pulling her with him, then broke away to look at her a moment, her mouth smiling, her body easily nestling into his. His head seemed ready to explode, his heart pounding; then he felt her taking off his glasses, as if she had undressed him. And then . . .

"Lila . . ." he said, almost choking.

He could feel her press in all along the length of his body. He was aware of her perfume, of her soft marvelous flesh, as she urged him along.

At last, he thought, he knew what Jake was talking about.

The next afternoon, Byron and Ed came by Purdy's. They weren't mad anymore, they said, but insisted Jamie go swimming in the river with them.

It was a strange feeling — being back in the spot where he and Lila had made love.

Jamie didn't have long to think about his new feelings; Burt Barton — to Jamie's amazement — stepped out of a cover of willows.

"Okay, boys," he said to the others. "You've done your bit, now get the hell out of here."

"What?" Jamie asked, looking from Ed to Byron and back again.

Byron, sheepish, wouldn't meet Jamie's eyes. Ed was defiant.

"I said get out of here!" Burt went on then, curling up his fists and shaking them at Ed and Byron. "I mean you, Pegleg," Burt snarled. He had swung his huge head, turning it on the bull-neck, his glance falling on Byron now. "And you! You wanta play football this season, get outa here . . . or I'll break your bones!"

"Jeez," Byron said now, and started to go. Ed looked angry.

"What the hell is going on?" Jamie looked from Ed to Byron.

"What's going on," Burt said, turning back to Jamie, "is that your friends here have done you dirty. Got you out here so I could give you what you deserve."

Jamie looked at Ed, who squirmed and looked embarrassed. "Yeah," he admitted.

"Good friends you have!" Burt mocked Jamie. "Maybe they'd like a little of what I'm gonna give you!"

And Burt hurled himself toward Jamie, throwing him to the ground. In one swift move, Burt had tackled him and landed a heavy right on Jamie's jaw. Jamie felt blood spurt out of his mouth.

"You stay the hell away from Lila," Burt said, breathing hard as he began pummeling Jamie with his fists. "She's my girl and you stay the hell away!"

Jamie tried to tell him, "You make me," but his mouth was so full of blood he couldn't form the words.

Jamie tried to poke at the enraged hulk looming over him and then he saw Ed pulling on Burt's back. Jamie felt the pain in his shoulder, then his chest. *Oh Christ*, he thought — as Burt was working his way down his body.

Instantly Ed's face appeared behind Burt's, and just before Jamie's eyes fogged over and he sank into unconsciousness, he saw Ed with his artificial leg in his hand. It soared up in the air with Ed's raised arm.

Jamie didn't even feel Burt fall senselessly on top of him.

"Roll him off," Ed hollered. ". . . Pull Jamie over here."

"Good idea you had, Ed," Byron told him sarcastically. "Just teach Jamie a lesson, huh?"

Jamie had barely recovered from his fight with Burt — less quickly than Burt recovered from Ed's attack — when Byron telephoned.

Purdy had been "nursing" Jamie, insisting he was far sicker than he really was, and didn't want him to take the call. "I'll tell him you're resting," she called up to him.

She liked having him sick, Jamie decided, liked to hover over people and tend them when finally, wish-fulfilled, disaster struck.

"No, let me talk."

"But it's just Byron. It ain't your lady friend . . ." she called back.

"It won't be my lady friend, Purdy," Jamie said then, getting out of bed and starting down the stairs for the phone. "It won't be her ever again."

"Saints be praised!" Purdy exclaimed, clapping her hands.

"Hey there, Jamie," Byron said when Jamie picked up the phone.

Byron's voice, in spite of the ritual, jaunty greeting, sounded strained.

"What's up?" Jamie asked.

There was no answer for a moment. Jamie thought he heard a muffled sob on the other end of the line.

"What?" Jamie repeated.

"Ed's dead," Byron said finally.

Jamie didn't think he'd heard right. "What?" he asked.

"Ed's dead!" Byron screamed, and hung up the phone.

When Jamie reached Byron's home, went in without knocking, Byron was on the horsehair sofa by the phone, crying.

"Byron," Jamie said, "What happened?"

Just then, Byron's father came in, looked at Jamie, shaking his head. "We just got the news from Will himself. Ed took the family car out last night, without permission, went to Harper, and . . . well . . . they don't know what happened — think maybe someone was tailgating him, bumping his car, but . . ."

Jamie couldn't believe what he had heard. In the back of his mind, he thought: Burt Barton.

"Ed lost control of the car." There was a long pause. "Cut off his head, it did. Cut that poor kid's head clean off!"

"Oh my God," Jamie said.

Leaving Byron sobbing, Oscar Smith staring at him, Jamie raced into the bathroom by the hallway, leaned over the stool, paroxysms of nausea consuming him.

Jamie had gone to the post office to get the mail for Purdy. He was surprised she would let him, since she would know from experience that Oscar Smith would be prognosticating around town, but it was too hot for her to go. Jamie could hear Oscar talking with someone; Atlas City like a pool whose ripples had been disturbed, the waves spreading to unknown shores, unknown distances.

"Yeah . . . last night. Cut his head clean off. Can you imagine?"

"Ed Harvey? Jeez — he lost his leg and now his head."

Jamie wanted to punch them, but he strained to hear better.

Oscar Smith was holding shop on the steps of the white-frame post office, snapping the rubber bands on his sleeves as he spoke. "Bad times ahead," he forecast. "Deaths always come in threes."

Oscar was not known for his optimism, Jamie thought.

The postmaster, to whom Oscar delivered his monologue, shook his head. "Dunno who's next," he said. "Anything can happen. We're living in a fast age."

There was a murmur of assent in the small crowd that had gathered around Oscar and the postmaster. There was also a shiver of fear traveling through every person present: death had been unleashed on the town.

"I'm a pallbearer," Oscar now confessed officiously. "And that's a fact."

"Who's fixing him up?" someone asked.

"Emmett Carter," Oscar replied, addressing his listeners importantly, turning his gaze on each one. "Emmett has a real challenge."

"They won't open the casket," a voice in the back predicted.

Oscar scratched his head. "Like as not," he agreed.

At Purdy Pratt's, Old Jessica was also expounding.

"No doubt he had a girl — was driving with one hand on the wheel and the other on God knows what."

Purdy *hmmphed*. "At least you're dressed for the funeral," she observed.

Jamie, standing in the hallway, mail in hand, was amazed that Purdy had not called to him to bring in what he had; generally she was so obsessed with the mail delivery. If the postmaster was late putting mail in the boxes, Purdy was likely to scold him mightily.

Now, however, she seemed to be thinking of other things. Jamie put the mail down on the hall table, turned to go up the stairs, but hesitated when he heard Old Jess speak.

"I'm *not* going to the funeral," Old Jessica declared. "Not on your life! Expose myself to all those curious hypocrites? Never!" She went on: "These kids — racing around like lizards in their low-slung cars. Listening to Elvis Presley, drinking beer. It's no wonder someone is always getting crushed to a pulp. Buggies were bad enough, but those four-wheel monsters with their engines big enough to pull a battleship . . ." Apparently appalled by her thought, Old Jessica didn't finish her sentence.

"Well, *I'm* going," Purdy said, getting up from the kitchen table Jamie knew because he heard her push back her chair. "I wouldn't miss it — it's my duty!"

"You probably just hope they'll open the coffin and you can poke your snoopy old head in!" Jessica accused.

Purdy didn't answer.

Upstairs in his room, Jamie sat with Ned and Byron. Ned kept crying, soiling handkerchief after handkerchief.

"You stay home," Jamie ordered him. "You can't go to the funeral and just sob all the time. It's hard enough," and Jamie felt his throat choke off suddenly, nothing coming out.

For answer, Ned gave a huge sigh and began bawling all over again.

"For God's sake," Byron complained. "Ed wouldn't like that."

His voice too, was shaky.

"You go to your room and lie down," Jamie told Ned kindly. "We'll come back to see you as soon as we get back."

"Now Rita Hayworth will *never* come," Ned said, his voice sorrowful.

"Rita Hayworth doesn't even know Ed," Jamie pointed out. "If she's going to come, she'll come."

At that, Ned perked up. He raised his huge head, put the bear-like paws of his hands on his knees, pushed himself up and went to the door. He turned back to Byron and Jamie. "Play with trains," he said.

"Okay," Jamie said.

Just as Ned went out, Jamie thought of something. "And stay out of the trees," he commanded. "We've got enough trouble without upsetting Purdy."

Ned shook his head and left, muttering, sniffling.

"Jeez," Byron said. "I don't know how you take that all the time, Jamie."

Jamie was suddenly defensive. "Ned's okay," he said shortly. "He's my friend."

They sat in silence for a moment, Jamie feeling as if a great weight were pressing on his chest, making it hard for him to breathe or swallow. Could it have been Burt Barton, getting even with Ed for rescuing him? It was undoubtedly an accident, and yet. . . .

"Do you suppose they'll bury his leg with him?" Byron asked.

"Christ!" Jamie exploded, gritting his teeth and closing his eyes tightly. "You *would* think of that!"

Byron was defensive. "Well, it's a thought. Maybe someone else could use it."

"They make them to fit one person, dummy," Jamie said.

He wasn't sure it was true, but he wanted to urge Byron away from the subject.

"I'm going to be cremated," Byron announced then.

"You said that before," Jamie drawled. "So what?"

"I'm not taking any chances," Byron said, shuddering. "What if you weren't dead?"

"Well, Ed's dead, if that's what you're worried about. You don't get a head cut off and live, for Christ's sake."

But Jamie had the feeling that Byron still wasn't sure. *Oh God*, he thought. *Why do I have to have Byron on the one hand and Ned on the other? Why couldn't Ed still be there? Why did it have to happen?*

"Let's go," Jamie said suddenly. If he didn't get moving, he knew he'd burst into tears. "Purdy says," his voice was mocking, "we have to get there early to get a good seat. Purdy acts like she's bought a ticket to a circus!"

"I still wonder . . ." Byron didn't finish his thought as they walked out the door.

Jamie didn't help him out.

Chapter
Thirty-Seven

*J*AMIE EASED LILA into a seat in the very back row of Atlas City's decrepit theater. He had tried not to go to her and ask for a date — he'd told himself that he would go see Jake, maybe ask him about the coughing incident on their recent trip — but once facing Lila in Parson's, her wide smile and wonderful body so close to him he could almost feel her soft roundness, his resolve collapsed.

Now Lila nestled up against him.

"Careful," he said, low. "Someone might see."

He didn't mention that the someone he was worried about was one Burt Barton. He didn't care to risk another set of blows from him.

Lila didn't understand, or didn't care. "So?" she said.

"So I don't want that."

"What's the matter with you, Jamie? You sorry you took me out . . . ?"

Her eyes were fierce in the reflected light from the screen, and she pulled away from him in anger.

"Naw, it's just —" now he tried to look in control, "there's a time and a place."

Lila jerked her arms into her lap and sat staring at the screen. But moments later, after gazing fixedly at the old James Cagney movie, Lila seemed to have forgiven him. She put her head on his shoulder, her hair soft and shining, perfume wafting over to him, singeing him with its promise.

Purdy had made some popcorn for them and Jamie reached into the brown sack, plopped some in his mouth. Lila sprang up from his shoulder.

"Good Lord!" she protested. "Do you have to do that?"

"You're not hungry?"

"Let's get out of here," Lila said then.

"But we haven't even seen the show!"

"Honey — don't you love me?"

"Shh!" came from ahead of them. Heads turned.

Jamie said, "Shh yourself!" But Lila took his arm. "Come on, let's go for a walk."

He followed Lila out of the hot theater and into the cooler night air. They followed the breeze down to the river, the night deepening in coolness the nearer they got to the water. Someone's cow was bawling in the night, and, faroff, they heard the wail of a coyote.

As they passed the Lutz house, Jamie swallowed, forcing himself not to look up. He supposed he shouldn't feel guilty, but outside of the usual Sunday dinners, he hadn't shown up there lately.

Lila said, "I thought I heard someone moan."

Jamie tensed. "Oh, surely not," he said. "It musta been a coyote."

"No," Lila insisted. "I'm sure I heard it. Maybe it was Jake Lutz. People have been saying he's not well."

"I tell you it wasn't!" Jamie said, and, seizing Lila's arm, he pulled her quickly into a run.

"Good Lord," she said, "what's the matter?"

Their footsteps rattled behind them as they crossed the rickety wooden bridge. In a moment, crashing through the underbrush, they had reached the spot of their first lovemaking; Lila sank against the bank, putting a hand to her chest, trying to catch her breath.

The moon had risen, round, full, shining like a coin in the sky, laying a white glow on Lila's face. She brushed back some hair that had fallen into her eyes.

"Leave it," Jamie said, crouching near her and catching her hand. "I like it."

She looked up at him, smiled.

Her eyes traveled over Jamie's face, then they swept away to look at the dark tangle of trees that jutted up on the opposite side of the river. Crickets and frogs, silenced at first by their intrusion, now began a cacophony, the sounds hollow and raw, filling the night. Jamie threw himself down beside Lila, put his arms behind his head, and looked up at the sky.

"It's like I said," he began, as though he had just been speaking about it, "I like this country when there aren't any people in it."

"Jamie!" Lila said, laughing. "*I'm* here."

"Yes, but I mean . . . well, you know."

He couldn't tell Lila about his concerns regarding Jake — he didn't want to add to the speculation of the town — though now, thinking about it, he decided he would surely have to go tomorrow and see what, if anything, was wrong.

Jamie's head lay by Lila's thigh and he saw how the moonlight outlined the warm shape of it, her dress gauzy and silvered, as if she wore a veil of light. She had taken off her shoes, her ankles, rather thick — surprising since her legs and body and face were so beautifully made — her ankles wiggled, turning her small feet in the cool air, then pitching them down to burrow in the sand.

"The river — this place — is nice," Lila murmured.

Now it was Jamie's turn to be dreamy, and his mind raveled back over the night: the show, the walk . . . the sound they'd heard at the Lutz place.

Abruptly he reached out for Lila. She gave a startled laugh, adding, "Aren't *you* in a hurry."

"Love me, Lila . . ." Jamie said, burying his head in her breasts. "Love me."

She began stroking his head, softly laughing, the motion causing Jamie's head to move back and forth, gently bumping on her chest. "Of course I love you, honey," she said. "Didn't I once say so?"

"But Jamie," she said, "what are we going to do?"

He didn't want to talk; he wanted to listen to the night, to feel her warm body close to his; he didn't want to talk or think.

"I mean . . . do you really love me?"

Jamie sat up then and ran his fingers through his hair. A cloud had moved across the moon and Lila's face was shadowed. She seemed to be frowning, her lower lip caught thoughtfully by her teeth.

"Do you or don't you?" she asked. The voice was petulant.

"I don't know, Lila."

"You don't *know*?" Her voice ascended, shutting off the sounds of the night.

"You don't want me to say things I don't mean, do you?" he challenged, hoping to gain some ground.

"Well, you said — I mean — what in hell do you think we're doing here?"

Jamie faced her. "You tell me." He looked at her until her eyes slid away from his.

"Whose idea was this, anyway?" he asked softly.

"Burt Barton would never have asked that," Lila blurted out angrily.

"So go find Burt Barton!" he replied, just as angrily.

"All right!"

She got up, pulling herself from the sand and brushing her dress with her fingers. She shoved back her hair, wiped her lips with the back of her arm as if wiping off Jamie's kisses, and began to stalk down the side of the bank, toward the path that led back up to the road and the bridge.

"You haven't changed at all this summer," Lila accused him. "You're just a two-bit teenager!" She was scrambling up the bank now. "And he can make love bettern' you," she hurled back at him, her teeth glinting in the moonlight.

Jamie laughed, the admission pleasing him: he didn't care now — he hadn't been the first or only one, he knew that.

"I don't doubt Burt is better," Jamie called after her retreating figure. "He's had more practice!"

"Oh-h-h, you!"

But her voice was fading, the sound of her steps diminishing into the night. He didn't feel sad at her leaving now — the whole affair had been wonderful for awhile, and he was not going to cloud it by unhappiness.

Jamie lay on the riverbank for hours. He saw a raccoon come idling down, stopping to wash itself in the shiny water, go on. And a deer — a young buck — the horns just rounded knobs, his immature shoulders muscling, growing strong for the mating contests to come. Deer were rare here, but still around in the wildest parts of the country.

The summer seemed to be going faster the past few weeks, and the thought struck him again that there would be roundup again this fall; he would surely be with Jake soon, and he had better find out if Jake were really ill.

Jamie took some sand in his hand, let it slip through his fingers.

Jamie and Ned walked along in the sudden coolness of the summer evening. Jamie had put off going to see Jake until the two of them had seen the Golden Express; he would have more time then to talk and not have to worry about Ned.

The sun was hidden behind a bank of clouds, the undersides black, the layers piled high like meringue, the rumble of thunder emanating from them and sudden shafts of lightning twitching through them. The wind had come up, just a thread of cooler air sweeping past them, sending little whirls of dust into the air like miniature tornadoes. Some of the men in Parson's came out as they walked past, beers still in their hands, staring at the sky and the change in the weather. One sniffed at the air, pronounced: "Trouble."

On the porch of the Manor, the old men rocked. One — the one he'd seen that first night with Lila — with a foolish grin, poked his cane at them. "Bang!" he cackled. "You're dead!"

In the distance, they heard the train.

"Train coming!" Ned sang.

"Yeah." Jamie nodded.

They were almost on the brick platform. Oscar Smith was out, adjusting the visor on his cap, fingering the note in his hand. "On time," he intoned in his nasal tenor, "on time out of Kansas City."

The sun glinted abruptly through a narrow slit in the clouds behind him, outlining him against the sullen sky, striping the horizon.

"Train coming!" Ned sang, his face red and flushed.

"Naw," a voice said, issuing from behind the door leading into the dusty sitting room, which no one ever used. "There isn't gonna be any train."

Jamie, startled, turned to see Burt Barton emerging from the depths of the darkened waiting room, Lila in tow, wearing the dressy blue frock, a sailor hat, sandals, and carrying a cardboard suitcase strapped with a leather belt. Burt had on a suit, an open shirt, brown and white shoes, and was carrying a men's shaving case and a sports magazine.

"I'm seeing Lila here," Burt declared, his head barely moving on top of the stocky trunk and the short neck, his face swelling with red at his importance. "I'm seeing Lila off to the city."

Still Jamie could not speak. He looked for a minute at Ned, saw the great face was furrowed and red like Burt's, heard low rumbles coming from within him exactly like the thunderclaps in the approaching cloud-bank.

"That boy hurt you?" Ned asked, pointing a huge paw in Burt's direction.

Ned never forgot anything, Jamie thought.

But Burt ignored Ned. "Train's a big thing to your boy, isn't it?" Burt asked then, looking only at Jamie.

"Aw, leave 'em alone, Burt," Lila said, digging a sandal into a crevice in the brick platform.

"That train's not gonna come. We're just here to see your face, big boy," Burt said, edging closer to Jamie and Ned.

Jamie felt a sudden chill. Ned was trembling beside him, and Jamie put out a hand to steady him. "You know it's coming," he told Burt, trying to warn him. "How else could you leave?"

"*I* show him!" Ned cried.

His face was deep red now, his brows wrinkled into a frown, and he was moving agitatedly on the platform, the overall strap flapping up and down. Suddenly, with a roar and a leap, like that of a charging bull, Ned swooped Burt up in his powerful arms.

"Hey," Burt said. "Put me down."

The engine had come around the bend and was approaching, whistle blowing. Oscar stood with the note ready to hand to the engineer, and Ned stood, hesitating for a moment, with Burt in his arms, Burt beating at Ned's shoulders, the blows falling off Ned's huge hulk as though they were struck by a child.

"Rail talks," Ned shouted then.

Before Jamie could quite gather what was in his mind, but with a sudden apprehension, Ned started running with Burt, directly to the rails.

"Jeez," Jamie said. "Ned *don't!*"

It suddenly struck him what Ned was about to do, and he pointed to the train, pulled futilely at the overall strap that hung down from Ned, Ned kneeling beside the track, pushing Burt's head onto the rail. Burt's body twitched.

"He hear train," Ned said, turning briefly to Lila. "Rail talks!"

Lila began beating Ned about the head with her suitcase, but her blows slid off his rock-like skull.

"Get out of there!" Oscar shrieked. "Oh, my God, you're going to kill him!"

There was a screech from the train as the engineer tried to apply the brakes, the whistle sounding as the great engine bore down on them, Lila's screams shredding the air. But Jamie knew the train never stopped on this side of the station and wouldn't be able to stop now. Lila was crying, Jamie pulling and pulling. He couldn't believe it was happening.

"Let him go, Ned! Let him go!"

Burt's face was growing fiercely red, his lips moving soundlessly.

"Rail *talks!*" Ned shouted.

Burt struggled, kicking his legs, but, like matchsticks, Ned pinned them down with his body. Burt's face was turning purple, Ned's fingers crushing his windpipe.

"Ned!" Jamie shrieked. "Ned!"

There was a tremendous roar of sound around Jamie then, the whistle one great blast, tears streaming from his eyes so that he could no longer see. His hands seemed welded to Ned, yet it was as if he were trying to move a mountain. He pulled and pulled, his and Oscar's hands tearing at Ned's back, while Burt gave a violent shudder and then lay still. Suddenly there was a fearful rush of air and suction and Jamie felt something give, the overall strap torn off in his hand.

Jamie remembered falling back and cutting his head on the cinders near the track, regaining consciousness to see the train was stopped and people were staring out the windows at him. He felt a huge weight on him and struggled to get up; he saw it was Ned and — his eyes swarming with tears of relief — Burt Barton. Burt was coughing, holding his hands to his neck while Lila assailed Ned with, "You stupid nut, you could've *kill*ed him!"

Jamie noticed then that it was beginning to rain, the first drops tentative, then streams of it lashed out of the clouds with abrupt force, whipping them.

"Get inside," Oscar said. "I gotta have time to think!"

The curious stares followed them and the train panted, waiting for

Oscar to give out the note intended for the engineer from the first. Oscar walked to the head of the train, poked his note in, shaking his head, standing to talk for a moment while the others went back inside the station. When he came back in the waiting room, shaking himself off like a wet dog, he told Ned: "You sit down there in that chair and don't you move! I'm gonna call the sheriff!"

"Please don't," Jamie begged. "He didn't know what he was doing."

"Alla same, he damned near killed a man!" Oscar shouted.

And he rang the phone for the central and, in a moment, was connected.

Jamie knew that Lucy, the central operator, would be listening, holding her breath.

Burt and Lila sat, the train pulling out without them, Lila looking at her cardboard suitcase and then bursting into tears.

"You ruin everything, Jamie Pratt!" she accused. "Just everything!"

The rain beat down outside while Lila cried and Burt rubbed his neck. Oscar paced the floor, Ned stared uncomprehendingly at his hands, as if they had acted of their own volition, had nothing to do with *him*, and Jamie wished he could pray.

Half an hour later the sheriff arrived, Oscar huddling with him in cozy conference, both looking out every so often — first at Ned, then Burt — Lila had gone home. Oscar was moving his hands around — back and forth, up and down. The sheriff took off his hat and rubbed his head. "I don't likely know what to do," he said. "I 'spect I better take him in."

So Jamie and Ned piled into the car with the sheriff, Ned saying, "We go to Harper for picnic?" and Jamie saying, "Not now. We're just going to Harper to see the town."

The sheriff turned on the police radio loud as they went down the slick highway through the rain toward Harper, the lights as they approached it, fuzzed on the horizon by the water. Jamie watched through the night fog, as the windshield wipers cut across the glass in front of him, over and then back.

"Train came," Ned sang.

"Yeah," Jamie said.

The police radio was on, but nothing was coming over it, except that someone was going to check in at a Harper cafe for coffee. The sheriff turned the radio down low and fiddled with the dials until music was suddenly blasting a plaintive cowboy tune into the car.

"I like that," the sheriff said. "You go to Texas now" — he said, "*Take-sus*" — "you hear it alla time. Oklahoma too. But here in Kansas we think we gotta be uptown and have the city music. Me, I like this!"

Jamie huddled in the seat beside Ned, a chill settling in the very corners of him, eating into his bones. He thought he would never again feel warm or secure.

The
Family
1958

Chapter Thirty-Eight

*J*AKE DROVE DOWN the highway from Granada, retracing his steps to Atlas City. Ilse's diary lay on the front seat with him; he couldn't believe its revelation: *Jamie!*

To think that all the time Jake had spent loving Jamie — yes, he realized, love was the word — Jamie was his son! *His son!*

The implications were enormous: he couldn't wait, he told himself, until he revealed it to Jessie and Jamie himself. And — oh my God, just wait until Molly and Fred found out!

Jake laughed, the laugh suddenly choking off as he was seized by a spasm of gripping pain. "Oh, God," he said aloud. "*Oh, my God.*"

The agony jerked his body, his hands leaving the wheel; abruptly the black Cadillac began to weave over the road. *Christ Almighty*, he thought, what was wrong with him? He couldn't seem to grasp the wheel, to right the car which was now plunging toward the shoulder.

Jake could hear the tires screeching, forced his hands onto the wheel and, without seeing, attempted to steer the car back to the road. Suddenly the right tire went off the asphalt; in desperation, Jake put his foot, hard, on the brake, tried to yank the wheel back.

The maneuver caused the car to spin. Jake just had time to let go, go limp, when he felt the car hurtle into space, his chest bursting as the Cadillac dived down the hillside, struck a tree, shuddered to a halt. Jake's head hit the wheel; before he passed out he knew that he was vomiting, the mess piling up on the floor of the car, a sharp acrid smell rising on the air. "Oh God," Jake thought, "am I going to die before I can tell Jamie?"

But he didn't die.

"You damn fool," Doc Harvey was saying to him as he lay in the hospital bed in Harper. "What the hell were you trying to do? Fly?"

Jake didn't quite take it in for a moment. "What?" he asked.

"You," Will Harvey said. He began to pace around the bed, glaring at Jake in the way he had when a patient had done something particularly asinine. "Do you think I want to spend the rest of my life patching you up?"

"Am I hurt?"

Jake felt dizzy. As if in answer to his question, a nurse entered the room, gazing at Jake as if she were accusing him of something. Silently she yanked his arm out from the sheet, sterilized a spot, plunged the hypodermic needle in, then, apparently satisfied, she spun on her white rubber shoes and left, including Doc Harvey in her final, disapproving glance.

"I must have committed a crime," Jake murmured. Then: "Are you drugging me?"

"Damn right," Will said. "You go around knocking your head on steering wheels and flying into the air with your car, and I've got to do *some-thing*! And," he added, "that nurse doesn't approve. She'd rather let you suffer for being an idiot!"

But Jake noticed that the jaunty air Will used to have when they argued like this was absent. Everything he said seemed forced. And Will's face was clouded — as it had been when Ed had died.

"What is it?" Jake wanted to know. "You're thinking something and I want to know."

But for answer, Harvey reached for Jake's arm, looked at the red spot where the shot had gone in, then dropped the arm back gently on the bed. He walked over to the window and stared out.

"I've kept the family out for awhile," Harvey said then. He paused. "I just have you here to be sure you didn't have any undisclosed injuries —

and for tests." He paused again. "You didn't do anything serious to your head — not even a concussion! Guess you're built just like your Dad, who managed to fall from that windmill so they say, and not hurt a thing!"

"He broke plenty of things," Jake said. "As I recall, he didn't break his back — something Mother thought would only have been fair, or so she told me." Jake laughed, weakly.

Will Harvey was silent.

"Well," Jake said then, "tests, you said. What's the verdict?"

Ordinarily he would have added, "Will I live?" but the question, now, was inappropriate.

For a long time, Will stood at the window looking out. He seemed to be following some scene with his eyes.

"Jessie and Fred are waiting to see you," Will said. "And Molly's there, Jamie's there."

"Oh," Jake said.

Again Will was silent.

Finally he turned to face Jake, looked at him across the room and then, focusing just above Jake's head, as if that made it less painful, he said, "It's worse than I thought, Jake. It's moving faster than I thought."

"Oh."

Now Jake felt as if another needle — a huge one — had been inserted into him and was being twisted back and forth. This time, the needle was not putting fluid in, it seemed, it was sucking everything out. Jake felt as if his stomach were hollow, collapsed in upon itself. Fear began to spread through him like a poison.

"Those damn cells," Harvey mused. "Those goddamn cells that we can't stop." Harvey paused, his voice tenuous and soft. "I ran some tests here — things showed up that didn't show in the x-ray."

"Don't!" Jake spoke out suddenly. "I don't want to talk about it!"

Now Harvey came over to Jake's bed, his face flushed, his voice openly trembling. He said, leaning over, shoving his face into Jake's averted one, "Damn it, Jake. You've *got* to talk about it. You've got to tell Jessie."

"No."

"Then I'll tell her."

"No!" Jake felt as if he were in a vise — why did it have to happen like this? Why did life have to be so unfair? What in hell had he ever done to deserve this?

"I — I have something to say to Jamie first," he said then.

Will looked at him, as if testing him to see if he were still delaying.

"You've got to face it, Jake," he repeated.

"Yeah," Jake said.

"It's the only way. It doesn't go away."

Now Jake exploded. "Goddamn it, Will, leave me alone! I'll tell them, but you just get your ass out of here now and let Jamie come in!"

Will folded his arms over his chest, studied Jake. "Okay," he said. Then, as he went out of the door, "But if *you* don't, I will."

Jake turned his face into the pillow.

Jamie came in, almost tiptoeing. Jake was amazed at the sudden rush of feeling he had for this boy — this blondish, slender boy with brown eyes solemnly staring out from behind the large eyeglasses, feeling that was now reinforced by the fact he knew he was Jamie's father. He still couldn't believe it.

"I've got something to tell you, Jamie," he began.

"Yes, sir?"

Jake had often told Jamie not to call him "sir," but his politeness, his awe around Jake, apparently kept him from dropping it. Jake knew the word was not meant to put distance between them; it was Jamie's way of showing respect and . . . love?

Oh God, Jake thought, *please let it all work out.*

"I don't really know how to tell you this," Jake began again. "But I've discovered something."

"Yes, sir?"

Jake swallowed.

"In 1940," he paused, cleared his throat, "well, really earlier than that, in the late 1920s after . . . ," again the pause, "after Louise died . . ."

He knew he was stumbling over the words, but he couldn't help himself.

"Yes, sir?" Jamie said.

"Well, Ilse Olson, a local girl, came to work for me. Take care of the house, etc. Fred was only five, Jessie seven, and old Henrietta was failing — never *had* been much good, according to Mother — and Mother . . ."

Jake looked at Jamie; he seemed uncomfortable at the mention of Old Jessica.

"My mother just couldn't cope with us all I felt, even though we were all in the house together. So anyway, I hired Ilse."

Again the voice drifted off, as if Jake himself were retreating.

"And then," now a huge sigh, "well, she was a nice girl, hard worker, intelligent . . ."

If Jamie wondered why the recital of Ilse Olson's virtues, he didn't say anything.

"Well, after several years — well more than ten actually — Ilse was like one of the family."

When Jake's voice dropped, Jamie offered: "Yes, I understand."

"And I found out I was going to have to go to war — we weren't in the war yet, but I was in Intelligence and we were already starting to gather information — you can't imagine the fear in that war — we were setting up the machinery for the terrible conflict we knew would come. Anyway," Jake pulled the sheet up under his chin, looked at Jamie, "well . . ."

But the voice had once again become inaudible.

"What, sir?" Jamie asked. "What did you want to tell me?"

Suddenly Jake looked squarely at Jamie, seemed to iron out the tremor in his voice, said, "You're my son, Jamie. Mine and Ilse's. I have her diary."

Before Jamie could react, Jake indicated the diary lying on the bedside table. His head seeming to spin, Jamie picked it up, looked at it, not opening it.

"I found out about all this through Maria Sanchez, in Granada," Jake went on. "She was a friend of your mother's."

If there were a fog in Jamie's mind, it apparently cleared abruptly, for the words drilled into Jake now as Jamie spoke.

"What do you mean, my *mother*?"

Jake noticed that Jamie's voice was trembling now, that the inflection was rising. He saw a flush rising to Jamie's cheeks.

"My mother is dead," Jamie said, coldly. "My mother and father — who adopted me — told me that."

Jake's heart was beginning to hammer. He put a hand to his chest as if to pin his heart in.

"Yes, she *is* dead, Jamie. But you didn't know — *I* didn't know — that I was your father."

Jake felt as if an enormous burden had been lifted from him. Now was the time to tell Jamie of the other, terrible secret he'd just learned. "And I, well, I'm not well, Jamie . . . I . . ."

But suddenly Jamie cut him off, his voice stiff and formal, bitter in a way that Jake had never heard. "You mean *you're* my father? All this time you've let me live with crazy Aunt Purdy and your mean old mother, and you didn't *do* anything about it? I've had to live with people who didn't care about me . . . ?"

"We cared about you, Jamie," Jake interrupted. "You know we did, Jess and I. And Purdy too."

"Like hell you cared about me!" Jamie blurted. The book in his hand, he began shaking it at Jake. "You could have told me!"

"I didn't *know*, Jamie, I swear. Do you think I wouldn't have taken you into my own life if I had? You were always like my own son. I had always *want*ed you to live with me, but Mother wouldn't have it. As long as she was living, I felt I could wait."

Jamie's voice was scoffing. "I don't believe you," he said, lips compressed so tightly together they were blanched. "I don't believe you!"

Intense pain gripped Jake then, Jake gasping and clutching his chest; he begged Jamie: "The call button, Jamie, please."

"Goddamn you, Jake Lutz," Jamie said. Stalking angrily over to the bed, he grabbed the call button, pressed it. "Goddamn you to hell!"

Jake's chest throbbed; he *was* in hell, Jake thought, pain wracking his mind and body. Oh God, why did it have to be like this? Why couldn't he stop anything that was happening? He'd never felt so powerless in his life, he thought, not even when he was little and his mother ruled over him.

"You let my mother go off alone, and didn't do anything to stop it! You let *me* suffer," the words were hurtling out of Jamie — he was listing things as, years ago, Old Jess had, cataloging Jake's faults.

"Jamie," he pleaded.

But Jamie wouldn't be stopped. "Goddamn you, Jake," he said again.

He turned, pulled open the door, and slammed it behind him.

It was the first time Jamie had called him Jake, he thought as he lay there in agony: why did the name have to be hurled at him like a curse?

"Okay, okay, relax now," Doc Harvey said.

The medication in, Jake felt it almost literally seep through his body. Like the cancer, he reminded himself, like the cancer.

But his thoughts were weakening, his pain lessening, and he seemed to be floating momentarily, a warm glow penetrating his chest and flowing through him. The pain blunted, he could focus on the real sorrows of the day.

"What in hell was Jamie in such a state about?" Will asked him now. "Never have seen the kid so mad!"

Jake turned his head on the pillow. "I've got a lot of things to tell you, Will," he said, "to tell everybody. Not just about the cancer."

Will pulled up a chair beside Jake's bed, smiled at him. "I'm listening," he said.

"I don't know how to tell you this — didn't know how to tell Jamie, don't know how to tell *any*body, but," Jake looked now at Will, "Jamie is my son, Will. Through some kind of trick of fate, Ilse had my baby and let it for adoption. Somebody — it wasn't you, was it, Will — let Willard, Jr., and Hazel take the boy. Somebody here in this town."

"I'll be damned!" Will said.

"I intend to find out who that someone was, because they must have known whose baby it was in the first place — that it was mine."

"Christ," Will said. "I can't believe it."

"Neither could I. But I was happy, Will; I've always loved Jamie. I even intended to leave some of my estate to him before I found out. You can't imagine how thrilled I was to know that this boy whom I've treated like family over the years, is my son! I was so happy!

"And now look what I've done. Jamie's furious with me. And I haven't told anyone about this stuff inside me yet . . ."

"I'll tell them," Will said with sudden resolution. "No need for you to have to do that too."

Jake closed his eyes, wished for a moment he were already dead, not just dying. "I can't bear it if Jamie doesn't forgive me, Will," he said. "If I have to die with the goddamn awful trick of Nature and Jamie hasn't come back to me, I can't stand it."

"We'll get him back," Will Harvey said then, standing up and heading for the door. "Don't worry, someone will."

But Doc Harvey wasn't able to catch Jamie before he left the hospital — to go where? Will told Jake he didn't know. Jamie'd ridden up with Jessie, Will said, so he was on his own.

Well, Jake thought, Will Harvey has to be the one to tell the family what's wrong with Jacob Lutz. He has to go into the little family room where Jessie, Molly, and Fred are waiting, he has to face Jessie and tell her that her father is dying. He also has to face Jessie and tell her that Jamie is his son, and he has to face — *damn it to hell* — Molly and Fred. At least, Jake told himself as he drifted off into half sleep, he didn't have to face Old Jessica. Not just yet.

Later, however, Will did.

They were in his room, Will and Old Jessica, Will having picked Old Jessica up at Purdy's and brought her to the hospital. He had told her everything on the way.

"What do you *mean* my son is dying?" Old Jessica snapped now. "I won't have it."

For once, Jake wished his mother could have her arrogant, determined way.

"You can't do anything about it, Mother," he said.

Through the years, he and Jessica — and Will and Jessica — had had a kind of live-and-let-live philosophy. Jake knew his mother never thought Will had any real ability as a physician — she had barely trusted Will's father, who at least had been her contemporary. But Jake also knew that Jessica trusted Will to express his real feelings and that she respected him for that. She couldn't manipulate him — he was too direct and open.

Will had been blunt. Jake was dying.

At first, he told Jake, his mother had refused to believe him. But Purdy would learn of it from his mother, Jake knew, and then it would be all over town. Purdy seemed possessed of the notion that she alone was responsible for dispensing any news in Atlas City, never mind that Oscar Smith — and sometimes the postmaster — might think *they'd* been chosen. Purdy would pass on the information to her cronies and then they would pass it on to their cronies. The town crier would be at it again!

But perhaps, he thought then, it would make it easier if everyone learned of his disease in one fell swoop. He would have to reveal nothing; the townspeople would undoubtedly tiptoe about him when they learned, as if stepping on eggs. Some of them would be afraid the cancer could be catching and would avoid him altogether; most would regard him as already in the grave and be surprised when he lasted — Will had told him he was guessing — six more months. They would study the effects of the radiation therapy Will had recommended to Jake, and they would shake their heads saying, "Can't believe he's still alive, he looks so awful!"

And Oscar Smith, who greeted each day and each person with the adage, "Things be a-changin' here," would be gripped by fear because at last things really *would* be changing. To have Jake Lutz gone would be something he and other old-timers couldn't fathom. The newcomers, those who were serving at the nearby fort and now lived in Atlas City because it was cheaper, the executives from the corporation that had bought the large farm near Jake's, all these people would not understand what the fuss was about. They would turn on their newly purchased TV sets and drown out Atlas City and everything about it, watching *Gunsmoke*. They would dream of heroes like Matt Dillon and characters like Chester. "That place musta been something once," they might say to their friends about Atlas City. "Can you imagine?"

"It can't be," Old Jessica murmured again.

For the first time, in spite of her stiff back and her imperious manner, Jake felt sorry for his mother. She looked genuinely grieved, and he reached out impulsively and touched her hand. She jerked it away as though she, too, was angry with him.

"You're supposed to outlive *me*," Old Jessica said testily.

Then Jake, too, was exasperated.

"Oh for God's sake, Mother," he protested. "I didn't ask for this."

As soon as Jake raised his voice, became angry, Jessica seemed to feel at home. Maybe, Jake thought, it was as if she were back in the years in which she and August had shouted at each other. Certainly she looked suddenly better, the blood rising into her face, any doubts apparently having been dissipated.

"I'm moving home," Old Jessica said then, stomping about the room with sudden energy, the cane boring into the floor. "I'm going to pack right up and move back and take care of you, *if*," and she still underlined the word with hesitation, "it's all as you say. Anyway, they need me over there."

Now Jake snorted, exactly as August used to. He shook his head. "I've got to hand it to you, Mother," he said. "You're one for the books."

But his mother ignored him. Turning to Will Harvey she said, "Please leave us. I've got things to do."

Jake heard Will chuckling as he left, and he knew his mother would bring something different into the home when she came back . . . but he wasn't sure precisely what it would be.

Chapter
Thirty-Nine

"NO, NO," JAKE said weakly as Molly and Fred hovered about him, trying to help him into his own, familiar room. "I want Jessie."

Now it was Molly's turn to tighten the screws. "She doesn't want to see you," she said.

She winked at Fred, who bent his head.

"*What?*"

Jake felt pain in his chest again — he never knew if the sudden pangs were brought on by the cancer, or by the terrible things that kept happening.

"What do you mean she doesn't want to see me?"

By now, Molly, stronger than Fred, had helped Jake into the bed.

"Oh, Dad Lutz," she said, tucking in the covers so that Jake had to — irritably — grab her hands, fling the covers away from his body, saying, "I'm not a damn baby. Leave me alone!"

But Molly went on. "Dad Lutz now," she said, "you just settle back and rest. Jessie's all upset over . . . ," now Molly's throat seemed to clog at some fearful thought, "she's upset over Jamie. We all are," she said, looking at Jake's furious face. "Well, kinda."

Jake didn't answer. He turned his face to the wall.

"She'll get over it," Molly predicted. "It's just that it's such a surprise to us all. In the end, we'll be one happy family."

"I bet," Jake said, suddenly despairing.

"Now you just go to sleep, don't worry about a thing. Fred and I will take care of your every need."

"I bet," Jake said again.

Molly sighed, gave a final, tentative pat to the bedcovers, then she and Fred left, closing the door softly behind them.

I've got to get well enough to get out of here, Jake thought then. He leaned back on the pillows, closing his eyes. *If anything is ever to be resolved, I'll have to get out of here.*

Doc Harvey had given him a sedative; he slept for hours.

When he woke up, Fred was sitting in the rocker, watching him.

"I thought I asked you to leave," Jake said.

"No, Dad," Fred said, his face clouding. "You didn't say that. And I want to take care of you. You've got to take care of yourself, now that . . . " Abruptly, Fred stopped talking.

"Now that I'm about to kick the bucket, eh? Is that what you were going to say?" Jake said, knowing he sounded a great deal like Old Jessica in his petulance.

Fred looked down at his hands, flushed. He began rocking. "I wanted to explain about Jessie," he said finally.

"What the hell is there to explain? I learn two secrets, divulge them, and now everyone's mad at me. I suppose she's mad because I have cancer too?"

Angry, he felt better. And that *was* like his mother, Jake thought. "The apple doesn't fall far from the tree," Old Jessica used to tell him as a child when he wanted to play with someone Old Jess disapproved of. Evidently not.

"And Grandmother's coming home."

"I knew she was planning it," Jake said, "but I can't really believe it."

"Oh, you better believe it," Fred said, the cords in his neck standing out. "And now she'll give us *all* hell!"

Jake found himself suddenly sitting bolt upright in the bed, more energy than he'd had in days pouring into him. "I suppose she wants to verify the wreck of my life for herself!"

"I don't know why she's coming back," Fred said evenly. "She didn't say. She only called to say she was coming."

Secretly, Jake was pleased. His mother would chase Molly out of his room and at least she wouldn't baby him. Bully him, maybe, but not baby him.

"You were going to tell me why Jessie is mad," Jake prompted.

"Well," Fred looked at his hands. He seemed to be stalling.

"For God's sake, spit it out. Don't be a mealy-mouth, Fred!"

"You sound so much like Grandmother, Dad," Fred said. "She always berated everyone close to her."

Jake realized Fred was right: he *did* sound like his mother and he was maltreating Fred just as he had been — or thought he had been — maltreated.

Fred's face had grown red when Jake spoke, then he stood up from the rocker and approached Jake's bed. "It was because of Ilse," Fred said. "She didn't think you should have played around. She felt you . . . sullied Mom's image."

"*Oh, God.*"

For a moment, Fred didn't know if his father was disgusted — or dejected. Jake knew Fred couldn't read his expression.

Then: "I wasn't playing around, Goddammit!" Jake said defensively. "And I didn't plan it. I didn't sully Louise! I loved her — but she was gone, Fred. And I was lonely. Neither of us," he finished finally, "planned it."

He was taken by a fit of coughing, Fred going over to him and pounding him on the back; the blows made Jake feel his ribs would burst. Weakly, he waved Fred away.

"*God,*" he said. "*Oh, God.*"

Fred's face looked frightened — as it always did when things were getting out of control. "Shall I call Doc Harvey?" he inquired, glancing nervously around the room as if seeking aid.

Now Jake felt numb, the spasm over momentarily. "I don't know," he said. "I really don't know."

"I'll call," Fred said. "I think I'll call."

"Do that," Jake agreed.

As Fred turned to go out the door to the hall phone, Jake called to him:

"And bring the books when you come back. There's a little matter of a transfer of $30,000 on the books that you and I have to go into. An 'error', shall we call it, that you'll have to rectify."

Fred's face blanched.

"I'll call Harvey," he said irresolutely. "It'll only take a minute."

"And if Wilbur comes here," Jake added with a snarl, "you keep him away from me!"

Fred shut the door, carefully.

"Why're you awake?" Doc Harvey assaulted Jake with the question as soon as he had pushed his way through the door. "I gave you a sedative, intending you to sleep all night."

"You may try to drug me," Jake said, abruptly pleased to see his old friend so soon again, "but I'll outwit you yet. You can't put this old lion down, you know."

Will grinned. "I know," he said. "That's what I'm counting on."

They were silent a few moments, Will settling in August's old rocker and looking out the window.

"Will I be able to ride again?" Jake asked then, his voice soft suddenly, his eyes having followed Will's glance. "Will I get out of this bed?"

Will didn't look at him. "You will," he said. "You'll feel better with the treatments."

"For awhile?" Jake guessed.

Will nodded. "You could get out of bed right now, but I think — for the first time in your life, you want to give up."

Jake ignored Will's observation. "And Jamie?"

Will looked at his hands. "Old Jessica tells me he's gonna join the Army."

"*What?*" Jake jerked himself upright in bed, stared at Will.

"Yeah." Will turned back to face Jake. "I didn't get a chance to tell him about . . . well . . ."

"Now who's evading?" Jake asked with a sour smile. "You didn't tell him about this stuff." He patted his chest. "My nice little present from God or the Fates or whatever."

The voice was bitter.

"No," Will said, shaking his head and coming over to the bed, pulling up a chair and sitting beside his old friend. "I didn't have time. He took off like a rabbit."

Jake pulled in his chin, studied the bedcovers. "Maybe it's better. If he comes back then, it won't be because he feels sorry for me."

"No," Will agreed, "it won't be because of that."

Jake was silent for a moment. His glance went back to the window as if pulled there by a current: the ranch looked the same — all the changes didn't seem to be reflected in it at least. He knew the cattle were out there on the pastures beyond the bluff, and that they were fattening for the fall roundup. He knew that calves had been born and now frolicked beside their mothers or, if there were problems, had been kept in the barnyard, unaware of what was in store for them.

Jake kept looking out the window, though from his bed he could only see the tops of the trees swaying in the hot breeze. Will too, seemed glued to the scene.

"If you were in my shoes, Will," Jake asked at last, "what would you do?"

Will coughed, cleared his throat. "I don't know," he admitted.

"I thought about — you know — the gun and all."

"Yeah."

"But it didn't seem right. It seemed cowardly."

"Yes."

"If things get bad — if I find I can't take it, take the pain . . ."

Will reached over, patted his hand. "I think we can control that, Jake. You've got some good times to come yet. I know this will not be easy, but you'll weather it."

"Not the disease? Just the other stuff?"

"I can't predict anything, Jake," Will said then, pulling a hand across his face as though he were trying to wipe off some vision. "The disease can't be beat. The other things — Jessie, Jamie — maybe they'll work out. We can only hope so."

Jake was pensive. "So you think Jessie'll come around?"

"I do."

"And Jamie?"

"I think so. It may take him a while longer."

"You *think* so."

"Jake," now Doc Harvey got up, like Jessica, to stalk around the room, "I'm not a seer."

Jake looked up at the massive headboard of the walnut bedstead; he remembered when he had had pneumonia, and his mother had worked furiously over him, only he hadn't known that until he'd awakened from the coma brought on by the fever.

"I guess I'm trying to run things still," Jake said. "It's so important to me now."

"Yes," Will said.

He paused, cleared his throat.

"Jake, I can't tell you anything about the way you should feel — emotionally, I mean," Harvey said. "But remember that I've had some experience with sadness too — and helplessness."

Jake knew he was referring to Ed, first losing a leg and then his death. He nodded as Will began again to talk, still walking around the room, as though propelling himself into action.

"I can tell you this, however. Everyone *dies* — we know that as soon as we get smart enough and old enough to know that death is not just something that happens to other people. It's there, waiting for us, but most of us don't see the end. Our lives are like a long string," now Will's glance again went out the window, then rested full on Jake's face, "and the end of the string is occluded. For some of us, however," Will paused briefly, the silence being filled suddenly by a calf bawling outside in the barnyard, the sound plaintive, "for some of us, *both* ends are apparent. It isn't easy to face that, and I'm not going to say it is, but we take what life deals us and we try to handle it. That's all we can do."

Jake was silent for a long time. "You're my best friend, Will," Jake said then. "Don't abandon me."

"You just try to get rid of me," Harvey said, picking up his black satchel and preparing to leave. "I like to give you shots too much."

Jake tried to laugh. Then, sobering, "When do I start the cobalt?"

"In a few days," Harvey said. "I've got to set it up first. That is, set you up with the specialist."

"I see."

And Harvey left the room.

Jake felt, somehow, much as he'd felt years ago when August had taken him down to the state college, dumped him off at the gate, pointed to the native limestone buildings clustered on the top of a gentle hill and said, "There it is, boy. Make the most of it."

Jake had felt very lost; he didn't know anyone. But he had joined the football team, played end, had done a good job. He was big, tall, and had good hands and instincts. Old Jessica had scoffed at his sporting prowess — "It's the muscles in your brain I'm interested in, Jake," she'd said — but August had seemed pleased. Oddly, August didn't attend any of the games, but Old Jessica did, in spite of her antipathy to the sport.

But Jake knew August loved him, and if he were still sometimes uncertain about the extent of Jessica's affection, he had learned to live with it. She never inquired about his college life; the only mention she ever made of it was when she exploded upon finding he and Will Harvey had enlisted in the Army in World War I. "Thank God you've finished your college," she'd said. "If you don't get gassed or blown up, you may emerge with your brains still in your skull!"

"Thanks, Mother," he'd said.

Now — in the present — he still hadn't seen his mother for long, just in that cryptic visit in the hospital when she had said she was coming back to take care of him.

Old Jessica had been busy cleaning up the house since she had returned home, with a huge steamer trunk full of her things. She had immediately started organizing the kitchen, or so she said. Though Jake was certain none of this was needed. Jessie didn't make a big point of it, but she was neat and orderly, and Jake felt sure that little organizing was necessary.

Jake could hear his mother's cane beating its way up and down the hall outside his room, going down the stairs, proceeding into the kitchen where there was usually some kind of shouting between her and Molly, neither of whom apparently wanted to give up the role of chief caretaker.

Molly was coming over more often, Jake knew, probably only to confront Old Jess and make life tough for her. But Old Jessica had survived a very long time, Jake thought, and in the end, Molly would be no match for her. His mother had vanquished stronger foes than Molly in her lifetime, and she had lost none of the strength of her voice or her character. Molly could only flutter protests and hope that Fred would extract her from the confrontations.

Jake chuckled.

Maybe that was his mother's role: to make him laugh.

He had something to ask Old Jessica, however, and he was waiting for the perfect moment. Someone had known about Jamie and that someone had arranged for him to be adopted by Hazel and Willard. He couldn't rest, he thought, until he found out.

But a sudden melancholy seized him then — he was no longer in charge of his own time schedule. He had to depend on the whims of Fate — and what little medicine could do.

Fred had brought Jake a book to read, one of August's, one he had retrieved from Old Jess's steamer trunk. In the book — a first edition of *Ben Hur* — Jake had found a letter. It was written by a friend of his father, and it was dated Arcatur, Illinois, December, 1861: "*They came today to take the few horses we have left — marched right up and spoke to my father, but I knew — and he knew — that they would take them anyway. I can't tell you how sad it made me feel to see ol' George go too — looks like he'd be too old for anything, but they took him as well. Ol' George turned his head when they led him out of the driveway and I knew they'd be wanting me next, even if I had to farm.*

"*There are some 'Copperheads' here and I've had several fights with them. They make me mad! We live in the North and they should not sympathize with the South!*

"*I saw Mom making bandages today . . . the women sat in Mother's kitchen and just kept rolling them. They looked like long cylinders of snow.*"

There was another letter, evidently from the same correspondent, though the signatures on both letters were either missing or torn off: "*Arcatur, April 5, 1861. Bob went into the Army last month. Mom cried and cried but there was no way he wouldn't go. I would've tried to enlist too but I know they need me at home. Little sister Amanda is sick, she's all broke out with something that itches awful. She looks terrible.*"

For some reason, the letters seemed to further depress Jake; it was as if troubles simply went on and on — war, plague, pestilence — and man struggled just to stay on his feet. Was there any reason for it? Any pattern?

Jake knew that Will would say no. They'd talked about it often enough — even years ago when his grandfather Herman had died. "It's a roulette wheel," Will declared always.

But somehow Jake — though practical enough not to embrace organized religion — somehow he felt now that it was no more unlikely for there to be a pattern than for there to be merely chaos. Man didn't live long enough to see it — he was like an insect, here and then gone, but whose species couldn't be obliterated. At least, Jake thought, it hadn't been yet . . . though there was always *the bomb.*

Yet even that was a manifestation of man's age-old destructive inclination — an impulse that ran parallel to his constructive self. It didn't make sense, but he really didn't feel the discovery of nuclear power would destroy man. The Chinese had invented gunpowder eons ago, and they must have thought then that it was enough to destroy their world too.

Jake felt lost in this conundrum, almost feeble!

"May I come in?" a voice said then.

Oh, God, Jake thought, it was probably Old Jessica and he didn't feel like confronting her yet. He had straightened up the store's books with Fred — just told him to put the money *back* — and that was enough for awhile.

But it wasn't Jessica, it was Molly, and for some reason, she looked almost human he thought. She'd bathed and changed into a dark dress, which made her look less like a balloon, and she didn't — thank God — have the simpering smile on her face. She had also, refrained from calling him "Dad" Lutz. He was grateful for that!

"You may come in," Jake said warily.

Molly walked slowly, closed the door behind her, asked, "Where should I sit? . . . I thought you might be lonely."

At her tone, sympathetic, his low spirits of the moment before still simmering within him, Jake felt a sudden empathy for her — a guilt for his incessant hostility. After all, Molly had been plunked down — protesting — right in the midst of his family, and she had to take it whether she liked it or not. She'd made it clear that she *did*n't like it. So perhaps he had misjudged her, Jake thought; she'd lost her father early in her life, Fred had said, and this may have accounted for her apparent eagerness, like his mother, to do battle with everyone. Though Molly's methods, he remembered, were even more devious.

Yet Molly seemed different this morning — almost normal! — and he was glad for the company. It kept him from dwelling on things.

"Sit in the rocker by the window," he said. "It's more comfortable."

Molly nodded, and went over to ease herself into the chair, her heavy rounded breasts sliding against the front of her dress as she did so. To his utter amazement, Jake felt a stir at the sight of them. *Oh God,* he thought, *what's going on here?*

Molly didn't say anything for a moment, brushed her hair back from her face — the gesture bringing the full breasts forward again. "Are you feeling any better today?"

For once, the question didn't make him angry. "Not much, really," he answered.

"It's hard, isn't it?" Molly asked.

She looked out the window as Jake and Will had done earlier; her face lined with light, exposing her very fair skin. She was actually rather pretty, Jake decided, though much too heavy. He'd never really looked at her, he realized, and he had not noticed that her face was unlined and even attractive. For the first time, he could sense what had drawn Fred to her.

"I don't know how I would take it," she smiled. "I'll help here all I can," she finished.

"Thank you."

They sat in silence for a moment, then Molly pitched herself out of the rocker and came over to sit on the bed. Her dress was rather low-cut, Jake thought, and he could see the bulge of her smooth white breasts swelling above the material. He swallowed.

She was so heavy she almost pulled him to her with the weight of her body as she sat down. Her perfume was heady. Jake felt his head spinning. Was it the drugs? No, it was almost time for a shot; it couldn't be that.

Molly reached out to touch his forehead, smiling. "You don't have a fever," she observed.

"No," Jake said. "Sometimes in the afternoon I do — a low one."

Jake found his glance riveting, insensibly, onto her chest, which seemed to fill his field of vision. He felt like a rabbit mesmerized by a snake, watching Molly deeply breathe, in and out, and feeling a sudden, overwhelming repulsion-attraction to her. She was so . . . *alive*!

"Come here, Jake," Molly said now, like a mother instructing her child. "Rest your head."

Without protesting, feeling that somehow, long ago, he had lost all control in this situation, Molly pulled his head onto her breasts.

"You're still so strong . . . and handsome," Molly was saying quietly.

Then Jake realized what it was that Molly was doing, as she reached under the bedcovers.

". . . Leave me *be*, Molly!" he shouted, taking her hand and yanking it away from him. "Get out of here!"

Molly smiled. Slowly, deliberately, she reached up to tousle her hair, then she took the material of her dress and, while Jake watched in amazement, tore it until there was a gaping rip down the front. At that precise moment, as though it had been orchestrated, Old Jessica burst into the room.

She took in the scene, flushed. "*Oh my God.*"

"Well it's *certainly* not what you think, Mother," Jake said weakly.

Molly, as though in slow motion, walked out of the room, her hands fluttering at the dress as if she were trying to put it back together. "He's an *animal*," she stated.

"*What?*" Old Jess demanded.

"*Oh, God,*" Jake said then, rolling his face to the wall.

He knew now what Molly had planned and he knew that she had been successful, at least in his mother's eyes. "Where there's smoke, there's fire," she had often said.

"*Oh, God,*" he moaned again.

Chapter
Forty

*J*AMIE COULDN'T believe how different he felt viewing Atlas City in his uniform. The past winter and spring he had not even written to Purdy, except for the first letter telling her that he was all right. He'd added that, just as he and Byron and Ed had once discussed, he hadn't been sent to a camp far away: he'd ended up at Fort Riley . . . Kansas! He remembered that Jake himself, and Will Harvey, had been there, at Camp Funston, during the First World War and, still angry at Jake, he didn't like being stationed in the same place.

Jamie had gone, in his uniform, to see Byron first thing on his return; Byron had been ecstatic. "Jeez, Jamie," he said, "you look so grown up and everything."

He had particularly admired Jamie's new "aviator"-tinted glasses: "They make you look handsome, Jamie," Byron marveled. "They change your whole appearance."

Jamie wasn't quite sure he liked that — what had he been before? But he knew that Byron meant to compliment him, so he accepted the comment in that spirit.

"Just wait 'til Atlas City gets a look at you now!" Byron predicted.

Jamie was again staying with Purdy and he was happy to find that Ned
was back in her care. The sheriff had committed Ned to the state asylum
for observation, but the resident psychiatrist, upon examining him, concluded he was no danger to himself or anyone else and that he could be
released back to Purdy if she promised not to let him leave the house without someone accompanying him. Purdy had also written that the minute
Ned got back to the house he had climbed up into the trees and swung
there all day.

"He couldn't understand where you were," Purdy had written. "But I
told him you would soon be home on leave and that made him happy."

Ned had hardly left Jamie's side since he had come back; now he sat in
Jamie's room, watching his every move, like a dog who's been temporarily abandoned by his master glues his eyes on the beloved object when he
returns. Jamie knew it would be hard for Ned to grasp why he would have
to leave again, but he told himself he'd worry about that later.

And just as Byron had predicted, Atlas City *did* respond to the new
Jamie, or at least, a representative of Atlas City did. The telephone rang in
Purdy's downstairs hall shortly after Jamie arrived, the sound jarring the
silence.

"It's for you," Purdy called up the stairwell. "Telephone!"

Ned and Jamie had gotten the trains out again and Ned was pushing one
engine around the track with his big finger. Then he had depressed the
electric switch and watched it go. When Jamie went out the door to take
the call, Ned followed him, almost bumping into him.

"Now wait, Ned," Jamie said, putting a hand on Ned's shoulders. "I'm
not leaving. I'm just taking a phone call."

"Not leaving?"

"No."

"Okay."

Ned gave a big smile and went back to the trains.

"Wait there for me, Ned," Jamie ordered. He heard Ned's "*Whee!*" as
the train flew around the track. He could picture Ned bent over the train,
overall strap flapping, his huge shoes stiff on his feet.

"I wait, Jamie," Ned called down.

"Good."

"I wait and not move."

"I'll be right back," Jamie promised.

As Jamie descended, the door across from the telephone stand opened.

He saw Nellie Nameless coming out into the hallway, heard her giggle. Of course, she was naked. His new image must have brought this on, Jamie thought, because Nellie only undressed for strangers. Or perhaps she was heading for Lars' old room — she couldn't seem to remember that Lars had died, Purdy had written Jamie. "She just stands there, looking around as though Lars has hidden himself somewhere, and when she can't find him, she takes off her clothes and leaves them on the bed as though they were her calling card!"

"Nellie," Jamie said sharply now. "You know bettern' that."

Apparently shocked by his tone — recognizing Jamie's voice — knowing he had never talked harshly to her before, Nellie's face crumpled.

Trying to sound less cross he added, "That's no way for a lady to dress."

At the word "lady," her head cocked up, her eyes looking into his, first one, then the other, with the nervous intensity of a sparrow. "Lady?" she questioned, as though tasting the word.

"Yes, *lady.*"

Nellie stared at him for a moment, then with a kind of self-conscious giggle, she bent her head up and down in agreement, turned and went back into the room, shutting the door.

"And now," Jamie called to her through the door, "behave like a lady. You mustn't take off your clothes."

Behind the door, he heard Nellie giggle.

He didn't know if she would mind him or not, but at least he'd tried.

Purdy's raucous voice shot out at him from the kitchen. "Jamie Pratt!" she shrieked. "I do declare you delay about everything! Telephone! You don't know but what it's Rita Hayworth!"

So it was a woman, Jamie thought. He had a suspicion.

"Take care, Nellie," Jamie said to the door and turned to pick up the phone.

"Lady," Nellie said behind the door. "Lady."

Purdy had come out of the kitchen and now hovered about the phone as Jamie picked up the receiver.

It wasn't Rita Hayworth. It was Lila Hildenbrand, just as he'd guessed.

She purred into the phone, and Jamie felt a strange pull in his stomach and an equal sense of irritation that she had called him. "Yeah," he said, trying to sound nonchalant.

"This is Lila."

For a moment, Jamie didn't speak. Then: "Yeah."

"Well . . ." He could hear a sharp intake of breath on the other end, looked over at Purdy, who was standing with her hands on her hips, brows raised, leaning forward as if to hear for herself what was going on.

"Just a minute," Jamie said to Lila then. "Purdy — *get out*," he told her.

"Get out? You tell me to get out? Well, ol' Purdy knows when she's not wanted. Imagine . . . !" Purdy was leaving the hallway, clucking to herself. "He tells me 'get out,' just as if he weren't the very young boy I took in from the goodness of my heart when he was still an orphan. 'Get out,' he says!"

As Purdy's voice retreated with her form, Jamie turned back to Lila.

"Is that all you can say?" Lila asked then, the voice petulant.

"Well," but Jamie couldn't think of anything else.

He had a vision of her as she'd been last year at the river, and he felt his throat go dry.

He realized Lila was talking. "And I thought we could get together tonight . . . maybe for the movies, don't know what it is, but . . ."

Jamie didn't say anything and Lila paused too. Finally she said: "You look great in your uniform, Jamie. I saw you walking down the main street. You look different somehow — all grown up and . . ." she paused, hurled through the telephone lines, "handsome!"

"Thanks," he muttered.

"Why don't we go out," Lila repeated. She made the words sound full of promise. She seemed to be breathing heavily into the phone.

"No," Jamie said then. "That's all over. You stick with Burt Barton." And he hung up the phone.

"I suppose that tramp wanted to see you," Purdy surmised, having rocked back into the hall with her lurching gait. "That figures. You'd do well to keep your distance. We've had enough trouble with her and Burt Barton!"

Jamie faced Purdy. "I'm grown up now, Purdy," he told her, his voice suddenly soft. "You're no longer responsible for me and you'll have to recognize that. I can take care of myself."

"Hmmph," Purdy said.

Jamie reached out to take Purdy's hand in his. "You heard me say *no*," he went on, "and I meant it. She won't bother us again."

Purdy seemed pleased at the "us."

She led Jamie into her little kitchen and sat down at the white table, rubbing at the enamel with her fingers as if she hoped to conjure some saving genie. "I guess you *are* grown-up," she said. "Old Purdy will have to remember that."

She smiled at him. Running her fingers around the table edge now, she said, "And I suppose," her eyes fixed on him once more, piercing him, "you and Jake Lutz can be grownups too. I mean, can you beat that cancer that he has?"

Jamie wasn't prepared for the abrupt, sickening sensation in his abdomen: he felt as if he'd been shot. Purdy had not written him about this.

"Oh, you didn't know?" Purdy said then, her voice mocking — she evidently still couldn't quite let him out of her clutches. "You had to leave so sudden you *didn't know*. Well, let me tell you, Mr. Grownup who says 'Get out' to his old aunt Purdy, that Jacob Lutz is busy right now . . . busy dying," she went on, as Jamie stared at her in astonishment. "Some just give him weeks."

Jamie hadn't known — but a small voice told him that maybe he *should have*. Yet he didn't think he could forgive Jake for what he had done.

"He's ill?" Jamie asked.

"Oh, it's been discussed, diagnosed, and dealt with, as well as his cancer can be," Purdy went on. "Right now he's taking nothing — he's had his x-ray treatments, and I can tell you, that's leaving him a wreck. He looks like he's 80 years old . . . thin as a rail!"

Jamie felt a rock in the pit of his stomach. Almost as if someone else were speaking the lines for him, he turned to Purdy. "He's dying?"

Purdy snapped her head up and down. "Would ol' Purdy lie? He's dying all right. Does that make a difference?" She watched him, hawk-like.

Why did she care, Jamie thought. Why did Purdy care *what* he felt for Jake?

As if she had read his mind, Purdy said, "You've had a lot of lovin', boy. Jake and Jessie love you, Hazel and Junior loved you, and *I* love you. So quit feeling sorry for yourself — you think ol' Purdy don't have sorrows?"

Jamie stared at her. It was almost as if they'd both retreated to that time, long ago. She *had* taken care of him, hadn't she?

Suddenly Jamie realized a face was missing in the old boardinghouse.

"And Old Jessica?" he asked stiffly.

"Oh, she's gone. Left the same day you did. Went charging right back to Jake's to manage things — or try to. But she can't manage *this*. No, he's gonna die all right."

Without responding, Jamie left the room.

As if to verify that Jessica had really gone, Jamie entered her old room, quietly, almost afraid he would suddenly find she hadn't left, that she had the cane ready to land a blow on his head, finish him off.

The room looked empty without her perfume bottles, without the shoebox with the letters; but when Jamie pulled open a drawer of the writing desk, he found a letter Old Jessica had written the very day they had both left, evidently forgotten in her haste to get back to Jake's.

Jamie sat down on the bed to read. He could feel the indentations of her pen on the back of the paper; she had evidently pressed very hard while she wrote. He could picture Old Jessica biting the end of the pen while she paused in thought, as if she might devour it.

"*Dearest Elsie, I need to tell you that Jake is very ill.*"

Jamie felt the pain in the pit of his stomach. "*Well, perhaps 'ill' is not the word. Doc Harvey has finally convinced me, well . . .*" Jamie had to look up from the letter suddenly, realizing his eyes were full of tears. "*. . . I now see that Jake is dying,*" the letter went on. "*He's not merely ill, he's dying!*"

Jamie wiped at his eyes, let the letter fall to his lap for a moment. He looked out the window in Old Jessica's old room, saw the trees where Ned liked to swing.

"*The things in this family are just too much! The family has found out about Jamie — remember I wrote to you that Jake — oh, damn him to hell all over again! — had had an affair — perhaps I should say liaison, with our maid. Well, Jamie was the product of that infamous match. . . .*" Now Jamie felt himself growing angry at Old Jessica's constant disparagement of his mother. "*But Jamie got mad at Jake for this very affair with his mother and he has gone stalking off to the Army. I don't know why I ever let Hazel and Junior take him as a baby — I should have known that the Fates would cross me up. But it seemed safe, and I did feel that Jake's baby, no matter how it was conceived, deserved at least that consideration.*"

So, Jamie thought. *That was how it had happened.* He could pity his adoptive parents, for they would have had to endure both the scorn of Old Jessica and her persuasion.

"So that problem of Jamie is solved, Elsie, at least for now. But then the awful thing that Jake has — I had to live after the deaths of two of my children and I never wanted to go through that again. I wish I could die. I'm too old and too tired to carry on."

I bet, Jamie thought.

He read on: *"Last spring, I talked to Jessie. 'Jess,' I said, trying to keep my voice calm and level as usual . . ."* now Jamie hooted in derision, *". . . 'why don't you just forgive your father and let it go? You know that he didn't mean to hurt Louise — he couldn't have hurt her — she was long dead when he took up with Ilse.'*

"Do you know what that silly girl answered? 'I don't care how long she'd been dead. It wasn't fair to Mother.'"

Jamie could understand Jessie's loyalty to her mother, but then — Ilse was *his* mother, and he felt great loyalty to *her*.

He almost regretted coming back.

"Well, Elsie, you know that I don't want to shake people up unnecessarily . . . ," again Jamie laughed scornfully, *". . . but it did seem to me that Jessie was judging in an area in which she had no right to judge. You know what I mean. So I caught her in the kitchen one day when I was over at Jake's, and asked her for a cup of coffee. She and I sat there at the kitchen table, drinking coffee, and suddenly I asked her: 'Do you think it's fair to blame your father for having a solitary fling when, after all, you did the same thing? For a much longer time?'*

"Well, I can tell you Elsie, Jessie has spunk. I've always admired her for that, and for a minute I thought she was going to strike me. She put down her coffee cup, <u>plunk</u>, like that — and looked me squarely in the eye. I swear those brown eyes were black with anger. Just then Fred came in — he's always barging in just when he's not wanted, and he asked Jessie, . . . Are you going to hire some hands now that Dad isn't up to working?'

"I waited for the explosion. But Jessie turned to him, quiet as could be and said, 'I don't know. I'll discuss that later. Grandmother and I have some business.'

"Of course, the mention of 'business' made Fred alert — he and Molly always think business means money (maybe it does), and he wanted to hang around. But I said, 'Get out, Fred.' He shrugged and left.

"Then I turned back to Jessie. 'Well, Jessie?' I said. I wasn't going to let her think she had frightened me off. If I'd had to hold her there with my

cane, I was going to make her answer me. And I really don't know why. I
don't know why I'm getting so soft in my old age (though even if I'm old
and want to die, I can't say I think of myself as in*firm*). Anyway, it seemed
to me that Jake had enough trouble right now without Jessie adding to it.
And she had no right, as I was trying to point out to her."

Jamie paused a moment, letting the letter sag in his hands. He knew that
something had happened to Jessie before he came to live with Purdy.

"*So finally Jessie took up her coffee cup again, stirred, sipped the cooling liquid, held the cup from her and said into the cup, 'I guess you're
right, Grandmother.'*

"*That was all, nothing else. And she hasn't mentioned it since. But she
said, 'Guess you're right.'*

Outside a breeze was beginning to stir; clouds had drawn across the sky
in the early afternoon, and it seemed they might have a summer rain. They
needed it; it had been hot and dry and the birds had crowded the birdbath
Purdy kept in her yard. She'd had to refill it over and over again.

"*Well, I'll have to see what the maneuvers are in Jake's house when I
get there. And you can be sure there are maneuvers. There are plots here
which would have put the Nazis to shame. And it might just be that it
would be to my advantage to stay quiet about Ilse and the past — to
choose my time to reveal what happened, or to choose never to reveal it at
all. I can keep a secret, you know. Because I have another one which I've
harbored all these years and not a soul — not a soul — knows it. Whether
I ever reveal it or not, I don't know.*

"*I must end for now, dear Elsie, and go back to the other house. Jake
needs me. Take care. Love from your fellow GG, Jessica.*"

Jamie didn't know quite what to think of the letter; he was happy that
Old Jessica's focus seemed to be on someone other than him.

But Jamie knew that something *was* happening to Jake. And he would
be as mean-spirited as Old Jessica if he didn't do something to mend the
rift between them.

He would go see Jake.

He would try again.

Chapter
Forty-One

*A*S HE WALKED along the quiet streets of Atlas City to Jake's house, Jamie thought of the time he and Jake had found a blind calf in the upper pasture. "Gotta take him in," Jake said. "He'll die out here because he'll wander off."

Jamie remembered how the poor calf kept going in circles, no idea of direction, how it shrank from their hands when they roped it and then picked it up to put it in the truck to take it back to the corral. And it still went around and around in circles in the corral, in constant motion.

"Some people are like that," Jake had said. "They never find what they want."

. . . Had he been like the blind calf, Jamie wondered now as he came to a stop in front of the Lutz place. All the time he thought he was moving forward, was he really going in circles? Why had he been so angry at Jake when, after all, maybe Jake *hadn't* known about his mother. The Lutz household, after all, was full of secrets.

Jamie swallowed. Looking at the old homestead, he let his eyes drift over it a moment, absorbing it, as though it had been years, not months, since he last saw it: the wide front porch on which he'd sometimes played as a child, the ivy that tenaciously clung to the porch posts, and which he and Jake had once yanked down only to find it creeping back up within weeks — the ivy had, no doubt, been there on the original home of August Lutz.

The warm breath of late spring had caused the honeysuckle bushes clustering around the house to spurt up, making a tangle in front of the foundation — something Jake would have attended to had he felt better. The overgrowth somehow seemed portentous.

And yet it was still orderly here, at least it was compared to the chaos of Purdy's house. Nevertheless, Jamie now felt he could understand Purdy and her clinging to her "dear little things" — her little white pump, the sewing machine, the wood stove. She had made her future secure by familiarity of place, Jamie decided, just as Ned did with his trains. Just as *he* had, with Ned. And if Purdy kept everything, as she certainly did, Jamie went on, she never had to find she had thrown away something she really wanted. It would still be there.

Jamie was glad that Ned didn't have to stay in the state hospital; he would have been afraid there, with the unfamiliar sounds and the strange people. Ned cared about Purdy, Jamie, Nellie — he wouldn't have wanted to feel abandoned by them nor to abandon them.

Jamie moved up on the porch, his footsteps sounding on the old boards so that old Prince shuffled over, eyes white and rheumy, legs dragging. He sniffed at Jamie, tail wagging suddenly as he recognized the scent, slavering in his excitement so that he left a streak of spittle on Jamie's trousers.

"Hi, old boy," Jamie said, rubbing the collie's ears affectionately. He felt a wash of anxiety: everything had seemed to grow old here while he was gone . . . *how* was Jake? "Lie down, Prince, and rest," Jamie told the old dog then.

As if relieved of his duty to greet guests, Prince collapsed in the shade of the porch and was soon snoring.

Jamie turned the handle on the door buzzer, over which the marker, gold letters on black, still read, "August Lutz." Jake had never changed it: in Atlas City, there was no need to.

He could hear the buzz of the bell echoing through the house. For a moment it appeared as if no one would answer, and Jamie felt his heart begin to beat faster, louder.

At last he heard footsteps on the other side of the door and then it swung open abruptly, Jessie's downturned face appearing in the blackness of the hallway.

"Jessie?"

At the sound of his voice, Jessie peered out, staring closely through the screen into the bright light of the spring day, her eyes searching (and looking very tired, he thought). As she recognized him, her face seemed to brighten with a smile, her voice excited. "Oh, Jamie, Jamie! Thank God you've come!"

"Is Jake . . . ?" But he couldn't finish the sentence. What had he wanted to say? "Is Jake . . ." Again he stopped. Finally: "How's it going?"

Jessie's face fell. She opened the door to sweep him into the hallway. "He'll be so glad to see you. He asks about you constantly. He's been wanting to see you so much. Oh, Jamie . . ."

She had thrown her arms about him, clinging to him, shaking.

"Let me look at you." She held him back to survey his uniform, study the new glasses. "You're handsome, Jamie," she said, "very handsome."

"I'm sorry, Jessie," Jamie said then. "I'm sorry for . . ."

But again he stopped, perplexed. Was he sorry for Jake — or himself?

"We all are," Jessie said, giving Jamie time to organize his thoughts, assuming from what he said that he was expressing concern for Jake. She went on, "But I guess that's life, Jamie. It never works out perfectly."

"No."

"Do you want to go right up or have a cup of coffee here. Or iced tea?"

Jamie looked hesitant at first, searching the upstairs balcony as if awaiting the once frightful face. Jessie followed his gaze.

"Old Jessica's resting in her room, Jamie," she said, as if she'd read his mind. "And Molly and Fred and Wilbur . . ."

"Oh God," Jamie interrupted. "*He's* here?"

"Unfortunately . . . but," Jessie went on more brightly, "we can put up with Wilbur too. This is no time for nit-picking."

"No."

"Coffee then? Or tea?"

She seemed desperately glad to see him and Jamie felt overwhelmingly ashamed; of course she would be lonely and sorrowing. She wasn't to blame for what had happened to him; why had he let himself be so selfish, thinking only of his own disappointments?

He remembered Purdy admonishing him: "You've had a lot of lovin', boy."

"Well," Jamie said then, "iced tea would be fine."

Jessie pointed to a white wicker chair for him to sit in — porch furniture moved in for extra company he supposed, though what extra company there would be, Jamie was at a loss to guess — only Wilbur, he surmised, and Old Jessica. The townspeople were evidently as remiss as he was in calling — cancer was dreaded.

Jamie strained his eyes briefly, searching the familiar corners of the room, tracing the wide, dark baseboards and the horsehair sofa, then looking up to see the fancy carved-wood moldings on the walls near the ceilings. Pictures hung with gold wire from the moldings: "The Horse Fair," and a watercolor that Old Jessica's mother, Lizzie, had done many years before. Jessie had shown the picture to Jamie just months ago, before he left; she'd dug it out of the attic where it had been languishing and put it back on display.

Now Jessie came back into the room, bearing a tea glass on a tray.

"How is he, Jessie?"

Jessie bent her head, hands pushing together. "Low," she said finally.

She put the tray and glass on a table near Jamie and he drank, put the glass down. There was a long silence — punctuated by the ticking of the grandfather clock August had made in one of his "saner" moments, as Old Jessica would have termed it. The clock was in the dining room and Jamie looked toward the sound, saw the big table still had a cloth and a bowl of flowers on it — as if awaiting Sunday dinner. On a sideboard next to one wall, matching crystal candelabra caught the weak light in the room, sending prisms of color onto the walls and floor.

"Pain?" Jamie asked at last.

"Yes . . . but the medicine helps."

Now Jessie pushed back a stray lock of brown hair, Jamie thinking she must have aged ten years since her father's illness.

When Jessie spoke again, her voice was almost inaudible. "You wish you could change things, that by taking thought, you could change things, but of course you can't."

Jessie sighed.

"No," Jamie said.

"Do you want to go up? Are you through with the tea?"

She inclined her head in the direction of the half-full glass.

"Yes."

Starting up the narrow stairway he was aware of Jake's labored breathing, punctuating the stillness. Forcing his attention elsewhere, he studied the carpet on the stairs, worn and faded, but which he knew must have once been — in Old Jess's time — magnificent, scrolled and heavy. At the door to Jake's room, Jessie put a hand on Jamie's arm, the bellows of Jake's chest seeming to vibrate the very timbers of the door.

"We let him set the tone of things," she said, looking into Jamie's eyes. "If he wants to talk, we talk."

"Yes. I understand."

And then Jessie opened the door and Jamie greeted Jake, wrenched over in bed, gasping for breath.

"Poppa!" Jessie called, running to him.

"The sheets hurt . . . the sheets *hurt* . . ." Jake was crying out, the words loud and angry, as if Jake couldn't believe what was happening.

Jamie felt anguish tear through him: Jake was a skeleton! How could he and Jessie have changed so much in the months since he'd been there? It was as if time had telescoped and rushed by, like the earth speeding past the side of a car when, looking farther out, one could see he was not traveling nearly so fast as it appeared.

"Help me turn him over," Jessie said then to Jamie, putting a finger to her lips to indicate he was not to express his dismay.

Jamie took Jake gently under one arm — such a thin arm! — and then, Jake groaning with pain as they turned him, flinching, perspiring, his eyes focusing suddenly on Jamie's face as he lay back in bed. Jake closed his eyes for a moment. "Let me get my . . . my . . . breath."

"Should I go?" Jamie whispered to Jessie.

It seemed the wrong time for a confrontation, or a discussion of the affair between Jake and Ilse.

Jessie shook her head. She retreated then to the rocker placed close to the bedside, a book opened, face down, pages spread to mark the place, on the bedtable there. Her reading glasses rested on top of the book. She must spend most of her time here, Jamie thought, his heart full with pity for her.

"Jamie? . . . Is that you Jamie?"

Jake's voice emerged up out from the pillow where his head had sunk. His eyes flicked open, searching the room, finding Jamie. They seemed watery, less brown, less firm.

Jake's hands trembled on the turned-back bedsheet.

"Yes," Jamie said.

"Hell, boy, what're you doing here? You're supposed to be mad at me!"

His mention of the anger suddenly brought it back to the surface. "I *am* mad at you," Jamie said then.

Suddenly Jake's eyes seemed to darken against the white face.

"What in hell for?" he challenged.

"You know damn well what for," Jamie said, the anguish abruptly coming out so that his voice was husky. "Why the hell didn't you take me in?" He was almost sobbing.

For a second, Jake was silent. Then he exploded, his face red, his voice as firm as it had once ever been. "*Goddammit*, Jamie," he said, trying to sit up, the action aborted, "you can go around mealy-mouthing like Fred if you want to, whining because you think I didn't do right by you, but *by God* I didn't know your mother had had a child — she wouldn't marry me — I know because I asked her. Just read her diary and you'll see — well, *by God* I would have taken you in if I'd known. So for Christ's sake — get it straight — I *didn't* know!!"

Jamie stood there, ready to make a retort. What could he say? That *he'd* made an awful error? That maybe he wanted to make Jake suffer because *he* had suffered?

"Jamie," Jessie said then. "Let it go. . . . What does it matter?"

Abruptly Jake became angry at Jessie too. "Goddammit, Jess," he said, "what matters is that I didn't *know*! Get that straight, for God's sake, both of you! *I didn't know*!"

And then Jake collapsed back against the pillow in another coughing fit. Jessie rushed to help him, holding the frail body in her arms, blood staining the sheet as it exploded from his lungs. Jamie blanched.

Moments later, when the fit had subsided, Jamie found all the anger had drained out of him. Perhaps it had never been real; all he could think of now was that there was very little time. He knew that Jake and he needed to make the most of it.

He edged closer to the bed. "You didn't know."

He cleared his throat, rubbed a hand over his forehead, temporarily dislodging his glasses. He straightened them. "I'm glad I'm here, Jake," he went on.

Jake could only nod agreement.

"So what do I call you?" Jamie asked after a moment. "I can't really . . ."

"*Jake*," Jake sputtered. "Just call me Jake."

Now Jake seemed to have become absorbed by his own pain. He had retreated from Jamie and Jessie, from the room. He said, at last able to speak: "This is a hell of a note to have this stuff taking over your body — to be on a timetable someone — or *thing* has set up. So don't you two dream up things to feel bad about. I haven't time for that!"

Then he was silent, Jessie and Jamie standing as if transfixed in the room.

"It'll be all right, Jake," Jamie said then. But Jamie remembered those words. . . It seemed whenever someone said, "It'll be all right," it *had*n't been. But he added anyway, "I mean, we'll be all right."

"Good," Jake managed to say.

And he closed his eyes again, lost in memories, lost in pain.

Jamie thought again of the blind calf as Jessie lowered her father onto his pillow — *their* father, he thought, he would have to get used to that — and gently pulled the blood-speckled sheet up over his chest, covering the bony protuberances. In that other scene, long ago, when he and Jake had taken the calf and cared for him, his fate was certain. . . . Nature had only foreshortened his life.

When Jake had told Jamie, years ago, that the calf would not be kept alive, his eyes had looked long and deeply out from the corral where the calf paced to the rolling hills back of the creek, to the place where the bull liked to stand and look out over the ranch.

"Where're *you* headed?" Jake'd asked Jamie suddenly that day. "You gotta have something in mind. What is it?"

And Jake's gaze had pinned him down — he was just twelve years old then — forcing him to stutter: "Get me out of this town. That's what I'm gonna do."

Jake hadn't said anything; he jabbed his hands in his pants pockets and looked up at the sky, as if searching for clouds. "It isn't all the town, boy," he'd said. "You come out here and live on this land, you'll never want the city."

But Jamie hadn't answered.

"When you coming to work for me? *Per*manently," Jake had queried then.

"I . . . I don't know, sir."

"Don't know, don't *know*?" He had shouted, neck veins straining.

Suddenly Jamie realized it wasn't just memory; Jake was shouting now. Propping himself up in bed, he railed at them, at the room: "What *is* this Christ-awful stuff anyway? Why? . . . Why?" his voice resounding through the room, the tirade ending in another spasm of coughing.

Jessie went to him, holding him once again. "Oh, Poppa," she said grimly. "When will you learn to keep your mouth shut?"

And, miraculously, as if she'd ordered it, the paroxysm left him and Jake's color returned to normal.

Jake looked at Jamie and smiled. "She's got my fire, hasn't she, boy?" he said with affection.

"Yes, sir."

"And so do you."

Jamie didn't answer. He realized he had never sat down and he went to perch gingerly on the side of the bed away from Jake; he could hear a young calf bellowing down in the barnyard, and the soft whinny of a horse.

"You haven't got another blind one, have you, Jake?" he asked.

"Blind?"

"You know — the blind calf like you had before."

"Oh." The words seemed to call forth the same ambivalent image Jamie'd had because he frowned. "No." Then: "You still heading for the city, boy?"

There was an urgency in his voice. Jamie looked over at Jessie. He studied his hands. "Don't know."

Jake said, "That's a fake world, boy."

Jamie was silent.

"I was thinking," now Jake's glance sought the window, went out to the space beyond, "I was thinking maybe you and Jess . . . maybe you could, you know?"

A cough separated them momentarily.

"Poppa, rest."

"Jake, maybe I'd better come another day."

"No. This stuff," he said again, waving vaguely at his chest. He didn't finish the sentence. Then, as if he had only just noticed, Jake asked, "What the hell's that uniform?"

But he knew, Purdy must have told him because he went on, "Fort Riley — Will and I were there — a long, long time ago."

He sighed. And then the spasm came again and wouldn't let him go. Jake's face twitched with pain, his eyes filling with tears, until Jessie flew to the bureau on the other side of the room, swept up the syringe there, sterilizing Jake's arm — why, Jamie wondered, did she bother? He didn't know that Jake had once wondered the same thing about his own father. Jessie plunged the needle in, again wiping the alcohol-laden cotton wad over the place the needle had penetrated. Gradually, even as Jamie watched, the distorted features relaxed, the head sank back against the pillow, and Jake slept.

Jamie found himself staring into his hands.

"Have you . . . ever thought of staying, Jamie?" Jessie asked him then.

Jamie brought his glance up to face her. "Yes," he said. "But I don't know."

She sighed. "It's not the same as it was," she admitted. "I mean —" and her own glance went out the window, escaping, as Jake's had. She didn't finish her sentence.

They were leaving a great many things unspoken, Jamie thought.

Outside, the sun was beating down, heating up for summer, and Jamie knew if he looked far enough, he could see past the creek up to where the great bull — or one of them — stood and surveyed his territory. Behind the bull, if he were there, would be the cows he protected, mated with, and beyond them, would be the rolling pastures and ponds and small ravines that he and Jake had searched on foot and horseback until they knew them as well as the parts of their bodies. Sometimes they had come across a spring, bubbling out of the earth or between the rocks of a cliff and Jake had told Jamie that his father had drunk from those streams and had never been ill.

"I do love this land," Jamie said at last. "It's just —" but he didn't finish his thought.

"Yes . . . " Jessie said.

She had barely spoken before the door was flung open and Fred's terrified face appeared.

"Grandmother's had a *stroke*," he announced.

Chapter
Forty-Two

HAD OLD JESSICA been able to see herself as others saw her, her alarm at her condition would have increased; but she couldn't see the perpetually astonished face she now presented to the family who trooped, one after the other, into the room. She couldn't see the mouth that sagged downward, she didn't know that her bodily functions were going on even as she lay beneath the huge walnut headboard — the one she had slept under as a bride. She felt secure in the old bed, it having been moved to this northwest room which had once been Jake's and Herman Lutz's. She and Jake had subtly changed positions.

And there were other things in the room that calmed her — thank God she was back from the Jesus Saves Boardinghouse — items which, like the bed, had come down through the years and remained in this room: the walnut dresser with the heavy marble top, on which her Shalimar and Chanel now rested, the gray and white pitcher and basin once used for morning ablutions. Even the ancient Swedish New Testament that had belonged to Olie. Olie, dear, dear Olie, had been in this room.

Jessica's eyes filled with tears. Olie — August — gone. And now she was about to join them.

Old Jessica knew she couldn't speak, and strangely, the inability was comforting to her: it had always seemed that she had to try to right things in the family, to control things, and now, she was relieved of that burden. She knew that when she attempted to say something, the words did not come out right. They were slurred, and inappropriate. At last she had retreated into silence. There was only the sudden welling up of tears now that demonstrated her emotion.

Fred came into the room.

"Oh, Grandmother!" he said, coming over to the bed, noticing that she was weeping. "Please don't cry. Things will get better."

Freddie always hoped for that, Old Jessica knew. And once again she found herself trying to say something, though from the moment she had regained consciousness it had been apparent that what she pictured in her mind as neat sentences came out as a garble. And now, as she tried, foolishly, it was all mumbles and mutters and nonsensical! *I sound like a goose*, she thought.

Good God, she told herself then, abruptly frightened. Would she ever be able to speak correctly again? Did she really *want* to? If she tried and it didn't come out, she would sound like those silly morons they used to drag along in the dreadful tiny circuses of her youth in Atlas City. Freaks, everyone called them, the "freaks" themselves seeming to like the designation, for at least it gave them some identity.

And if she were now placed back in her youth, would carnival operators want to display her before an insensitive public, make signs for her reading: "Come See the Freak Who Cannot Speak!" *Oh, God.*

"Grandmother," Fred was comforting her, reaching over to plant a kiss on her masklike face, "Grandmother, you mustn't cry. Doc Harvey will fix you. He will."

He made her sound like a lawnmower, Old Jessica told herself. Or some kind of mechanical monster.

But at least Fred was now calling her "Grandmother," Molly too, instead of the awful "Gran." It was only Wilbur — dumb, foolish Wilbur — Jessica had revised her earlier estimate of him — who insisted still on "Gran."

"I'll send Wilbur in to cheer you," Fred said then. "You know how you've always responded to Wilbur."

Oh God.

While Fred was searching through the house for Wilbur, Jessica thought, she and Jake were dying in this house and all about them boobies raced. It was too late to tell Jake that at last she loved him, that all through the years — when she was mourning her dead children and somehow blamed Jake for everything — she had loved him. Why was it, Old Jessica wondered now as tears once again washed over her eyes, seeped over them and streaked down her face, why was it that exactly when she began to understand things, to reach reconciliation with life, Fate struck her down so that she could do nothing about her revelations. That was the one painful thing about not being able to express herself. At first, she had felt like snatching a shotgun from somewhere, exactly like her brother, poor, weak Willard, Sr., and blasting herself out of this world. It seemed she was in a living hell.

But gradually, an understanding came over her. Perhaps this was retribution for her many unkind acts in life, acts which she had not always seen as unkind. Perhaps if she suffered in this life, she would not have to suffer in an afterlife. For Old Jessica now believed in an afterlife, and she did not want to have to endure eternal agony.

She was willing to suffer speechlessness when she really wanted to say something, and to glory in the lack of speech when she did *not* want to say something. Her life still had some kind of purpose evidently, for the Good Lord had not seen fit to take her.

She thought then, if she and August were together in the afterlife, she would enjoy their further battles. Surely going into the "Great Beyond," did not destroy every earthly relationship. How she would enjoy a good verbal joust!

And strangely, one of the comforts now came from an unlikely source: Jessie. Jessie did not insist on treating her like some demented idiot; she seemed to sense that the mind, which tried to force the mouth to shape sentences — and failed — was not crippled. Beneath the blur of her babbling, or her silence, there was order.

Wilbur now projected himself into the room, with a leap. He seemed to feel that exhibiting stout good health would somehow force Jessica into recovery, would, by some unknown osmosis, seep into his great-grandmother and make her well. *He acts like a seal*, Old Jessica thought as she watched the thin, wiry, continually smirking Wilbur go through his antics.

"Dad said you needed brightening, Gran," Wilbur said, now thrusting his face directly before hers, as though she could not see him perfectly well. "Do you?"

Wilbur looked into each widened eye, seeming to be looking through her at the pillow. What was he thinking, Old Jessica wondered. Was he planning his next year at the Denver high school he attended? Was he plotting to do away with Jamie, now that he had been established as Jake's son? Did he believe his mother, that she had had an affair with Jake? What did he think about *that*?

And suddenly Old Jessica knew that what Molly was trying to intimate around the house was all wrong. Jake would not be such a fool, if he even had been capable of what she claimed; and surely Wilbur would not believe it either.

While Wilbur cavorted about the room, sentences — as nonsensical as hers, though Wilbur seemed not to care — spilled from him like water over a dam. Jessica let her thoughts rove. There was one other advantage to being considered an idiot she found; people did not expect answers. No, they per*for*med for you, inflicting themselves on you and expecting to find you delighted with the attention. But you did not have to follow them in their rantings — you could lie back and say to yourself: what a busybody you are, my boy, and not a flicker of an eyelash, not a non sequitur from your mouth, would give them a clue that you did not consider them vastly entertaining.

And if you wanted, you could pretend great sleepiness, close your eyes, pretend to drift off. If she did that, Old Jessica thought with a wry inward laugh, Wilbur would probably hold a mirror up to her mouth to see if she were still alive!

Well, Wilbur *was* entertaining at times. Like a clown, he pranced fatuously about the room, touching things — the gray and white pitcher, the marble top of the dresser, as if he were about to appropriate them.

"I know you don't want Jamie to have this, Gran," Wilbur was saying to her then, placing a proprietary hand on the marble of the dresser. "So when you get your speech back — or your writing — you can simply assign it to me."

He seemed proud of himself for his cleverness, folded his hands under his shirt, regarded her, nodding assent for her. His hair was faintly red — everything about Wilbur was faint, she decided now — a fact that infuriated her as much at the moment as it had when Willard, Jr., was born with the tinge of red. It was, again, her sense that red hair belonged to *her*, the family icon, and no one else. It was also the sensation she had that part of her family were, perhaps, kind of cretins, some offspring of dull parents, a streak that ran through them like the brown line down the spine of a buckskin.

What was he saying now?

"Yes, Gran, we must keep Jamie from putting his hands on everything. You know Mom and I are concerned. I know you were too because . . ."

And Old Jessica rolled her eyes shut and pretended sleep.

But Wilbur did not leave. He seemed to think she was still listening to him.

Jamie.

It had been hard for her to reconcile her feelings about Jamie. She couldn't help but feel he was an interloper — she could never change that, but she was somehow glad the whole stupid secret was out. If she could write Elsie — and she could, she did, in her head — she would say that she was happy to be through with all the machinations of the past. "Things will out," August once said, and he was right.

One thing that remained buried, however, but which she might have confessed to Jake had she been able to, was the part she had played in getting Jamie adopted by Junior and Hazel. She suspected that Jake had centered on her as the go-between, but that knowledge, the certainty of it, would be buried with her. It would remain a family mystery.

There were so many mysteries in her family, she thought — in families in general. People act from certain motives and perhaps years later, the motives are gone, but the actions remain — like furrows in the soil — and reactions have taken place that cannot be called back. Pain makes an imprint that lasts forever.

"I'm studying nuclear energy," Wilbur was saying now as Old Jessica briefly allowed his voice to penetrate her thoughts. "Well, not really studying — I'm looking into it. I can see myself as a great scientist."

That was the trouble with Wilbur — and Fred and Molly, and had been the trouble with Willard, her brother — as well as other Pratts and Lutzes. They saw themselves as great, but did nothing to attain their vision.

Oh the way a family weaves its webs!

Was she just tying up loose ends in her mind now, Jessica wondered. She turned her head slightly, to take in Wilbur's pacing about the room, seeming to follow him with her usual devoutness. She thought: if you but knew how my feelings have changed toward you! But Wilbur, misinterpreting her studied gaze on him for fondness, smiled at her and winked. He flung himself into the chair by the window, then flung himself out once again to come over, touch her bedcovers, run a hand over the headboard directly above her so that she caught the scent of some men's cologne he'd sprayed on. She would wrinkle her nose if she could, Jessica thought; she tried, the plastic face not responding to her signals.

"Don't consider your life over," Wilbur was saying, philosophic. "You have many years left."

His tone clearly indicated he thought she had *weeks*.

"And Jake?" Wilbur seemed to think he had to play both their parts — his and his grandmother's — so he was apparently constructing conversation.

He leaned back from the bed and returned to the chair by the window, plunking down in it. He placed his chin on one hand. He seemed to be reaching into his most reclusive depths for ideas. "Jake won't last as long as you will."

If he thought that was comforting to her, Jessica told herself as tears once more filled her eyes, the poor boy was clearly wrong. *Oh wretched child,* she thought, *leave me be!*

"Don't cry about Jake," Wilbur advised. "He's lived a full life."

Jessica wanted to ask him what he knew about it. Did Wilbur think that anyone — even herself at ninety — was ready to just drop off into the afterlife? . . . Would there be anyone there to greet her if she did?

Oh, Wilbur, how much you have to learn, she thought.

And while she watched Wilbur, as if prodded by her silent feelings, finally get up and leave the room, Old Jessica thought that perhaps it didn't matter at all. Perhaps nothing mattered. Perhaps life was only the putting of one foot before the other, no matter what happened.

All of which took an incredible amount of courage.

"I won't have it," Old Jessica heard Jessie say.

She was talking to someone just outside Old Jessica's door, and the ears, which Old Jess had always been famous for, had not been affected by the stroke. Apparently people forgot that.

"She should be in a home," Wilbur was announcing, seemingly to the closed door, for his voice was so loud he must have been facing her room.

"You don't take care of her, *I* do," Jessie said. "And I won't have it. So just go back to your own house Wilbur Lutz, and think up your deviltry there. We don't need you."

"Suit yourself," Wilbur said with a mocking half-laugh. "But don't come to me for help when Jake gets even worse and Old Jessica's wetting her pants every fifteen minutes."

"Get *out*!" Jessie shouted.

Thank God someone was shouting, Old Jessica thought. The house was made for shouting.

And then Jessie came into the room, fed Old Jessica, tenderly wiping off the morsels which Jessica couldn't clutch in her recalcitrant lips, sponging up the drools which insisted on coming, which raced down her chin, coagulating onto the napkin Jessie'd put around her neck. *Oh God, Jessie*, Old Jessica said silently, *I wronged you all*.

Chapter
Forty-Three

"WHAT DO YOU MEAN?" Jessie was demanding. "How can you just force yourself in here and start spouting off?"

Jessie and Jamie were in Jake's room. He had been resting from a particularly fatiguing coughing spell, when Fred had burst through the bedroom door, his face fiercely red.

"Okay, Dad" — he nearly shouted in fury — "it's time for talk. . . . Molly told me!" — as if he'd forgotten Jake's condition.

Jessie turned to face Fred, her voice as furious as his. "What do you mean?" she punctuated each word.

Rambling on, Fred blurted, almost irrational, "I'm a descendent too. A relative. . . . Don't tell me you and Jamie there," he cast a malevolent glance at Jamie, who had stood up as if to protect Jessie — or Jake — or himself — "are the only le*git*imate heirs?"

He thrust the word "legitimate" at both of them.

"And don't tell *me* you're not going to try to pull something out of your hat," Jessie shouted back with sarcasm. "Don't tell me you and little Molly haven't been hatching plans again. . . . If your schemes were golden eggs, you'd be rich!"

Her anger was hurled across the room at him, but Fred deflected it. "If Grandmother could talk, she'd tell you. *That bastard* — my own father — seduced my wife. She came in here to console him and then he just got himself all riled up and . . ."

Fred was blubbering now, his words almost as garbled as Old Jessica's.

Jessie looked as if Fred had slapped her. "What *do you mean?*" she said for the third time.

For a moment, Fred just looked down, shook his head, then put his face in his hands.

Jake, staring out from the bed at them, felt paralyzed, as if a knife had gone through him. The incident with Molly had been shoved from his mind — he knew her scheme had been to turn his mother against him. And Molly knew there was nothing to her accusations. But he had apparently underestimated her again, he thought.

Yet Fred's ranting seemed to pump some new life into him. If Fred *wanted* him to die — and he couldn't be certain, ever, how Fred really felt about him — he had just done the wrong thing. Fred had never learned that with his father, with his grandmother, with Jessie and Jamie, opposition gave them strength.

"*I* can tell you," Jake said, his voice firmer than it had been for weeks, "*nothing* happened between Molly and me. If you prefer to believe her trash, that's up to you. . . . My conscience is clear."

Jessie and Jamie turned their heads to look at him, as if they were not quite certain who to believe.

Jake went on, trying to prop himself up on the pillows, but finding he was unable. "Molly came in here . . . I didn't know what for, but I certainly know now!" He shot a glance at Fred, who had dropped his hands from his face and glared at his father. "She came in here with a purpose, but she didn't accomplish it. Doesn't it seem a little odd that she took so long to tell you about it? Just when Jamie gets back?"

From the doorway came Molly's voice. "Old Jessica saw us! You know that, Dad Lutz."

So she was back to that, Jake thought, *Dad Lutz*. Well, he didn't care anymore what she or Fred thought. And his mother certainly couldn't express what she saw, or thought she saw.

Now Fred leaped into battle. "Don't you dare try to make Molly out the villain," he shouted. "Don't you dare sully her name! She said you tried to seduce her and I believe her!"

"You can think what you like, Fred," Jake calmly said. "You will anyway. But she's lying. *Why*, I don't know. I can only guess."

Jessie began to cry and without another word, she ran from the room.

Jake, exhausted by the effort it had taken to try to clear his name, leaned over, abruptly caught by a fit of coughing, pulling the sheet up to his face to try to stifle the cough. But it wouldn't stop. Jamie went over to him, tried to touch him. "Not my ribs," Jake screamed, "not my ribs!"

"Get out of here," Jamie almost shouted then, turning to Fred. "You've done all the damage you can, . . . so get out of here."

"I'll get out," Fred shouted back. "You damn bet I'll get out. And Dad can just damn well separate the store from the ranch because I'll never work for him again. Or for *you*, you little bastard!"

"Get *out*," Jamie ordered.

Jake could hear him start to walk over to Fred. He would hit him, Jake thought; but just as Jamie reached him, Fred, apparently sensing the danger, scooted out the door. Jake heard him call back: "You'll regret this! Dad can't manage without me!"

Ha, Jake thought.

Jake lay in the bed, staring at the ceiling as if it would give him some answers. The pain now was intermittent — steadily intermittent — coming back with a stab, then fading, sometimes like a shock of electricity, sometimes more slowly, more fully, rounding out into something dreadful so that he had to grip the sheet, hard, to keep from crying out. The injections finally released him to rest or sleep.

Will came often; he liked to visit with Jake, and Jake liked to visit with him, even under the circumstances neither of them could change. Jake remembered a poem from the *Rubáiyát*: "The Moving Finger writes, and having writ, moves on. . . ." It was an expression of the futility of action, sorrow, regret. And it was so true. Jake only wished — *Goddamn!* — that it didn't have to be a choice between pain and clearheadedness or absence of pain and muddled thinking.

It angered him to have his thoughts blunted! He hated when he would search for a word, his glance seeking help from Jamie's face — for Jessie had not come back since the altercation with Fred and Molly. Jake would seem to search the corners of the room, as though the word — *something*

— would be revealed to him. *Damnation*, he thought, this was rough! If only he could compete with it as he had everything else in his life.

He felt a twinge in his side, like a gentle reminder, of its superiority, and he took one hand and covered the place with it, patting the pain as though familiarity made it a friend, made it better. For some reason, his mind lurched back to the calves that had to undergo the branding iron. Well, this thing was branding him now, and unlike the hot iron, it didn't let up.

But Jake was no longer afraid of the pain. It was only that he seemed to have to meet death on unequal terms — in fact, on no terms at all.

How much time did he have?

What he did have now, he told himself, were memories — of Louise, of his mother, of Fred and Jessie, of Ilse, of Jamie. For some reason, those of Jamie were among the best.

When Jamie was still very small, Jake used to take him out on snowy mornings in the cutter. Jamie would sit, huddled under a blanket on the seat, watching Jake while he harnessed the horses, the harness stiff with cold, the horses' nostrils steaming. Jamie's nose, protruding into the cold, would grow chill and Jake would hear him whimper; then Jake would take off his muffler and wrap it over Jamie's face. Frost clung to the bushes and fence posts. As they rode along, Jake would watch, and Jamie too, as the horses' haunches churned, now right, now left, the hooves striking the hard-packed snow, the sled gliding smoothly over it.

When they came back from the ride, Jessie would have baked bread, the delicious yeast smell permeating the air, the butter sinking into the warm bread as he and Jamie sat at the kitchen table and stuffed it in their mouths, some rivulets of melted butter running down the sides of their lips to their chins.

Jake would tell Jamie tales: of his father, August, and his father's father, Herman — on those wintry evenings when the sun sank down so hurriedly in the sky and darkness took over the land. "My father's father, my grandfather, Herman, was adopted; and my great-grandpappy Jacob Lutz was a minister, believe it or not," he'd say. "I sometimes think I must have inherited the antidote to that!" Then Jake would throw back his head and roar with laughter, and Jamie, seemingly catching it like a plague would laugh too, both of them shaking their sides and howling.

"Old Jessica claimed my great-grandfather got an education from the church. And *I* told her," and Jake knew Jamie's eyes would grow round then, impressing the boy with his seriousness, "*I* said, 'He got some *learning.* . . . Some folks *call* that an education!'"

And then, Jamie, delighted, would laugh and they would stare into the fire that snapped in the kitchen fireplace, Jake's eyes thoughtful. "Now *I* got my education down there in the store — sleeping underneath the coat racks when we stayed open until midnight on Saturday nights — and here," and he would bang his fist on the kitchen table for emphasis so that their plates jumped, "here on this ranch!"

The pain twitched, nagging him. Moaning, Jake turned his face on the pillow, sweat prickling his forehead. . . . He wanted to put off the shot as long as possible, as if he were testing himself. But it was more than that, he thought now. He didn't want the painkiller to become ineffective. Doc Harvey had told Jessie how often he could have the shots and he would stick with that.

Jake's mind wandered again . . . he imagined himself riding Cannibal, with Fred behind him on the gelding. Suddenly the gelding reared, bucked, made ready to bolt, and Jake turned to hear Fred scream, "*Help,* Dad! . . ." Jake felt the tremor within himself whenever Fred called for him, because it was always demanding something, it seemed, that Jake could never fathom.

Fred's face hung before him, pleading, the voice resounding in his ears, "*Help,* Dad, *help!*"

"I *can't* help you!" Jake shouted into the room. "I *can't.*"

"Easy . . . Jake," a voice said softly. "Easy now."

"Who?"

"Jamie."

"Ah . . ."

He sank back into the pillow then — he must have sat up, he decided. It was such a long way down. He seemed to be able to roam the bedroom, stand near the treasured rocking chair where August had said William Jennings Bryan had sat, walk up behind Jamie, who now, he saw, was leaning over him and holding his hand. As if he were in a dream, outside himself, Jake could see he was lying in the bed, eyes wide, head almost obscured in the depths of the down pillow that swelled around him.

This was dying, wasn't it?

With everyone busy elsewhere, but Jamie here beside him, the oxygen tank in the corner, at the ready, to prolong the last moments . . . this was dying.

Well, he thought, it wasn't too bad. The pain was stilled for a moment, perhaps even now he was merely in a haze of drugs, suspended above the petty cares of the world . . . almost euphoric. Sounds came back to him as though they had issued from great distances, problems no longer churned in his mind. His nostrils detected the faint scent of cooking and he thought to himself that of course the mortals out there in the room had to eat and drink and sleep, but he no longer had need of those things. It was as if his body and his soul had already been separated.

The bright, orange nasturtiums in the vase on the corner table caught his eye and he wondered . . . *what month was this?*

Then suddenly another image pressed in upon him: Louise, her face swollen and unrecognizable. Had he heard Louise now? Was she calling for him?

"*Louise . . .!*" Jake called out to the void.

But the image was cut off and instead Jamie was leaning over him, his hands on Jake's shoulders, gently holding him back in the bed.

"Relax, Jake," he said. "Everything's all right."

Jake remembered reading a story once of an old person dying, who kept asking the people around him to do something for him, something that actually had been done years earlier, and the people did not know how to respond. They kept saying it was "*all right.*" Finally a little boy in the room went up to the dying man and said, "I'll take care of it. I'll do it." And he went out of the room to do whatever it was, or seem to do it, and the old man died in peace.

But of course, Jake gathered his thoughts now, there was nothing to do. And he no longer could direct anything anyway.

For a split moment, he was angry. People around dying people, he thought, were always asserting themselves. Do this, do that, relax, don't fret . . . *it's all right.*

Why don't they leave us alone? He wanted to bang his fist down on the sheet, but of course he couldn't even raise it.

"Get *out*," he said then.

Jamie must have misunderstood, for he said, "I'm sorry, Jake. Of course I'll leave you alone."

"No, *no!*" Jake corrected him; he didn't know what he had meant when he had said that, *"Get out."* Was it to the thing that was swallowing him?

"I didn't mean you."

So Jamie sank into the rocker and watched the fan he had set on the window to suck in air, keep it moving in the room, apparently listening to its little internal squeak, setting the tempo of time. Jake closed his eyes and lay quietly, his chest slowly moving up and down. From time to time, he quivered, twitching slightly, like a dog having dreams.

In his mind, Jake was again remembering far, far back to the time when his father, August, and another man from Atlas City had decided to start raising and racing Greyhounds. "No-No" Neil was the name the towns-people gave to August's partner. No-No's opinions were always gloomy. "Worms," he'd say of some Greyhound August wanted to buy. "See that white in his gums? *No, no.* Won't live three months."

Often August would buy the dog anyway, Neil's dire prognostications resounding in his ears, and just as often August proved to be right and Neil wrong. But it never changed Neil's opinions. "A mere stroke of luck," he'd maintain. *"No, no.* The dog will die soon, mark my words."

No-No always wore a tan surplus Army shirt and khaki pants, his mouth wrapped around the stub of a cigar, which he chewed and sucked on and pushed around with his tongue. It reminded Jake of August, before he gave up smoking. When Neil spoke, he merely shifted the stub onto the back molars, pulling his lip aside, his teeth gleaming yellow. No one ever saw him with a fresh cigar in his mouth; no one ever saw him without a cigar.

It was an epidemic of leptospirosis that ended the racing career of August and Neil. One day they awoke to find the kennel sick, the dogs dragging their hind legs around, the bitches not feeding their puppies. And hours later, the entire kennel was dead. Jake recalled that August kept shoveling dirt on the large, communal grave; they buried the puppies, nine of them, with the two bitches. Neil kept shaking his head and saying, *"No, no.* I told you. It's a crazy world we live in."

Jake's mind jumped back to the time that August had encountered the "World Rebels." He read — he sent for the classics, books on Nature, anarchist pamphlets. Old Jessica used to demand of August, Jake had overheard as a boy: "Why don't you just settle down and be an ordinary person?" And August had replied: "T'ain't my nature!"

The World Rebel Movement was one of the doubtful enterprises August had gotten into — discovered on one of his trips to Chicago: "*The seat of iniquity,*" Old Jess had declared. August saw the lettering of the World Rebels on a door in an almost abandoned building, with a directing hand pointing upward. He climbed the dingy staircase and faced two men running off pamphlets on a duplicating machine.

"What's the *World Rebel Movement?*" he'd asked.

"A group . . . non-conformist . . . for the purpose of establishing a single tax on land . . . to promote the welfare of the common citizen . . . and to urge revolutions — *of the mind,*" one of the men answered.

His father was enchanted.

"How much does membership cost?" he'd asked.

The two men looked at one another, and one reached down for the pamphlet they were printing off, "Duties of Membership."

"Are you Communists?" August demanded.

"We're *rebels,*" was the answer.

August signed the membership card and handed over the $10 dues for the first year.

Again . . . Jake smiled, remembering.

He knew that for a time after August had returned to Atlas City, it had amused him to talk of his connection with the World Rebel Movement, to frighten local landowners with the prospect of a single land tax!

"You're a *damn* fool," one irate farmer reportedly yelled at him one day.

Jake remembered that August's involvement with the World Rebels was an undulating course, determined by his speculative mood at the moment. For several years his father had given the movement nothing, then he donated $500 — while Old Jessica screamed they'd soon be in the poorhouse — then nothing again for years. Always he received polite letters from the group, which told of their plans and their minor triumphs.

Jake could even recall that as August grew older, he sometimes would have a pang of emptiness — loneliness — Jake could empathize now. He would see August pacing the room, unable to keep still.

"What is it, Dad?" Jake would ask.

But August seldom answered. And when he did, he would confess that he felt he should go out and chop wood — or haul water — or maybe tear up the ground and plant a huge garden. But sometimes it was winter when this happened to him, and the ground was frozen; even if it were summer, he would indulge himself only briefly . . . and the notion would pass.

"Sometimes I feel," he told Jake, "like *I'm* a rebel — I don't fit in."

"But you like Atlas City!"

"*Yes.* Yes! But I want to *do* . . . something . . . only — I don't know what there is to do."

August went through his Nature books, Jake could recall, learning the names of the common varieties of plants and trees and birds in the countryside around Atlas City.

He would read Thoreau . . . "*Yes!*" he would say, "you can spend an entire afternoon watching ants and insects, noting the life that moves around you. We don't see it until we look for it . . . and then, there, reflected in Nature, are all the fundamentals of knowledge."

Looking at a winter-brown landscape, Jake could remember that August might say: "See the tiny red berries that stay on that bush? You don't notice them until you get close. It's like a Chinese painting — spare brushmarks, color that becomes apparent only when you search for it — elusive beauty."

Jake would be surprised by August's artistic intuitions; it was a part of him he never expected — one that Jake knew his mother would never have believed. In fact, Jake mused, trying to focus his mind now, there had been many things about both his parents he had never understood. But one thing he knew: they did not understand each other.

Perhaps that was part of their mutual attraction, the glue that held them fast.

Refocusing again, Jake recalled that this lack of understanding had resulted in one especial unfairness: August had refused to recognize Old Jessica's legitimate claim to the property they had built up, and he had bypassed her with his will. Jake regretted later that he had gone along with his father's wishes, presuming at the time that August had wanted only what would be "best" for Jessica — no burden, no responsibilities, knowing Jake would take care of her.

Jake's thoughts seemed to collect and hover over him, as though he could reach out and pluck one to reconsider. In his more lucid moments, he felt, somehow, that he should organize his life now — at least in his mind — before it was too late. He needed to trace it, see the pattern. But the images refused to be put into order, and they slipped back and forth with a will of their own.

Jake's glance sought Jamie in the rocker, the plane of Jamie's face sagging, his eyes closed, his glasses askew. He's asleep, Jake realized. He looks tired. *And I . . .* he thought *. . . I will soon be in the deepest sleep of all.*

Already he felt a detachment to the things in his world, a drawing within, a retreat to his innermost self.

Suddenly it seemed to Jake that he was being transported, to a place within Jamie, the room, the land, the house, the sky, while another part of him began a journey elsewhere down a long empty corridor. He pulled back from the walk down this hallway — it wasn't quite time.

"I'm tired," he thought.

Jamie must have thought Jake had spoken, because he awoke with a start.

"What, Jake? . . ."

Instantly Jamie was beside him almost whispering, "What is it?"

But Jake didn't know and he didn't answer.

Chapter Forty-Four

*A*S IF MOLLY and Fred had planned it, the rains came. Spring and summer downpours had always been threatening on the ranch, with the river flowing through it. But this summer the rains had begun early and continued day after day.

"It's already flooding upstream," Jamie reported to Jessie early one day. "It's only a matter of time. The radio reports the trains can't get through at Darby's Crossing, and the highway past Harper is flooded."

"I can't do anything," Jessie said, shaking her head, and seeming to miss the point, "I can't forgive him."

"You'd better act," Jamie said. "*We* had. Or we'll lose the calves, the wheat, the hogs . . ."

But Jessie couldn't — or wouldn't — pull herself together.

"In *our* house," she said. "Under *our* noses!"

"Jessie," Jamie said now. "Why do you believe what Molly said? You know she's lying . . . and I think you *want* to be angry at Jake, but for something else. He can't help it if he has cancer, you know."

Jessie flushed, but she didn't answer.

By the noon hour, Jamie had been down to the river to inspect it, riding Duke. He hadn't been prepared for the torrent that was rushing full between the banks, nor for the water inching up that would soon spill over onto the trees near the creek and then on into the wheat fields. He saw a raccoon clinging to a tree limb, floating past, the sharp little face looking at him with terror.

"Jessie," Jamie said when he returned to the house. "I'm calling the neighbors."

"They'll be busy with their own problems."

James insisted. "The ones who live upland — the Beningas can help us. And Sandy'll help."

Jessie was unresponsive.

"By now, it's over the banks," Jamie said, "and spreading in the wheat fields. It's come up six inches in the last hour. We've got to get the sows and their litters out of the barn. We've got to see that the cattle aren't down in the creek area."

Jessie finally seemed to comprehend what he was telling her as Jamie took her arm, led her to the kitchen table, seated her. "This is serious and it's going to get worse. We've got to do something or we'll lose every-thing. We can't just sit here."

By afternoon, Jamie had called Will Harvey and the Beningas and even the soldiers at the Fort were helping out. Sandy was there of course — he'd taken some of the sows and, because the water was high, guided them by their tails until they got their footing. The little pigs swam beside their mothers, snorting fearfully, but negotiating the water until they, too, were secure. Sandy was putting them behind the fence at the homeplace, right in the lawn, and then he began sandbagging around the fence to keep the rising waters out. Some of the soldiers were helping him; at first they seemed tentative, uncertain what to do, but Sandy shouted orders like a Sergeant and soon they were working as a team.

Jamie got on Duke again, called to the other men on horseback to fol-low.

"The cattle're in trouble down there," one of the Beninga boys had said.

They followed Jamie down the lane as far as they all could go be-fore they heard the powerful roaring of the river, the crack of the huge cottonwoods, downed, banging up against the banks, knocking still more earth into the raging waters. They heard the bawling of the cattle.

As the men approached the angry torrent they saw that the cattle indeed were in trouble. Three calves, little ones, new this past spring, were crowded together on a sandy islet as water rushed against it, an uprooted chicken coop crashing onto it, banging off, and sailing on into the current. Dead chickens floated on the water as if in pursuit of their home. As Jamie watched, the chickens were pulled under by the current, as if they were being whipped into a giant beater.

Looking out over the area, Jamie could see just the tops of the trees now, the water having risen so fast it lay like an ocean sprouting greenery.

"*My God!*" Will exclaimed. "Look at it! It's as bad as '51!"

That had been the last major flood; even Harper had sections of town inundated then, and had since built a dike to try to keep the high waters out.

Jamie realized they couldn't help the calves now; the water would be well over their heads. He pointed down at Duke's hocks, which were forming little dams against the current. They were standing in nearly two feet of water themselves.

"We're not even near what was the bank," Jamie went on. "Out there, it's over eight feet deep. We can only hope their island holds out."

That question was settled in the next moments. With a sudden surge, the water raced up and over the islet on which the terrified cattle stood; in seconds, as Jamie watched, the sand began giving way, then, with a roar, the whole hillock collapsed and the calves were swept downstream. Two white faces emerged, but in seconds, they too, disappeared.

The men watched in an awed and fearful silence, then turned their horses and rode back up to the wheat fields. The rest of the herd had evidently reached safety; there was no sign of them.

Jamie caught sight of a barn cat clinging to a tree and as he rode up to it, the cat trembling with fear and ready to lash out, Jamie gently, carefully, pulled it from its perch and held it near the saddle horn.

Most of the wheat fields now were under water; clumps of yellow grasses clung to the lower fence posts where the current had hung them like decorations. Jamie noticed the telephone poles were sagging and he wondered how long they would hold up. The water was pounding them, then flowing on.

"I guess we won't get a wheat crop," Jamie said.

Jamie didn't know that Sandy had already gotten the hogs out of the barn until the men approached the house and saw that Sandy and the soldiers were almost finished sandbagging the fenced yard.

He looked out toward the barn, saw that some of the cats had made their way to the roof and were safe. If the water stayed up, they could take food to them, he thought, but hopefully it would recede before that was necessary.

Jamie looked up at the window of Jake's bedroom. He thought he now knew how Jake felt about this place.

Surprisingly, Jessie had come out of the house to help finish with the sandbags; she had said nothing about the sows and their litters, who were investigating all the corners of the yard and seemed happy to be there. Of course they were rooting up some of her petunia bed, but Jamie figured she could overlook that.

Jessie was almost as strong as a man, and she began lifting the heavy sacks of sand, piling them against the fence. At first she worked slowly, almost reluctantly Jamie thought, but as time passed and the edge of the water in the fields crept slowly toward them, she reached her usual, swift pace.

"Sometimes I wonder why we stay here," she said to Jamie. "Maybe Fred was smart to pull out." She stopped to wipe her forehead, a smudge of mud splaying out across it. "It's such damn hard work. And then something like this happens, and wipes out everything we've done!"

"You stay because you like it," Jamie said. "And because Jake wants you to."

Jessie frowned, but didn't answer.

Maybe, Jamie thought, just maybe that was the reason Jessie was so provoked with Jake: it really had nothing to do with Molly — Jessie could hardly take *her* word over her father's — it had to do with the feeling she was trapped.

He had felt that too, he knew. But he had also understood, later, that it wasn't Jake who was causing the problem within him; it was himself.

"You know, it's a hell of a note," Sandy said then. "We live in this

Goddamn country and take its floods, and tornadoes, and blizzards, and we still think of it as 'God's country.'"

"It *is*," Jamie said. "I think it *is*."

But back when he had thought of leaving, Jamie remembered, he had forgotten that a place could so indent itself on your consciousness that you would forever be a part of it.

"Well," Sandy went on, "if you say so. Right now, that's hard to believe."

"Me," Sandy was saying as they piled more bags against the fence, "me — I'm just living here because I've always known it. I wonder what'll happen if our kids ever decide they want to try something else, if they can't really make a living here."

Jamie didn't answer, and Sandy didn't continue. Finally, he straightened up and concluded, "That should do it."

Now all they had to do was wait . . . and hope.

Hours later, when Jamie and the men and Jessie were having coffee, the crest had finally passed. The rain had stopped, and radio reports indicated that the dike had held in Harper, preventing major damage there; but the train tracks were washed out. Countless animals — wild and domestic — had died, and those that remained would have to look earnestly for food. This might be Nature's way, Jamie thought, but it seemed to cause hardship for the entire food chain.

Though the news from Harper about the train tracks was bad, the worst was that the railroad company did not plan to rebuild them into Atlas City — the train was being pulled out. "Inadequate usage," the company had concluded.

"Oscar won't know what to do," Will Harvey said.

"Ned won't know what to do either," Jamie added. "Seeing the train has been part of his life."

A lot of things were over now, Jamie thought. As Jessie moved about the kitchen, refilling coffee cups, he remembered that he was due back at the Fort in two more days, his leave up. He might not be with Jake when he died, he thought, and it made Jake's passing all the harder to bear. He couldn't even imagine Jake not being in his world.

He had promised Jake that he would somehow find a way to stay, and for a moment, Jake looked his old self. He smiled, and reached out to touch Jamie's hand. "I can't ask for more than that," he softly answered.

Jessie, Jamie, and Will had come into Jake's room, all of them standing near the bed, as if they wanted to be as close as possible to Jake. Making idle conversation, Jamie told Jake that the flood had taken the old chicken coop. Jessie, ever the manager, added, "We can use it for firewood if we find it." Then remembering, laughed, "August was always wanting firewood — guess he just got used to it in his boyhood." Will too laughed, recalling those times.

Jake spoke up, "We didn't have furnaces at first — and we didn't have bathrooms. I can't say I regret civilization's improvements on those two things." A smile broke across the thin, pained face. Then, ". . . But what we gain on the one hand, we lose on the other. . . ."

Jamie remembered reading Emerson's *Essays* to Jake a long time ago, with the same thought, and Jamie had wondered at the time if it were true. Now he was certain it was.

He looked over at Jessie. He couldn't tell what she was thinking. Jessie looked up at Will, then away, and Jamie could see the tears in her eyes. She was kneading her hands, as if she hoped to wring something good out of them.

"I think I'd better get some lunch ready," she told them. "We've all worked hard and there's nothing to do but wait."

Jake, Jamie saw, had closed his eyes. He didn't seem concerned how things were going.

Chapter Forty-Five

"POPPA," JESSIE SAID, walking over to the bed and taking his hand, "I'm sorry. . . . I should have known better . . ."

She saw Jake's eyes studying her face, then he weakly smiled at her. "I couldn't bear you being angry, Jessie."

"It was silly," she admitted. Then, "How is it going today, Poppa?"

Jake didn't answer for a moment. She had noticed one thin hand trembling on the bedcovers; Will Harvey had said it might go to the brain and if it did, there would be neurological problems. Jessie felt a tightness in her chest; she knew she had no control over this thing, no one did, and it made her impossibly frustrated and angry. She had always thought people could handle things; now she knew that life had a beat that she couldn't interrupt nor change.

"Poppa," she said, "is it all right if I sit on the bed?"

Jake nodded.

Gingerly, Jessie eased herself beside him. "I remember how I used to do this," she said.

"Yes," Jake murmured.

"I used to think there was a protective caul around us after Mother died. I thought that maybe all the bad things had happened to us and that the rest of our lives would be okay. But," her voice grew low, "I was wrong."

Jake didn't speak, tried to clear his throat, put his hand there as if to stop a cough, the hand trembling.

"Still," Jessie said, "I wouldn't exchange my life for anyone's."

"I'm glad," Jake said. "You were always a strong one, Jessie."

"I never thought of myself that way," Jessie admitted. She bent her head, reached out to straighten the bedcovers and steady her father's hand. She felt the light quiver he couldn't control.

"I was lucky to have you, Poppa," she said.

Jake didn't answer, but he slowly smiled.

"I got a letter a while back," Jessie said then.

She didn't know why she was telling her father this; she had always been withdrawn about her personal life, but there had been this letter and it was something she was going to have to think about, answer.

"It was from Pete Johnson."

Her father's brow wrinkled for a moment, as if he were trying to recall the name.

"You didn't know him, Poppa," she said. "He was someone I met during the war."

Jake nodded.

"I think I've decided what to do," she said, just as though her father knew what she was talking about.

Now she saw he was staring at her, almost without seeing. She wondered how far he was dropping away from her, what images he saw in the room; it was almost as if he were there, but not there, traveling someplace, exploring, a destination she couldn't share.

"I'll let you rest, Poppa," she said then, getting up gently from the bed so she would not disturb him.

She didn't know if he had heard her or not; he seemed to be content, wherever he was.

Before Jessie went back to the kitchen to prepare the lunch, she stopped in her room, at her writing desk, which had once been her grandmother's, looked out the window onto the scene Jake could also see from where he

lay. Sighing, she pulled out the letter she had pushed into one of the cub-
byholes in the desk. *"Jessie Lutz,"* the address read, *"Atlas City."*

And of course it had reached her. In Atlas City everyone not only knew
where she was, but what she was doing!

As Jessie held the paper, it began to tremble in her hand, like the bedcovers that had quivered in Jake's grasp.

"Dear Jessie, I know you will be surprised to hear from me."

Jessie looked up from the paper; she *had* been. She never thought she'd
see or hear from Pete Johnson again.

*"I'm writing to you because I haven't been able to get you out of my
mind. What happened between us so long ago was not a thing I could ever
forget — I love you, Jessie, and I always will."*

Now Jessie looked out the window, saw that a slight breeze had come
up and was stirring the branches of the elm. She saw the glimmer of the
water in the distance and hoped, prayed, that it was going down.

*"Jessie, I want you to marry me. I hope to God you haven't found some-
one else — no, let me rephrase that. That's selfish of me, but I guess what
I'm trying to say is that if you have, I'm happy for you and I hope you're
happy. But if you haven't — and I can't help but wish for that — I want to
be a part of your life. A permanent part.*

*"If you want to see me, talk with me, think about this whole thing,
please write to me at this address."*

Pete had then given an address in Kansas City.

*"My wife died several years ago. I re-enlisted at the end of the war,
spent several postwar years in Germany, and returned to the States in the
early fifties. I moved my wife to a private institution here, where she died.
It took me a few years to get up the courage to write you. Please write me,
no matter what you have to say."*

It was signed, *"With love, Pete."*

For a long time, Jessie hadn't known what to think. A portion of her
past had opened again, leaving her vulnerable and exposed. At first, she
had thought she wouldn't answer, and she had thrust the letter into its hiding place; then events in the Lutz household had taken over so that she
couldn't answer.

Jessie pressed the letter to her chest. She still loved Pete; that hadn't
changed. But what kind of life could they have together?

She knew that her place was here, on the ranch, which she hoped to
share with Jamie. If Pete wanted to join them here, then maybe they could

make it work. If he didn't — well — she would survive, wouldn't she? It wouldn't be the first time she had had to make a difficult choice. And if there was anything she had learned over the years, it was that one choice determines the next.

She couldn't bear to leave the ranch.

Old Jessica was in the wheelchair and Jessie was rolling her into Jake's room. Jessica felt her face was molded — she couldn't seem to move the muscles as she wished, but she realized she was able to force a tiny, lop-sided smile.

"Here's Grandmother," Jessie told her father. "I think she wants to see you."

Damn right I do, Old Jessica thought.

Jessie left her grandmother, the wheelchair pushed to the edge of Jake's bed, just as if they could carry on a conversation.

He's so thin, Jessica thought.

She saw that Jake was looking at her, his head seeming much too large for his body, his eyes piercing. Without warning, he began to cry, not great tears, just a gentle stream.

Don't cry, Old Jess ordered him. *There is no need to cry.*

She was able to reach out with one hand and stroke the bedcovers, just as she had so many years ago when he had pneumonia and she had washed his forehead with damp cloths.

As quickly as the tears began, they stopped. "I'm sorry," he said. "I don't even know why I'm crying. . . . For you? . . . For myself?" Then he announced, "Jamie's changing his name to Lutz. You'll be glad there's one less Pratt!"

Jake smiled at her — feebly, she thought — then his gaze went out the window, seeking the pastures that lay on top of the bluff and which she knew he could see, even as he lay in the bed.

She remembered how she herself had lain in this bed and looked out; how it had seemed to calm her. Perhaps it was the same with Jake.

"There it is, Mother," Jake was saying. "There it all is."

Old Jessica followed his gaze; she could see the bull on his lookout point, just as if it were a century ago and it was not a bull, but an Indian. Wagon trains had gone past here, she thought; one of them had been followed by August's father. He was only twelve; he had followed them all the way to Colorado, where he made sandwiches in the mines and sold them to the miners. He had to walk behind the wagons in the trains, though they carried his belongings. Once, he had told them all, he had seen a wolf cross between him and the last wagon and he thereafter kept closer behind the train.

As Jessica watched, the bull turned and slowly made his way down from the hillock and back to the pasture.

Jessica sighed. Jake's glance came back to her and once again, he smiled.

"I'm glad you're here, Mother," he said, an almost breathless voice.

Again she stroked the bedcovers; Jake wiped his eyes, erasing the tears of the moments before.

"Fred hasn't come back, has he?" Jake asked then.

Old Jess tried to shake her head no; it tilted askew, like a spun-out top.

"Well," Jake said, "it's all right. He's on his own two feet at last."

Old Jessica looked at him with her large, round eyes.

"I'm not sure I understand it all . . ." Jake said then. ". . . But I'm glad I was witness to a part of it."

What did he mean, Jessica wondered. Was he talking about the family? . . . The ranch?

She wished she could tell him that she loved him. She wished she could tell him that she was tired too.

But she had to content herself with the silent stroke of the bedcovers.